STATE OF BLISS

FIRST FAMILY SERIES, BOOK 6

MARIE FORCE

State of Bliss
First Family Series, Book 6
By: Marie Force

Published by HTJB, Inc.
Copyright 2023. HTJB, Inc.
Cover design by Kristina Brinton and Ashley Lopez
Cover photography by Regina Wamba
Models: Robert John and Ellie Dulac
Print Layout: E-book Formatting Fairies
ISBN: 978-1958035535

The First Family Series

Book 1: State of Affairs
Book 2: State of Grace
Book 3: State of the Union
Book 4: State of Shock
Book 5: State of Denial
Book 6: State of Bliss
Book 7: State of Suspense (Coming April 2024)

More new books are always in the works. For the most up-to-date list of what's available from the First Family Series, go to *marieforce.com/firstfamily*

CHAPTER ONE

The all-hands message arrived with a loud chime right after midnight on Friday morning.

Urgent notice! Chief Farnsworth will be briefing all members of the MPD on an important matter at zero eight hundred. Commanders should report to the chief's conference room at zero seven thirty. Anyone not on annual leave is expected to be present either in person at HQ or remotely via the secure link provided below. Thank you for your attention to this matter.

Sam groaned as she read the message.

She and Nick were due to depart on their anniversary trip at noon. Technically, she was on leave for the next ten days.

But...

The curiosity would kill her. Usually, she was in the know on most things that went on in the department, but she had no clue what this urgent meeting was about.

"What's up, babe?" Nick asked as he yawned.

"All-hands meeting at zero eight hundred. Commanders at zero seven thirty."

"Over what?"

"No idea."

"You don't have to go, do you?"

"I don't *have* to, but it might be better for both of us if I did so I don't die of curiosity."

His grunt of laughter made her smile as he put his arm around her and snuggled up to her. "I agree it's better if you go, as long as you're back in time for our very important date. I can't wait to get the hell out of here."

"I know." She put her hand on top of his. "I promise I won't be late."

"I have the dreaded national security briefing at ten, so it's fine. We'll leave when you get back. Did you remember to tell your detail you have a meeting?"

"I was just getting ready to do that."

He poked her side, startling her as she laughed. "Sure you were."

"I was!"

She grabbed her phone off the bedside table and sent a text to Vernon, her lead agent. *Urgent meeting at HQ at zero seven thirty.*

Even though it was after midnight, he responded right away. *Will be ready for transport at zero seven ten.*

You're the best.

I know.

Sam laughed at his cheeky reply. "He's awesome."

"I'm so glad you like him."

"I do like him and Jimmy. They're fun to be with."

"Do they have any idea how lucky they are that you like them?"

"Duh, of course they do."

"How silly of me to ask."

"Freddie tells them all the time how lucky they are, because I hate people in general."

"It seems to me, and I could be wrong, that you like a whole lot more people than you hate lately."

"That's not true, and I'd better never hear you say that outside the confines of these four walls."

"Yes, dear."

"Are you laughing at me?"

"Would I do that?"

"Yes, I'm quite sure you would, and the fact that I can feel you shaking is a dead giveaway."

"My wife is funny. What can I say?"

"Nice recovery."

He held her tighter and kissed the back of her shoulder. "Get some sleep. You're going to need to be well rested when we get to Dewey."

"Thanks for the warning."

"I can't wait for *days and days and days* alone with my wife."

"Same, except for with my husband."

"Whatever happens at the meeting, you can't let it mess up this vacation."

"I won't."

"Promise? My life depends on it."

"Since your life is critically important to me, I promise."

AT SEVEN THIRTY, the department commanders gathered in Chief Farnsworth's conference room.

Lieutenant Archelotta from IT glanced at her. "What's this about?"

"No idea."

"Huh, I figured if anyone would know, it'd be you."

"You figured wrong."

Captain Malone stood at the head of the table. "Thank you for coming in. The chief has called the all-hands meeting to provide an update on new information uncovered regarding former Lieutenant Stahl."

Sam bit back a gasp. *Holy hell. What now?*

"We've received a credible tip tying him to as many as twenty missing women." Malone pressed a remote that put photos on the screen at the front of the room. "Over a seventeen-year period, the following women have gone missing."

The slide show provided an array of young, attractive women.

"Each of them was known to the MPD as a drug addict and, in some cases, had a history of prostitution."

Sam was filled with sadness as she watched the faces of one woman after another go by. They were a variety of races with few similar characteristics to tie them to a type. What they'd been, she realized as Malone recited their names, ages and some of the details that were known about them, was vulnerable.

Stahl had preyed on those vulnerabilities.

But had he killed them? They could've gone missing and ended up dead by any number of means, but she knew from experience Stahl was certainly capable of committing murder. The thought had her stomach turning as memories of him trying to kill her came surging to the surface.

Dear God... To think he might've actually killed other people while employed by the department was almost too big to process. The first time, he'd nearly succeeded in strangling her on her own doorstep before the Secret Service had intervened and saved her life. Later, he'd wrapped her in razor wire and threatened to set her on fire. He was now serving a life sentence at Jessup with no chance of parole for both crimes.

Sam tried very hard to never think about her former lieutenant or how he'd tried to kill her. Twice. Just hearing his name made her clammy and light-headed.

"Sam."

Archie's voice dragged her out of the rabbit hole she'd fallen into as she relived her near-fatal encounters with the disgraced former lieutenant.

Sam glanced at him.

"Are you okay?" he asked quietly.

"Yeah."

Her hands were shaking, so she tucked them between her knees. As if that could stop the cold wave of dread that overtook her whenever she thought of that day in Marissa Springer's basement when she'd been certain she was about to die in the most horrific way possible.

That'd been his goal, of course.

He'd been outraged by her refusal to engage with him in any way as he went about his sinister task.

Maybe he'd hated her because he couldn't just kill her. She wasn't someone he could "disappear" the way he might've done to these other women.

"Needless to say," Malone continued, "we're taking this new information very seriously and plan to devote significant resources to reopening the investigations into the disappearance of each of these women. After the all-hands meeting at eight, Crime Scene detectives will be descending upon Stahl's home. We expect this to be a major local and national story."

As he said the word *national*, he let his gaze land on her.

The national media would salivate over the news that the first lady's former boss and assailant might be a serial killer.

Sam looked away, mortified that her stature on the national stage would add to the media frenzy that was sure to ensue after these new suspicions went public.

"How do we plan to handle the media on this?" Lieutenant Max Haggerty from Crime Scene asked.

"We're not saying anything publicly until we know more. Stahl's attorneys have been notified about the warrant to search his property. Apparently, the home once belonged to his grandparents and was left to him when they died. For whatever reason he didn't live there, possibly because he used the place for nefarious purposes."

The thought of that turned her stomach.

His property wouldn't have been searched in the earlier cases because neither of the attempts on her life had taken place at his home.

Sam hadn't known much about his life outside of work. She'd tried to avoid anything having to do with him during the miserable years she'd worked for and with him.

From the first day she'd been put under his command, she'd tried to stay as removed from the nasty lieutenant as she possibly could. That he couldn't goad, rattle or intimidate her was part of why he hated her. Her last name hadn't helped.

He'd hated her father almost as much as he hated her. Though they'd started out together, Skip Holland had rapidly advanced through the ranks to deputy chief, while Stahl had remained a lieutenant.

"Lieutenant Holland."

Sam's gaze snapped up to meet Captain Malone's. "Yes, sir?"

"Are you still going to Delaware this week?"

"Yes, sir."

"Please stay after this meeting for a minute, if you would."

She nodded.

"Your teams will have questions," Malone continued. "As we will do in the all-hands meeting, please tell them no one is to speak to the press about this case. That's all."

After the others had left the room, Malone sat next to her and handed her a sheet of paper. "Two of the missing women are originally from Delaware. We'd like you to see their family members and update them on the reopened investigation while you're out there, if you don't mind."

I mind, she wanted to say, screaming on the inside at the thought of anything interrupting her time alone with Nick, let alone something having to do with Stahl.

"We know it's a lot to ask, but everyone will be on this, and it would be a huge help."

"No problem."

The chief sat across the table from them. "Are you all right, Lieutenant? We know this news is difficult for you, in particular, to hear."

"I'm fine. Are you?"

They both looked exhausted, as if they'd been awake for days. Maybe they had been.

"I've been better," the chief said. "I'm mad as hell that this guy keeps besmirching the reputation of this department and the hardworking men and women who show up and give it their all every day."

Sam glanced at Malone. "I assume the tip is from a credible source..."

"One of my longest-standing informants was told by

someone he trusts that Stahl was well known for looking for women who wouldn't have anyone sounding the alarm if they went missing, which they always did."

Sam shivered as she contemplated the pure evil it would take to do what he was accused of doing. "Can you tell me what specifically you were told?"

"That we should look at Stahl for any missing-women cases over the last twenty years."

"God, twenty years..."

"Our thoughts exactly," Farnsworth said. "We've worked for forty-six hours straight to make a list of missing women and figure out a plan to deal with this latest nightmare he's brought to our door."

"Do you think he did it?" Sam asked.

"Before he wrapped you in razor wire and threatened to set you on fire, I would've said no way," Farnsworth replied. "But now we know he's capable of anything, even mass murder."

"After everything that's happened, it shouldn't shock me," Sam said, "but still... It does."

"Us, too."

"We were going to give you a heads-up," Farnsworth said, "but we know you don't like special treatment."

"No, I don't, so thanks for that."

"The others were looking for your reaction," Malone said. "They saw the shock."

"How can he still shock me? How is that even possible?"

"Trust me," Farnsworth said. "We get it."

"We're going to ask your squad, in conjunction with Special Victims and Crime Scene, to head up the investigation with Gonzo taking the lead to avoid any potential conflicts of interest," Malone said.

He meant because she was the victim in the two crimes that had already put Stahl away for life.

"That's a good idea. Gonzo is more than ready for something like that."

"We agree," Farnsworth said.

"Where's Jeannie?" Sam asked, referring to Deputy Chief McBride. "I thought she'd be at the commanders' meeting."

"She's preparing for the all-hands," Malone said.

"Okay."

"We're sorry to ask you to work during your vacation," Farnsworth added.

"It's no problem. I can knock it out in an afternoon."

"You don't have to stay for the all-hands since you're on leave," Malone said.

"I'll be there. Appearances, you know..."

Malone nodded, and the three of them got up to attend the second meeting. While Malone and Farnsworth headed toward the chief's suite, Sam went to her pit to watch the meeting with her team.

The Homicide squad was seated around their conference room table with the TV set to the meeting, which would begin shortly.

"Morning," Sam said when she joined them.

"What're you doing here, LT?" Sergeant Tommy "Gonzo" Gonzales asked. "You're on leave."

"Curiosity got the best of me."

"Can you give us a preview?" her partner, Detective Freddie Cruz, asked.

"Nope."

"When do you leave on vacation?" Detective Cameron Green asked.

"High noon."

"Ah, I'm so jealous," Detective Gigi Dominguez said. "You'll have the best time."

"That's the goal, and I'm happy to see you here. How're you holding up?"

"We're okay." Gigi glanced at Cameron, her boyfriend. "Thank you for giving us your lawyer friend Andy's number. We're going to reach out to him soon."

They were recently sued, along with the department, for the wrongful deaths of Cameron's ex-girlfriend and her mother. The two had been killed after they took Gigi and

Jeannie McBride hostage in separate incidents. Both were clean shots, and Sam had full confidence that the lawsuits would go nowhere. But she felt for Gigi and Cam, who were dealing with the awful stress of a looming Internal Affairs hearing and a lawsuit while managing a relatively new relationship that had been making them both very happy until his ex-girlfriend intervened.

"When's your IAB hearing?" Sam asked her.

"Wednesday," Gigi said.

"Shit, I wanted to be there. I'll be sure to put in a good word ahead of the hearing."

"I'd appreciate anything you can do."

"Of course. Don't lose any sleep over this stuff. You survived. That's what matters."

"I've been trying to tell her that," Cam said.

"It's a tough thing to take a life, even if it was done to save your own," Sam said. "If you get so jaded you aren't affected by that you should hang up your gold shield and call it a day around here."

"Thank you, Lieutenant," Gigi said softly. "I needed to hear that."

"Stay strong. You're on the side of right here."

"We're trying," Gigi said with a warm look for Cameron.

"The whole thing is so fucked up," Gigi's partner, Detective Dani Carlucci, said. "Gigi was taken hostage in her own home and fought back. How is that grounds for any of this nonsense?"

"It's not," Sam said, "but she has to go through the motions and see it through, unfortunately."

"It's bullshit," Dani added.

"Agreed," Sam said. "Unfortunately, it's how our world works."

Jeannie's face appeared on the screen.

"Look at our pal," Gonzo said, smiling at the sight of their close friend, who'd been recently promoted from their squad to second-in-command.

"I'm bursting with pride," Sam said.

"Thank you all for being here this morning, whether you're in the building or logged in remotely," Jeannie said. "We've called this meeting to pass along important information about a former member of the department, Leonard Stahl."

Sam appreciated that Jeannie didn't give him the courtesy of referring to him by his rank. He didn't deserve courtesy of any kind.

"Jeez," Gonzo said. "What now?"

Sam's team watched in stunned silence as Jeannie went through the presentation the commanders had been shown earlier and discussed the tip Captain Malone had received from a trusted source.

"We'll be asking Detective Sergeant Tommy Gonzales, on behalf of Homicide, to lead the investigation along with Detective Erica Lucas from SVU and Lieutenant Max Haggerty from Crime Scene."

As Gonzo glanced at Sam, she gave him a smile and a thumbs-up.

"Holy crap," Freddie uttered after the last photo had been shown. "He's a freaking serial killer."

Stahl was also facing numerous other charges for failing to perform even the most perfunctory investigations in several cases, as well as fabricating evidence that put an innocent man in prison for twenty years on bogus rape charges. "We don't know for sure that he's done any of this," Sam said, "but if he did, we'll nail his ass to the wall—again."

Sam had no sooner said those words than Gonzo's radio crackled to life with a call from Dispatch for Homicide detectives to report to a dormitory at the George Washington University on Foxhall Road Northwest for a student found dead in her room.

CHAPTER TWO

Gonzo could see that Sam was deeply torn as their team mobilized to respond to the call at GW. "Get going," he said to her. "We've got this."

"I know."

"You guys need a break. Enjoy it."

"Okay, I'm leaving. Keep me posted?"

"Nope."

"Come on!"

"Go be on vacation, you whacko."

"I'm noting this insubordination on your next review."

"Whatever. Cameron, stay here and work the social media and online angles. We'll send you the names. Also, get whatever Deputy Chief McBride has on this latest situation with Stahl and start to work on a plan of attack. Gigi and Dani, go on home. The rest of you, let's go." Gigi was on administrative leave until her case wound through the Internal Affairs process, and Dani worked overnight.

Gonzo could feel Sam watching them as they left the pit and headed for the morgue exit to tend to yet another murder victim, this one a college student. The younger ones were the worst, and they'd just closed a case that had included four dead kids.

"Why'd you leave Cam behind?" Cruz asked.

"He's no good to us in the field until this shit with Gigi and IAB is worked out."

"That's true. He's a red-hot mess over it."

"I feel awful for them," Gonzo said. "They've been so happy together, and now this."

"Hopefully, it'll blow over soon," Cruz said.

"You ready to lead another case?" Gonzo asked him.

Freddie balked. "*What?* No, I'm not ready for that. The last one almost killed me." He'd recently taken the lead for the first time, on the Blanchet case.

Cackling with laughter, Gonzo said, "Relax. I've got this one."

"Don't mess with me. I'm on vacation from my ball-busting partner."

"She told me not to let you go soft while she's away."

"She did not say that!"

"Maybe she did. Maybe she didn't."

"Whatever you say, boss. Can you even believe this shit about Stahl? I mean..."

"It's unreal, but not totally unbelievable. We've known he was a son of a bitch for a long time."

"But possibly a serial killer? We didn't know that."

"Anyone who can wrap someone in razor wire and threaten to set them on fire has issues beyond what you and I can imagine."

"Yeah, for sure. As horrifying as that was, though, I could apply some logic to it. He hated Skip, so naturally, he hated Skip's daughter. Sam refused to give him an inch, so he snapped and tried to kill her. Twice."

"Are you trying to say that makes sense?" Gonzo asked.

"Not to you and me, but at least there was rationale behind it from his demented point of view. What reason would he have to kill other people while pretending to be an upstanding Homicide commander?"

"That's anyone's guess. If you're trying to understand it, don't bother. It'll never make sense to people like us."

"No, it won't, and yet... I'm still trying to wrap my head

around how he could've been doing all this while we worked for him. How did no one notice?"

"When you know how to solve the crimes, you also know how to hide the crimes."

Freddie thought about that for a minute. "I suppose that's true."

Gonzo was aware that his friend's emotions had been all over the place since his wife, Elin, had suffered a miscarriage. Shortly after that, Freddie had been thrust into the role of lead detective on the Blanchet case, which had involved the murders of four children and their parents.

"Not sure I've got the bandwidth for another dead kid," Cruz said.

"I hear you, brother. It's been a lot lately."

"When is it not a lot?"

"Never. It's always a lot. And speaking of shit happening, I've been waiting for the right time to tell you—"

"Tell me what?" Cruz asked, brows furrowed.

"Christina is pregnant."

"Oh," Cruz said on a long exhale.

"I'm sorry about the timing."

"Don't be. Of course I'm thrilled for you guys."

"She's starting to show, and I didn't want you to hear it from someone else."

"All good, man. When's she due?"

"In the fall."

"Alex must be excited."

"He can't wait to be a big brother."

"Do you know what you're having?" Cruz asked.

"A girl."

"Oh damn. You're going to be a girl dad."

"I know, and I'm terrified. She'll rule the roost."

Cruz laughed. "I can't wait to meet her. Congratulations."

"Thanks. It's going to happen for you guys, too. I feel that in my bones."

"I do, too. As Sam said, it's good news that Elin can

conceive, and we're trying to make peace with the one we lost being not meant to be."

"It's heartbreaking, though."

"Yes, it is."

Gonzo brought his car to a stop outside the dormitory, which had been blocked off by the Patrol officers who'd answered the call for help. "Here we go again."

Business was always brisk for murder cops in a major city.

"What've we got?" Gonzo asked the first Patrol officer they encountered as Detectives Charles and O'Brien arrived on the scene in O'Brien's vehicle.

Officer Youncy, a young Black female officer Gonzo had met before, greeted them. "Hey, Sarge, so the body was found on the third floor, room 322. A twenty-year-old junior named Rachel Fortier. Her roommate became concerned when Rachel didn't get up for her eight o'clock class. Apparently, she never misses class, which is something her friends teased her about."

"Do we know where she's from?"

"St. Louis."

Gonzo ached for the parents in St. Louis, who'd soon be receiving the worst call any parent could ever get.

"Sergeant Gonzales and Detective Cruz," Youncy said, "this is Officer Sandoval from GW Campus Police and Grant Kingston, the residence hall coordinator."

"Take us up." Gonzo nodded to the two men, who'd probably do more to complicate the investigation than help it. To Charles and O'Brien, he added, "Start with the security footage and the canvass."

"Uh, about the footage," Kingston said haltingly. "Our monitoring system went down on Friday. We're still waiting for the repair people."

Nothing is ever easy, Gonzo thought with growing frustration. He was still processing the news that he'd be leading the new investigation into Stahl possibly being a serial killer and now this, too. "Do the canvass," he said to Charles. "Find out who was working the front desk last night and get us a list of who was in and out of here."

"You got it, Sarge," Charles said.

Gonzo liked working with her. She was sharp and understood the mission. The jury was still out on O'Brien. He had potential, but he reminded Gonzo of his late partner, Detective AJ Arnold, in that he was a bit clueless at times. That fleeting thought of Arnold, who'd been shot dead right in front of Gonzo, sent a shaft of pain lancing through him. God, he missed that big doofus and would mourn his tragic loss for the rest of his life.

As they followed Youncy up two flights to the third floor, Gonzo tried to shake off the feelings of despair that came over him any time he thought of Arnold, which was often.

Room 322 had been taped off to keep everyone out, and Gonzo recognized Youncy's partner, Officer Clare, a young white officer who still had acne, positioned outside the door. Clare lifted the yellow tape for Gonzo and Cruz.

They stepped inside a room divided in half—one side featured pink and purple, the other was black. Someone had taped a yellow traffic line straight down the middle of the room, which Gonzo found odd. Did that mean the roommates hadn't gotten along?

The victim, who had blonde hair, was still in her bed, and at first glance, he might've thought she was asleep until he noted the bluish tinge to her lips and skin.

"Have you called the ME?" Gonzo asked.

"She's on her way," Youncy said. "Crime Scene is delayed with most of their team now deployed to Stahl's house."

The Patrol officers had done the right thing calling them, Gonzo thought, if for no other reason than to rule out murder. Whenever someone died under suspicious circumstances, they got the call. Once in a while, they later determined the person had died by natural causes.

"There's no way someone got in here and murdered her, if that's what you're thinking," Kingston said. "We pride ourselves on world-class security."

"But your cameras are down," Gonzo said. "Interesting."

"That doesn't mean one of our students was murdered!"

"It sure as hell doesn't help us figure out what happened here."

Gonzo withdrew his phone and called Malone.

"What've you got?"

"Twenty-year-old college student dead in her bed. No outward signs of struggle or trauma, but we haven't looked closely yet. I'm hearing CSU is straight out at Stahl's. Can we request mutual aid?"

"I'll put out the word and let you know."

"Thanks."

"Keep me posted."

"Will do."

Local departments called on one another when they needed assistance. Hopefully, someone could provide crime scene help ASAP. Time was of the essence in these situations. Who knew if the scene had already been compromised?

He pointed to Rachel's phone, attached to a charger on her bedside table. "Bag that," he said to Cruz. To Kingston, he said, "Where's the roommate?"

"In the lounge with others from the suite. Three rooms share two bathrooms and a common living area."

Pretty sweet setup, Gonzo thought as he followed Kingston to the lounge, a large public space with foosball tables, a coffee station and vending machines.

A group of young women were huddled together, their faces swollen from crying.

Officers Phillips and Jestings, who were watching over the young women, nodded to Gonzo and Cruz as they approached.

Phillips introduced him and Cruz to the young women.

"Who's the roommate?" Gonzo had already zeroed in on the one dressed all in black. The strikingly beautiful young woman had brown skin, dark hair and eyes dramatically lined with black makeup.

Kingston gestured to the one Gonzo had guessed. "Harley Flores. She's the one who called 911 when she realized Rachel was dead, not asleep."

"Could we have a moment with Harley, please?" Gonzo asked the other girls.

They hugged Harley as they got up to give the detectives room.

Gonzo sat on a chair that faced Harley. "Again, I'm Detective Sergeant Gonzales, and this is my partner, Detective Cruz. We're very sorry for your loss."

Harley wiped tears off her face. "Thank you."

Gonzo noted that her makeup remained unaffected by the tears. Christina had taught him the pro and con of waterproof mascara. Pro: it didn't run. Con: it was a bitch to get off. "Can you tell us what happened?"

"I have no idea. I woke up as usual around seven thirty to go to work and realized Rachel was still in bed, which was very weird. She never sleeps past six. She was a high school swimmer and had practice every morning before school. She said it ruined her for sleeping in."

Harley wiped away more tears. "I called over to her, and she didn't answer, so I went to look closer and saw that... She was... Her lips were blue. I started freaking out. I called 911 and ran out of there."

"Did you touch her at all?"

Harley shook her head. "I was afraid to."

That's good news, Gonzo thought, relieved to know the body was undisturbed.

"What went on around here last night?" he asked.

"Nothing out of the ordinary. She did homework while I went to dinner with some friends. When I came home around eleven, she was already asleep, which isn't uncommon. She conks out early, too." Harley seemed to stop herself when she realized she was speaking of Rachel in the present tense. "Well, she did. I can't believe she's gone." She looked up at them with heartbreak in her eyes. "How is that possible? She's only twenty."

"Do you know of her having any visitors or guests while you were at dinner?"

"She didn't mention having plans."

"We noticed there was a line down the center of your room," Cruz said.

Harley nodded as she swiped at tears. "We got off to a rough start as roommates. I put that line down the middle to make a point. But freaking Rachel... She couldn't let it be. She had to keep at me until I decided to like her, which took about two days, because you can't *not* like her. Pissed me off."

Gonzo would've been amused by her under any other circumstances.

"Everyone loved her. She was like the mother hen around here, checking on everyone, making sure we were all right. I can't believe she's gone."

He wasn't entirely convinced this was a homicide, as the victim was so universally well liked, or so it seemed. "Did she have any health problems that you know of?"

"No, she was ridiculously fit and tried to swim every day."

"Did she swim competitively still?"

She shook her head. "Only for exercise and because she loved it so much. She tried to talk me into taking up swimming, but I told her to stand down. This girl doesn't do pools."

"Did she have trouble with anyone that you know of?"

"Not at all. Like I said, people liked her even when they didn't want to."

"Did she have a boyfriend?"

"There is this one guy. They've been kinda on-again, off-again."

"His name?"

"Gordon something? We made fun of his name. One of the other girls said her grandfather's name was Gordon."

"Do you know where we can find him?"

"He lives in the building next door." She pointed in the direction. "Over there."

"Would anyone here know his last name?"

"I think Kristy would."

"Can you get her for us?"

"Sure."

As she got up to go get Kristy, Gonzo turned to Cruz. "Send

the names to Green so he can start looking at the social media. Also, let's see if any of the neighboring buildings have cameras pointed this way or if the department has anything."

Cruz stood to leave the room. "On it."

Harley returned with another girl, this one with light brown hair and freckles. Her face was red and swollen from crying. "This is Kristy. She was close with Rachel."

"We're very sorry for your loss."

"Th-thank you."

"What can you tell us about Gordon?"

"She really likes him. Or, um, I guess I should say she *liked* him. I'm sorry. I'm in shock. She was so amazing. Never had a bad word to say about anyone." When Kristy broke down into heartbreaking sobs, Harley put her arm around her.

Cruz returned. "ME is here."

Gonzo nodded to him. "What's Gordon's last name?" he asked Kristy.

"Reilly."

"Can you spell that for me?"

"I think it's R-E-I-L-L-Y."

Gonzo wrote that down. "Had she been seeing him for long?"

"Since the fall, but it was complicated."

"How so?"

"He has a longtime girlfriend at home, and even though they agreed to see other people while they were in college— she goes to the University of Georgia—she's been super clingy and stuff. He's been saying he's going to end it with her once and for all. Rachel told him to let her know when that happened, and she's been keeping her distance from him in the last few weeks. She was upset about it."

Gonzo took notes as she spoke. "What do you know about the girlfriend?"

"Not much except she's extra, and he's been looking for a way out of it. At least that's what he told Rachel."

"Thank you for the info," Gonzo said.

"Do you think she was murdered?" Harley asked.

"We don't know anything yet."

She crossed her arms and looked madly vulnerable.

"Do you have contact info for her parents?" Gonzo asked.

"I have her mother's number," Harley said. "Our mothers insisted that we have each other's digits." She withdrew her phone and recited the number.

Gonzo wrote it down as a feeling of dread came over him. There was nothing worse than having to make that call to an unsuspecting parent. "What's the mother's first name?"

"Caroline."

He handed her his notebook and pen. "Can you please provide your names and numbers, too?"

Both girls wrote down their info.

Harley passed the notebook back to him.

"Thank you for your help. We'll be in touch."

CHAPTER THREE

G onzo felt bad leaving the young women in such distress, but he had a job to do. If Rachel had been murdered, he would do everything he could to get justice for her. That was how the job was supposed to be done. People like Stahl gave them all a bad name when most of their department was out busting their ass on behalf of the citizens they served every day.

Before he left the lounge, Gonzo approached Kingston and the university cop. "I don't want anything about this case released to anyone. This is our investigation. The school and its personnel are out of the loop now. Do I make myself clear?"

"Who will notify her parents?" Kingston asked, sounding miffed.

"We will. I want you to ask these kids to keep the news of Rachel's death off the internet until we're able to notify her family, which will happen in the next hour or so. If anything gets out about this before then, I'll hold you personally responsible."

"You can't do that!" Kingston said. "These kids live on their phones."

"Want to try me?"

Gonzo walked away, leaving the two of them staring after him in disbelief. He hoped he'd made his point. Not that he could do anything to Kingston if Rachel's friends chose to post about her death, but hopefully he'd incentivized Kingston to get them to hold off. Speaking to Rachel's parents was his top priority after they finished at the campus.

When he returned to Rachel's room, Lindsey McNamara and her team were working the scene. They had Rachel's body on a stretcher.

"What're you thinking, Doc?"

"I'm not sure yet. There's no obvious trauma, but sometimes trauma isn't obvious. I'll know more in a few hours."

"Keep me in the loop?"

"You got it."

Gonzo took a call from Malone. "What's up, Cap?"

"PG County Crime Scene Unit is on the way."

"Okay, thanks."

He ended the call and looked to Cruz. "PG County Crime Scene is coming."

Charles and O'Brien found them in Rachel's room.

"We may have something," she said. "The young man working the desk overnight, Tucker, said there was a ten p.m. pizza delivery for Rachel from a company he hadn't heard of before. He said the deliveries tend to come from the same ten or twelve places."

"The roommate told us she goes to bed early just about every night and was asleep when she got home at eleven," Gonzo said, consulting his notes. "Did you get a description of the delivery guy?"

Charles nodded. "Tucker said he was a big dude, like someone who'd played football. His dark hair was buzzed. He had brown eyes and a goatee. The interesting thing was that Tucker said that usually the pizza deliveries make his mouth water even when he's not hungry because they smell so good, but he couldn't smell anything coming from that one."

"Let's get back up to Rachel's suite and see if there's a pizza box to be found anywhere," Gonzo said, "and if there is, let's get it bagged and to the lab."

"On it," Charles said as she and O'Brien headed for the stairs.

To Cruz, Gonzo said, "Let's go talk to the boyfriend."

NATURALLY, the whole world went mad when Nick was counting the minutes until he could escape the gilded cage of the White House for ten blissful days with his beloved.

The North Koreans decided to test yet another long-range missile, the Iranians were doing something with plutonium, and an uprising in Niger was causing concerns around the world.

He wished there was an "unsubscribe" button he could push to disengage for a few days, but that button didn't exist for the president of the United States. Everything was his problem, whether he wanted it to be or not.

Following the national security briefing, he consulted with Secretary of Defense Tobias Jennings about the situations in North Korea and Iran and with Secretary of State Jessica Sanford about Niger.

Satisfied that his team was managing the latest flashpoints and would keep him in the loop, he left the Oval Office and headed upstairs to finish packing.

He and Sam had said their goodbyes to the kids before they left for school.

Aubrey's tears weighed on him. They'd promised to FaceTime every night until the kids joined them at the beach for the second weekend next Friday. That had seemed to satisfy her as she'd headed off to school with her twin brother, Alden, and their Secret Service detail.

"Have a great time and don't worry about the kids," Scotty had said. "I'll take good care of them."

Not that long ago, Scotty would've been the one who was teary-eyed at them leaving for a week. Now he was stepping up to help with their Littles. Scotty was such a bright light in their lives, and the twins looked up to him with near-hero worship.

They'd be in good hands with him and Sam's stepmother, Celia, this week.

When he entered their suite in the residence, Nick was surprised to find that Sam wasn't back from her meeting yet. He hoped that whatever had resulted in the unusual all-hands meeting wouldn't mess up their trip.

After this vacation, he was making it his goal to get out of the White House at least once a week to go *somewhere*, whether it be an official or unofficial outing. He'd been sticking close to the office since he'd been sworn in, fending off enemies near and far who were looking to undermine his fledgling administration.

The latest surreal event had occurred when he'd caught wind of a potential military coup orchestrated by the Joint Chiefs of Staff. They'd since been relieved of their duties and dishonorably discharged from the military. Despite this swift action on the part of Secretary Jennings, the media was like a pack of dogs with meaty bones as they continued to report on the story, with huge daily headlines describing each new development.

Nick had tried to keep his head down to stay focused on the endless demands of the job while others took care of the situation with the now-disgraced Joint Chiefs. The betrayal had cut deeply. He was well aware of his status as only the second unelected president. Chosen to replace an ailing vice president, he'd risen to the top job after President Nelson's sudden passing last Thanksgiving.

Four months later, he was still fending off claims of illegitimacy, despite being confirmed by the Senate on a bipartisan vote of one hundred to zero to fill the vacancy created by Vice President Gooding's departure.

The Constitution had worked exactly as the framers had intended after President Nelson's death, and yet, here he was still dealing with illegitimacy bullshit.

Despite the furor, his plan was to keep doing the job, regardless of what anyone had to say about it.

He put his shaving bag in the suitcase he'd left open on the floor and zipped it closed just as Sam came rushing into the room, her cheeks red from the chilly March day and her eyes a bit wild looking.

"That took way longer than I thought it would. Have you been waiting long?"

"Just got back to the residence a few minutes ago."

"Oh, good. Well, not good. But I'm glad I didn't keep you waiting."

"You're well worth waiting for, babe. And besides, I can't very well go on an anniversary trip without my better half."

Her smile was everything. When she looked at him that way, he forgot all his worries and frustrations.

He reached out a hand to take hers and kissed the back of it. "Are you all mine for the next ten days?"

"For the most part," she said, biting her lip.

His heart sank. "What does that mean?" *For the most part* was nowhere near enough.

"The meeting at HQ?" she said, sighing as they sat together on the bed.

"What about it?"

"We've received a credible tip that Stahl might be responsible for the disappearances and presumed deaths of upward of twenty women."

"*What?* Holy shit."

"I know, right? Just when we think we've seen it all with him, there's more."

Nick couldn't even think about how close he'd come to losing her to that madman, or he'd break into a cold sweat. He still had nightmares about razor wire and fire, not that he'd ever tell her that. She had enough to worry about without adding his fears to her plate.

"So what do you have to do?"

"Update two families in Delaware on this latest development. I should be able to knock it out in an afternoon while you tend to world domination." She gave him a wary look. "I'm sorry about this. I know we strive for as little work as possible on these trips, but—"

He leaned in to kiss the concern away. "It's no problem. I have no doubt that my job will be a much bigger cockblocker than yours this week."

"You said bigger cock."

Smiling, he said, "So I did. What're you going to do with it?"

"Everything I can think of, but first you need to get me to Delaware. Stat."

After another quick kiss, he got up. "I'll let Brant know we're ready to roll."

WITH CHARLES and O'Brien looking for an abandoned pizza box in Rachel's dormitory, Gonzo and Cruz went to the dorm next door to find Gordon Reilly.

They showed their badges to the student working at the front desk, introduced themselves and asked where they might find Reilly.

"What do you want with him?"

Gonzo gave the cheeky kid a don't-fuck-with-me look intended to make the kid's balls shrivel. "What room is he in?"

"Uh, 212."

"Thank you."

The young man's Adam's apple bobbed in his throat, which gave Gonzo tremendous satisfaction.

"I love how he thought you were going to tell him what we want with Reilly," Cruz said as they hoofed it to the second floor.

"Idiot."

When they opened the door at the top of the stairwell, they stepped into a crowd.

"Whoa," Gonzo said. "What's going on?"

"Big fight in 212," a female student with red hair said. "Been going on for hours now."

"Is there an RA around?" Cruz asked.

"They're all in classes," someone else said.

"Step aside," Gonzo said, adding, "*Now*," when the group didn't immediately react to his direction. He held up his badge so they could see it. That got them moving out of his way. "Everyone back off." He pounded on the door. "Police. Open up."

"Now see what you've done?" he heard a male voice shout inside the room.

"Open the door," Gonzo said. "Right now!"

The door opened to reveal a handsome, dark-haired young man with high color in his cheeks, like he'd been exerting himself.

Gonzo showed him his badge. "Step back into the room."

He shoved the kid back and followed him into a room with a twin-size bed.

Cruz came in after him and shut the door.

A woman with braided blonde hair sat on the bed, her face tear-stained. She looked freaked out to see cops.

"What're your names?" Gonzo asked.

"Uh, Gordon Reilly, and she's Tori Stevens."

"What're you fighting about?"

Gordon glanced at her. "We... We're breaking up."

"No, we're not!" Tori shot back.

"Which is it?" Gonzo asked.

"I am breaking up with her. She says it's not over. Thus the fighting."

"How long has this fight been going on?"

"Most of the night." Gordon ran his hand through his hair. "But she was just leaving."

"I'm not going anywhere until we work this out! We're not throwing away seven years like they meant nothing!"

"I told you hours ago there's nothing left to work out, and I'm done talking about it. Now there're cops here, which is the last freaking thing I need. Will you please just *go*?"

She crossed her arms and gave him a mulish look.

"Have you both been in this room all night?"

"I was," he said. "She stormed off for a while at one point. I'm not sure when that was."

"Where'd you go?" Gonzo asked her.

"For a walk to get some air."

"When?"

"Sometime last night."

"How long were you gone?"

"I don't know. A while."

Gonzo glanced at Cruz and saw that he was having the same thoughts. "We'd like you both to accompany us downtown to get this sorted out."

"To get what sorted?" Gordon asked, sounding panicked. "We had an argument. No one was hurt."

"Rachel is dead."

Gonzo watched the words land on the young man like a bomb detonating right in front of him. "*What?*" he asked softly. "What did you say?"

"Rachel was found dead in her bed this morning."

When his legs gave out under him, Gonzo grabbed the kid and kept him from crashing to the floor. He emitted a roar full of pure, guttural grief. "Rachel. No. No. *No.*"

Gonzo nodded to Cruz and used his chin to point at Tori.

He went over to Tori. "Stand up."

"Why?"

"Because I told you to."

She stood reluctantly.

He put his hand on her arm, intending to escort her from the room.

"*You're arresting me?*" she shrieked as she landed a hard kick to his shin. "For what?"

"Assaulting a police officer, for one thing," Cruz said as he cuffed her. "You have the right to remain silent. Anything you say can be used against you in a court of law."

"I haven't done anything! You can't just arrest innocent people."

"You kicked me. That's called assault of a police officer. I could also charge you with obstructing a homicide investigation."

"Homicide? I haven't killed anyone! You can't do this!"

He recited the remainder of her rights. "Let's go."

"Why do I need handcuffs?"

"We cuff everyone we arrest, and we can't trust you to behave yourself while we're transporting you."

Gonzo couldn't have said it better himself. "Gordon, we need you to come with us, too."

"Wh-what happened to Rachel?"

It said something about him that he was more concerned about her than he was with his own plight, Gonzo thought. "We don't know yet."

"She's really dead?"

"She is. I'm sorry."

Gordon bent at the waist as if someone had punched him. The sound that came from him reminded Gonzo of hundreds of other people who'd lost the person they loved the most.

If Gordon loved Rachel the most, had Tori known that? Could that be why Rachel was dead?

"Does it really take twenty vehicles to safely convey the first couple to a beach vacation?" Sam asked Nick an hour later as they headed east on US-50, ensconced in The Beast, the presidential limousine that'd been built to withstand just about any kind of attack. Sam hoped they never had to test those parameters.

"Apparently, it does," Nick replied. "What do we care? We're alone and finally away from La Casa Blanca for ten glorious days. I don't care if it takes a whole armada to get us there."

"As you once told me, armadas are for ships," she retorted, thrilled to see him already relaxing in a way he hadn't in months.

"You do listen to me!"

"Hush. No one listens to you the way I do."

"Have I told you yet today that I would cease to exist without you right here next to me to keep it real?"

"Not yet, slacker. I'm here for all the sweet nothings you've been saving for this time away."

"I've got a lot of sweet nothings in inventory with your name on them."

"I thought we'd take Marine One to Dewey."

"I told them I wanted to drive because that's the only way I could be completely alone with you for the time it would take to get there."

Sam leaned across the console between their seats to kiss him. "You know what we haven't done yet?"

"There's something we haven't done?"

"Uh-huh." She released her seat belt and moved over to straddle him, loving the look of surprise in his sexy hazel eyes. "Beast sex."

He put his hands on her ass and pulled her in tight against his instant erection. "Alarm bells are sounding at Secret Service headquarters because the first lady isn't seat-belted, and there's extra weight on top of the president."

Sam froze. "Really?"

Nick laughed so hard, he had tears in his eyes.

Pretending to be mad, she tried to pull back from him and found out once again that he was much stronger than her. Not that he ever used his strength inappropriately.

"Are you done laughing at me yet?" she asked on a huff of annoyance.

"Not quite."

Smiling, Sam planted a kiss on lips still quivering with laughter. "I might take back my offer of Beast sex since you laughed at me."

"I was laughing *with* you. Not *at* you."

"You were the only one laughing!"

"This is the best hour I've had since Thanksgiving."

"That's very offensive. I've done some of my finest work in the White House residence."

"Yes, you have, but I'm so happy to be out of there for more than an hour or two. I'm going to start traveling more after this vacation. I can't take being cooped up in there."

"I was thinking about that. You should start running again. It'd get you out of there every day."

"That would be such a production."

"Not for you. Tell Brant what you want to do, and he'll make it happen. Stop worrying about putting them out. That's their job—to make it so you can do what you want."

"That's true, and you're right that I spend too much time worrying about inconveniencing them."

"We'll work on your mindset shift when we return. But for now..." She pushed against him suggestively. "Are we for or against Beast sex?"

"I'm scared there might be cameras."

Again, she froze. "For real?"

"I'm not entirely sure."

"How can we find out?"

"We could ask Brant, but that'd be the same as saying, 'Hey, Brant. We want to have sex back here. Is anyone watching?'"

"And you'd be opposed to coming right out and asking him that?"

He gave her a look that said, *Seriously?*

"What? He knows we have sex. Hell, the whole world knows that. Exhibit A: *Saturday Night Live.*"

"Funniest thing ever." He hummed the tune to "My Humps" by the Black Eyed Peas, which had become their anthem on the comedy show, much to her horror and his amusement.

Sam smacked him on the shoulder. "No, it wasn't."

"Yes, it was."

"Are we going to fight about that or have Beast sex?"

"You can't ever say the words 'Beast sex' outside of this vehicle. Do you hear me?"

"Yes, Mr. President. The mood for Beast sex is slipping away..."

"Please hold." He raised the cover of the center console and pulled out a phone she'd never noticed before. "Random question for you, Brant. Are there cameras back here?" He listened to whatever Brant was saying while Sam basically gave him a lap dance that had the fingers on his free hand digging into her hip. "Okay, got it. Thanks."

"What's the verdict?"

"There're cameras, but they're used only in an emergency, not during routine conveyance."

Sam shivered dramatically. "I love when you say things like 'routine conveyance.'"

"I love when you lap-dance me when I'm on the phone."

"I can do that more often, if you'd like."

"I'd like." He unbuttoned her blouse and freed her breasts from the black lace bra she'd bought for the trip.

"Someone has been doing some shopping, I see."

She could barely think, let alone speak, when he touched her breasts and ran his thumbs over her nipples. "Perhaps."

"You're the sexiest first lady in history."

"I have nothing on Eleanor Roosevelt."

He snorted with laughter.

"Her brain was sexy."

"Yours is, too. Every part of you is sexy."

"I never thought so until you made me believe it."

"That's a crying shame." He buried his face between her breasts and seemed to breathe her in as she wrapped her arms around his neck and let her head fall back in surrender.

No one had ever made her feel the way he did.

"It's okay." She gasped as he drew her left nipple into his mouth, running his tongue over it until she was breathless. "I never cared about such things until I cared about you."

"In case I've forgotten to say so... You caring about me has made my life worth living."

"Two whole years married. And they said it would never last."

He pulled back to look at her, his expression stunned. "Who said that?"

Sam laughed. "No one. It's just a saying." She framed his face and kissed him with the love and desire that had powered them through two of the most wonderful—and tumultuous— years of their lives. As she kissed him, she worked on his belt, button and zipper.

"Careful. Don't injure him. We're going to need him a lot this week."

"Then help me!"

They worked together to free all the important parts.

Sam gasped as she took him in, slowly, methodically, going for the ultimate effect.

"Babe. Come *on*." His hands dug into the flesh of her ass as he tried to move her along.

But Sam was in charge and planned to enjoy every second. "Don't be hasty." She glanced out the window. "We're not even to the Bay Bridge yet. We've got plenty of time."

"Not if you want this to end in a satisfactory way for you. It's about to end very satisfactorily for me."

"Oh, that does sound like a problem."

"Not for me."

She slid down on him in one swift stroke that had him moaning and gripping her even tighter.

"Holy shit, that was hot."

She loved seeing his head back against the seat, eyes closed and as relaxed as he ever was these days, even if one part of him wasn't. That was her goal for this week. To get him as relaxed as she possibly could. Well, except for at times like this, of course. Then she wanted him fully engaged with her and not thinking about any of the many things that regularly weighed on him.

With that in mind, she picked up the pace until they'd fully consummated the Beast and were pulsing with aftershocks as they clung to each other.

All at once, Sam had a worrisome thought. "Do they check this thing for DNA?"

Nick laughed. "Stop thinking like a cop."

"That's like asking me not to breathe."

"They won't be checking for DNA."

"You're sure of that?"

"Fairly certain."

"That's not what I want to hear!"

"Relax, babe. They work for me. It's all good."

"Oh, listen to you. Mr. Powerful President."

"Eh, whatever. It's my car to do with as I please, and if I want to f—"

She kissed the word right off his lips.

"—my wife in the back seat, then that's what I'm gonna do."

"Well, all righty, then."

"Wanna do it again?"

CHAPTER FOUR

While Freddie got Gordon and Tori settled in interrogation rooms, Gonzo returned to the pit, where Captain Malone waited for him.

"Who'd you bring in?"

"The vic's on-again-off-again and his so-called longtime girlfriend, who he was trying to break up with."

"You like him for this?"

"Not him so much as her. She seems a bit undone by him breaking up with her, and his reaction to hearing about Rachel's death was genuine shock."

"When you get things handled here, I need you at Stahl's."

"Let me take care of a few things, and then I'll get over there."

Malone handed him a slip of paper with the 15th Street Northeast address, which Malone had noted was in the Brookland neighborhood.

"Is that the one they call Little Rome?" Gonzo asked.

"Yep. Catholic U, Basilica of the National Shrine and Franciscan Monastery of the Holy Land in America are all up there."

"Interesting area for a sinner like Stahl to call home."

"The irony isn't lost on me." Malone held out a sheet of paper. "This is the release that the Public Affairs team came up with. Let me know what you think. It'll go out after we've paid visits to the families. The chief will add a quote expressing his outrage and commitment to getting answers for the families of the missing women—no matter where those answers may lead."

The Metropolitan Police Department has received credible information tying former Lieutenant Leonard Stahl, who is serving two life sentences in prison, to as many as twenty missing women. Crime Scene detectives have been dispatched to Stahl's DC-area home to execute numerous search warrants. This investigation is in the earliest stages, and we'll have more information as it becomes available.

We are investigating Stahl's possible connection to the following missing persons:

Gonzo scanned the list of women, who ranged in age from nineteen to thirty-two. Their cases predated his tenure with the department, so he didn't recognize any of the names.

Anyone with information about Leonard Stahl and his ties to any of the missing women is asked to contact the MPD information line.

Gonzo handed the page back to Malone. "It looks okay to me."

"We're hoping to notify the families in person in the next few days, and then we'll release the statement to the public. We expect there to be a lot of anger from the families, which is certainly understandable."

"I can't even imagine what the reaction will be."

"We're hoping we can keep a lid on it until we're ready to comment. We've got people dispatched to each of the twenty families to provide the update within the next two days."

"God, what a mess."

"You said it. Get with Lucas and Haggerty as soon as you can."

"Will do, Cap."

Gonzo used his key to unlock the door to Sam's office and then shut it behind him. He left the light off and went straight to her desk to get the most dreaded task handled. As a parent himself, he simply couldn't fathom being on the other end of a phone call like this. He hoped to God he never was.

He stared at the phone for a minute, preparing himself as well as he could, before he picked up the receiver and dialed the number in St. Louis that Rachel's roommate had given him.

A woman answered, sounding wary after seeing the MPD number on her caller ID. "Hello?"

"Mrs. Fortier?"

"Yes. What's wrong? Why are you calling from the Metro PD? Is that in Washington?"

"Yes, ma'am. This is Sergeant Thomas Gonzales."

"Oh God! What? Is Rachel okay?"

"Ma'am, I'm sorry to have to inform you that she was found dead in her bed this morn—"

The woman's shrieks pierced his heart and touched his soul.

How did anyone survive such a thing?

He could hear a man's voice in the background before he came on the phone. "Who is this? What's happened?"

Gonzo closed his eyes as he was forced to repeat the news.

"Oh my God. Not Rachel."

"I'm so sorry to have to tell you this news."

"If the police are involved, does that mean... Was she murdered?"

"We won't know that for sure until the medical examiner completes her work."

"What do we do?"

"I'll get back to you when we have the ME's report."

"Should we come there?"

"Not unless you want to, of course. The funeral home you choose will arrange transport home to you in St. Louis."

"This can't be true. We just spoke to her yesterday. Everything was fine."

"We're so sorry for your loss. You said everything was fine yesterday, but could I ask if Rachel was having any challenges or concerns lately?"

"She... This has been a very difficult school year for her."

"How so?"

"She started seeing that guy Gordon in the fall. We met him when we were there for parents' weekend, and he seemed like a nice young man. She was very excited about him, but the ex-girlfriend was harassing them."

"How so?"

"Somehow she got Rachel's number and was texting her that she was fucking around with someone else's boyfriend and how would she feel if someone did that to her."

As Gonzo took notes, he wished he'd turned on the overhead light.

"We ended up getting her a new phone number, but the ex-girlfriend got ahold of that number, too."

"Did you report the harassment to the police?"

"Rachel didn't want to. She said Gordon was taking care of it, and she wanted to give him the space to do that."

"Why didn't she block the other woman's number?"

"For a while, it was so Gordon could see what Tori was saying to her. Then she did block her, but she continued the harassment from other people's phones. She was relentless. But it had dropped off lately, so we'd hoped she'd given up on bothering Rachel."

"Can you give me both of Rachel's phone numbers?"

"Hang on a minute."

Gonzo heard him comforting his wife before he came back to the phone and recited the two numbers.

"The second one is the new one. We... We never thought her problems with Gordon and his ex-girlfriend would put her in danger. If we had..." Sniffing and sounding tearful, he said, "I mean, we thought it was typical college drama, and she told us it was under control. Do you think they hurt her?"

"We don't know anything yet. We have Gordon and Tori here and plan to question them about their dealings with Rachel."

"The girlfriend is *there*? She goes to school in Georgia. What's she doing there?"

"From what we've learned so far, she was visiting for the weekend."

"So she and Gordon were still together. What the hell? They must've been involved in this."

"We're very early in the investigation. I'll keep you apprised of any developments, and again, we're so sorry for your loss."

"Thank you."

"I'll be in touch."

After he put down the receiver, Gonzo thought about what Mr. Fortier had told him and how he wanted to deal with Gordon and Tori. He picked up the phone again and dialed Archie's number.

"Hey, Sam, I thought you were off."

"It's Gonzo in Sam's office."

"Ah, okay. What's up?"

"I need to dump two phones ASAP. Let me give you the numbers." He recited them both.

"We need a warrant."

"I'll take care of that."

"Let me know when you have it, and I'll get right on it."

Next, he called Malone to ask him to expedite the warrants. "While you're at it, I want to get warrants for two other phones. I'll be right back to you with those numbers."

"I'll get it started," Malone said. "What're you thinking?"

"Love triangle gone wrong is the obvious conclusion. I just need to prove it."

"I'll let you get to that and will keep you in the loop about the goings-on at Stahl's."

"Great, thanks." Gonzo put down the phone just as a knock sounded at the door. "Enter."

Cruz stuck his head in. "Gordon and Tori are set in interview one and two."

"Did you take their cell phones?"

"I did, and I got the numbers, too."

"God, you're the best. Let me have them."

Gonzo wrote them down and then called Malone back to give him Gordon's and Tori's numbers. "I've got their phones and Rachel's and will get them upstairs to Archie." As he spoke, he gave Freddie the signal to go ahead and deliver the phones.

After he finished the call, Gonzo went to the pit to talk to Cameron. "Anything on the socials?"

"Tori Stevens is a piece of work. Nonstop ranting about people who steal other people's boyfriends and how there ought to be a code among women that other people's boyfriends are off-limits."

"I really like her for this," Gonzo said. "I'm just trying to figure out how she could've gotten into Rachel's building and her room, killed her without making a mess and returned to Gordon's room like nothing ever happened."

"I asked Archie for pings as well as data," Cruz said when he returned. "And I asked him to prioritize Tori's phone to see if the pings put her in Rachel's building."

"Text Lindsey and tell her to let us know the minute she has a time of death."

Cruz sent the text. "I heard from Charles that they weren't able to find any abandoned pizza boxes in the suite or in any of the garbage cans in the building. PG County Crime Scene detectives are looking for them in dumpsters and other garbage cans on campus."

"Is it strange that there were no pizza boxes to be found anywhere in a college dorm?" Gonzo asked.

"I thought so, too," Freddie said. "Made me wonder if someone went through floor by floor looking for them or something and then got rid of them all together."

"It's a theory. Pass it on to the PG County detectives."

"I'll text the lieutenant."

"Anything else on the social media?" Gonzo asked Cam.

"Not yet. Will let you know."

"Thanks." To Cruz, he said, "Let's go talk to Gordon."

THE MOTORCADE ARRIVED at the house in Dewey Beach around four, with Sam and Nick looking perfectly respectable when the Secret Service agents opened the door for them. They'd been forced to wait until the agents had fully inspected the house ahead of their arrival.

"Who do they think is lying in wait in there?" Sam asked.

"Could be any number of people."

His list of enemies had expanded exponentially in the four months he'd been president, a fact that terrified her if she allowed herself to think too much about it.

This was no time to be terrified, so she pushed those thoughts to the back of her mind and slammed the mental door shut on negativity so she could fully enjoy this time away with her beloved.

The house was just as she remembered it, with comfortable furnishings and seaside décor.

She walked to the sliding glass door and opened it to step onto the deck that overlooked the dunes, beach and ocean.

A sharp, cold breeze greeted her. "Yikes."

Nick followed her and wrapped his arms around her from behind. "It's not August anymore, Toto."

"Nope, but it's still gorgeous and perfect. You want to walk on the beach?"

"Sure, that sounds good."

Nick went to notify Brant that they wanted to take a walk. "He said they need fifteen minutes."

She could hear the frustration behind the words, so she went to him, put her hands on his chest and kissed him. "It's fine. We can certainly entertain ourselves while they make sure no one is waiting out there to harm my husband."

He put his arms around her. "Or my wife."

"I'm thankful for everything they do to keep us safe. We have to let them have the time it takes to do that."

"Yes, dear."

"Could I please record you saying that so I can play it back any time I need it?"

"And how are you going to record anything on your antique flip phone?"

"My husband has an iPhone."

"Now you want to borrow my phone to use it against me?"

She giggled as she hugged him, loving the silliness, the laughter, the ease of being with him that made this relationship different from all others.

"While I have you in such a good mood, I need to give you a heads-up that we're being featured on *Saturday Night Live* again this week."

Her good mood deflated. "Come on. No way."

"Yes way."

"Why? Why? Why?"

"Um, is that a rhetorical question?"

"I don't hate you for being president, but I hate you for making me an *SNL* target."

"You really hate me?"

"I really do."

He put his arms around her, letting his hands slide down to cup her ass and bring her in tight against him. "I bet I could change your mind about that."

She turned her face away from his kiss, which he then directed to her neck. "That'll depend on how badly I'm humiliated by *SNL*."

Damn if she could resist those neck kisses.

"All set Mr. President, Mrs. Cappuano," Brant said from the front door.

Nick extended his hand to her. "Let's walk, love."

"I still hate you."

"Duly noted," he said with a chuckle.

They had the beach to themselves, except for the White House press corps, which had apparently accompanied them on their trip. Sam wanted to scream at them to leave him alone, for God's sake, but she bit her tongue so she wouldn't be the lead story around the world.

Nick tuned in to her outrage. "Just ignore them."

"Easier said than done."

"I know, but what do we care if they take pictures of us?" He put his arm around her shoulders. "Let the whole world see how much I love my wife."

She put her arm around his waist. "And how much I love

my husband."

"Just no grab-ass, you hear me?"

"Buzz killer."

"I'll make it up to you later."

"I'll look forward to that. In the meantime, how is it still so freaking cold?"

"Supposed to get warmer in the next few days."

"I can't wait for that. I'm so over the cold."

"The cold air feels amazing to me. Better than the stale White House air."

"I'm sure it is."

They walked until their faces were numb from the cold and then turned back, coming face-to-face with the gaggle of photographers and camera-people who were stalking them.

"Ignore," he said under his breath.

"Ignoring. Since they're in front of us, is this allowed?" Sam dropped her hand to squeeze his ass.

"Not allowed."

"Just checking."

"Don't be fresh."

"You like when I'm fresh."

"Watch what you say. I'm sure some of them are accomplished lip readers."

"For fuck's sake."

"Sam!"

"Whoops. Sorry."

He shook with silent laughter.

"I'd like to remind you that I warned you *way back* at the *very* beginning that I'd be a political liability, and you chose to take me on anyway. Oh wait, was that when you were promising me one year in the Senate? Hmmm…"

"Are you angling for a"—he put his hand over his mouth—"spanking, by any chance?"

"Oh yes, please."

"Knock it off. I don't want photos of me with a"—he covered his mouth again—"boner on the front of every paper in the world."

"Then quit talking about things that will cause that."

"This walk was a terrible idea."

"You might want to explain things to me ahead of time in the future."

If there was anything more fun than sparring with her gorgeous, witty, sexy husband, Sam had yet to discover it. Even hunting down murderers couldn't compete with him on the scale of the most fun she'd ever had.

As they walked up the beach to the path that led to their house for the next ten days, reporters started yelling questions at them.

"Mr. President, have you met with the new Joint Chiefs yet?"

"Do you have a comment on the statement issued by General Wilson?"

"Is it true that former Lieutenant Stahl has been connected with missing women?"

"Did you pay your mother's bail?"

That last one had Nick going tight with tension.

His mother had made bail? That was news to Sam—and apparently to him as well.

"Don't react," she said through gritted teeth. "Just keep walking."

They went up the stairs and through the sliding door that Brant opened for them.

"We're in for the night," Nick told him.

"Very well, sir. We'll be next door and will have agents positioned around the perimeter. We took the liberty of lighting the fire for you. Please enjoy your evening."

"Thank you. We will."

The White House chef had sent meals for the next couple of days, with more shipments coming in a couple of days.

Sam was also determined to go out to dinner at least one night while they were there. She went to the fridge to find out what the chef had sent. "What do you feel like? Tenderloin with mashed potatoes and green beans, or shrimp and pasta?"

"Tenderloin for the win."

"That got my vote, too."

Per the instructions that had been affixed to the containers, Sam set the oven on 350 and put the meals in to warm for thirty minutes. Then she poured a glass of the rosé that Tracy had told her about. She'd added it to the food-and-beverage order she'd placed through the chief usher, Gideon Lawson, ahead of the trip.

She'd wanted Nick to have all his favorite things.

As she opened a bottle of Sam Adams for him, she glanced at him standing at the slider, looking out on the beach. His hands were in his pockets, but his shoulders told the true story of a man burdened by things no one else on earth had to deal with.

Sam put their drinks on the glass coffee table. "Come sit with me."

He came over to join her.

She pointed to the floor in front of her. "There."

When he was seated, she began to knead the tension from his shoulders. "I need you fully relaxed and not thinking about anything but me and us."

"This is a good start." After a moment, he added, "You heard what they said about my mother making bail."

"I did, and we don't care about her. What goes on with her is none of our business."

"Right."

She was painfully aware that this particular topic didn't work like that for him. Sam hoped if she kept reminding him that his mother was nothing to him that he might be able to forget about her. Nicoletta had been arrested for prostitution and racketeering in Ohio more than a week ago. Since then, Nick had struggled with her being in jail when he could fix things for her with one phone call.

Sam had carefully encouraged him not to make that call. Everything involving his mother was like an emotional minefield that she had to tiptoe through to help steer him away from involvement with the woman who'd repeatedly broken his heart. If Sam had anything to say about it, she'd never get close enough to him to hurt him again.

"How do you think she made bail?" he asked. "I heard they froze her assets."

Sam wanted to weep from the vulnerability in his voice as they talked about Nicoletta. It was like he had a whole separate tone reserved only for his mother—one filled with heartache. "Does it matter?"

"I guess not. I was just wondering."

Sam rested her chin on the top of his head as she continued to massage his tight shoulders and neck. "I hate this for you. I hate everything about it."

"I know, and that helps." After a pause, he said, "Will you be annoyed if I want to know the details?"

Yes, she wanted to say, but that wasn't what he needed to hear. "Of course not. I'm here to support you in any way that I can. You're in charge of how you handle her."

"It makes no sense to you. I get that."

"It doesn't have to make sense to me. And don't forget, I've had my own mother struggles." Things with her mother were much better these days after twenty years of silence between them after her parents' divorce. Sam had sided firmly with her father, but had later learned there were two sides to the story, and her mother hadn't been entirely to blame. "Nothing like what you've endured, but it hasn't been easy."

"True. Would you care if I asked Avery to make some subtle inquiries into how she posted bail?"

"I wouldn't care if it gave you peace of mind to know the details."

"Thank you for understanding and for sticking with me through all the bullshit."

"I've provided a good dose of bullshit to this marriage, too."

"Thank God all the bullshit is out there," he said, gesturing outside their cozy bubble, "and never in here."

"Never in here."

"Come down here with me."

CHAPTER FIVE

S am moved from the sofa to the floor, sitting next to him as they leaned back against the sofa. "Nice fire."

"I love the way it makes your cheeks rosy."

"Does it?"

"Uh-huh." He nuzzled her face. "So, so beautiful."

Other men had told her she was beautiful, but when this man said it, he made her believe it. He didn't see her flaws, of which there were many, in her opinion.

She leaned her head on his shoulder. "I thought I'd be disappointed not to go to Bora Bora, but this is almost better."

"Because you didn't have to spend twenty hours on an airplane to get here?"

"That's one very big reason, but we don't need to go somewhere fancy to have a good time together. This is all we need."

"And it doesn't take twenty hours on a plane to get here."

She bumped against him as she laughed. "At least you won't have the media critiquing your carbon footprint."

"There is that."

When Sam's phone rang, she ignored it.

"Go ahead and take that. It's fine."

She got up from the floor to retrieve the phone from the kitchen and took the call from Freddie.

"Hey."

"Sorry to bother you on the getaway."

"It's fine. What's up?"

"I wasn't going to call you, but Elin said I should, that you wouldn't care."

"Elin was right. Are you okay?"

"I'm trying to wrap my head around having worked closely with a man who might be a serial killer. I mean, we haven't proven anything yet, but we all know he's capable."

Sam wasn't surprised that her kindhearted partner was undone by this latest development. "It's disbelief on top of disbelief."

"Yeah, exactly that. I didn't think he could shock me any more than he already has. I read the report Malone filed with the info provided by his informant. It's believed that Stahl was using the women as part of his various schemes to pin crimes on innocent people, such as Eric Davies. Tiffany Jones, one of the missing women, was used to entrap him and was never seen again after he was convicted."

"Jesus." Sam felt sick. "And Stahl had the perfect cover as a police officer."

"Right. They've scheduled a hearing on the Davies case for a week from Tuesday."

"That man shouldn't spend another night in prison." Evidence showed that Stahl had framed Davies for rape after he complained about Stahl's treatment of him during a traffic stop years earlier.

"These things take a minute, as you know."

"It's sickening, revolting and every other word that means disgusting that I can think of."

"And it's going to make every hardworking police officer in America look like crap," Freddie said, "the way it always does when something like this comes to light."

"We just have to keep our heads down and do the job. That's all we can do."

"Do you think there're others like him? Ramsey, for

example. Was he running a criminal enterprise on the side while on the job?"

"There're probably others, but the one thing I know for certain is that there're more of us than there are of them, so try not to surrender to despair."

"It's hard not to when our job is to uphold the law, and people in our ranks are criminals."

"I know, but what do we always say? The only things we can control are our own actions and how we react to the actions of others. By keeping our focus where it belongs, we'll get through this."

"Elin was right. I feel better after talking to you."

"Likewise, my friend. Let me ask you a favor. I have to run down the families of two of the missing women. Would you mind taking a look at what you can find out about them beyond what's in the reports?" She gave him the two names.

"No problem. Do you have a way to print there?"

"Yeah, Nick has a whole office set up here."

"I'll do it first thing and send it to you."

"Thank you. Now go have a big drink and enjoy your evening with Elin. Tomorrow is another day."

"Thanks for taking the call."

"I'll always take your call, grasshopper."

"Have a good time at the beach. See you next weekend."

"Call me if you need me this week."

"I will. Later."

Sam closed her phone and thought about their conversation. It was impossible for Freddie, who did the job with honesty and compassion, to understand the actions of someone like Stahl. Hell, it was hard for *her* to understand them, and she was far more jaded than her partner. She'd learned not to expect the best of people when she saw so much of the worst. That was part of her nature, while kindness and compassion were part of his. Those qualities made him exceptionally good at a difficult job, but made him question every choice he'd ever made for his career at a time like this.

"Is Freddie okay?" Nick asked.

"He's reeling over the latest disclosures about Stahl."

"As he would."

Sam returned to her spot on the floor next to him. "He's almost too good for this world sometimes."

"That's why we love him so much."

"Indeed, but he takes things like this extra hard."

"You said all the right things. I'm sure he feels better after talking it out with you."

"He said he did." She put her head back on Nick's shoulder. "Why do people have to do stuff like this? I mean, at what point do they go from being innocent little children to people who would falsely charge a man with rape and then disappear the woman he used to secure the conviction, as well as a bunch of other women? When does that happen?"

"It's hard to say, but if you ask me, that's in them from the start, and life brings it to the surface."

"I suppose. I'm glad it's not in me. What a dreadful way to live."

He moved her head from his shoulder only long enough to put his arm around her. "I'm glad it's not in you either. You have just the right amount of kindness, compassion and meanness to be good at your job and your life."

"Had to toss the meanness in there, huh?"

"It's what makes you you, my love."

"Hardy har har."

"Freddie lacks that edge, so he suffers that much more when others inflict harm."

"You have us all figured out."

"Am I wrong?"

"Not at all. Does it make me mean to admit that when I heard there were others, I was glad it wasn't just me he came after?"

"I think that makes you human."

"I feel terrible for everyone who ever tangled with him and lost."

"A shrink would have a field day with a guy who had trouble getting along with people on and off the job—you have to assume he had the same issues off the job, including with women—turning out to be such a prolific criminal."

"I need to talk to Dr. Trulo about that. I want to try to understand this."

"You'll never fully understand it. Tell me you know that."

"I do, but I still want some insight into how this happens."

"Can you let it go for the time being so you can enjoy your vacation?"

"Absolutely, but there's apt to be more calls like that one."

"I'm sure I'll get a few calls, too."

Sam laughed at the absurd understatement. "I'm sure you will."

WHEN GONZO and Cruz walked into the interrogation room, Gordon Reilly was halfway lying on the table, his head on his arms as his shoulders shook with sobs. The face of the man who looked up at them when they entered was ravaged with grief.

"What happened to her? To Rachel?"

"We don't know yet."

Freddie turned on the recorder and noted the three people in the room.

"How can she be dead? I saw her in class on Monday. She was fine. What could've happened?"

"Did you speak to her when you saw her Monday?"

He shook his head. "She asked me to stay away from her until I resolved the situation with Tori. I've been trying to work that out, but…"

"Did Tori know you were seeing someone else?" Gonzo asked.

"Not specifically, but we agreed to see other people when we went to college."

"Whose idea was that?" Cruz asked. "Yours or hers?"

He wiped away tears that streamed down his face. "Mine, but she agreed to it. It was fine for the first two years. I mean, I hung out with other women, but it was nothing special until I

met Rachel. Everything about her was different from the start."
He looked crushed as he seemed to once again recall that she
was dead. "She's the sweetest, kindest person I've ever met."

Gonzo sat across from him. "How much did you tell Tori
about her?"

"Not much of anything."

"You never mentioned Rachel to her by name?"

"Not specifically, no. I mean... She's had a lot of struggles
since we've been apart. She hasn't made many friends at
Georgia, so that's been tough, and she said she didn't date
anyone else. I, uh, I think she tried to transfer up here, but she
didn't get in because her grades at Georgia haven't been that
good."

"Would Tori have noticed you pulling away from her since
you've been seeing Rachel?"

"I, uh, I don't think so."

Gonzo gave him a skeptical look. Of course she'd noticed.
"Did you visit her in Georgia?"

"Not this year, but I've been there a couple of times the past
two years."

"Other than this week, did she visit you here?"

"A few times freshman and sophomore year, but only this
once this year. I saw her when we were home at Christmas,
too."

"Where's home?"

"Milwaukee area. We went to high school in Franklin."

"Is there any chance that Tori could've harmed Rachel?"
Gonzo asked.

He sat up straight, his face registering shock. "No! She
didn't even know about her!"

"And you're sure of that?" Gonzo asked.

"I'm positive. I never mentioned Rachel's name to Tori."

"Is she in touch with any of your friends here?" Cruz asked.

"Not really."

"If she checked your social media or Rachel's or one of your
friends, for example, would Tori have seen photos of you with
her?" Cruz asked.

Gordon thought about that, seeming a bit stunned by the possibility. "I don't think so. Rachel and I mostly hung out by ourselves and not in groups."

"Did you ever socialize with others?" Cruz asked.

"I, uh, I don't think—" After a few seconds passed, he said, "There was a party before Christmas break. My friend Jeff had everyone over. Rachel went with me."

"Had Tori met Jeff before?"

"Maybe on one of the times she was here freshman or sophomore year? I'm not sure."

"Were pictures from the party posted online?"

"I... I'm not sure. I don't do much with social media. I have an old Facebook account, but I rarely check it."

"What's Jeff's last name?"

"Montgomery."

Gonzo glanced at Freddie, who got up and left the room to have a look at Montgomery's social media.

"You... You don't think Tori did something to her, do you?"

"Do you?"

"No! She wouldn't do that."

Gonzo said nothing, hoping the young man might come around to believing it was possible on his own.

"She couldn't have. She was with me all night. Well, except for when she went for a walk last night. But how would she even know where Rachel was?"

That was a question Gonzo would like an answer to as well.

"Tori couldn't have hurt her. She just couldn't have. Yes, she was upset about our breakup, but that wasn't about Rachel."

"What was it about?"

"We'd grown apart. The long-distance relationship was hard to maintain when we were both meeting lots of new people."

"But you said Tori wasn't really interested in new people."

"I encouraged her to get out there and enjoy herself. She said she couldn't do that without me."

"I'm going to talk to her. Stay put."

Gonzo left the room and met Cruz in the hallway.

"This is what I found. Took me all of three seconds."

He handed Gonzo a printout of a December post that showed friends gathered at a holiday party. In one of them, Gordon had an arm around Rachel, who smiled as she leaned into him.

"There it is," Gonzo said. "Let's pull Tori's financials and see what she's been up to behind the scenes."

"I'll take care of that."

"Has everyone else left?"

"It's six thirty."

"Oh shit." He was supposed to have been at Stahl's house hours ago. "You can go if you need to get home."

"I'll stay until we're done."

"Let me know what you find on the financials."

"I'll do it right now."

"Great, thanks."

Gonzo nodded to the Patrol officer standing outside the other interrogation room. When he stepped inside, Tori shot to her feet.

"You have to let me out of here."

"Have a seat." He turned on the recorder and recited his name and hers.

"I want to leave."

"I understand that, but you're not leaving until you're arraigned."

"For what?"

"You kicked my partner. Assaulting a police officer is a crime."

"He scared me coming at me all hostile and shit when I had no idea what was going on."

"You can tell it to the judge. Hopefully, we'll have someone here tomorrow. Otherwise, you'll be our guest until Monday."

"I have class on Monday! I have to get back to Georgia."

Gonzo ignored that. "Tell me about your relationship with Gordon."

"Wh-what business is that of yours?"

"Have you ever been anywhere near a homicide investigation?"

Her eyes bugged. "*A h-homicide investigation?* No, I haven't."

"Then you wouldn't know that everything is my business when I'm investigating a potential murder."

"You think Rachel was *murdered*?"

Gonzo found it interesting that she spoke of Rachel like she'd known her when Gordon had been so sure she didn't. He'd get back to that.

"About you and Gordon..."

"We... I... We met in middle school... We were good friends until tenth grade when we started to date. Everything was fine... Everything was *great*, until it was time to leave for college. I wanted to go to the same school as him, but my parents were adamant that I not choose a college based on a boy."

Gonzo had to give the parents credit for having some sense.

"I didn't want to be away from Gordon. I love him."

"How did you feel when he suggested you two see other people while in college?"

"I was devastated. I don't want anyone but him, and hearing that he could want other girls... It broke me."

"But you agreed to it?"

"I wanted to do whatever it took to get through school so we could be together again. That was my only goal."

Gonzo put the picture of Gordon and Rachel on the table between them. "Seeing this must've really upset you."

Her expression turned thunderous when she saw the photo. She immediately pushed it away.

"Well?"

"Well, what?"

"What did you think when you saw that photo online?"

"What do you think I thought? I was upset."

"Even though you'd agreed to see other people?"

"I never agreed to that. It was what *he* wanted. Not me."

"So when you saw him in a photo with his arm around another girl, that must've made you angry as well as upset."

She shrugged. "I was devastated."

"Did you tell him you'd seen the photo?"

"No, because we were home for the winter break, and I wanted to enjoy the time we had together."

"Even though you now knew he was seeing someone at school?"

"I didn't know that. I saw a picture of him with a girl. That's all I knew."

"I'm going to put this right out there. I don't believe that. I've known you two hours, and I have absolutely no doubt you did a deep dive on her the second you saw that photo. I'll bet you had her birthday and possibly her Social Security number in a matter of minutes."

Tori shifted restlessly in her seat.

Gonzo wouldn't call it a *squirm*, per se, but it was close.

"You also just referred to her by name as if you knew her."

"When did I do that?"

"When you asked me if Rachel had been murdered. If you didn't know of her, you might've said 'that girl Gordon knew' or something like that. Instead, you very specifically asked me if Rachel had been murdered. Interesting, wouldn't you say?"

"I didn't know her!"

"You know what I think, Tori? That you had motive and opportunity to kill Rachel in the time you were away from Gordon's room last night."

"I didn't kill her!"

Freddie came into the room with a stack of pages with highlighted details.

"No, but you harassed her for months with threatening messages about what would happen to her if she didn't leave your boyfriend alone," Freddie said, putting the pages in front of Gonzo.

"Well, look at this," Gonzo said. "'Leave him alone, or I'll fucking kill you.'"

"That was before Rachel had to switch phone numbers to make it stop." He handed Gonzo another stack of pages. "This is what happened once Tori got ahold of the new number. And how did you do that, anyway?"

Tori had her arms crossed and a defiant expression on her face. "I want a lawyer."

Gonzo gathered the papers, turned off the recording and stood to leave.

"Where're you going?" she asked in a high-pitched screech.

"I can't speak to you any further until your lawyer is present. Let us know who you'd like us to call for you."

"How should I know? I don't live here."

"Would you like us to call the public defender's office for you?"

"No, I want to call my parents. They'll get me someone."

"Give me their number. I'll make the call."

She seemed to hesitate, as if trying to decide if she should argue further with him before she recited the number. "Tell them I didn't do anything."

"I'll be sure to let them know."

Gonzo left the room, with Cruz following him. "What a fucking piece of work she is. I feel sorry for Rachel—and for Gordon—for having to deal with her."

"You think she killed Rachel?" Cruz asked.

"I think she had a beef a mile wide with her, but until we know the results of the autopsy, we won't know for sure if she was murdered."

"She was," Lindsey said as she joined them in the pit. "It took me a bit to figure out how, but I found it."

CHAPTER SIX

After a dinner he'd barely touched, Cameron sat at his kitchen table with Gigi to finally read the full text of the lawsuit against them and the department, charging the wrongful deaths of Jaycee Patrick and her mother at the hands of Gigi and Fairfax County SWAT. The suit tracked both wrongful deaths back to Jaycee's relationship with Cameron and how Gigi had shot Jaycee after Jaycee attacked Gigi in her home.

He'd put it off for days because he couldn't bear to look at it. But because it required a response within fourteen days, he'd run out of time to pretend it wasn't happening.

"This feels like a nightmare that refuses to end." Cam sipped a beer as he tried to wrap his head around a ten-million-dollar lawsuit. If they both sold everything they owned, they wouldn't be able to come up with a million, let alone ten, not to mention the attorney fees that could bankrupt them.

"It'll end eventually," Gigi said, "but first we have to deal with it. It's time to call Andy."

"I wanted to talk to you before I made the call to make sure you didn't have someone else in mind."

"I don't know too many lawyers except the criminal ones we encounter on the job."

They needed a top-rate civil defense attorney for the lawsuit.

Cameron glanced at her warily. "I know I've said it a million times, but I'm so sorry to have brought this bullshit into your life."

She put her hand over his, her touch instantly calming him. "You didn't. She did, and we'll get through it together."

"At what point does it become too much?"

"What do you mean?"

"My ex-girlfriend attacks you, assaults you in the most invasive way possible, leaves you fighting for your job and now your financial future. When will you decide that being with me isn't worth it?"

"Um, never? The only one blaming you for this is you, not me. Never me."

"You're being *sued*, Gigi. Fucking *sued*."

"I have every confidence that we'll prevail against this ridiculous lawsuit. She entered my home uninvited, held me hostage, assaulted me and forced me to defend myself. If the whole thing happened again, I wouldn't do anything differently. What choice did I have? I'll continue to share my truth with anyone who needs to hear it, from Internal Affairs at work to the Patrick family members suing us, until this whole thing goes away."

"Your courage astounds me. I'm like a quivering mess of anxiety over being sued, and you're cool as can be."

"Don't get me wrong. I'm worried and stressed about the cost of defending against this, but I'm not at all concerned about whether we'll win. We didn't do anything wrong, and we know it."

"Keep reminding me of that, okay?"

"Any time you need to hear it. Why don't you call Andy and get his take on it? We might feel better when we have some solid legal advice."

Cameron checked the time and decided to text the attorney rather than calling after hours.

Hi, Andy,

My boss, Sam Holland, suggested I get in touch. I'm in need of an attorney after having been sued, along with my girlfriend and fellow detective, Gigi Dominguez, over a fatal incident involving my ex and a secondary fatal incident involving her mother. Would love to touch base to discuss representation with you or another attorney you might recommend. Needless to say, this is a first for us, and we're unnerved by the prospect of being sued. Look forward to hearing from you. Det. Cameron Green

He shared the text with Gigi. "Does that sound okay?"

"Perfect."

Cam sent the text. Not even a minute later, his phone rang with a call from Andy. Cameron put the call on speaker. "Hi, Andy. Thanks so much for calling after hours."

"No such thing in my line of work, or yours, right?"

Cameron liked him immediately. "That's right."

"Fill me in on the details of what happened."

Gigi took hold of Cameron's hand. "Let me."

She told Andy about Jaycee's multiple attempts to undermine Cameron's new relationship with Gigi, culminating with the attack in Gigi's home, the details of Jaycee putting her fingers inside Gigi, saying she wanted to know what Cameron saw in her. Then, when the incident escalated and Gigi realized that Jaycee intended to kill her, how Gigi had used her service weapon to kill Jaycee. Cam was filled with revulsion over what Jaycee had done and awe for Gigi's cool, unemotional recitation of events that had left her shattered.

Cameron picked up the story with how Mrs. Patrick had taken their colleague, Deputy Chief Jeannie McBride, hostage in her home and was killed by Fairfax County SWAT. "The Patrick family is asserting that their deaths were my fault and Gigi's, which is ludicrous."

"Certainly sounds that way. I assume you have these incidents fully documented?"

"We do," Gigi said. "We can get you copies of the official reports of everything with Jaycee and her mother. I should add I'm currently on paid leave until an Internal Affairs hearing this week."

"Have you secured representation for the hearing?" Andy asked.

"Not yet. I was planning to fly solo, actually."

"I wouldn't," Andy said. "These things can go south quickly. I'd be happy to represent you there and to help try to make this lawsuit go away. I can offer you the friends-and-family rate since Sam recommended me."

"Thank you so much, Andy," Cameron said. "It's a huge relief to have someone of your caliber helping us."

"I'll do everything I can for you."

"We'd be so thankful for that," Gigi said.

"Send me a scan of the lawsuit, the reports you mentioned, along with contact info for both of you, and I'll be back in touch in a day or two." He recited his email address, which Gigi wrote down. "Also, give me the information about when and where your IAB hearing is."

After they said profuse thank-yous and ended the call, Cameron said, "Well, that's a huge fucking relief, huh?"

"Sure is. As is the friends-and-family rate."

"Thank goodness for friends in high places."

Gigi held up her wineglass in a mock toast. "No kidding." She put down her glass and held his hand between both of hers. "Can we put this madness aside for now and enjoy the weekend?"

"We can sure as hell try."

Lindsey gestured for Gonzo and Freddie to follow her to the conference room, where she placed several printouts on the table. "I was leaning toward natural causes, even though she's young and her friends said she was in good health. Believe it or not, sudden, unexplainable death happens at all ages, even with people who appear to be in perfectly good health."

Gonzo wanted to tell her to get on with it, but he'd never say that out loud. Lindsey was the best of the best, and she'd get to the point. Eventually.

"I had to think like a killer to figure out what happened."

She pointed to a photo that had been zoomed in. "Do you see this faint bruise on her neck?"

They leaned in for a closer look.

"What about it?" Gonzo asked.

"I believe someone pressed on her neck hard enough to restrict her carotid artery, which would lead to brain death after a sudden decrease in cerebral blood flow. I put her time of death around ten o'clock last night."

"So whoever restricted the carotid artery knew what they were doing," Gonzo said. "We need to ask Tori what her major is at college."

"I checked her social media, and it's nursing," Freddie said.

"Very interesting," Gonzo said. "Anything else of note, Lindsey?"

"One thing... There was a print on the bruise, but nowhere else on her body. The print isn't in CODIS or IAFIS."

"Thanks for another great job, Doc."

"You got it," Lindsey said. "I'll send my full report to your email."

After she left the conference room, Freddie said, "I just got Tori's financials, and they're also very interesting. There's more than fifty thousand dollars in her checking account, even after she wrote a check for ten thousand dollars that cleared a week ago."

"How in the hell does a college kid have that kind of money?" Gonzo asked.

"I looked into her family. The dad made a fortune in the steel business. He's the founder and CEO of a company in the Milwaukee area."

"I want to know who she wrote the check to," Gonzo said.

"Maybe she hired someone to get the competition out of the way," Freddie said.

"It's certainly possible, especially since she had access to that kind of money."

"I'll scroll back a couple of months to find out if there were other payments made to someone to keep tabs on what the boyfriend was up to in DC while she was in Georgia. I also think we need a warrant for her computer, which may be in Gordon's dorm room."

"Good idea," Gonzo said. "While you get that started, I'll call the parents about getting her a lawyer, and then I've got to get to Stahl's."

"You want me to go with you?"

"You don't have to."

"I know I don't. I'm offering."

"I won't say no to any help I can get with that."

"I'll let Elin know it's going to be a late one."

"Thanks, Freddie," Gonzo said as he went into Sam's office and closed the door to call yet another set of parents with news that would rock their world. However, in this case, he wondered if they'd reaped what they'd sown with Tori. "Mrs. Stevens, this is Detective Sergeant Tommy Gonzales with the Metro Police Department in Washington, DC."

"What's wrong? Did something happen to Tori or Gordon?"

"No, something happened to Gordon's new girlfriend, and we're investigating your daughter's activities over the last twenty-four hours. In addition, she's being charged with assaulting a police officer."

She released a loud gasp. "*What?*"

"You heard me, ma'am. Gordon's girlfriend at GW, Rachel Fortier, was found dead in her bed this morning. We have Tori in custody, and she's requesting an attorney. She told us to call you about getting someone here for her."

"Gordon doesn't have another girlfriend, and I don't know of any attorneys in Washington! Tori never would've had anything to do with something like this!"

"I can assure you that Gordon *did* have a new girlfriend in DC. Tori knew about her and had been harassing her by text for months. She was nearby when Rachel was murdered. I'm sure your local lawyer can direct you toward someone who can help, or you can consult the local DC Bar Association for a list of attorneys. Until she has representation, Tori will be our guest at the city jail."

"You can't just hold her on suspicion."

"We're holding her until she can be arraigned on the assault charges. We're continuing to investigate the murder of Rachel Fortier and Tori's possible involvement. The sooner you send someone to represent her, the sooner we can determine next steps."

"I want to talk to her."

"That's not possible right now. We'll have her call you tomorrow. You can call me at this number to let me know when there's an attorney on the way." He gave her his extension.

"I don't know who you think you are, but I'll have your badge for accusing my daughter of something so sinister. She's a college student! Not a *murderer*."

"I'll wait to hear back from you about the attorney." He ended the call before she could make any other threats. At least now he understood where Tori's sense of entitlement came from. He sat back in Sam's chair and ran both hands through his hair, exhausted from the long day that wasn't over yet.

Freddie knocked on the door and came in. "Found some more payments from the account—five hundred here, a thousand there. I think we need to ask her about them and see what she says when the lawyer gets here. In the meantime, I asked Malone to request a warrant for her canceled checks and to search her computer. I asked Charles and O'Brien to go back to Gordon's dorm room and get the computers. We'll ask Gordon which one is his and which one is hers, if she brought it with her."

"Good work, Freddie. Thanks."

"How'd it go with her parents?"

"Their darling princess had nothing to do with any of this."

"Of course not."

"I recommended the parents get an attorney here sooner rather than later." Gonzo glanced at the clock, which was heading toward seven thirty, which meant he wouldn't get to see his son, Alex, before bedtime. That made him sad, as Alex was the highlight of his days. "Let's get to Stahl's house and see what's going on there before we head home."

"I'm with you, Sarge."

When they were in Gonzo's Charger on the way to Brookside, he looked over at Cruz. "Shoot the LT a text giving her an update on the Fortier case, will you? She asked to be kept in the loop."

"Yep." He tapped away on his iPhone. "All set."

"Thank you."

"I told her we were headed to Stahl's. I wasn't sure if she'd want to know that."

"She would. I'm glad she's on vacation and not here for this, though. She doesn't need to be anywhere near this madness."

"No, she doesn't. I was surprised they asked her to brief two of the families while she's in Delaware."

"I think that might've been their way of keeping her involved, but not in the middle of it."

"Possibly. I feel for her. This must bring it all back for her."

"Seriously. I thought we'd seen the last of him when he was convicted and sent to prison, but it turned out we were just scratching the surface. At least they've finally got the Davies hearing on the calendar for next week."

"That case makes me sick."

"Me, too."

Even though it was dark, the area around 15th Street Northeast was lit up like daytime. They had to park blocks from the scene, which was surrounded by police and public safety vehicles.

"Jesus," Gonzo said as they took in the surreal view of their former lieutenant's home.

"I never had the first clue where he lived," Freddie said.

"Me either. The less I knew about him, the better."

"Yeah, same."

SVU Detective Erica Lucas was conferring with a Patrol officer when Gonzo and Freddie walked up to the gate outside the house. Due to Christina's addiction to HGTV, Gonzo recognized it as a Craftsman style, with a large front porch and a dormer on the second floor. The house was painted yellow with blue shutters and matching flower boxes under the first-floor window. Someone had taken some time to make the place attractive. Gonzo was sure the credit for that did not go to Stahl.

"Hey." Lucas looked and sounded as exhausted as Gonzo felt.

"How's it going?"

"Slow and methodical. The sister and her kids had taken over the first floor, so that part of the house is completely compromised. Interestingly, there was a lock on the door to the basement that the sister didn't have a key to."

Gonzo's stomach took a weird drop at hearing that. What fresh hell would they find in that basement? "Did Haggerty get in?"

"The warrant came through an hour ago, and they broke the lock."

"Any word from them since?"

"Not yet."

"I'm terrified to go in there," Gonzo said.

"Right there with you," Lucas said. "The sister is losing it over being forced out. Threatening all sorts of legal action. She says her brother signed the house over to her before he went to prison. We're looking into that now, but in the meantime, we've told her the house is a possible crime scene, and she won't be allowed back in for quite some time. We recommended she find somewhere else to live in the meantime. She didn't like that. I'm worried she'll blow the lid off this situation with the media before we have a chance to control the narrative."

"Where is she?"

"We put her up in a hotel near the kids' school for now."

"After I leave here, I'll swing by and have a chat with her."

Lucas handed him a page from her notebook that had the address on it. "I'd be forever thankful to you for handling her. I know it's shocking to hear, but she's not very nice."

"Runs in the family," Cruz muttered.

"I'll take care of it." Gonzo glanced at the house. He *really* did not want to go in there.

"I can take this if you want to see the sister," Cruz said, probably picking up on his dread.

Gonzo would never delegate a task like that to anyone, let alone one of his best friends on and off the job. "It's okay. I'll do both. You can split if you want."

"There's no way I'm leaving you to deal with this by yourself."

"I won't be by myself. Lucas is here."

Freddie stared at him without blinking. "I'm staying."

Gonzo would never admit to anyone other than himself that he was relieved. He wouldn't have blamed his friend for running far away from this nightmare.

"Erica, if you want to ask the sister what they need from the house, we'll take it to her. Maybe it'll help to smooth things over with her and keep her quiet."

"I'll ask her and text you."

Gonzo glanced at Freddie. "Let's get this done."

They walked through the gate in the white picket fence.

"This looks like something out of a sitcom or something," Freddie said.

"My thoughts exactly."

At the front door, they showed their badges to the Patrol officers, two young women who were not familiar to him.

"Sergeant Gonzales, Detective Cruz from Homicide."

One of the officers lifted the crime scene tape across the door and held it for them as they ducked under it.

Against an entryway wall, two backpacks hung from hooks.

"We should take those to the sister," Gonzo said.

"I'll grab them on the way out."

They went to the hallway where the basement door stood open. The low hum of voices from below had them heading down the stairs. A musty smell reminded Gonzo of the creepy basement in his grandparents' West Virginia home. He and his sisters had once played hide-and-seek down there. He'd been so freaked out that he'd never gone down there again.

The memory of that smell gave him goosebumps as they landed on a concrete floor.

It took about two seconds for him to want out of there.

Usually, it took a lot to spook him. Knowing what might've happened down there only added to his anxiety.

"What've you got?" he asked Crime Scene Lieutenant Haggerty.

"Nothing out of the ordinary. Yet."

That last word—*yet*—told Gonzo the CSU lieutenant fully expected to find *something*.

"Is there anything we can do to help?"

"Not at the moment, but I was told to keep you in the loop. I'll send you an update later. We're operating around the clock here until we're done."

"Say the word if there's anything we can do."

"I will. Thanks. I heard PG County is covering us at the GW thing?"

"Yes."

"I'll send along my thanks."

Gonzo checked his phone and found a text from Lucas with the list of items Stahl's sister and her kids needed from the house. It included clothing, medication and the backpacks they'd noticed on the way in. It took about fifteen minutes to gather everything, which they put in bags they found under the kitchen sink. On impulse, he grabbed a few stuffed animals from each of the kids' rooms and put them in the bag, too. Regardless of what he thought of Stahl—and the sister, who'd given his colleagues such a hard time—none of it was the fault of innocent kids.

CHAPTER SEVEN

Gonzo drove to the hotel on Massachusetts Avenue, where they met the Patrol officer standing watch at the lobby elevators.

They showed him their badges.

"Room 413, Sarge."

"Thanks."

They hoofed it up the stairwell because it was faster than waiting for the elevator.

Another Patrol officer guarded the door to the room. They showed him their badges.

"She's very upset, Sarge."

"So we've heard." Gonzo knocked on the door. "Open up."

The heavy-set woman who came to the door bore a faint resemblance to her brother, with the same full face and eyes that could only be described as beady.

"Can you give us a minute?" he asked the Patrol officer, who nodded and moved down the hallway.

They handed over the bags of things they'd brought from the house. "I'm Sergeant Gonzales, this is Detective Cruz. Could we speak to you for a few minutes?"

She took the bags from them and put them inside the room. "I've already told the other cops that I know nothing about anything Lenny did at the house."

"We'd still like to speak to you."

"My kids are sleeping."

"Can you step outside?"

"Do I have to?"

"We can either do this here or at the station. Your choice."

Her scowl reminded Gonzo of her brother as she stepped outside the room, leaving the door propped open. "What do you want to know?"

Gonzo pulled his notebook from his coat pocket. "Your full name."

"Cindy Stahl Brenner."

"Age?"

"Forty-five."

"Are you Leonard Stahl's only sibling?"

"I'm his only living half sibling. We shared the same father."

"Is your father still living?"

She shook her head. "He died more than ten years ago of cirrhosis of the liver."

"So the two of you didn't grow up together?"

"Lenny came to live with my family when he was thirteen and I was a baby."

"Where did your family live?"

"Right here in the District, about four blocks from here."

"And where did he live prior to coming to your home?"

"Somewhere local. I'm not sure where. We weren't exactly close. He was out of the house before I went to kindergarten."

"Why did he come to live with you when he did?"

"Something happened with his mother. I'm not sure what, but the police were involved. I never have heard the whole story."

"You said you were his only living half sibling," Freddie said. "There were others?"

"One other," she said on a sigh. "I had another brother, Michael. He was four years older than me."

"What happened to him?" Gonzo asked.

"I don't know. He disappeared when he was in high school.

Lenny always said Michael was why he became a police officer. He said he never stopped looking for Michael."

Or, Gonzo thought, *Lenny knew exactly what happened to Michael and became a police officer to cover up his crimes.*

"What was your relationship with Lenny like as adults?"

"Distant. I talked to him once or twice a year. After his trial, I received a letter from an attorney telling me he'd deeded the house to me and the kids."

"Did that surprise you?"

"Very much so, but it came at a good time. I had recently gotten divorced and was struggling financially."

"Were there any caveats or special instructions included in the letter?"

"Just that his things were stored in the basement, so that needed to remain locked and off-limits to me and the kids." Her eyes darted between them. "Am I going to lose the house?"

"I'm not sure what's going to happen. It's possibly a major crime scene."

"What does that mean for me? That's our home." Her chin wobbled. "I don't know what I'll do if we can't go back there."

"Have you seen or talked to your brother since he went to prison?"

She shook her head. "I wrote to him to thank him for the house and asked if he'd like us to visit, but I never heard back. I took that as a no."

A young girl opened the door. "Mommy?"

"I'm here, honey." She looked up at Gonzo. "Is there anything else?"

"Not right now. If you'll give me your phone number, I'll be in touch about the house."

She took the pad and pen he held out to her and wrote her number. "Whatever my brother did, it had nothing to do with us."

"We understand. We'll do what we can for you."

Cindy nodded, ushered her child back into the room and shut the door.

"I tend to believe she knew nothing about what he was up to," Cruz said as they went down the stairs.

"Same. I also tend to believe he knows exactly what happened to their brother."

"Oh my God, I thought the same thing."

"Another potential victim to add to our list," Gonzo said with a sigh. "Crazy that she kinda looks like him, though, huh?"

"Yeah, seriously."

"I want to know what happened with his mother that involved cops."

"I'll get on that in the morning. See what I can find out."

"You want me to drop you at the Metro?"

"Sure."

They were quiet on the short ride to the Rhode Island Avenue-Brentwood station.

Gonzo pulled up to the curb. "See you in the a.m."

"Yeah, see you then." Freddie reached for the door handle, but didn't get out. "Whatever happens at Stahl's, it has nothing to do with us. I think it's important that we remember that so we can continue to do the job."

Before Gonzo could formulate a reply, Freddie got out of the car and jogged toward the station, eager to get home to his wife.

Gonzo pulled into traffic and directed the car toward home, thinking about Freddie's parting words. He was right. It had nothing to do with them, even if it felt like it did.

He used voice commands on the Bluetooth to call Captain Malone.

The captain picked up on the third ring. "Hey, what's up?"

"I'm on my way home after having been to Stahl's and then to talk to his sister at the hotel. She told us something interesting. He was thirteen when he was sent to live with his father after something went down with his mother that involved the police. The sister doesn't know what happened. She's thirteen years younger than him and barely remembers him living in their house. She had only sporadic contact with him and was surprised when he deeded his house over to her after he was convicted. And there was another brother between her and Stahl who disappeared while he was in high school. She said Lenny became a cop because he wanted justice for their brother, Michael."

"Jesus. Another potential victim."

"Our thought exactly. Although, Cruz and I both came away from the meeting with her agreeing that whatever her brother has done doesn't involve her."

"Good to know."

"Cruz will look into what happened with Stahl's mother."

"That was my next question."

"Also, we've booked Tori Stevens on assaulting a police officer and obstructing a homicide investigation. We found some large payments from her account made by check."

"I've requested a warrant for the canceled checks from her bank."

"Great, thanks. She requested an attorney, so I notified the parents in Wisconsin and heard all about what a good kid she is, how she couldn't have had anything to do with hurting her boyfriend's new girlfriend, etc. I told them to get her an attorney, and we'll see where we stand with that in the morning."

"Good work today, Sarge."

"Thanks. Have a good night, Cap."

"You, too."

Gonzo pressed the accelerator as he headed for home. Some days were longer and more difficult than others. Today had been rough as they processed the possibility that someone they'd once worked closely with could be capable of repeatedly committing the unspeakable crime they'd spent their careers investigating.

He'd never understand the mind of a killer, how they could take someone else's life without thinking a thing of it in some cases. Sure, he'd seen the cases where something went terribly wrong, and someone ended up dead at another person's hands —and the killer was absolutely devastated. But those instances were rare. Most of the time, it was someone like Tori who wanted someone like Rachel out of the way, and they thought murder was the best way to achieve that goal.

Murder would never make sense to him, which was a good thing, he supposed. The minute the urge to kill another person made sense to him, it would be time to hang up his badge.

He pulled up outside his apartment building and parallel parked. After the recent incident at the home of FBI Agent Avery Hill and his wife, Shelby, Sam had urged their team to make sure their residences were as secure as possible. People Hill had arrested years ago had shown up looking for him and had taken his pregnant wife and young son hostage. The incident was a good reminder that something similar could happen to any of them. Over the course of a career, they arrested a lot of people who'd like to blame the police rather than themselves for their troubles.

It wasn't unheard of for them to come out of prison seeking retribution from the people who'd sent them there. Avery and Shelby had had a close call, and it had to serve as a wake-up call to the rest of them.

Gonzo needed to find a more secure home for his family. The thought of something happening to them because of his work was unbearable. He truly felt for Avery Hill, who was planning to move his family to a gated fortress in the city's Northwest quadrant. Since they were still in debt from his long stay in rehab, Gonzo and Christina couldn't afford anything like that. But they could do better than a building in which the security cameras didn't work more often than they did.

He charged up the stairs toward the people he loved the most, both of whom were sound asleep when he checked on them. Alex had a smile on his face even when he was asleep, Gonzo noted as he kissed his son's sweaty forehead. The kid was the sweatiest sleeper ever, which brought his daddy endless amusement. Everything he did amused Gonzo. For now, anyway. He knew the years were coming when his son would challenge his father's patience. But even that was something to look forward to.

In the months since he'd gotten sober, he was drowning in

gratitude, most especially for the woman who'd stood by him in his darkest days. He sat on the edge of the mattress to brush the hair back from her face. Pregnancy was kicking her ass, leaving her exhausted at the end of every long day as a mother and Nick's press secretary at the White House.

Gonzo leaned in to kiss her cheek and then got up to take a shower, needing to wash the grime of this day off his body and soul. Sometimes, it was just too damned much, and lately... As they uncovered more and more crimes committed by their former lieutenant, Gonzo carried a perpetual knot in his belly at how much worse it might get before the full picture was revealed. And what would the fallout be for the department, for people he cared about and respected, such as their chief of police, Joe Farnsworth?

Like it or not, many of Stahl's crimes had taken place on Farnsworth's watch. Would their beloved chief be held accountable for that? Would Farnsworth be forced to resign? And if so, who would take his place, and how would that change everything?

The questions gnawed at him as he stood under the warm water.

He startled when the shower door opened, and Christina stepped in behind him, wrapping her warm, naked body around his. "You're supposed to be sleeping," he said as he covered her hands with his.

"I fell asleep five minutes after I tucked Alex in. I didn't get to shower." She rested her head on his back. "Rough day?"

"Rougher than most."

"What can I do?"

He leaned back into her. "This is helping. How was your day?"

"Long. Still dealing with the bullshit about Nick's mother and her arrest, and the nausea has become an all-day event."

"I'm sorry, sweetheart. That sucks."

"Sure does, but she'll be worth it, or so I'm told."

"I can't wait to meet her."

"Me, too."

Gonzo moved carefully to turn so he was facing her, tipping her chin up for a kiss. She had dark circles under her eyes and was paler than usual, which worried him. "Should you check in with the doc about the nausea?"

"There's nothing much they can do about it. Hopefully, it'll pass before too much longer."

"Let me take care of you." He moved so she could stand under the water while he washed and conditioned her blonde hair, tossing in a scalp massage that made her purr.

"Feels good."

He soaped her up, added a rubdown of her shoulders and noted her larger, heavier breasts and the gentle swell of her abdomen. "Pregnancy looks hot on you, babe."

She grunted out a laugh. "I feel like a swollen whale, and nothing fits."

"Don't talk about my gorgeous wife that way, and if you need new clothes, get them. Whatever you want or need."

"Do you still want to move?" Her brows came together as she frowned. "The thought of that is so overwhelming right now."

"I want us to find somewhere safer after what happened to Shelby and Noah. We can hire packers and movers. I'll take care of everything. The only thing you have to do is help me find the place."

"I can do that," she said on a yawn.

"Let's get my baby mama to bed."

"Yes, please."

Gonzo completed his shower service by blow-drying her hair while she seemed to sleep standing up. Then he directed her to the bedroom, where he put one of his oversized T-shirts on her and tucked her into bed. She was asleep before her head hit the pillow.

After he made himself a sandwich and brushed his teeth, he climbed into bed and put an arm around her from behind.

As he breathed in the clean scent of her hair, he was so damned thankful for her, for Alex, for their life together, for surviving the challenges of the past so he could live this happily ever after with her and their children.

He'd do whatever it took to protect his family and keep them safe.

Nicoletta walked into the luxury high-rise apartment on Saturday morning and took a good look around, calculating the value of each object and determining that many were priceless works of art. She turned to take a closer assessment of Collins Worthy, the man who'd brought her here after she'd finally been arraigned and released on bail that he must've put up for her, since all her assets were frozen.

"What is this place?"

"My home."

"Oh. I see. If you're hoping I'll repay you in sexual favors—"

"Whoa." He smiled as he held up his hands to stop her. "I'm hoping for no such thing. I brought you here because your home is surrounded by media. I thought you'd be safer and more comfortable here."

"Oh. Okay. Well, thank you."

"You're welcome. Can I get you anything?"

"I'd really like a shower." She feared the filth and stench from her time in jail would stick to her forever.

"Right this way."

He led her deeper into the two-story apartment, past a beautiful gourmet kitchen to a hallway. "This is the guest suite. I asked my assistant to pick up a few things for you, and she left them on the bed. Please make yourself at home."

She entered the comfortable, well-appointed bedroom with an adjoining bathroom done entirely in Italian marble. "Why are you doing this for me?"

"You need help. I provide help for my clients. That's what I do."

"You bring them home, have your assistant buy clothes for them and put them up in high style?"

For the first time, he seemed slightly uncertain of himself. "Well, this is a first, but I'm happy to do what I can for you."

The man was too handsome for his own good, with silver hair, a tanned face and piercing blue eyes that seemed to see right through her bullshit. That was unsettling, to say the least. He was wearing yet another suit that she suspected had been custom-made for him. This one was gray pinstripe. She'd always been a sucker for a well-dressed man. This one had the added distinction of being the first to ever make her mouth water at the sight of him, a truly unsettling development that had left her off her game and vulnerable. She hated being vulnerable, especially around men.

"Why?"

"Because it seems like you need it. Am I wrong? Are you not in a boatload of trouble and the source of a media circus due to the office your son holds?"

"I am, but it's certainly not your problem."

"I think we can agree this is a unique situation, with you being the mother of the president. The press coverage has been frantic, to say the least."

"I wouldn't know."

"Take my word for it. You're better off staying here, where no one would think to look for you."

"It's that bad, is it?"

"You know how the media likes to sink its teeth into a juicy story. The arrest of the president's mother is as juicy as it gets."

"What has my son had to say about it?"

"Nothing directly, but through his spokesperson, he's claimed to have no relationship with you. Is that true?"

"I'm sure that's how he sees it," she said with a note of bitterness.

"We should discuss that further, but first, I'll leave you to enjoy your shower. When you're ready, come have something to eat."

Nicoletta had learned at an early age how to tell when a man wanted something from her. She couldn't read this one, and that, along with her unprecedented attraction to him, had her questioning her own judgment. "Thank you."

"You're welcome," he said, leaving her with a charming smile that sparked another unprecedented feeling of pure desire.

What was it about him that made her blood run hot? She was fifty-four years old and had never experienced such a pure, natural attraction to a man as she did to him the first time they'd met. It had been immediate and primal, the kind of thing she'd read about and seen in movies but never experienced for herself.

She went into the bathroom that was right out of a dream, with a steam shower and high-end fixtures.

Someone had stocked it with shampoo, conditioner, body wash and lotion from one of the best spas in town. Had that been done for her or another guest? And why did it matter, anyway? She wouldn't be here for long.

She luxuriated in the best shower of her entire life, scrubbing the filth of jail from her hair and skin. Never again would she take being clean for granted. She'd rather die than ever go back to that hellhole. If this Collins Worthy fellow could keep her from that fate, she'd tell him anything he wanted to know.

But would she give him anything he wanted?

He swore that wasn't why he'd brought her to his home but come on. She'd lived long enough to understand men and their ulterior motives.

As she smoothed on sage-scented lotion, she finally felt like herself again. A woman like her didn't belong in jail. She belonged among the crème de la crème of society, not the dregs. Perhaps if she played her cards right with this Worthy fellow, he could help her get back to where she belonged.

Nicoletta was tired of the rat race, the struggle to survive and thrive in a world in which the game was rigged against women like her. Though she'd shamelessly used men to suit her own purposes since she'd first understood her own power, in the end, they always won. They held the ultimate power. It was exhausting swimming upstream against the patriarchy and always coming out on the losing end of the race.

She studied her reflection in the mirror, noting the appearance of a few fine lines around her eyes and mouth that hadn't been there before her incarceration. If a few days without her special face cream could lead to that, then it was only a matter of time before she lost the stunning beauty that was her hallmark.

Time was running out, and if she didn't want to end up alone and broke, she needed to act quickly. Fate had brought the handsome, debonair Collins Worthy into her life for a reason. As she ran a brush through her thick dark hair, which stayed that way thanks to monthly visits to a pricey salon, she realized she was fresh out of options.

With the scrutiny that would come from her arrest, her business was finished, and with it, the lucrative income she'd recently enjoyed. If she could somehow fend off the charges and stay out of prison, she had to come up with a new way to survive. For her entire adult life, she'd resisted relying upon a man.

The very thought of it revolted her.

Though she'd spent only a few minutes in his presence thus far, she already suspected she could swallow her revulsion with Collins in a way she couldn't have with any other man. There was something different about this one, and he could turn out to be her ticket to the future she deserved.

She was about to reach for the hair dryer that had been left on the counter, but stopped herself. Let him see her for who she really was—unvarnished, unpolished, unadorned. He would either want that version of her, or he wouldn't.

What if he didn't? she wondered with an unusual lack of confidence.

"He will," she said to her reflection. "They all do."

And that was the fundamental truth of the matter. Yes, there might be something different about this one, but at the end of the day, they were all the same, ruled by their cocks and their insatiable lust for sex. If she was good at anything, it was that, and if he took her for a ride, she'd have him right where she could best manipulate him to do her bidding—in court and out.

She smiled at her reflection. "You've got him on the hook, girl. Now go get him."

CHAPTER EIGHT

Worthy's assistant had somehow provided clothing in all her sizes, including the high-cut briefs she favored and the double-D-cup bra. How had they known? She chose a pair of leggings and a soft long-sleeved top in a shade of light green that would make her eyes pop. How often had she been told they were among her best features? Her legs, tits and ass were also on that list, and she used each of them to maximum effect.

Leaving the guest suite, she walked to the main area of the apartment, her feet snug and toasty in a brand-new pair of Ugg slippers. They'd thought of everything she might need.

Nicoletta was stunned to find Collins standing watch over a pan of eggs he'd obviously made himself. He'd removed his suit jacket and tie and rolled up the sleeves of a crisp white dress shirt.

"Hope you like scrambled. That's my specialty when it comes to eggs." He flashed that disarming grin. "Well, that's not true. I don't have a specialty, per se. More like a go-to."

He was rambling like a nervous boy making breakfast for a woman for the first time, when that couldn't possibly be true.

"Scrambled is perfect." Her mouth watered at the scent of decent food after days of that crap they called food in jail.

"Toast?"

"Sure, thanks."

He popped four slices into the toaster and poured her a cup of coffee, pushing it across the counter, followed by cream, sugar and artificial sweetener. "Wasn't sure how you take it."

"Black is fine."

"That's how I like it, too. Not sure why people put all that garbage in it when it's perfectly good as is."

"My sentiments exactly." She took a seat on one of the plush stools that lined the longest island countertop she'd ever seen. It had to be twenty feet.

"Did you find everything you needed?"

"And then some. How did you know all my sizes?"

"My assistant is very good at these things. I have to give her full credit."

"Please tell her thank you for me."

"I'll do that." He served the eggs and toast with butter, jam and a bowl of fruit.

"This is lovely. Thank you so much."

"My pleasure."

He brought his plate with him and sat next to her.

They ate in companionable silence, which she appreciated. She'd grown weary of men who felt the need to be entertaining every minute they were with her out of fear she might lose interest. What they'd failed to realize was that she'd never been interested in the first place. So there'd been nothing to lose but her patience with their endless yammering about themselves.

This man knew how to work the silence, which made her even more intrigued.

After they'd finished eating, he cleared their plates and offered her more coffee.

She nudged her mug forward.

"We need to talk about your case," he said gently after he'd refilled both their mugs.

Her bubble of contentment burst with those words. "Must we?"

"I'm afraid so. The DA has reached out with a possible deal that would keep you out of jail."

"What kind of deal?"

"The kind where you might have to turn over your client list."

She gasped. "Never."

"I understand your reluctance, but here's the thing. Your business is dead. The only way you can save yourself is to deal with the prosecutors. They've offered to clear the charges from your record in one year, provided you're not charged with the same crimes again, in exchange for the client list. It's a very fair deal, Nicoletta."

"Fair to whom? To save my own skin, I have to sacrifice thousands of other people?"

"That's about the gist of it."

"I can't do that, Collins. I simply cannot."

"Then you'd have to take your chances at trial, which would be a national media circus the likes of which you can't begin to fathom."

The thought of that was unbearable, even if she did relish being the center of attention. That kind of attention, however, was not the kind she enjoyed.

"What about the federal charges?"

"Those are a bit trickier."

"How so?"

"The Feds have indicated they're planning to play hardball on the money laundering."

"Are those the same Feds that work for my son?"

"Indirectly. The Justice Department is supposed to be independent from the president."

"Could he tell them to back off?"

"He could, but it wouldn't be a wise move on his part. It would be seen as an inappropriate use of presidential power."

"He never does anything inappropriate."

"He does seem to color inside the lines, from what I've seen thus far."

"He gets that from his father."

Collins chuckled. "I think it's safe to assume there's no help coming from him."

"Agreed. We're not on the best of terms."

"We may have another option."

"What's that?"

"If you agree to community service and make a huge donation to a youth crisis organization, we may be able to plead the federal charges down to a misdemeanor with probation."

"How big of a donation are we talking?"

"A million dollars?"

"I don't have that!"

He raised a brow.

"I don't!"

"Not even in offshore accounts?"

How did he know about them? "I, uh..."

"You have the money to buy your way out of this, Nicoletta."

"But that's my nest egg. My security."

"Which is worse? Being penniless or being in jail?"

"Is that a multiple-choice question?"

His smile made her weak in the knees. Good thing she was sitting, or she might do something mortifying, such as swoon.

"This is all my bitch daughter-in-law's fault. She sent the FBI after me."

Collins was taken aback. "Do you know that for certain?"

"She would've been smart about it, but I know it was her. She hates me."

"Why does she hate you?"

"I can only assume it's related to certain... failures, you might call them... as a mother to my son."

"Is that why you're on the outs with him?"

"I suppose so. Look, I was sixteen when I got pregnant with him. So I wasn't mother of the year. He had everything he needed."

"And since he's been an adult? Have you tried to mend fences with him?"

"I've tried, but he's not receptive."

"In what way have you tried?"

She began to squirm under his penetrating gaze. She

couldn't talk to him about these things and hope that he'd still find her appealing.

"Do you have kids?"

"Three."

"Are you close to them?"

"They're my best friends."

Great. So how could he possibly understand her situation with Nick? "Where's their mother?"

"She died of cancer fifteen years ago."

"Oh. I'm sorry."

"Thank you. It was a very difficult loss for all of us, but it's made me closer to my kids than I already was."

"You're lucky. It doesn't always happen that way."

"No, it doesn't."

"Look, I've made some mistakes in my life. A lot of mistakes. I don't deny that. I tried to be a good mother to my son, but what did I know about motherhood? My own mother was in and out of psychiatric hospitals the whole time I was growing up."

That wasn't entirely true, but he didn't need to know that. Her mother had had one breakdown after her father left them, but she was never the same afterward. That was the first time Nicoletta had seen what men were capable of, and it was why she'd never allowed herself to love one of them so much that she'd be destroyed if he left.

It was easier not to care. The philosophy applied to her son, too. If she didn't care, she couldn't be hurt.

Collins seemed to listen carefully to everything she said. If he was judging her, she couldn't tell. "I think you should consider pleading out the charges, paying the fines, doing your community service and starting over with a clean slate."

"Is there any other way for the state to get the info it wants without me handing it over to them?"

He thought about that for a second. "Where's it kept?"

"My business records are in a safe-deposit box at the bank."

"There may be a way to steer them in that direction without your obvious involvement. Let me see what I can do. In the meantime, I want you to think about how you might repair your relationship with your son."

She looked at him with pure shock. "Why?"

"Because you're missing out on one of the best things in life."

"Why do you care?"

He gave her another of those penetrating stares that seemed to see right through her. If that was true, would he like what he saw?

"I'm not sure yet, but I'll let you know as soon as I figure it out."

Nicoletta had no idea how to take that, but since she needed him and his help, she decided she could be patient.

For now, anyway.

SEVERAL MEMBERS of Nick's national security team arrived after breakfast to provide his daily briefing. While he was cloistered with them in a secure room next door, Sam got out her laptop to read the latest emails about the Stahl investigation.

Included in one that Captain Malone had sent to all personnel was a photo of Stahl's home in Northeast, shrouded now in a tent and yellow police tape. The photo, taken by drone, also showed a crowd of people gathered outside the police perimeter. Lookie-loos, they called them. It was human nature, she supposed, to want to know what was going on. That was until disaster struck their own home, and then they asked for privacy.

She read Malone's email update. *Crime Scene detectives arrived at the Stahl home to find that his sister, Cindy, and her two young children were living there. The sister put up a fight when asked to leave and was told she'd be taken into custody unless she and her children vacated the premises immediately. She swore at the officers, told them they had no right to enter her home (despite having been presented with the warrant) and was generally uncooperative. Lieutenant Haggerty gave her ten minutes to pack the family's belongings and expelled her from the house.*

Sam wasn't surprised to learn that Stahl's sister was unpleasant, but Sam felt for her for being booted from her home thanks to her good-for-nothing brother.

The sister demanded to know what the police wanted at the house and was told they had no obligation to discuss that with her as she isn't the subject of the investigation. She said her lawyer would be in touch, as Stahl made her the owner when he went to prison. Once the occupants were removed from the house, Haggerty and his team started in the basement with a full investigation that may involve the breaking of the concrete floor and excavation of the yard. We expect this investigation to take several weeks to complete.

Detectives have been assigned to reopen the cases of each of the missing women who may be tied to Stahl. More information will be shared with you as it becomes available. Needless to say, we are carefully managing the distribution of information to the media until such time as we have more concrete evidence of the former lieutenant's involvement in these cases or until we rule him out. Gonzo and Cruz talked to the sister last night, learned there was a brother between her and Stahl who went missing in high school. We're adding the name of Michael Stahl to the list of potential victims. In addition, Cindy, who is thirteen years younger than Stahl and shared his father, told them that Stahl came to live with them when he was thirteen due to an incident with his mother that involved the police. We'll be looking for more information about that today.

Sam responded to him to let him know that reporters traveling with them in Delaware had asked about Stahl's connection to missing women.

He wrote right back to that. *Great.*

In a separate email, Malone had sent the files for two of the missing women, both of whom were originally from Delaware.

Brittany Carter had grown up in the Wilmington area, the third child in a family of six siblings. Her father had worked in finance and her mother as a school librarian. After high school, Brittany moved to the District to work at a bank and had been arrested for public drunkenness and disorderly conduct on several occasions.

According to the report, at some point she'd been fired from the bank and had become an escort. The family hadn't learned that detail until much later. They'd suspected she was taking and possibly selling drugs, but had been unable to confirm that. Despite her troubles, they'd made the effort to stay in touch and to offer help that she'd rebuffed.

And then she'd stopped returning their phone calls.

Her parents had gone to DC to look for their daughter and had called the police when they were unsuccessful in locating her.

Detective Leonard Stahl had responded to their call.

Sam sighed as she sifted through the brief notes Stahl had made in the file about contacting her friends and known associates, interviews with her roommates at the time and the frustrating conclusion that she was known to go missing for days at a time before showing up like nothing had happened. Sam found no indication that he'd followed up.

As she studied the photo of the young woman with pale skin, big green eyes and light brown hair, she was filled with despair to know he'd done so little to "investigate" her disappearance.

And now Sam had to go see her parents, reopen the wound and remind them all over again how her department had failed to find their daughter. In fact, if current suspicions were true, the officer who'd investigated her disappearance might've killed her.

Sam was astounded that she could still be shocked by anything Stahl had done—or not done. The sheer scope of his crimes was overwhelming.

Caren Hans was originally from Newark, Delaware. She'd done a semester at Howard University before dropping out to work at a District restaurant. She'd quit her job a few months later and gone missing shortly after that, although her disappearance hadn't immediately been reported by anyone. A few months had passed before her grandmother had reached out to the MPD. Again, the case had been assigned to Detective Stahl, who'd done the most basic investigation.

It made Sam sick to think that he might've investigated crimes that he'd committed with no one the wiser that a killer worked among them.

She did a quick search online and learned that Caren's grandmother had died five years ago without ever knowing what had become of her grandchild. A sister had since checked in with the MPD only to be told there was no new information.

Sam wrote down of the sister's name—Cristen Hans Reid—and her address in the Newark area. Then she did a search to see how far Wilmington and Newark were from Dewey. About two hours each way. At least the two cities were close, so she could do both interviews in one trip.

The last thing she wanted was burn a precious vacation day running down a cold case tied to that son of a bitch Stahl, but this was an all-hands-on-deck situation, and she was determined to help get answers for families who'd waited far too long already. The second-to-last thing she wanted was for anyone she worked with to think that *she* thought she was special because of her role as first lady. She wasn't special on the job, and she was determined to stay that way.

So she picked up the phone and called Brittany Carter's mother, Theodora.

"This is Lieutenant Sam Holland with the DC Metro Police Department."

As usual these days, the recitation of her name was met with silence.

"Mrs. Carter?"

"I'm here. You caught me off guard. The last thing I expected today was a call from the MPD or the first lady."

"I'm just a lieutenant on the job, ma'am, and I wanted to let you know we're taking a fresh look at Brittany's case. I wondered if I might come by tomorrow afternoon to go over a few things."

"You want to come here."

"Yes, ma'am. Would that be okay?"

"Um, sure, I guess. Have you found her?"

"No, we haven't, but we're pursuing some new leads."

"Why, after all this time, do you suddenly care about my daughter?"

"I'll explain that to you when I see you, if that's all right. What time is good for you?"

"Any time is fine."

"Would two o'clock work?"

"Sure."

"Could I ask that you not tell anyone that I'm coming? I don't want our meeting to turn into a three-ring circus. I'm sure you can understand."

"I won't tell anyone but my husband."

"Thank you."

After Sam confirmed the address with her, she said she'd see her tomorrow. Next, she called Cristen Hans Reid and got the same stunned silence after she introduced herself.

"We're taking another look at your sister's case, and I was wondering if I might come by tomorrow afternoon to go over some of the details with you."

"You want to come to my home after all this time to discuss my sister's case?"

Sam found the hostility in her tone more than understandable.

"Yes, that's correct."

"Why now?"

"We've uncovered some new information that we're actively pursuing. I wanted to update you on that and to fill in a few blanks on the original investigation."

"What investigation? The guy they assigned didn't do shit to find her. We've had our own investigator working on it ever since, but he's never come up with anything either."

"I'm deeply sorry for the failings of the officer who was assigned to your sister's case. We're trying to rectify that now."

"He's in prison, right? For trying to kill you?"

"Yes, that's right. May I come by tomorrow between three and four?"

"I guess."

She confirmed the address. "Thank you for your time. I appreciate it."

"I hope this time we might get some answers."

"I do, too."

Sam's stomach ached when she thought of what those answers might be. With her appointments made, she called Vernon, who was part of the detail sent with them to Dewey.

"Good morning, ma'am."

"Sam."

"I'm with other agents."

"Ah, I see. I'll let it slide this time, then."

She appreciated his low chuckle and the fun groove they'd found with each other.

"What can I do for you?"

"I have to make a work trip to Newark and Wilmington tomorrow. Two hours each way."

"What time would you like to leave?"

"Around eleven thirty? That gives us some extra time for traffic. My first appointment is at two."

"We'll get you there in time. I assume just you and not the president as well?"

"Right. Just me."

"Very well. We'll have the car ready to depart at eleven thirty."

"Thanks, Vernon."

"You're most welcome."

Sam slapped her phone closed and stood to stretch. She walked to the windows at the back of the house to look out at the beach.

That's where Nick found her when he came in from the briefing next door.

He wrapped an arm around her waist and rested his chin on her shoulder. "Are you stressed?"

"A little."

"Not exactly the peaceful break we'd hoped for, is it?"

"Nope, but I suppose we were delusional to hope it might be. What's the news from La Casa Blanca?"

"Nothing good. Apparently, General Wilson is teaming up with former Secretary of State Ruskin to make the rounds on any shows that'll have them to spew about my lack of fitness for the presidency."

"Oh, Nick. Honestly. I can't believe the networks give them the airtime."

"Why wouldn't they? Controversy sparks ratings."

"I'm sorry you have to deal with that on top of everything else."

"Goes with the territory, or so I'm told. My team is on it."

"What can they do about it?"

"They can remind people that both of the people spouting off about me left office under less-than-honorable circumstances, which no one can say about me."

"That's true, and a very good point to hammer home as often as possible."

"That's the plan, but enough about that crap. What've you been up to?"

"Crap of my own. Making appointments to see two families that hate my department because of the deplorable way their missing-person cases were handled years ago."

"Ouch."

"Yeah, the reception was a bit chilly, but that's to be expected. They were done dirty by Stahl and the department." She crossed her arms and turned to him. "I miss my dad all the time, but at times like this, I yearn for five minutes with him to ask how Stahl could've gotten away with everything he's apparently done. It boggles the mind."

"I'm sure it does for those of you who work inside the lines, rather than outside."

"For sure," Sam said. "I wonder more than anything how he did all this without anyone questioning him."

"From what I know about him, it seems like he was a lone wolf. People didn't like him, so they gave him a wide berth, which created opportunity."

"That's very true," Sam said. "I remember being a kid and my dad ranting about what a son of a bitch he was."

Nick drew her into his embrace. "I hate the thought of you having to work under his command and put up with his crap."

Sam shivered as she breathed in the familiar scent of him, the scent of home. "Those were some of the most difficult years of my life. Between him and Peter, I was utterly miserable." Sometimes she still couldn't believe she'd actually married Peter Gibson while Nick Cappuano was out there somewhere.

"I wish I'd been there for you."

"Me, too. I wouldn't have been miserable if I'd had you to come home to."

"Enough of this sad-sack stuff," he said. "We're here to celebrate two years of the best marriage in history, so what do you say we get back to it?"

"I say yes, please."

"How about another walk on the beach? I need some exercise."

"Let's go."

Smiling, he kissed her cheek. "You know it's never that simple. Let me talk to Brant."

As she watched him go, they were anything but relaxed, as she'd hoped they'd be on this getaway. It seemed as if the whole world was conspiring to keep them from enjoying their vacation. The reemergence of Leonard Stahl and his evil acts wasn't helping anything, nor were Nick's concerns about the people constantly coming for him. Not to mention wondering about how his mother had made bail or where she was hiding out.

At this rate, it would take an act of Congress to save this vacation.

CHAPTER NINE

Nick was still processing the information that'd been conveyed to him during the latest briefing. A military coup was taking place in Niger, Russian and Chinese ships were positioned off the coast of Alaska, intense storms were expected in the Midwest, and a standoff was underway at the southern border between immigration officers and armed bandits. Any one of those things would be a lot on a given day, but taken all together, they had him buzzing with stress as he contemplated the ripple effects of each situation.

Thankfully, he had an amazing team of experts working on each issue, as well as a host of other concerns, even as they planned a state dinner for the Canadian prime minister and his wife that would occur next week.

So many things were happening all at once. It made his head spin as he tried to keep up with it all while making high-stakes, consequential decisions that affected people around the world. No matter where he went or what he did, there was no escaping the staggering weight of that responsibility. He understood now why American presidents aged dramatically during their time in office. The burden was heavy and relentless.

He opened the front door to the rental house and found his

lead agent right where he expected him to be. Brant was nothing if not predictable.

"What can I do for you, Mr. President?"

"We'd like to take a walk on the beach."

"I'll get that set up for you right away."

"Thank you."

"No problem, sir."

Asking for permission to leave the house reminded Nick of the tiny apartment where he'd grown up with a grandmother who hadn't wanted the bother of raising her son's child. But she'd also wanted to know where he was every second of every day, which had driven him mad the older he'd gotten. The memories of those years had been front and center since his mother's arrest, which had resurrected emotions tied to that time in his life that he'd much rather forget. Why was it that the most painful events in a lifetime were the ones that never seemed to fade with time? If anything, they became more vivid as the years went on.

Using his personal phone, he texted their friend Avery Hill, who worked for the FBI, asking for an update on his mother's case. Every text had to be carefully considered, pros and cons weighed against the fallout of a text being made public. Despite a rough start to their friendship, when Avery had barely managed to hide his feelings for Sam, Nick had come around to being tight with him, especially since he'd married their close friend Shelby.

The list of people Nick trusted beyond a shadow of a doubt was short. Avery was one of them, as unlikely as that might've been at the outset of their relationship. Back then, Nick had thought about ways to have the pesky agent killed for daring to look at his wife with anything other than professional respect.

That seemed like a long time ago now that they'd all moved on. If anyone had the lowdown on what was happening with his mother, Avery would. He was the reason she'd been arrested in the first place. In a fit of rage over a horrific interview his mother had given, claiming all sorts of bogus insider info on Nick, Sam had asked Avery to look into her, certain Nicoletta was up to no good, as usual.

When Sam had finally told him about the investigation, his mother had been about to be arrested on prostitution and racketeering charges. Just what he'd needed after spending months trying to convince the American people to accept him as their unelected president.

He'd briefly been angry with Sam for keeping the investigation from him, but he'd forgiven her once he realized her heart had been in the right place, her focus on protecting him from being hurt any more by his mother.

Sam came out of the bedroom, carrying the long down jacket he'd bought her for when she attended Scotty's hockey games. She called it the blanket coat. With her hair pulled back into a ponytail, he was able to fully appreciate her showstopping face. He never got tired of looking at the woman he loved with all his heart.

She caught him gazing at her. "Do I have toothpaste on my face or something?"

"Or something," he said, smiling. His worries melted away when she came into the room. She was the only one who could relieve some of the intense burden, and he was thankful for her every minute of every day.

"What?"

He went to her, put his hands on her hips and peppered her face with soft kisses. "You have pretty all over you."

"I bet they make a scrub for that."

Chuckling, he said, "Don't you dare scrub the pretty off your face. It's my favorite face in the whole world."

She looked up at him with her heart in her gorgeous eyes. "How lucky am I?"

"How lucky are *we*?"

A knock on the door interrupted the moment.

Nick kissed her and went to answer it.

A huge bouquet of flowers greeted him.

"These just arrived from the White House," Brant said, "along with meals for tomorrow."

"Come on in," Nick said, stepping aside so Brant and Eric could bring in the items.

"Flowers came with a card," Brant said, handing it to Nick.

The card read, *Happy anniversary to the best parents in the whole wide world. Thank you for our amazing family. Love you forever and ever, Scotty, Alden, Aubrey, Eli, Candace and Skippy.*

"We're told that Scotty organized the delivery with the White House flower shop," Brant said.

"That's amazing," Nick said, sharing the card with Sam.

"Aw," she said after reading it. "I love that. What a kid."

"We need ten more minutes," Brant said.

"That's enough time to call home to thank him for the flowers," Nick said.

"Let's do it." Sam put through the call, setting her phone to speaker. "Don't tell me you're still asleep," she said when Scotty answered.

"Okay, I won't."

"It's almost noon!" Sam said.

"I'm fourteen, and it's Saturday, Mom. I need my rest."

Glancing at Nick, Sam fanned her face the way she often did when Scotty called her by her favorite title. "Thank you for the flowers. They're gorgeous. And the card made me teary."

"Glad you like them. It sure does come in handy having an in-house florist with an out-of-state delivery service."

"Don't get too comfortable with the trappings, son," Nick said, grinning. "They're temporary."

"I'm well aware, and I'm enjoying it while it lasts. How's the vacation? And don't tell me anything that will scar me even more than I already am."

"We're having a very nice time," Sam said. "We're about to take a walk on the beach."

"Isn't it too cold?" Scotty asked.

"Nah, it's fine."

"Has Skippy been outside yet?" Nick asked, cringing at the thought of puppy pee all over the residence.

"Alden came to get her earlier and brought her back."

"That's very nice of him."

"He supports my need to sleep in, unlike some people I could mention."

"You've wasted half a day you'll never get back," Nick said as Sam rolled her eyes at him.

"Listen, Dad, we can't all be the overachievers that you've been your whole life. Take it down a notch, will you?"

Nick bit his lip to keep from laughing out loud.

"I'm with you, kid," Sam said. "Sleep in while you can."

"Sam!" Nick feigned outrage. "We're supposed to set a good example."

Scotty's laughter made them smile. "You two are a mess. Don't you know that parents are supposed to be on the same page, so the kid doesn't end up receiving mixed messages?"

"Where does he get this stuff?" Sam asked.

"Duh, I know things."

"All right, smarty-pants," Nick said. "Get your butt out of bed and do something productive with your day."

"I've got hockey practice at five. Is that productive enough for you?"

"That's something, anyway," Nick said. "What about that social studies paper you have due on Tuesday?"

"Don't ruin my weekend by talking about Tuesday."

"I want to see a first draft before you go to bed tomorrow, you got me?"

"How you can be such a buzzkiller when you're not even here?"

"That's my job."

"Fine. Whatever. I'll send you a draft."

"Make it a good one." He smiled and winked at Sam. "I'm on vacation with my best girl. I don't have time to clean it up."

"Ew."

"What?"

"The grossness was implied."

Skippy started barking.

"I have to go deal with Her Royal Highness. Happy anniversary, you guys. All kidding aside, you're pretty great, even when you're sending mixed messages."

"We love you madly," Sam said.

"Back atcha."

"Love you, buddy," Nick said. "Text me after practice."

"Will do. Love you, too."

"What a kid," Nick said after Sam had slapped her phone closed to end the call.

"The best kid ever."

"Thank God for Alden coming to rescue Skippy," Nick said.

"I'm sure Celia suggested that."

"Thank God for her, too."

Having Sam's stepmother living with them at the White House enabled them to juggle their many responsibilities and get away from it all this week while knowing she would be there to help keep the kids on a schedule.

"Asking her to come to the White House with us was the best idea Freddie ever had," Sam said.

"Absolutely. It's worked out well for her, too. It's nice to see her smiling again."

"Definitely. Hard to believe my dad is gone six months already next month."

"I know. I feel like we haven't seen him in years."

"I miss him so much. After that all-hands briefing yesterday, all I wanted to do was call him to share the latest developments with Stahl. *And* I want to ask him how it was possible he was doing all this crap while pretending to be an upstanding officer."

"What do you think he'd say?"

"He'd be as shocked as the rest of us are, and he'd remind me how they went through some very tight budget years in the late '90s and into the 2000s. They were under a hiring freeze and were forced to work with available resources while crime was surging. Since the department was spread so thin, a lot of detectives worked without a partner. Supervisors were stretched to the limit. No one had time to be constantly checking the work of their subordinates. It was a perfect storm of opportunity for him."

"I guess so."

"It's all so unbelievable, and yet, it's not, too."

"I'm sure."

Brant knocked before sticking his head in to gesture they were ready for the walk. "Sorry that took so long. We had to relocate some tourists."

"I'm sure they appreciated that," Nick said.

"They were happy to assist."

As they followed Brant from the house, Nick said, "Good to know I have a few supporters left."

"You have more than a few, so don't focus on the naysayers."

"It's hard not to when they're organizing coups and such."

Sam curled her hands around his arm. "Let it go for now. It'll all keep until later."

"Yes, it will. Thank you for the reminder."

"That's what I'm here for. Any time you need to hear it."

Sam was right. The madness would keep. This day was about celebrating their second anniversary, which was actually the next day, and he planned to fully enjoy every minute of the time with her.

WHEN THEY RETURNED from their walk on the beach, Sam was determined that Nick would have the rest of the day off from the worries that sat on his shoulders like ten-ton boulders.

They enjoyed the deli lunch the White House had sent, which included the best chicken salad Sam had ever had.

"I'm going to need the chicken salad recipe for when we move out," she said. "I'm completely addicted."

"I'll bet Mario would be delighted to continue to make it for you even after we're out of office. He has a crush on my wife."

"He does not! He appreciates that I like to eat."

"That's not all he appreciates."

"He's seventy, Nick."

"And his eyes still work just fine."

"I had no idea you were jealous of the executive chef."

"Now you know."

The silliness was just what he needed. "I might just leave you for him and his chicken salad."

He popped a potato chip into his mouth. "You'd miss the things I bring to the table."

"Like what?"

"You know."

"I have no clue what you're referring to."

"Sure, you don't. Do you need me to refresh your memory?"

"I might."

He moved so fast, she had no time to prepare before she was slung over his shoulder as he headed for the bedroom. They were afraid to get busy anywhere else in the house during the day out of fear of long-range camera lenses from the beach.

"What have I told you about hauling me around like I'm a side of beef?"

"You've indicated that you quite like it."

"No, I haven't! I'm going to puke chicken salad all over you."

"That's sexy, babe."

Standing next to the California-king-size bed, he let her slide down the aroused front of him. He brushed the hair back from her face and kissed her before she could continue her protest over the way he'd slung her about.

Truth be told, his strength was a huge turn-on, not that she'd ever tell him that. She was hardly a waif, but he made her feel weightless as he kissed her with the wild desire that had become such a critical part of her daily life. How had she lived before she'd had him to make her feel this way? His love had become as essential to her as oxygen, food and water. The old her, the pre-Nick her, would've laughed at such a thought. But as he undressed them both with impatience, she was overwhelmed with gratitude for him, for them, for their family and their chaotic, ridiculous life.

He eased her down onto the bed, hovering above her with his sexy hazel eyes full of love as he gazed at her. "Two years."

"And ten lifetimes."

His smile was a thing of beauty. "Remember when you said, 'I do,' to a lowly senator from Virginia?"

"That was a total hoodwink."

Chuckling, he bent his head to plant a kiss between her breasts. "No way."

"Yes way."

"Best day of my life, bar none."

"Same."

"Whenever things are too much for me to deal with, which is often lately, I let my mind wander back to that day. That's all it takes to make me feel better about whatever I'm dealing with."

"I love that."

"It was perfection, from start to finish."

"Well, not completely…"

He knew she was referring to his mother's attempt to crash the wedding. "It was perfection in all the ways that mattered, because at the end of the day, you were my wife, and we had forever to spend together."

Before she could reply, he had drawn her nipple into his mouth, stealing every thought from her brain that didn't revolve around him and this.

"Are you recalling why you can't leave me for the chicken salad man?"

"Not quite there yet."

He bit down on her nipple, making her gasp as she laughed, and then she moaned when he pushed inside her, stretching her to capacity. "Is it coming back to you yet?"

"Starting to," she said breathlessly.

"I'd better be very thorough so you never forget again."

"That would probably be for the best. That chicken salad is *good*."

"My filet mignon is way better."

Sam laughed so hard, she could barely function, and even in the midst of hilarity, he had her on the verge of orgasm so quickly, her head spun from love, amusement and desire unlike anything she'd ever experienced.

Nothing could compare to him, and he knew it.

Afterward, they stayed wrapped up in each other as their bodies cooled and their breathing returned to normal.

Nick raised his arm and reached for something on the bedside table. "Happy anniversary." He placed a small, wrapped package on her shoulder.

"You expect me to function after that?"

"Uh-huh."

She groaned, reached for the gift and turned onto her back. "You wore me out."

"I had to make sure you weren't fantasizing about the chicken salad guy."

"You know there's no one but you, and there'll never be anyone but you."

"Likewise, my love."

"What is this?" she asked, tugging on the red ribbon that formed a bow at the top of a box wrapped in silver foil paper.

"As you may or may not know, the traditional second anniversary gift is cotton. I racked my brain trying to come up with something fabulous enough for my bride, but cotton wasn't doing it for me. So I wrapped something fabulous in cotton."

"Oh, I love fabulous things." She tore off the paper, opened the jeweler's box and pushed aside the soft cloth to find a platinum watch. "That's beautiful." The face was adorned with tiny diamonds.

"Read the engraving on the back."

Sam took it out and tilted it toward the waning light coming through the blinds. THANK YOU FOR THE BEST TWO YEARS OF MY LIFE. NDC

Her eyes filled. "I love it. Thank you so much."

"Thank *you*." He went up on his elbow to kiss her. "You've given me something I've never had before—a family to call my own. And despite all the unforeseen wrinkles—"

Sam raised a brow in his direction. "Is that what we're calling the presidency? A wrinkle?"

"A very *temporary* wrinkle."

Sam snorted out a laugh.

"As I was saying, despite the *many* wrinkles, I've never been happier or more content than I am since you and the kids came into my life. As long as I have you and them, I have everything I'll ever need—and then some."

"I love seeing you as a dad. I've never loved you more than I do when you're with them. Your groove with Scotty is something to behold. Your sweetness with the twins and your guidance of Elijah... It's so wonderful."

"As is watching you be a mom."

"I'm not as good at this parenthood gig as you are. I'm the one telling Scotty to sleep in and don't worry about math."

"You're great at it. They know how much you love them. One of my favorite things ever was when you had to go to school to pick up Scotty. Telling the office people that you're his mom made you cry."

"That was the best. I was finally a mom. Not like I thought it would happen, but I couldn't love him any more than I do if I'd given birth to him. Same with the twins and Eli."

"Me, too. It's amazing when you think about how we didn't even know the three of them a year ago, and now they're so much a part of us."

"Life is strange and wonderful." Sam leaned over to pull the bag she'd brought for him from under the bed. "What do you buy the leader of the free world? I asked myself. And the cotton presented a challenge for me as well."

"What could it be?" He smiled as he pulled the tissue paper out of the bag and removed the heather-blue cotton T-shirt she'd bought him online.

On the front it said: I LOVE YOU MORE. THE END. I WIN.

She loved him all the time, but especially when he laughed. He'd had such a hard go of it with his screwed-up family that seeing him laughing and surrounded with love made her happy.

"I love it, babe. I'll wear it all the time so you can read the message from me to you."

"No, that's not how it works. That message is from *me* to *you*. I am the winner of this fight."

"I want to have this fight every day for the rest of our lives."

"As long as you concede that I'm the winner of the fight."

"I'll concede to whatever you want as long as I get to have you and this and all the rest of it forever and ever."

"Does that mean I win?"

Smiling, he kissed her and held her close. "It means we both win."

CHAPTER TEN

At eleven thirty, they turned the bedroom TV on to watch the latest horror unfold on *Saturday Night Live*. Sam could barely stand to look. Yes, she knew it was a tradition for the comedy show to skewer the latest occupants of the White House, and she'd found it funny before those occupants were her and her husband.

"Here we go," Nick said.

Once again, they were featured in the cold opening.

Sam took one look and screamed at the sight of the same actress who'd played her before, this time made up to be a big-boobed blonde with a dark spray tan and teeth so white they probably glowed in the dark. She wore a hot-pink bikini with a police belt around her waist and a gold badge pinned to the right side of the barely there bikini top.

"You motherfucker," she muttered as Nick rocked with silent laughter.

And then the actor who played him came on the screen, wearing a banana-hammock bathing suit with a large bulge and an equally dark spray tan with the same sparkly white teeth that would be visible from outer space.

They landed on a single lounge chair on the sand, umbrella drinks on a table next to them.

"Not so funny now, huh?" Sam asked.

Nick had a slightly horrified expression on his face. "It's, um…"

Then the actors started talking, and it got worse.

She rubbed tanning oil on him as she basically humped him from behind. "I'm so excited for our beach vacation."

He moaned as she rubbed the oil into his shoulders.

"Those mean old Joint Chiefs can go bleep themselves." She bit his neck. "They *wish* they were as sexy as you are."

"I'm most definitely going to kill you for this," Sam said.

"Who needs Joint Chiefs, anyway?" the Nick actor asked as he beat his chest. "I'm the commander in chief."

"That's right, baby. You're the big boss, the big hoss, the *main man*."

"Death won't be good enough for you," Sam muttered as her phone buzzed madly with texts. She could picture everyone she knew howling with laughter.

"How should we celebrate our second anniversary?" the Nick actor asked with a gleam in his eye.

He turned toward the camera to reveal the bulge in his teeny-tiny suit had gotten bigger.

"Oh my God," Nick muttered.

"I have a few ideas," the Sam actor said as she wrapped herself around him in a passionate embrace just as "Why Don't We Get Drunk and Screw" by Jimmy Buffett started to play. The couple gyrated to the beat as they made out, hands all over each other.

They emerged from the revolting kiss to flash their bright white smiles as they said, "Live from New York, it's Saturday night."

"I want a divorce," Sam said.

He shut off the TV. "You do not."

"No, I really do."

"You'd miss me."

She crossed her arms. "I don't think I would."

He cozied up to her, kissing her neck and making her melt. "Yes, you would."

"Wouldn't."

"You'd miss the bulge in my banana hammock."

"That's the only reason I'm still here."

His laughter rocked them both.

"I still hate you."

"I hate me, too."

"Good."

Their phones went wild with texts.

"We'll never be able to show our faces again," she said on a moan.

"Eh, it's funny."

"No, it isn't! It's mortifying."

"It's really concerning how well they seem to know us."

"Can't you pass a law or something against *SNL* making fun of the president—and the first lady?"

"I wish I could, babe, but there's this pesky First Amendment thing that would preclude such a directive."

"Don't be presidential with me. It's annoying."

He nudged at her crossed arms. "Let me in. It's cold out here by myself."

Only because she actually loved him more than she hated him, she yielded to allow him to cozy up to her.

"That's better."

"You're going to pay for this for the rest of our lives."

"I know."

"Do you? Do you understand that any time I tell you to jump, you're going to say, 'How high, my warrior princess?'"

"It's come to that, has it?"

"It came to that last Thanksgiving. It's just gone nuclear."

"Don't say the word 'nuclear.' You'll set off an international incident."

"Don't deflect. You'll be my beck-and-call boy for the rest of our natural lives and into the next one. You got me?"

"I got you, babe, and I'm never letting go of my warrior princess."

. . .

VACATION WASN'T what it used to be. That was for sure. Nick had been occupied since shortly after eight with a series of security briefings surrounding the situation off the coast of Alaska and the uprising in Niger.

Sam had spent the morning sipping coffee with a view of the ocean as she sifted through texts from literally everyone she knew, cracking up over the latest *SNL* skit. She was glad they were amused. She was mortified.

She'd hoped to see Nick before she left for her two appointments, but he didn't return from the house next door in time.

If it seemed like everything that happened in the world was somehow his concern, that's because it was. Sam couldn't imagine having the kind of responsibility that he did, or having to make decisions that could affect millions of people. It was better if she didn't think about what her husband had to deal with as she rode in the back of a Secret Service SUV to the first of her appointments in northern Delaware.

Despite the frivolity of the night before, she had her own concerns today and was dreading meeting with families who'd been further victimized by the very person who should've been helping them.

It made her skin crawl to think of Stahl taking missing-person reports from the distraught families of women he might've killed.

"I was surprised to hear you're working today," Vernon said, glancing at her in the mirror.

"I'm assisting in an investigation that has all hands on deck."

"That sounds serious."

"It's the worst kind of serious. One of our own suspected of mass murder."

"The guy who hit us?"

He was referring to Sergeant Ramsey. "No, the one who tried to kill me."

"I've read about that son of a bitch."

Sam appreciated his forceful tone. "How is it that some of

the people who wear the badges and swear the oath do everything *other* than uphold the law?"

"Officers like us can't understand that mentality."

"I'll never comprehend it. I worked closely with him for years. I detested the guy, and he detested me right back. But never in all that time did I think he was capable of the things we already know he's done, let alone what we're investigating now. We just thought he was a miserable coworker, not a psychopath."

"It has you questioning your instincts because you didn't see it."

"Yeah, kind of."

"Don't do that. Psychopaths hide in plain sight. When I was with the FBI way back in the early part of my career, I worked on a unit that tracked a serial killer in the Midwest. Our team became subject-matter experts and ended up consulting on a number of other similar cases."

"Wow. I had no idea."

"I didn't just land on your detail out of nowhere."

Sam laughed. "I suppose that's true."

"He had a really cool career with the FBI and ATF before coming to the Secret Service," Jimmy said.

"Don't tell all my secrets at once, young Jimmy," Vernon said. "I need to retain my aura as an international man of mystery."

Sam and Jimmy laughed.

"All right, then, Mr. International Man of Mystery... Tell me what you know about psychopaths."

"They tend to fall into four categories—narcissistic, borderline, sadistic and antisocial."

"I can see Stahl in the last two—sadistic and antisocial. He seemed to take great pleasure in tormenting the people who worked for him, and no one liked him."

"Not to mention what he did to you the second time," Vernon said, glancing at her in the mirror.

"Not to mention."

"Anyone who can do something like that to another person is

a textbook psychopath," Vernon said forcefully. "They also lack compassion and empathy, but can phone it in when needed, such as a police officer on the job doing the bare minimum while satisfying his psychopathic tendencies on the side. I think if you were able to go back to examine his childhood and life before he joined the department, you might see the signs were there."

Sam made a note to have someone investigate Leonard Stahl's earlier life. "Wouldn't that have shown up in the due diligence the department did before they hired him?"

"If they did it," Vernon said. "We're talking thirty years ago, right?"

"Yeah, about that."

"Who knows how thorough they were in vetting people back then, especially if they were desperate for officers? That tends to happen after times of unrest when people get to see the downside of policing or in cases of police behaving badly, which gives potential officers pause about wanting to join a department."

She wanted to talk to Dr. Trulo about what sort of psychological tests had been given to prospective officers at the time Stahl was hired. Sam recalled a rigorous screening after she applied, but who knew what they did thirty years ago?

Her father would have known, and she wished more than anything that she could call him to ask. Since she couldn't, she sent a text to Captain Malone. *Question: What kind of psychological testing did you guys go through before joining the department?*

He replied a few minutes later. *Not much. Wasn't as big of a thing back then as it is now. The department was vigorously recruiting when our group came in following a hiring freeze that had left them seriously shorthanded.*

We need to do a deep dive into Stahl's past, his childhood, etc. Especially in light of what Gonzo and Cruz learned yesterday.

Will ask someone to do that and report back.

Thanks.

Next, she texted Dr. Trulo. *In light of the new info on Stahl,*

I'm wondering if there's any insight from your end that might help us to wrap our heads around the possibility that a serial killer was working in our midst.

Aren't you supposed to be on vacation?

I'm on my way to Wilmington & Newark DE to brief families of two of the missing women.

Oh wow. Ok... Well, I don't have much on him that you don't already know. He was always an enigma around here. No one was particularly close to him (that I knew of).

Did you suspect he was unbalanced in any way?

I had suspicions that something was "off," but without being able to fully evaluate him, that's all it was. Suspicions. Until he confirmed them, that is.

This is helpful. Thank you for sharing. I'm really struggling with how he could've done the things he did right under the noses of all the good cops we work with.

I'm sure that was part of the thrill for him. That he was deceiving his fellow officers with his criminal behavior while pretending to be an upstanding member of the department. We don't think to look for criminals under our own roof. We like to think we're all on the same side with the same goals, but we've seen that isn't the case.

It's demoralizing.

Yes, it is, and it's something I'll be addressing with the entire team as we go forward. It's important we don't lose sight of the overall goal while dealing with the transgressions of a very few.

True.

We'll be discussing it more in small group settings in the coming weeks. I want to give people the chance to share their feelings in a positive forum, so they don't fester.

I appreciate you, Doc. I really do. If you'd asked me before you saved my life and my career—more than once—if I thought shrinking was for me...

Haha. Thanks for the kind words. It's taken a long time to earn the trust of my colleagues. A skeptical group, to say the least. I'm proud of the strides we've taken as a department to address the mental health challenges that come with a stressful job. Still much more work to be done.

Thank you for doing that hard work. It's badly needed.

Try to enjoy the vacation.

Will do. See you next week.

He responded with a thumbs-up.

With an hour still to go, she sifted through the notes in the Carter file along with the updates Freddie had emailed her. In his message, he'd written:

Wilmington is the largest city in Delaware, with just over 70,000 residents. The Carters live in a suburb west of Wilmington called Elsmere, which has about 7,000 residents. Solidly working-class community with median home value around $184K and median rent at $1100. Bart Carter is retired from Merrill Lynch, and Theodora Carter is retired from the Elsmere School District after working for twenty-five years as a school librarian. I've attached a clip I found from a local paper when she retired. I took a look at their social media... Their five adult children live close by and have at least six children among them. Lots of photos of the parents with their grandchildren and a group shot of the whole family taken at a family reunion last summer. (See enclosed.) They post photos of Brittany on her birthday each year and had an age-enhanced photo of what she might look like now done two years ago (also attached). From what I can see, they've never stopped looking for her or hoping for a break in her case.

That last line broke Sam's heart. How did people live for decades without knowing what had happened to their missing child? She would go mad within days if it took that long.

Next, she studied the additional report Freddie had sent on the Hans family. Caren and her sister, Cristen, had been raised by their late grandmother in Brookside, outside of Newark, after their parents died in an accident when the girls were very young. They both graduated from Christiana High School.

There's not much to be found about Caren after graduation, but Cristen graduated from the University of Delaware with a business degree and is married to Paul Reid, a firefighter in Newark. They have two young children, a boy and a girl, ages four and one (based on a recent Facebook post). She runs an online business from home, providing apparel to local teams, schools and other organizations. Caren and Paul reside in Brookside, about six blocks from the home where the sisters were raised. I went back several years on her social media and found no mention of her missing sister.

Sam's phone chimed with a text from Freddie. *Cadaver dogs have picked up on scents in Stahl's basement and backyard. Excavation equipment is being brought in.*

Her heart sank at that news. "Cadaver dogs have identified scents in the yard and basement at Stahl's house," Sam said to Vernon and Jimmy.

She had such mixed feelings about the news. On the one hand, she wanted closure for the families of the missing women. On the other, she dreaded the fallout of this case for the department, its leadership and the rest of them.

It made her sick to her stomach.

"Keep doing what you do, Sam." Vernon's gaze met hers in the mirror for a second before he returned his attention to the road. "You're on the side of right. You always have been and always will be. Stay focused on what you can control."

The words touched her deeply. That was exactly what her dad might have said under the circumstances. "Thank you, Vernon."

"Any time you need to hear it, you know where to find me."

"I do, and I'm grateful for you."

"Likewise."

They arrived at the Carters' neat ranch house a few minutes later. Two Honda sedans were parked in the driveway, and the flag was up on the mailbox at the curb. For some reason, that little flag caught Sam's attention as she marveled at the mundane details of life marching forward even though someone you loved was missing. After the worst thing had happened, bills still had to be paid, people needed to be fed, grass had to be cut, and life went on like nothing had changed when everything had.

Vernon opened the back door for her.

"Thank you, Vernon."

"My pleasure. I assume you don't want us going in ahead of you."

"You assume correctly."

"Had a feeling."

Sam left him with a warm smile and headed up the sidewalk to the front door.

Theodora met her at the door. "Come in."

Sam didn't bother showing her badge or making the usual introduction. "Thank you for seeing me."

"I'd say it was no problem," she said, "but we suffer every time there's interest in Brittany's case, especially when nothing ever comes of it." The woman looked like a stereotypical librarian, with short gray hair, glasses, a neat appearance and an aura of efficiency about her.

"I'm very sorry for your suffering. I'll do everything I can to try to get you some answers."

Theodora gestured to the kitchen table, where her husband was already seated.

"We appreciate that you have good intentions," Theodora said. "You'll understand if we don't get our hopes up."

"I understand." Sam took a seat at the table. "I know you've been disappointed by members of my department for years and have no reason to believe this time will be different."

"Not members of your department," Bart said. "*One* member. Leonard Stahl lied to and deceived us at every turn. We're well aware of your own troubles with him and how he was convicted of trying to murder you."

"Yes, he was."

"And yet, you're still working on cases that involve him?" Theodora asked.

"Yes, I am, because I want to make things right—or as right as they can be—for the other people he harmed."

"How will you make this right?" Bart asked. "Our daughter has been missing for twelve years. What's different now?"

"I'm here to inform you that we've received credible information possibly tying former Lieutenant Stahl to

Brittany's disappearance and that of several other young women."

For a long time after her words landed, they stared at her in apparent shock.

"So the man assigned to investigate her disappearance might've been the one who took her?" Bart asked, his every word laced with outrage.

"We believe that might be possible. As we speak, Crime Scene detectives are at his former home and tearing apart every aspect of his life."

"How is it possible, in light of his crimes against someone like you, that his life hasn't been torn apart before now?" Bart's face had gotten very red, and a vein in his forehead pulsed.

Theodora placed her hand on top of his. "Take it easy, Bart. Remember your heart."

"I don't care about my heart, Teddy. Did you hear what she said?"

"I heard her."

"This is an outrage!" Bart sputtered. "All this time, we've been waiting to hear something, *anything*, about what happened to our daughter, *and it was him*? The whole time? Why didn't anyone else take over the investigation after he was arrested? Why does *no one care* that our daughter was abducted and probably murdered after withstanding God knows what level of torture?"

It'd been a while since anyone had screamed at Sam like that, not that she didn't feel it was warranted. Still, the outburst unnerved her.

Bart got up so quickly, his chair toppled over.

Sam and Theodora both startled at the crashing sound.

He kicked the chair aside and went out the back door.

"I'm sorry," Theodora said.

"Don't be. He has every right to feel the way he does. It is an outrage. I want you to know... And this is not an excuse for the inexcusable. I swear it isn't. But there're so many cases... It's not possible for us to keep up with everything we have going on currently as well as the cold cases that should get more attention than they do. I'm very sorry that your daughter's case hasn't received the attention it deserves. I vow to you that I'll stay involved until you have answers. However long that may take."

"I accepted a long time ago that she's probably dead and that we may never know the truth of what happened to her." Theodora spoke softly, but with conviction. "I had to accept it to keep moving forward. I couldn't dwell in that sadness and anger for the rest of my life. It was killing me. Bart, though... He refuses to accept anything until he knows for sure. He continues to hope..." She shook her head. "It's ruined our lives, Lieutenant. It's ruined our marriage. It's ruined everything."

"I'm so sorry." Sam was on the verge of tears listening to Theodora's heartbreak. "I wish I could go back in time and change what's happened. I would if I could. We've been working to right a lot of wrongs where Stahl was concerned. The magnitude of his crimes is only now becoming clear to us. I don't say that as an excuse, because there isn't one."

"It helps me to see that a good police officer like you is sick over this."

"I am," Sam said. "We all are. It's inconceivable to us that we worked next to a man who was capable of the things we already know he's done. That it keeps getting worse..."

"It means a lot to me that you came here today. That you told us the truth, even though it caused you tremendous pain and probably significant humiliation to do so. You certainly didn't have to do that."

"Yes, I did. And I mean it when I tell you I'm going to stay on this case for as long as it takes, until we get you some answers."

"I say this with all due respect to you and the other good officers you work with, but answers aren't going to change anything for us now. Our daughter will still be gone, and our lives will forever be shattered because of how we lost her."

"I understand."

"I hope you never truly understand this pain, Lieutenant. I wouldn't wish it on anyone."

Sam swallowed the huge lump that suddenly appeared in her throat at the thought of one of her precious children going missing, let alone falling victim to a monster like Stahl. "Thank you for seeing me." She glanced at the door through which Bart had escaped. "If you'll tell him thank you for me, I'll see myself out."

"I'll tell him."

"We'll be in touch."

Theodora nodded, her posture and expression one of grim acceptance that answers might be forthcoming and that her fragile pact with grief might be upended.

Sam exited the house and took deep breaths of the cool air as she went down the sidewalk to where Vernon held the door for her.

His brows furrowed with concern. "You okay?"

"That was brutal," Sam said softly. "Absolutely brutal."

When she was settled in the back seat, he stood there for a minute after handing her a bottle of cold water. "Anything I can do?"

She shook her head as she took a sip of water. "Let's get this next thing over with."

CHAPTER ELEVEN

The Reid family lived on a cul-de-sac where kids rode their bikes under the watchful supervision of parents, who stood in a group in one of the driveways.

When the Secret Service SUV pulled onto the street, everything came to a halt.

Children moved their bikes to the side of the road, and the parents stared as the vehicle came to a stop outside the Reids' home. The bricks had been painted white, and wooden accents gave it a fresh, modern look. Matching window boxes stood ready for spring blooms.

A woman with shoulder-length hair, brown skin and a trim frame broke away from the other parents. She was waiting for Sam on the sidewalk when she emerged from the SUV.

"I'm Cristen Reid."

Sam shook her hand. "Thank you for seeing me."

She nodded and led the way toward the house.

Sam glanced over her shoulder to find the other adults staring at her as she followed Cristen into an immaculate, nicely designed home.

"Your home is lovely."

"Thank you. Can I get you anything?"

"I'm fine."

They sat together at the kitchen table.

Sam assumed the neighbors were watching Cristen's kids or they were with their father.

"I've come to update you on a major development in your sister's case."

"What development?"

"We've received credible information that the officer who investigated her case may be responsible for her disappearance. We're actively investigating these new leads and hope to have more information to share before much longer."

Looking stunned, Cristen sat back in her seat, her gaze fixed on framed black-and-white photos of her family. "Is there anything else?"

"No, just that."

"Okay, you've told me. You can go now."

"I want to extend our apologies—"

"Please." Her heated gaze shifted back to Sam. "Save it. There's nothing you can say that would make this right."

Sam stood and headed for the door. "Thank you for seeing me," she said as she exited the house less than five minutes after she entered.

The people across the street did the staring thing again as she made her way to the SUV. "Let's get back to the beach, Vernon."

"You got it."

After he closed the door, Sam glanced toward the house, where Cristen was in the doorway glaring at the SUV.

Her phone rang, and she took the call from Malone.

"How'd you make out with the Carters and Hans's sister?"

"They're very, very angry, and with good reason."

His deep sigh said it all. "You heard about the cadaver dogs?"

"I did. How soon will we know anything?"

"It'll take a while to recover the bodies and have them tested. A couple of weeks, probably."

"I hated having to tell those poor people about this."

"Everyone is getting the same response you did as they update the other families."

"I fear this is going to make all our previous scandals look minor."

"I fear you're right about that." He took a beat before he continued. "I go over it and over it in my mind. What was I doing when he was on this lawless rampage?"

"You were running around doing the job while he cut every corner and operated as a lawless criminal in plain sight."

"Joe and I have lost a lot of sleep over this. Trying to figure out how he pulled it off."

"Do you think he had help other than Gibbons?" Sam referred to the former IT lieutenant who'd recently been charged with aiding some of Stahl's criminal activity. It'd turned out that Stahl had somehow found out that Gibbons had been carrying on an extramarital affair with one of his subordinates. Stahl had threatened to expose him, which had led to Gibbons hiding some of Stahl's dirty work in the IT annals.

Gibbons now faced charges.

"I suppose it's possible," Malone said. "But listen. None of this is your problem this week. We appreciate you updating the families in Delaware. Now go enjoy the rest of your vacation."

"Keep me posted. I want to know what's going on."

"I will."

Sam closed her phone, put her head back against the seat, closed her eyes and tried to decompress. She didn't blame either family for their anger toward her, the department, Stahl and police in general. They all had good reason to feel the way they did. She hadn't been surprised to hear that everyone charged with delivering this news to the families had received the same reception.

It was just another reason to hate Stahl for the many, many things he'd done that the rest of them were now trying to make right while knowing that some things could never be made right.

Lulled by the movement of the car, Sam dozed off and was

thrust back into Marissa Springer's basement, where Stahl had wrapped her in razor wire and threatened to set her on fire. She could feel the sharp wire cutting into her flesh as he splashed gasoline on her and lit matches to torment her.

She couldn't move out of the fear of being sliced to pieces, which gave him great pleasure. His beady little eyes glimmered from the thrill of having her right where he wanted her. All she could think about was Nick and Scotty and how much she loved them and wanted to go home to them.

She'd closed her eyes and focused on their faces, the beautiful, perfect faces of the two people she loved the most. She'd also thought of her dad and sisters, her nieces and nephews and the squad of friends and colleagues who were like family. But it was Nick and Scotty who'd carried her through the ordeal, her thoughts of them soothing her during the most excruciating hours of her life.

The smell of sulfur permeated her senses and burned her nose.

If he dropped one of those lit matches, she'd burn to death, unable to do a thing to defend herself without ripping her skin to shreds. She was already bleeding from numerous places where the razor wire had cut her, and she had to pee —urgently.

Stahl had planned his torture meticulously. He wanted her to die in the most painful way possible.

She was driving him mad by ignoring him, by not making a single sound as he methodically went about his diabolical plan.

The next thing she knew, someone was shaking her and calling her name.

"Sam. Wake up. Sam!"

She opened her eyes to find Vernon out of the car, standing inside the open back door of the SUV while Jimmy looked back at her with concern from the front seat.

"You were dreaming," Vernon said.

"Well, that's mortifying." Sam wiped a spot of drool from the corner of her mouth. "What did I say?"

"Nothing specific, but you sounded distressed."

"I'm sorry."

"Don't be. Are you all right?"

"Yes, I'm fine." The images from the dream were front and center in her mind, but she played it down for the sake of the agents who'd become her friends.

Jimmy handed her another bottle of cold water.

"Thank you."

"Watch your fingers and toes," Vernon said as he prepared to close the door.

"All clear."

He closed the door, got into the driver's seat and pulled onto the highway.

"How much longer to Dewey?" Sam asked.

"Thirty minutes."

After this hellish day, Sam couldn't wait to get home to Nick.

NICK CHECKED HIS WATCH, wondering what time Sam would be back. He was in his second-to-last meeting of the day, with his chief of staff, Terry O'Connor, who'd been transported to Dewey by helicopter.

"While you're away," Terry said, "I'm sitting down with every cabinet member, one on one, to discuss the concept of loyalty to you and the Constitution. So far, I've had productive conversations with secretaries of the Interior, Veterans Affairs and Education. I've got Agriculture, Commerce and Energy coming in tomorrow."

"Thank you for taking that on."

"It needed to be done. I'm asking each of them what they think of the situation with the Joint Chiefs as a way to gauge their true feelings. If I get the slightest indication they're not on board with you and your administration, I'll ask for their resignation."

"Go get 'em, tiger."

"I'm fed up with the bullshit. People are either with us, or they're not. If they're not, we'll show them the door. We need to get past this illegitimacy nonsense and get busy doing the job. I'm all done fighting these petty battles. We've got shit to do."

"Yes, we do, and I appreciate you taking care of those conversations. I wasn't looking forward to having to deal with that."

"I've got you covered."

"That means everything to me. You know that, don't you?"

"I do, and it's my pleasure to serve as your chief of staff. When I think about where I was a couple of years ago and where I am now..."

Nick had encouraged Terry to confront his drinking problem in rehab, while holding a job for him as deputy chief of staff in his Senate office after Nick took the place of Terry's late brother, John O'Connor. Since then, they'd taken a wild ride all the way to the White House together, and there was no one Nick would rather have by his side than his late best friend's brother.

"I owe you everything," Terry added.

"No, you don't."

"I really do, Nick. You gave me a reason to get sober and to stay sober. I'll never forget that."

Smiling, Nick said, "What do you think John would say if he could see us now?"

"He'd love it. I have no doubt about that."

"Yeah, he would."

"I'll let you get back to your vacation, such as it is."

"Sam reminds me frequently that this is temporary. What's a few messed-up vacations in the grand scheme of things?"

"I'll try to keep the mess to a minimum this week."

"That'd be good. Are you and Lindsey still planning to come out this weekend?"

"Hoping for the day on Saturday, unless work interferes."

"Glad to hear it."

"I'll talk to you tomorrow, if not before."

Nick laughed at the way Terry put that. There was a very

good chance they'd talk several times before the morning. "Sounds good."

After Terry left, he sent a message to his close friend and White House social secretary, Shelby Faircloth Hill, that said, *I'm free. Call whenever you can.* She'd asked for a minute with him whenever he had time.

Shelby called five minutes later.

"Hi there," he said.

"How's the vacation?"

"A little less relaxing than we'd like, but we're enjoying the view and downtime when we can get it."

"Glad to hear that. Happy anniversary to my dear friends and my favorite wedding of all the ones I've planned."

"That's quite an honor."

"It was quite a wedding."

"Yes, it sure was. How're you feeling?"

"A little better every day. My hands have finally stopped shaking, so that's progress. We really appreciate being able to stay in the fortress while we look for a new place to live."

"We're very happy to have you. Scotty and the twins love having Noah to play with."

"They were in the pool with Noah last night. He had a blast and slept for ten hours."

"Wow!"

"That was a record."

"The pool has that effect on the twins, too."

"Eli and Candace arrived late last night for spring break. The twins are so thrilled to have him home."

"We're looking forward to seeing them this weekend. Are you guys still coming out?"

"Just for the day on Saturday. We're looking at houses on Sunday."

"We'll take what we can get."

"We need to talk about the state dinner next Tuesday."

"Are you sure you're up for being back to work so soon?"

"It helps me to stay busy. It gives me less time to think about what could've happened."

"If you need extra help, please ask for it."

"I will. Thanks for the concern, but I'm doing okay as long as those creeps are locked up. Avery says there's no chance they'll be released before the trial on these latest charges."

"I'm glad to hear that."

"Now, about the state dinner. I wanted to give you a rundown of how the night will unfold and what will be required of you and Sam."

"You've got my full attention."

"The prime minister and his wife will arrive at the White House at three o'clock for meetings with you and Sam."

Nick needed to remind Sam that she had be back at the White House ahead of that meeting. He was certain her chief of staff, Lilia, was on it, but it never hurt to add his own two cents.

"After your meetings, you and the prime minister will host a joint press conference at four thirty. Then he and his wife will return to Blair House to change for dinner while you and Sam do the same. After that, you'll reconvene with them in the East Room for a reception with Congress at six before leading the procession into the State Dining Room."

She went over a number of other protocol items and promised to send him a copy of the final guest list so he could review it and prepare himself to meet luminaries from the entertainment, media and political spheres.

"Sam's staff will be sharing the list with her, too. I talked to Lilia today, and she's working with Marcus, Sam's favorite designer, to make sure the first lady is prepared to dazzle, as usual."

"Excellent. Thank you, Shelby, for a wonderful job."

"It's been a lot of fun to prepare for this. I keep wanting to pinch myself that this is my job. I can only imagine how you must feel."

"Most days, I want to kick myself—and Sam wants to kick me, too—for agreeing to be vice president, especially after *SNL* had its way with us—again."

They shared a laugh.

"That was too funny," Shelby said.

"No, it wasn't."

"Whatever you say, sir. Hopefully, next Tuesday evening will make all the crap and mockery worth it. You and Sam will shine."

"I proposed to her at a state dinner, so they do tend to work out well for us."

"Ah, yes, I remember that. I hope this one is equally memorable."

"With you in charge, I'm sure it will be. See you on Saturday."

"See you then."

Nick put down the phone and stood to stretch out the kinks after hours of meetings. Since Sam had had to work that afternoon, he'd made himself available to take care of some business. He hoped it would allow them some peace for the rest of the week. It was funny to think about how weekends were often just another day at the office in this 24/7 job of his.

He went to the front door to ask Brant for an update on Sam's ETA.

"They're ten minutes out," Brant said.

"Thank you."

"No problem, sir. Will you be staying in for the evening or going out?"

"We'll stay in tonight and go out to dinner tomorrow. I'll let you know the plan in the morning."

"Thank you, Mr. President."

Nick went to take a quick shower before Sam got home and was there to greet her wearing basketball shorts and the T-shirt she'd given him the night before.

She walked through the door and straight into his arms.

He held her close, breathing in the scents of fresh air, lavender and vanilla that came with her. "What's wrong, love?"

"Very rough day."

"What can I do?"

"This," she said on a long exhale. "Just this."

"This is my specialty."

They stood there for a long time before he gently helped her out of her coat and relocated them to the sofa, bringing her down on his lap and wrapping her up in his love. At times like this, he wished she'd give up the job that took so much from her even if he knew she wouldn't be her without the job.

It was the ultimate Catch-22.

And if he never again heard the name Stahl, that'd be more than fine with him.

"You want to talk about it?"

"It was more or less as expected. Just brutal having to tell more families about our major failings as a department."

"They're not your failings."

"They belong to all of us who ever worked with him and didn't see what he was doing."

"How could you have seen it? He was your boss. It wasn't your job to investigate him. It was all you could do to handle your own job while dealing with him."

"It's hard to explain how this feels like a failure for all of us. We're cops. We're supposed to rid the city of crime, and it was happening right under our own noses. He could very well be a serial killer, and we had no idea. We had no clue that Conklin was sitting on info that would've solved my dad's case years before we finally got to the truth. We didn't know Hernandez was aware of Conklin's involvement and didn't tell anyone or that Ramsey was mentally unbalanced. The collective whole of it makes us look incompetent."

"No, it makes *them* look like that. Not the rest of you, who are out there doing the work and solving the cases day after day. You're keeping the rest of us safe. People should appreciate that."

"They should, and many of them do. But the negatives have far outweighed the positives for a while now."

"That's not true. You're doing what you can to right the wrongs of the past, and that's appreciated by so many. Marcel Blanchet's mother is grateful for how quickly your team solved the murders of her son and his family. I saw the note she sent you on the desk at home. Those things—and those people—

matter, Samantha. You have to take the small victories where you can get them while you fight the larger war."

"You ought to be a politician when you grow up. You've got a way with words."

She always made him laugh, even when she was having an existential crisis.

Then she looked up at him with that one-in-a-million face, her eyes full of the vulnerability that only he ever saw from his badass supercop. "You really do. You always know what to say to make me feel better."

"That's my most important job." He tipped her chin up for a kiss. "You, my love, are the best cop in the whole world. You care so much about crime victims, their families, your community, the people you work with and for. No one could ask for more than what you give to a thankless job. You should never feel diminished by the sins of others."

She seemed to think about that for a beat. "Thank you. I needed to hear that. I do care. Probably more than I should."

"Nah, you care just the right amount, and that comes through to everyone you deal with on the job. Well, maybe not receptionists or people with obnoxious doorbells or certain officers who shall not be named."

Again, she laughed, and the sound filled him with joy. He loved to make her laugh, especially when she was feeling down.

"The ones who shall not be named are criminals," he said. "Is it unfortunate and disappointing that they worked among the honorable men and women who make up the MPD? It sure as hell is, but the rest of you have nothing to be ashamed of."

"Are you sure about that? They got away with murder, literally in Stahl's case, and it happened while he was surrounded by the very people charged with preventing such things.

"I'm sure about it. Don't forget he—and the others—knew all too well how to work the system so he wouldn't get caught."

"I guess."

"You know what you need?"

"What's that?"

"A nice bubble bath, a glass of wine, some TLC from your favorite husband, a fire, dinner, a movie, some epic snuggling. How does that sound?"

"Yes, please, to all of that."

CHAPTER TWELVE

"I want to talk about your son," Collins said over dinner of tender pork, risotto, salad and crusty bread fresh from the oven.

Nicoletta took a sip of the rosé wine he'd gotten for her after she told him it was her favorite. "What about him?"

"Your son is the president of the United States."

"I'm aware."

"I find that fascinating. Especially in light of your current... challenges."

"So what you're wondering is how a criminal like me has a son like him?"

"You said that, not me."

"It's what you meant." She took another sip of wine. "If you want the truth..."

"The truth would be good."

What was it about this man that made her feel ashamed of her propensity to lie? "I wasn't a good mother. I admit that. Like I said, I was sixteen when I had him. His father's mother raised him. I had very little to do with him being where he is now."

"Is that why he says you're not in his life?"

"Partially." She wanted Collins to like and admire her the way she did him, but after she told him the rest, he'd be revolted.

Then his hand came across the table to rest on top of hers. "I'm not judging you, Nicoletta. I swear I'm not. I wouldn't have been prepared to be a parent at sixteen either."

"I let him down," she said on a sigh. "Frequently. I never intended to disappoint him. It seemed that I couldn't help it. I was so, so selfish. I wasn't about to let a child get in the way of my hopes and dreams, even if he was the cutest little guy." She smiled when she thought of young Nick. "He was so serious and earnest. From the time he stepped foot in school, he was an outstanding student. He was everything I never was. I sort of resented him for that, you know?"

"I can see how it would've been difficult for you."

"I wanted to do right by him. I really did. I love him. I always have. I just was such a fuckup. And Nick... He just kept excelling at sports and school and everything he did. He played varsity hockey in high school and won a full academic scholarship to Harvard, of all places. My son was going to *Harvard*. I told everyone I met about that, as if I'd had anything to do with it. That was all him. He was on fire with ambition and drive. Over time, I started to feel ashamed to be around him. I was scraping the bottom of the barrel to survive, and my son was earning academic achievements at the most prestigious college around. I felt dirty next to him."

She'd never said these things out loud to anyone.

"I'm sorry you felt that way."

Nicoletta shrugged. "I've always been nothing compared to him. You may as well know that I've taken advantage of his soft heart a few times by shaking him down for money. I also was paid to give interviews full of falsehoods about him. It's no wonder he wants nothing to do with me."

She was almost afraid to look at him after confessing her deepest sins.

"People make mistakes, Nicoletta."

"There're mistakes, and then there are sins, Collins. There's a big difference."

"Are you sorry for the way you've treated your son?"

"I've always been sorry. There's an ache in my heart with his name on it. I wish things were different, but it's too late now."

"It's never too late to make amends to the people you love."

"In this case, it might be. He'd never see me or listen to me."

"Would he listen to me as your representative?"

"What're you suggesting?"

"That I reach out to him on your behalf, indicate your wish to make amends and to start fresh with him and his family."

"His bitch of a wife would never allow it. She's the reason the FBI investigated me in the first place. I'm sure of that."

"If you wish to truly make amends with him, Nicoletta, you have to stop calling his wife a bitch and blaming her for your troubles."

She felt chastised, the way she had when her mother used to tell her to quit being mouthy and promiscuous. She should've listened to her.

"I don't mean to be harsh," he added. "But the bond between the first couple is obvious to anyone who has even the slightest awareness of them. If you mean to make things right with him, you'll have to also make things right with her."

Nicoletta hated the woman her son had married and the way she'd been treated by her when she'd shown up, uninvited, to their wedding. The thought of that day made her seethe with resentment.

"Nicoletta?"

"I'm not sure I can make things right with her. I can't stand her."

"Why can't you stand her? Is it because she's gone to great lengths to protect her husband from someone who's hurt him repeatedly?"

She wanted to curl up in a ball and die at the way his words sliced through her, leaving her bleeding on the inside. The saying *the truth hurts* had never been more relevant. "I suppose."

"Can you blame her? After what you've told me, I'm not surprised that she's tried to protect him where you're concerned."

She put down her wineglass and stood. "I should go."

"Go where?"

"Anywhere but here."

"Have I said anything that isn't factual?"

She shifted her weight from one foot to the other, shame boiling up inside her and making her face feel overly warm. "I don't want to be here anymore."

He stood and came around the table to face her. "You have nowhere else to go. Your home is considered a crime scene. The media is camped out there, awaiting your return. In addition, your assets are frozen indefinitely, pending the outcome of legal proceedings."

"I have friends," she said defiantly.

"Unindicted coconspirators?"

"What does that mean?"

"It means, my dear, that your so-called friends have been encouraged to testify against you to keep themselves out of prison."

"They'd never do that!"

"When looking at decades in prison, you'd be surprised what people will do."

Hearing her friends had turned on her was devastating. She'd helped them make a lot of money. "Are you suggesting I make amends with my son so he might get me out of this jam? Because I doubt that's going to happen."

"Not at all. I'm suggesting you make amends with him to find some peace for yourself—and for him."

She gave him a skeptical look. "Why do I feel like you're selling me a bill of goods? Being all supportive and encouraging while you wait to pull the rug out from under me."

"I hate to have to say it so inelegantly, but there's no rug under you. I'm your best chance of dealing with these charges. I want you to think about fixing your relationship with your son so you'll have something to look forward to when this is behind you."

"When will it be behind me? To hear you talk, I'm going to die in prison."

"Not if you're willing to entertain a plea deal."

"You mean the deal that will require me to ruin other people's lives to save my own?"

"Yes, that one. I had a thought about that. If we were to nudge the prosecutors in the direction of the safe-deposit box, they could get a warrant for the contents, which would keep you from having to give up the info."

"Would the people on those lists be charged?"

"At most with misdemeanor solicitation."

"That'll ruin their lives."

"They knew that was a risk when they paid for sex."

"I want you to know that no one has ever paid me for sex. I was just the facilitator."

"That's good to know."

Once again, her weight shifted from one foot to the other, and she felt exquisitely uncomfortable as he directed a warm, sexy glance her way. She tingled all over when he gave her his full attention. She could never let him know he had that kind of power over her. "What's in this for you?"

"Other than helping you to avoid a lengthy prison sentence?"

"Yes, other than that. Are you hoping I'll be so grateful that I'll sleep with you?"

His laughter only added to the tingles attacking all her most sensitive places.

"What's so funny?" she asked indignantly.

"You are. If I sleep with you, it'll be because we both want that. I've never had to pay for sex, and I'm not about to start now."

"Don't worry," she said on a bitter-sounding note. "I wouldn't charge you if you get me out of trouble."

"No quid pro quo, Nicoletta."

"What is that?"

"I've already told you I don't expect sex for legal work."

"According to you, I don't have any money. So how will I pay you for your legal work?"

"With the pleasure of your company."

She shot him a skeptical look. "What does that mean?"

"I like you. You're not only strikingly beautiful, but you're interesting and entertaining. I find myself intrigued by you."

"Intrigued. I see."

"Do you? I want to help you. And in exchange for that help, I want to spend time with you."

"What's the catch?"

"No catch."

"There's always a catch."

"Not this time."

"You'll pardon me for questioning your motives."

"I understand you're preconditioned to think the worst of people. I assure you that you have nothing to worry about where I'm concerned. I want only to get to know you better and see what happens from there—while keeping you out of prison and possibly helping you find a path back to your son." After a pause, he said, "What do you think?"

"There's really no catch?"

"None whatsoever."

"You're not angling to get in with the president, are you? Because that's not going to happen through me."

"Of course it would be a thrill to meet him, but my life will still be fine if that never happens."

"I still don't understand why you'd do all this for a perfect stranger."

"You're not a stranger anymore." He took a step closer to her, leaving only a foot or so between them. "Are you?"

She held her breath, torn between wanting him to touch her and fearful for what would happen to her if he did. His rich, sexy scent had her wanting to lean in closer to him, but she held her ground, still suspicious of things that seemed too good to be true.

"I guess not," she said in response to his question.

"If you follow my advice, I can probably get the charges

pled down to misdemeanors with probation and community service."

She curled her lip to let him know what she thought of community service.

"It beats prison, doesn't it?"

"Does it, though?"

He laughed, and again her mouth watered. This man was dangerously attractive, seemingly kind and thoughtful with a quick wit and razor-sharp intelligence. A potent combination, to say the least.

"What do you say, Nicoletta? Shall we see what we can do to get you out of this mess so we can find out what else might be possible for us?"

Rarely had she found herself with so few options. She prided herself on always having a plan for whatever might arise. This, however, was bigger than her. She couldn't charm or cajole her way out of this kind of trouble. Here was a man—a devastatingly gorgeous man—offering her a way out in exchange for the pleasure of her company. She still wasn't convinced that he wasn't looking for sex as payment for his legal services. But it wasn't as if sex with him would be a hardship.

If anything, sex with him could change her life in ways she'd never before imagined.

She'd been on her own for her entire adult life, fighting to survive, to thrive in a man's world. She was exhausted and flat out of schemes to solve the problem of the moment. She needed what he was offering, and, if she were being honest, he intrigued her, too.

"Nicoletta?"

"Yes, please, Collins. I accept your kind offer."

"Excellent. I'll get to work in the morning and see what I can do about a plea deal—and then we'll figure out what to do about your son."

· · ·

SAM SLEPT like a dead woman and woke up rested and refreshed at nine o'clock the next morning. Clearly, there was something to be said for bubble baths, wine, sex and snuggling with her favorite man to make a girl feel better after a rough day. If Nick had one special gift, it was his ability to make anything better than it would've been otherwise. She'd become addicted to his healing powers and would be lost without him.

Her thoughts naturally shifted to her sister Angela, who was coping with the loss of her beloved husband, Spencer, to an accidental fentanyl overdose. While Sam wanted to support her sister, niece and nephew in every way she possibly could, she found it excruciating to be around Angela as she lived Sam's worst nightmare.

It wasn't about her. She told herself that every day while she showed up for Angela, Jack and Ella and helped Angela cope with being pregnant with a third child, due in June. She'd done and would continue to do everything she could think of to make this time easier for Ang while her sister's loss forced Sam to confront her own greatest fear.

At one time, she would've said losing her dad would be the worst thing that could happen, and that had been brutal. It still was. She missed him every day and yearned for his wise counsel and insight on all things. But nothing could compare to what it would be like to lose Nick. Now she had four kids to dread losing, too.

Sometimes it was all too much.

Nick came into the bedroom, carrying a tray and wearing only the snug boxer briefs that put his muscular body on full display. Knowing him, he'd already had a security briefing and a workout while she'd been sleeping in.

"Breakfast for my wife as we begin our third year of marriage." He placed the tray on her lap and leaned in to kiss her. "Good morning."

"You're awfully chipper."

"That's because I get to spend this beautiful Monday with my favorite person." He sat next to her in bed and reached for one of the two mugs of steaming coffee. "Good news. It's supposed to be sixty today. We can sit outside, and later we can have a bonfire."

"That sounds fun." Sam took a bite of veggie omelet. "Did you make this?"

"I didn't. It was delivered this morning from the White House, along with lunch. We'll be going out for dinner tonight."

"We're so spoiled with meal deliveries."

"It's the thing I like best about being president. The amazing White House staff and how they make everything so easy for us."

"Yes, they do. Did you have your briefing?"

"I did."

"How was that?"

"The usual shop of horrors, but it seems that China and Russia have removed their ships from the coast of Alaska, so that's good news."

"What were they doing there?"

"That's a very good question, and my national security team is hard at work figuring out what the deal is. Today, I've decided it's not going to be my problem."

"Every time you say that, something else becomes your problem."

He thought about that for a second as he popped a grape into his mouth. "You're right. I need to pass a law forbidding myself from ever saying that again."

Sam loved to see him in such a lighthearted mood.

They shared the omelet as well as the chocolate croissants that'd been baked at the White House and finished off a bowl of fresh fruit.

"What were you thinking about when I came in?" he asked as they relaxed with their coffee.

"Nothing much."

"You're never thinking about nothing much. It's always something big, so what gives?"

"I was thinking about you and us and how happy I am that

I found you again after all those years I spent wondering what'd become of you."

He winced. "I hate thinking about that. I get so mad at myself for not going to HQ to find you. I should've done that. That I didn't is my biggest regret in life."

"I think it all happened the way it was meant to. I had to go through what I did with Peter to appreciate this for the magnificent relationship it is."

"That's bullshit. You didn't need him and his nonsense to know we have a good thing. We both knew that the night we first met."

"Yes, we did, but I was so immature then. I probably would've screwed it up."

"You always say that, and I always say I wouldn't have let you."

"Is part of being married having the same conversations over and over?"

"It's fun to talk about the things that've happened."

"Even the bad stuff?"

"All of it. I like to talk about everything that makes up our unique story. Why are you dwelling on the bad stuff?"

"I was thinking about Ang and Spence and what I'd do if that happened to me."

"Don't do that, babe. I'm right here, and nothing is going to happen."

Sam barked out a laugh. "You say that as if you're not the most coveted target on earth."

"Who's surrounded by the best security money can buy. I don't want you to worry about me."

"Can't help it. I'm preconditioned to worry."

"Cut that out." He took her mug, put it on the tray and moved the tray to the floor. Then he turned on his side to face her. "I don't like it when you worry about me."

"I don't like when you worry about me."

"Maybe we should get ourselves a padded room where we can be safe and secure at all times."

"We'd go stir-crazy in there, and so would the kids, because we'd have to take them with us."

"True." His lips pursed as he seemed to think about something. "I suppose the only alternative to the padded room is to live our lives and hope for the best."

"I don't like that alternative."

"It's all we've got, babe." He leaned in to kiss her. "My goal is to live to be a hundred and ten and still be pestering you for nonstop sex."

Sam laughed. "Won't you be tired by then?"

"I'll never be too tired for sex with my love. Besides, you'll only be a hundred and eight. A spring chicken next to me."

She laughed helplessly at the picture he painted. "People will be paying us not to have sex at those ages."

"They could give me all the money in the world, and I'd say 'no, thank you' if it meant I couldn't make love with my wife anymore."

"Charmer. Will you still have all your teeth?"

"Will you?"

"Where would they go?"

"I have no idea."

She laced her fingers through his. "It's fun to think about getting really, really old with you and driving the kids crazy with our shenanigans."

"It'll happen. I feel it in my bones. We're going the distance. We'll be married so long, people will feel sorry for us being stuck with the same person for that long."

"I'm so happy to be stuck with you," she said, smiling.

"Same, babe. Now how about we go outside and sit in the sun?"

"Let's do it."

CHAPTER THIRTEEN

After a relaxing day with few interruptions from either of their jobs, they got dressed for dinner out.

"Will this be a shit show?" Sam asked him as she ran a brush through hair she'd straightened for the occasion.

"Probably, but what do we care? It's date night. That's our only focus. The good news is that it's quiet here this time of year, so there shouldn't be gawkers."

"'Shouldn't be' are the key words there."

He flashed a goofy smile. "We'll hope for the best."

"Let's call the kids before we go."

Nick used his iPhone to FaceTime with Scotty.

"Is it safe to look?" Scotty asked when he accepted the call.

"Of course it is," Nick said. "What do you take us for?"

"You really want to know?"

Nick smiled at Sam. "No, I don't think I do."

"How's the vacation?"

"Good. Relaxing. For the most part. Work keeps interfering."

"That's what you get for being the president."

"So I'm told. How's the social studies paper coming?"

"We don't need to ruin a perfectly nice conversation with that topic."

Sam bit her lip to keep from laughing out loud as Nick scowled at her.

"Mom thought that was funny, right?"

"I can neither confirm nor deny," Sam said.

"You did, and I'll send it to you in a little while." Scotty grinned as Skippy's face came on the screen. "The Skipster says hello. She misses you."

"We miss her, too," Nick said. "And you guys."

"You don't miss us. You're too busy kissing and other gross stuff."

Sam shook with silent laughter.

"We do, too, miss you!" Nick said. "Where're the twins?"

"They're having a great time with Eli. I'll get them. Come on, Skip."

They watched Scotty leave his room and call for the twins, who came running down the stairs from the third floor.

Their cute little faces filled the screen.

"How're our favorite six-year-olds?" Nick asked.

"We're good," Aubrey said. "We had ice cream with Celia upstairs. She said we can stay up an extra half hour because we did all our homework without help."

"That sounds like a fair deal to me."

"When are we coming there?" Alden asked.

"Right after school on Friday," Sam said.

"Can we go to the beach?" he asked.

"We sure can," Nick said. "It's too cold to swim, though, but we can have a bonfire."

"What's a bonfire?" Alden asked.

"It's a big fire on the beach," Scotty said. "We can make s'mores."

"Oh, I love them," Alden said.

"I stink at toasting marshmallows," Aubrey said.

"I'll do it for you," Scotty replied. "Don't worry."

"My heart," Sam said.

"Knock it off," Scotty said. "That's what big brothers do for little sisters."

"I repeat. My heart."

"You're the best big brother ever," Nick said. "We'll see you guys on Friday. We can't wait."

"Neither can we," Aubrey said. "Lijah is coming, too!"

"Yes, he is."

"Is he bringing *her*?" Alden asked.

Sam was taken aback by his tone. "You mean Candace? Yes, he is. She's his wife now."

"I don't like her."

"What?" Sam asked, glancing at Nick, who seemed equally baffled. "Why?"

"He's weird when she's around."

"You have to give her a chance, buddy," Nick said. "Eli loves all of you."

"We don't want to share him with her," Aubrey said.

"Guys..." Sam was truly astounded to hear them say these things. "Eli was going to get married eventually. You need to be nice to his wife. That will mean a lot to him."

"I guess," Alden said. "Can we go have ice cream now?"

"Sure, go ahead," Nick said. "We'll see you soon. Love you."

"Love you, too," they said as they ran off.

Scotty juggled the phone and then reappeared on the screen. "I wasn't going to tell you about this situation until I see you, but they've been super chilly to Candace since they got home."

"Oh jeez," Nick said.

"We had a long talk about it last night after I read their books to them. They asked why he had to marry her. And they said he's stupid when she's around. I think, more than anything, they're bent out of shape having to share him with anyone."

"Has Eli noticed?"

"I think he senses something is off, but not specifically that it has to do with her."

"Should we give him a heads-up?"

"I say no," Scotty said. "Let's deal with the twins and help them accept her. They've had a lot of change in a short amount of time. I'm not surprised they're feeling weird about him getting married, because they're no longer his sole focus."

"When did you get so wise?" Sam asked, impressed and amazed by his insight.

"Duh. I've always been wise. You're just now realizing it."

"Haha, whatever you say, sport. But thank you for your advice, which we'll follow." Sam glanced at Nick, who nodded. "For now, anyway."

"We'll see how the weekend goes," Nick added.

"I can't wait to come there. This is the part of the year where school starts to seem like it's never going to end."

"The end will be here before we know it," Nick said. "Keep your head down and your eyes on the prize of summer vacation."

"If I must."

"You must. You're going to Harvard, right?"

Scotty's snort of laughter was infectious. "Only cuz you're the president."

"You'll get there on your own," Nick said. "I have no doubt."

"I have enough doubts for all of us."

"You've got this, buddy," Nick said. "And now I have to take my best girl on a very romantic date."

Scotty made a face to let them know what he thought of that.

"Your day is coming, my friend," Sam said. "Get all your homework done and sleep well. We love you."

"Love you, too. Have fun tonight."

"We will," Nick said. "Love you."

"What a kid," Sam said after he'd disconnected the call.

"He's the best of the best. How'd we get so lucky? What he said about the twins and Candace was brilliant."

"It sure was. He's very insightful. He pays attention to what goes on around him, unlike most kids his age who are oblivious."

"I'm sure that's because of what he went through after he lost his mom and grandfather."

"I wish I'd found him sooner," Nick said, "and spared him from that."

"I do, too, but his past has made him who he is, and we love who he is."

"We sure do."

Sam's phone rang with a call from Freddie. "Hey, what's up?"

"Sorry to bother you on vacation. I thought you'd want to know that Haggerty and his team have uncovered bones in Stahl's backyard. They're bringing in a special forensics team to process the yard and basement."

Sam sat on the bed as all the air left her body in one whoosh. "I was so hoping it wasn't true."

"Me, too."

"What do we know about the informant who passed the tip to Malone? How did he or she know about this?"

"We're looking into him. Malone wants to be careful not to burn a bridge there, but if he's known about this all along and didn't tell us, that's a problem."

"Yes, it sure is. What's being done about the media?"

"They have a statement ready to go out soon. In the meantime, the brass is keeping a tight lid on it."

"It'll be thermonuclear when it gets out." Sam wondered how many more hits Joe Farnsworth could absorb before the mayor or city council called for new leadership at the MPD. She couldn't even think about him leaving without wanting to wail. He was an amazing leader and supportive boss, not to mention he was her beloved uncle Joe.

"People are worried. It's a lot on top of a lot."

"Isn't it always?"

"That's what has them worried. The constant chaos from within the ranks. It's not a good look."

"No, it isn't, but don't forget that's not the only thing happening. There's a lot of good, too. Nick reminded me of the letter we got from Graciela, thanking us for the quick resolution the Blanchet family's case. She said that while nothing can bring them back, it provides a measure of comfort to know that the people who took them from her will be punished. We have to stay focused on the wins as the chaos swirls around us."

"You're right, and so is Nick, but this is just…"

"It's devastating."

"Yeah, for sure. Anyway, I thought you'd want to know the latest."

"I do, and I appreciate you calling. Hang in there, okay? At times like this, my dad used to say, 'This, too, shall pass.' As bad as something is right now, it won't always be this bad."

"That's true, and I know it. It's just hard to fathom how this level of evil worked right next to us."

"If you need to see Dr. Trulo, Freddie, do it. There's no shame in asking for help. This is a lot to process."

"I know. I'm thinking about it."

"Remember this, too. People like you and me will never understand what motivates someone like him or Ramsey. So don't go crazy trying to understand. You never will."

"I hear you, and that's for sure."

"We just have to keep showing up and doing the job for as long as it makes sense to us. We're good at what we do. We make a difference. We should never question that."

"It helps to be reminded. Thank you."

"Any time, my grasshopper. Go have a nice evening with your wife and forget about it all until tomorrow."

"Will do. How's the vacation?"

"Excellent. We're going to attempt a dinner outing tonight. Watch for us on the eleven o'clock news."

Freddie laughed. "Will do. May the Force be with you."

"And also with you. Talk to you soon."

"Yes, you will. Later."

"Is your grasshopper upset?" Nick asked as he put on a sweater to go with well-faded jeans that did wondrous things for his ass. "Sam?"

"Huh? I was thinking about how hot you are in those jeans."

"Shut up about that and answer the question."

She laughed the way she always did when he bristled over her commentary about his hotness, which was, in fact, sizzling. "He's very upset. They uncovered a burial ground in Stahl's backyard and are bringing in a special forensics team to work the site."

"Jesus."

"That about sums things up."

"I'm sorry, Sam. I know how awful this is for you guys."

"It's devastating. Even though we knew he was a creep, we never thought he was capable of the things he's done." She exhaled a long deep breath. "It'll be a nightmare when this goes public."

"You don't have to think about that right now."

"No, I don't. Let's get this party started."

"Only if you feel up to it."

"I wouldn't miss date night with you for anything. Let's go."

Nick kissed her cheek. "I'll let Brant know we're ready."

NICK WATCHED her try to rally for their date, but he could tell by the furrow in her brow that she was deeply troubled. And with good reason. Even from prison, that son of a bitch Stahl continued to be a cancer within a department of hardworking, dedicated officers.

People like Sam and Freddie, who put their whole hearts and souls into the job, would take this latest blow harder than most.

Nick had chosen a local steakhouse that had decent online ratings. The Secret Service had been there the day before to secure a private room for the first couple. In exchange for the restaurant staff keeping the visit quiet, Sam and Nick would pose for a photo with them. He could only hope they'd abided by the agreement.

He was heartened to find no gaggle of reporters gathered outside on the way in. No doubt, they'd be there on the way out, as quite a few White House reporters had traveled to Dewey to cover their week away. Nick would never get used to everything he did being a news story, but it went with the office. People were interested in their president and his family. Even a casual night out with his wife was news.

In a few years, he would have fulfilled his duty and could return to semiprivate life. Nothing would ever be like it had been before he was president, but the intense scrutiny would recede. He couldn't wait for that.

He followed Sam out of the SUV and placed a hand on her lower back as they made their way inside.

The restaurant owners, Jim and Andrea, waited to greet them with excitement that could only be described as giddy.

"It's such an honor to welcome you to our humble establishment," Jim said. "We've got a special spot all set up for you. Follow me right this way."

Everything in the restaurant came to a stop as Sam and Nick walked through with the owners.

At least fifty cell phones were pointed at them.

They nodded to the other diners and shook hands with the waitstaff as they made their way to a private room in the back. He was thankful for that arrangement so they wouldn't have people staring at them while they ate. In his old life, he might've found the private room a bit pretentious. Now it was necessary if they were to have any prayer of privacy.

Nick held the chair for his wife and bent to place a kiss on her neck that she didn't see coming. He loved the way she startled and then laughed. He enjoyed catching her off guard, and more than anything, he was delighted by her laughter, especially since she'd been so low earlier.

When he sat across from her, she gave him a sly grin.

"That was a dirty trick, my friend."

Nick returned her grin and thanked Andrea for the cloth napkin she handed him.

"It's such a delight to see you're every bit as real in person as you are on TV," Andrea said. "We're huge fans."

"Thank you so much," Nick said. "That's nice to hear."

"You keep doing what you're doing, Mr. President," Jim said. "We're rooting for you."

"We appreciate it."

She handed them each a printed card that had the presidential seal at the top. "We took the liberty of preparing a special five-course meal for you, based on the information we were provided by the culinary team at the White House. We hope it sounds good to you."

"This looks wonderful," Sam said after she'd glanced at the special menu. "I can't think of anything I would add."

"Same," Nick said. "Thank you."

"We've also chosen wine pairings for each course."

"I love this place," Sam said.

"We were hoping you would," Andrea said, beaming. "We'll be right back with your wine and your first course."

"Lobster-stuffed mushrooms," Nick said. "That doesn't sound good at all."

"I'm drooling."

"Don't do that, love. It's unseemly for the first lady to drool in public."

"Ha! I'll try not to let anyone see it." She took a sip of her ice water. "I like to hear people say they support you. We need to get out more often so you can hear right from the people you work for that they approve of the job you're doing."

"We'll hear from those who don't approve, too."

Sam waved a hand to dismiss them. "That's fine. They have a right to their opinion, but you need to interact with real people outside the gilded cage so you get the kind of positive reinforcement that Jim and Andrea provided."

"You're right. I'd like to get back to school visits, too. I really liked doing that when I was VP."

"Then do it. You're the boss of the whole world, babe."

"Not quite, but your point is well taken."

"There were a lot of phones pointed at us on the way in. Do you think there'll be a mob on the way out?"

He was certain Brant and the other agents would take care of any crowd control. "Nah. I doubt it. Don't worry about it. Just enjoy the evening."

She raised her wineglass to him. "That's what I'm going to do."

Andrea returned with the lobster-stuffed mushrooms, which were delicious.

Nick spiked a bite with his fork and fed it to Sam.

"So, so good."

Next was a Caesar salad made tableside, followed by scrumptious filet mignon, grilled shrimp, scalloped potatoes and a delicious vegetable dish made with zucchini, squash, broccoli and snow peas.

The wine kept coming, too, until Sam had to cover her glass to keep them from giving her more. "I'm drunk on food and wine."

"And love," Nick said. "Don't forget that."

"Mostly love." Sam looked up at Andrea. "This was an exceptional meal. Thank you so much."

"It was our pleasure. Dessert will be out in a few minutes. Would you like some coffee?"

"I will," Nick said.

"Decaf for me," Sam added.

"Coming right up."

They lingered over a chocolate soufflé and coffee.

"I'm so full, I'm apt to burst," Sam said after they'd eaten most of the rich dessert.

"We can't have that." He signaled for the check.

Jim came over to the table. "It's our pleasure to have you, Mr. President, Mrs. Cappuano. Dinner is with our compliments."

"Absolutely not, Jim," Nick said. "We insist on paying for your amazing food and service."

They could see the man was debating what to do.

"Please." Nick handed him a credit card. "We insist."

Jim took the card. "As you wish, sir. I'll be right back."

Nick reached across the table for Sam's hand. "My wife looks particularly beautiful in the candlelight."

"I was thinking the same thing about my husband."

Jim returned with a black leather folder that he handed to

Nick. "It's been an honor to have you visit us. We hope you'll come back again."

"We definitely will," Nick said.

As he added a big tip, signed the receipt and returned the credit card to his wallet, he felt "normal" for the first time in months. For a few hours, he was just a guy taking his best girl out for a fancy dinner on their anniversary.

Before leaving their private room, they posed for photos with Jim, Andrea, their chef and the entire staff. They shook hands with everyone and signed a few autographs.

"We'll treasure this evening for the rest of our lives," Andrea said as she hugged them both.

"As will we," Sam said. "Thank you again."

CHAPTER FOURTEEN

Brant waited for them outside the private room, along with several of the agents who made up their details. "We've attracted a bit of a crowd out front." Brant sounded stressed. "We're going to take you out through the back door."

"I don't think we should do that," Nick said. "People want a glimpse of the first couple. We can at least give them a wave."

"It's a lot of people, sir."

"All the more reason to say hello. If you don't mind, Samantha."

"I don't mind."

The feeling of normality he'd briefly enjoyed evaporated as soon as they stepped into the cool evening air to find hundreds of people gathered outside the Secret Service perimeter, hoping for a glimpse of them.

As Sam and Nick waved to the gathering to the left of the restaurant, people called out to them.

"Mr. President, I love you!"

Out of the corner of his eye, Nick saw a sign raised above the crowd that said NOT MY PRESIDENT. He'd no sooner registered what the sign said than they were pelted with flying objects. Something red smashed against Sam's face. For a second, he thought it was a bullet.

Everything seemed to happen fast as Sam cried out and the

agents surrounded them, hustling them into the car with precision Nick hadn't experienced before now.

Brant and Vernon were practically on top of them as they landed in the back seat of The Beast.

"What the hell?" Sam asked as she rubbed her face where a red spot was visible.

Brant stared at them, looking a little wild in the eyes. "Are you all right?"

"Sam got hit by something, but she's not cut." Nick was extremely relieved to realize that.

"I'm so sorry, ma'am," Brant said. "Our officers will determine what was thrown and by whom."

The car was already moving to get them out of there when something hit the window with a loud thud and a splat.

"I think that was a tomato," Sam said.

"Do you require medical attention, ma'am?"

"No, not at all. I'm fine. Just a little rattled."

"I'm sorry, babe. Brant was right. We should've gone out the back." When Nick thought of what might've happened, he felt sick.

"You were both right," Sam said. "The crowd was larger than expected, and you can't hide from the people you represent."

Nick put an arm around her and drew her in close to him as their lead agents sat across from them, looking upset. "I'm sorry you got hurt."

"I'm fine."

What if they'd had a gun rather than a bunch of tomatoes? Nick realized his hands were shaking. There were no metal detectors when people showed up spontaneously.

He told himself that everything was fine—this time.

One thing he was certain of was that he'd be talking to Brant about increased security before he took Sam on another date in public.

. . .

SECRET SERVICE AGENT John Brantley Jr. was seriously undone by the chaos outside the restaurant. The minute he had the first couple safely back at their rental home, he went to the house next door call his supervising agent.

"What happened at the restaurant?" his boss barked.

Brant wasn't surprised that the word was already out. "Something was thrown from the back of the crowd. The first lady was hit in the face. She said she believed it was a tomato after another was thrown at the car."

"What the hell? Didn't you secure the crowd?"

"Of course we did, sir. But it grew exponentially while the first couple was inside the restaurant."

"Why weren't they taken out a secondary exit?"

"The president insisted on saying hello to the people who'd come out to see them."

"He's not in charge in a situation like this, Brant. You are. You make the call about what he's allowed to do and what he isn't."

"Yes, sir. I'm aware of that. The plan was for them to give a quick wave on their way to the car, which was exactly what happened until the objects were thrown from the back of the gathering."

"I'll need a written report on this incident."

"Yes, sir. I'll have it to you right away."

"I've already received a call from the director. He's not pleased."

"Nor are we, sir. We have several officers working to determine who threw the objects, and they'll be charged accordingly."

"Keep me posted."

Before Brant could reply, the call ended. This was just great. The first time the president and first lady had gone out in public in months had turned into a fiasco, and it was all his fault. He should've insisted on using the back door. His boss was right about that. He couldn't defer to the president at the cost of his safety or that of the first lady.

"Wasn't your fault, Brant," Eric, one of the other agents on the president's detail, said. "No one saw that coming from what seemed like a friendly crowd."

"If it's not my fault, whose fault is it? No crowd is entirely friendly. That shouldn't have happened."

"I understand, and I'd feel the same way. I just want you to know I think you do a brilliant job. We all do."

"Well, thanks, but I don't feel too brilliant tonight."

"We'll do better next time."

"Yes, we will."

Angst churned in his gut at the thought of something happening to POTUS or FLOTUS on his watch. They had been so very good to him from the first minute he'd started on the VPOTUS detail, and the president had gone to bat to keep Brant as his lead agent after he'd become president.

Brant would willingly give his own life to keep them safe if it came to that.

He prayed every day that it never came to that.

NEXT DOOR, Nick held a cold compress to the area of Sam's face where the tomato had struck her.

"I really don't need that," she said.

"I need it, so please let me."

She was reclined against his chest on the sofa.

Their happy buzz had worn off quickly.

"When I think about what could've happened..."

"Don't go there," she said. "Everything is fine. It was just a tomato."

"When I looked back and saw something red on your face, I thought you'd been shot. I almost fainted."

"Oh God, Nick. I'm sorry."

He kissed the top of her head and continued to hold the compress against her cheek. "Don't be. It wasn't your fault."

"I don't want this to discourage you from other outings. We were having such a good time until one stupid person ruined it."

"That's what terrifies me," he said. "That one stupid,

deranged person could ruin everything—and not just a night out."

"As you like to tell me, we're surrounded by the best security in the world. They did everything right by having the crowd held back from us and getting us quickly to safety."

"I hope there won't be a big uproar over it."

"Let's not think about it anymore. We're both fine. The agents are fine. They'll figure out who did it and slap a felony charge on them that'll make them regret getting out of bed this morning. Let's get back to enjoying our evening." She gently removed his hand and the compress from her face. "I'm getting frostbite."

"Oh, sorry."

"It's okay. Thanks for taking care of me."

"Always."

Nick's phone rang. "It's Scotty."

"He's probably heard what happened."

Nick pressed the green button to take the call. "Hey, buddy."

"Are you guys okay? It's all over the news that someone threw something at you outside the restaurant."

"We're fine. A tomato hit Mom in the face, but she's okay."

"Oh my God! *What is wrong* with people?"

"Are we supposed to answer that question?" Sam asked.

"I mean, really. Who throws tomatoes at the first couple?"

Nick's lips quivering with amusement at Scotty's outrage. "People who don't like us?"

"I'm sorry, but that's total bullshit. You can disagree without getting violent."

"You're right."

"I'm just glad you guys are all right. It scared me to see the news."

"Sorry, buddy. We should've called you."

"I'm okay as long as you are."

"We are."

"All right, then."

"I read your essay. It's very good."

"Really?"

"Really."

"No typos?"

"None that I saw. You made a compelling argument for the importance of access to voting for all citizens. You should consider posting it to your social media."

"No way."

"Way. You could be a voice for young people getting engaged in their government."

"Wow. I can't believe you like it that much."

"I really do."

"Thanks, Dad."

"You got it. Now get to bed so you're ready for school in the morning."

"Had to go and ruin it, didn't you?"

Sam and Nick laughed.

"Peace out."

"Peace out." The minute the call was ended, Nick's expression became serious. "I hate that he was upset. That infuriates me."

"I know. Me, too. What can we do to get your mind off it?"

"I can't think of a single thing."

Sam smiled as she turned to face him.

He ran a finger gently over the spot on her cheek, which didn't hurt. It had stung when it first happened, but was fine now. "That anyone would dare to strike my favorite face in the whole world."

"It's nothing compared to some of the things that've been done to this face."

Nick leaned forward and gently placed a kiss on the spot where the ice had been. "Chilly."

As he'd already removed his sweater, she unbuttoned his shirt and pressed her cold cheek to his chest.

He gasped and buried his fingers in her hair.

"I bought something new and slinky for this trip. You want to see it?"

"Uh, yeah?"

She laughed.

"Have you been holding out on me?"

"I didn't want to show all my cards on the first or second day." She kissed his chest. "I'll be right back."

"I'll be right here."

She went into the bedroom to change into the see-through gown she'd bought online and sent to Tracy's house for delivery. Thankfully, her sister accepted the packages Sam sent there and never asked any questions. She wouldn't dare buy something sexy and have it sent to the White House. The very thought of the mailroom receiving that package sent her into a fit of giggles.

When the slinky gown was on, she went into the bathroom and applied some bright red lipstick and fluffed up her hair, summoning her inner siren—another thought that made her laugh. Did she have an inner siren?

"Let's find out, shall we?"

She walked out to a dark room, lit only by the fire in the hearth, which cast a warm, cozy glow.

Nick was sitting on the floor in front of the fire, on his phone, his expression serious. He'd removed everything but his boxer briefs. As she took in the sight of him in the firelight, she thought he resembled a Greek god. If the rest of the world could see him now...

"Everything okay?" she asked.

"Brant is very upset about what happened."

"I hate that for him. He's so diligent."

"Yes, he—" Nick looked up at her, and whatever he was going to say died on his lips. His phone dropped to the floor with a soft thud. "Wow."

Sam loved his reaction. She'd wanted him thinking of nothing but her. Mission accomplished.

He reached out a hand to her. "Bring that over here."

She took his hand and let him draw her down next to him on the soft rug in front of the fire. "I'm here, Mr. President. Now what?"

"Let me take a good look at this goddess who's appeared before me."

"You mean me?" she asked, batting her eyes at him.

Smiling, he drew her closer. "No one else can dazzle me the way you do." He kissed her neck and made her shiver. "But I would like to know how my first lady goes about acquiring such a scandalous garment without setting off an international incident in the White House mailroom."

"I had it sent to Tracy."

"Ah, good call."

"I thought you had enough problems to deal with without a mailroom scandal."

"You thought right, and let me just say that you chose a winner from wherever you got this sexy thing."

He ran his hand down her side, over skin and silk. "I look at you sometimes and wonder how in the world I got lucky enough to find you twice."

"I do the same thing. I used to dream about you after the first night we spent together. Whenever things were horrible with Stahl and Peter and then my dad's awful injury, I would close my eyes and go visit you. You always made me feel better."

"Same, babe. I'd think of you and that one perfect night and wonder where you were and what you were doing and why you never called me back."

"Ugh. It still makes me so mad. I should've killed Peter myself."

"Nah, you look washed out in orange."

Sam laughed. "I never get tired of thinking about the first night we met, and even though the second time wasn't under the best of circumstances, the first instant I saw you in John's apartment, I knew that six years hadn't changed anything."

"You've never told me that."

"I have, too."

"I don't think so."

"Well, now you know."

He nuzzled her neck again. "You made me work awfully hard for it, if that's the case."

"Because I was afraid of blowing up my career by sleeping with a witness right after a kid died on my watch."

"Semantics from my Samantha."

Sam moved so she was straddling his lap.

With his hands on her ass, he pulled her in tight against him.

"I want to tell you something else I've never confessed before."

"What's that?"

She could barely think with his lips skimming over her neck, which he knew was her kryptonite. "If it had come down to a choice—you or the career—I would've chosen you."

He pulled back so he could see her face. "No way."

"Yes way. I would've found something else to do. I already knew there was no one else like you. I wouldn't have let you go again. No way." She kissed his neck this time, adding some teeth that made him groan. "What we have now, the family we've created together, would've been worth any sacrifice."

"I'm glad it didn't come to that."

"I am, too, but if it ever does, just know that I'd never hesitate to choose you."

"That makes me the luckiest guy who ever lived."

"And me the luckiest girl."

"You're all woman, babe. And all mine."

As their lips came together, Sam was relieved they'd managed to recapture the magic they'd found earlier in the evening before things went sideways outside the restaurant.

Somehow he managed to turn them so she was under him, reclined on the thick, cozy rug.

"Hello there." He kissed the spot where the tomato had hit. "How're you feeling?"

She put her arms and legs around him. "I'm feeling quite good, thank you."

The amazement she experienced when he joined their bodies was one she couldn't easily describe in mere words. It was spiritual, magical, the one perfect thing in her life—and his. As he gazed down at her with his heart in his eyes, she thanked whatever god had brought him to her twice in one lifetime.

She was startled out of the blissful state when the phone he always had to answer rang.

"No," he said. "Ignore it."

"You can't."

"It can wait for one more minute. Look at me."

Sam tried to ignore the ringing phone and the spike of adrenaline that went through her at knowing he was needed for something urgent.

"Samantha. Stay with me. It'll keep."

"I'm trying."

"Ugh." Realizing the moment had been lost, he withdrew from her and went to get the ringing phone. "Yes?"

His terse one-word greeting made her smile as she took in the sight of him, naked, aroused and furious at the interruption.

"What? When?"

Sam sat up and reached for the blanket on the sofa, wrapping it around herself.

"Yes, I'll be right there." He ended the call. "That was Terry. We've had a shooting at Fort Liberty. Two service members are dead and sixteen are wounded, some critically."

"Oh no."

"I'm sorry, love. I have to go next door to the mobile Situation Room."

"I understand. It's no problem."

"Yes, it is, and I'll make it up to you."

"It's really not, Nick. Those poor families getting that news. They need you."

"At some point, I'll have to make a statement. It'd be nice to have you with me if you're willing."

"Of course I am. Just tell me when. I'll be there."

He leaned down to kiss her. "I'm nominating you for wife of the year."

"Ha! I'll lose in a landslide."

"The only vote that matters is mine, and you win every time. I'll make it up to you."

"You bet you will. Go. People need you."

He groaned as he tore himself away from her and went to the bedroom to get dressed.

Sam tightened the blanket around herself and gazed at the fire, her body still vibrating with unfulfilled desire. How often did an encounter with Nick leave her unfulfilled? Never.

"I'll be back as soon as I can," Nick said when he emerged from the bedroom dressed in jeans and a sweater.

"I'll be here."

"Counting on it."

CHAPTER FIFTEEN

When Nick opened the front door, Sam heard him talking to Brant. Did the agent ever sleep?

Since she'd been left to her own devices, she checked the messages on her phone. One was from Avery Hill, asking her to call him when she got a chance. She sent him a text to see if he was still up.

He replied that he was, and she called him.

"Hey," she said. "What's up?"

"Just heard about Fort Liberty. I don't envy him things like this."

"Me either."

"I wanted to let you know that Nicoletta's new lawyer, Collins Worthy, has been in touch with state and federal prosecutors about beginning plea discussions."

"Will she slither out of trouble once again?"

"I'm not so sure. The racketeering charge is serious."

"If they deal with her," Sam said, "people will think it's because Nick intervened for her."

"I'm afraid that's true."

"Even though he's had nothing to do with it."

"Right. By all accounts, the attorney is very well respected. His goal is to get her free of these charges with probation, fines and community service."

"I want them to lock her up and throw away the key."

"I understand that, and you have good reason to feel that way, but... I'm saying this as a friend and not an FBI agent... It may be better for all involved for this to go away sooner rather than later. Having the president's mother on trial or in prison isn't a good look for him, even if he has no relationship with her."

"I hate to say you're right, but you're right."

"I'll keep you posted about what I hear."

"I'd appreciate that. How's Shelby?"

"A little better every day. I've found a house that might work for us with excellent security features. I'm taking her to see it on Sunday."

"That's great news. You know you're welcome to stay with us as long as you need to."

"I do, and we appreciate that. But it's better for all of us to get me out of the White House as soon as possible."

"Why?"

"The Justice Department and its many branches work hard to maintain separation from the White House. It's not great for me professionally to be cozied up to the president."

"Even if you were one of his closest friends long before he was president?"

"Even if."

"Ugh, sometimes I hate this town."

"Only sometimes?" he asked with a laugh.

"Ha! Most of the time, but it's home sweet home regardless of its many deficiencies."

"Yes, it is. I won't keep you any longer. Just wanted to pass along what I was hearing."

"I appreciate you, Avery. And thank you for taking such good care of our girl."

"That's my pleasure. She amazes me with her strength and fortitude."

"She's a steel magnolia."

"Yes, she is. I just wish I could be more like her. I still can't even think about what happened—and what could've happened—without getting the shakes."

"I totally understand that. The people you love best were threatened because of you and your work."

"Yeah, that. Exactly. And the people involved are the scummiest of scumbags. That they were anywhere near Shelby and Noah makes me crazy. I feel like I could kill them if I got the chance."

"Don't do that. They're where they belong, and they're not getting out any time soon."

"But how many others just like them are out there blaming us for their troubles?"

"Too many to count, I'm sure, but they can't stop us from doing the job and living our lives."

"Can't they?"

"What're you saying, Avery?"

"This incident took me over an edge of some sort. I'm not sure yet what that means, but it could be that I'm done with the job."

"Come on. No way! What will you do with yourself?"

"Be a husband and father. Protect my family."

"Even if you aren't working anymore, Avery, you can't be with them all the time. Shelby will still be coming to work at the White House. Noah will be starting school before you know it. The new baby will, too. Don't make a rash decision that you might regret later."

"I'm trying not to, but I'm having a very hard time coping with this."

"Maybe you should consult with a therapist?"

"Yeah, I've thought of that."

"You need to find a way through this that doesn't involve giving up your very successful career."

"I hate that career right now. You ever feel that way?"

Sam snorted. "Is that a rhetorical question? Of course I do, especially lately with all this crap with Stahl."

"We had a briefing about the latest because we were

involved in several of the missing-person cases back when they first happened. It's unbelievable."

"Did you hear they found human remains in his backyard?"

"God. No. I hadn't heard that."

"Keep it on the DL until it comes through official channels."

"I will. But you guys must be reeling."

"We are."

"It's unreal. Truly."

"And it's embarrassing. That he was doing this shit while pretending to be an upstanding police officer is so revolting to the rest of us."

"I know. We've seen some of it in the Bureau, too. It always hurts more than you think it will."

"Yeah, it does."

"Speaking of scumbags, what's going on with your friend Ramsey?"

"I haven't heard much from that front lately. He's out on bail awaiting trial on multiple felonies after he rammed his car into my Secret Service SUV. Did you know that attempted murder of a federal agent is a big deal?"

Avery chuckled. "I've heard that rumor. Not to mention trying to off the first lady."

"Not to mention. As if getting rid of me would solve all his problems."

"No kidding. He'd still be an asshole."

"I do worry about him suing the department over the shooting of his son. The last thing we need is more negative publicity surrounding a criminal within our own ranks."

"Yeah, for sure. I worry about Joe being able to hang on through all of this."

"Me, too. I can't imagine work without him in charge. Once in a while, he and Malone talk about retiring, and it gives me hives."

"It'll happen at some point."

"Shut your filthy mouth. It will not."

"Oh damn. I've got the TV on. They're saying three are dead at Fort Liberty. More than twenty injured, many seriously."

"Oh God."

"Fucking guns. It's insanity."

"Yes, it sure is. At work the other day, I heard that we're having trouble recruiting new officers for the first time in decades. It has to be because everyone is armed and angry, and because of officers like Stahl and Ramsey, who make the entire profession look bad."

"Nick's gun task force is just what we need, but change won't happen in time to stop what happened at Fort Liberty tonight or the next mass shooting."

"I feel sick."

"Me, too. On that happy note, I'll let you go. I'll keep you posted on what I hear about your mother-in-law."

"Thank you, Avery."

"Sure thing."

Sam closed the phone and reached for the remote to turn on the TV. The faces of the Capitol News Network anchors were grim as they reported the latest from Fort Liberty. "My God," she whispered.

Nick texted via the secure BlackBerry. *Briefing in thirty min. Can you come next door?*

Yes, I'll be there. I'm so sorry, love. It's terrible.

You have no idea.

Her stomach dropped as she read those words. What now?

THE NEWS GOT WORSE by the minute. More than seventy-five had been wounded, and four were now confirmed dead, including the shooter, who'd been taken out by military police. But not before he'd changed the lives of hundreds of his fellow service members, who'd been gathered for a comedy show at the post auditorium.

The weapon had been an M-16, a weapon of war, designed to kill many people as quickly as possible.

"Mr. President," Terry said.

Nick tore his gaze from the TV, where he'd been monitoring the news reports.

"We have an update for you, sir." His chief of staff had been brought back to Delaware by helicopter after the Fort Liberty news broke.

Nick followed Terry into their mobile Situation Room, which had been soundproofed and outfitted with all the necessary communications technology ahead of his arrival at the beach. He felt guilty at what had to be done, and the taxpayer money spent, so he could take a vacation away from the White House. But he had to get out of there once in a while, or he'd go mad.

He took a seat at the head of the conference table.

Terry pressed a couple of buttons that brought Vice President Gretchen Henderson, Secretary of Defense Tobias Jennings, Secretary of Homeland Security Madeleine Brill, acting Army Chief of Staff General Roger Kaull and General Hilary Stern, the commanding officer of Fort Liberty, onto screens on the wall.

"Thank you for joining us," Terry said, introducing Nick to Kaull and Stern.

"Mr. President, I'm so sorry to hear this terrible news," Gretchen said.

"As am I. What do we know, Tobias?"

"Corporal Tyson Briggs, a five-year Army veteran, has been identified as the shooter."

"General Stern, what can you tell us about him?"

"Mr. President, he was involved in an altercation in his workplace earlier today after the email came out from Secretary Jennings offering service members a dishonorable discharge if they're unable to faithfully serve under the commander in chief. From what I'm told by Briggs's superior officers, he was outraged that the discharge would be dishonorable simply because he couldn't stomach being sent to war by an unelected president."

Oh God, Nick thought. *Oh my God.*

"Apparently, others in the squadron fought back against his claims, calling him a traitor and other names that outraged Briggs. His commanding officer asked Briggs to step outside to get himself together. He stormed out of the building, and no one heard from him again until the shooting in the auditorium. The commanding officer had never seen any sign of anger or hostility in Briggs before today. He'd expressed some opinions about the current state of our politics, but nothing that would lead to what happened tonight. We have chaplains available to provide counseling to Briggs's coworkers and chain of command as well as others who were in the auditorium, sir."

"Thank you for the update, General Stern," Terry said. "What's the latest on casualties?"

"Four dead, seventy-five injured, two of them with life-threatening injuries."

"We appreciate the update and ask you all to stand by in case you're needed again tonight," Terry said.

"Thank you everyone," Nick added. It was all he could do to speak over the massive lump in his throat. Four people were dead and many others seriously injured all because a service member didn't want to work for him.

"Thank you, Mr. President," the others said as they signed off for now.

After the screens went dark, Nick stared at the far wall.

"I can feel you blaming yourself for this when it is not your fault," Terry said. "Corporal Briggs decided to express his views in the most violent way possible. That's in no way tied to you."

Of course it is, Nick thought. But he didn't share that comment with Terry, who was trying to make him feel better about the unimaginable. "We need to make a statement."

"Trevor has already sent over something for you to review." Terry pushed the page across the table.

Nick read the statement, feeling dead inside. "This doesn't mention the connection to the email sent by Secretary Jennings."

"We don't need to make that public yet."

"Yes, we do. Enough people know about Briggs's motivation. I'd rather control how that's made public than react to it later."

"Good point. I'll have Trevor add it to the statement. Is there anything else you'd like to change before we have it put on the teleprompter?"

"No. The rest is fine."

"I'll take care of it. Will Sam appear with you?"

"Yes, she's coming over."

"Very good."

None of this is good, Nick wanted to say. He was bereft over the loss of service members who'd voluntarily signed up to defend their country only to be struck down by a colleague who didn't approve of how his commander in chief had attained the presidency.

He would have to call the families of those killed or injured, and they'd know he was the reason their loved one was dead.

Sam came into the room, raising his spirits ever so slightly with her presence. She walked over to him and slid onto his lap, wrapping her arms around him.

He breathed in her vanilla-and-lavender scent, taking comfort from her.

"I'm so, so sorry, Nick. What can I do?"

Tightening his hold on her, he said, "Just this for now."

"Have you heard any details?"

"Yeah, and it's bad."

"How so?"

"It's because of me."

She raised her head from his shoulder so she could see his face. "What? How?"

He filled her in on what'd happened with Briggs earlier in the day. "Terry says it's not my fault, but I feel responsible just the same."

"Terry is right. Tell me you know that."

"Intellectually, I agree. I didn't pull the trigger and kill and injure those people. But he did it because he objects to me and the offer of a dishonorable discharge to anyone who doesn't want to report to me as their commander in chief."

"If you're looking for someone to blame, look no further than the ex-Joint Chiefs who sparked the need for that email in the first place with their talk of overthrowing your government."

He forced a smile for her benefit. "I love when my first lady gets fired up on my behalf."

"Then you must love me often because that's how much I've been fired up since you got this job. People suck. That isn't your fault. It's theirs. You're working so hard to do the right thing for the American people, to keep them safe and healthy and prosperous. I honestly believe, in the final analysis, the people who appreciate you will far outnumber those who don't."

"That would be nice."

"It'll happen. Just keep doing what you're doing. Lead with your heart. Show people who you really are and that you care about the same things they do. And whatever you do, don't take responsibility for the actions of others. You have no control over what other people do. You only control how you react to it. You have to go out there and project strength and resolve and fortitude. That's what people need from you right now."

"Thank you for the reminder and the pep talk."

She kissed him. "Any time you need it."

A knock on the door preceded Terry's return to the room. "Sorry to interrupt. We have a final statement drafted for you, Mr. President."

Sam got up from Nick's lap and stood behind him to read the statement over his shoulder.

He glanced up at her. "Do you approve?"

"I do."

"Thanks, Terry. That's good to go."

"We'll have it ready for you in ten minutes, sir. Trevor and his team have set up a room for you down the hall."

After he left, Sam turned to Nick. "Do you need to change your clothes?"

"Going to do that now."

"Do you have a suit with you?"

"I think Hank packed a couple," he said of his personal valet. He still couldn't believe he had a personal valet, but Hank was great in making sure he had what he needed no matter where he was. "He said we needed to be ready for anything, even when we're away."

"I suppose this evening is proof of that," she said as he changed.

"And I was hoping it would be so relaxing."

"I suppose we ought to forgo any thoughts of relaxation for the next three or so years. Possibly seven…"

"Three."

"Don't rule anything out."

"*Three.*"

Sam laughed. "We'll see."

Terry returned to the room. "Mr. President, Mrs. Cappuano, we're ready for you."

CHAPTER SIXTEEN

Sam found it jarring when Terry, one of their closest friends, was so formal with them, even if she knew he was simply doing his job.

She took the hand that Nick extended and followed him down the hall to a bedroom that had been cleared of all furniture other than a podium with the presidential seal affixed to it and American flags positioned on either side of it. A TV camera had been set in front of the podium, and electrical wires snaked through the room. They stepped carefully over the wires on their way to the podium.

Nick was outfitted with a microphone that was clipped to his lapel by a young technician dressed all in black. From the way he approached Nick with the microphone and helped him get it situated, it was obvious they'd done this dance before.

"This is amazing," Sam whispered to Nick after the tech had stepped away. "It's like we're at the White House."

"I suppose that's the idea."

Sam couldn't imagine what went into making sure these things were available if needed while Nick was on vacation. She was glad it wasn't her responsibility to manage those logistics.

Nick stepped behind the podium and read over the

statement one more time before giving Terry a subtle nod to say he was ready.

"We need the first lady to step closer to the president," the cameraman said.

Since there was nowhere she'd rather be than close to the president, she moved in next to him and placed her hand on his back, hoping he would take comfort from her nearness.

"That's great. Thank you, ma'am."

She did what she could for the people, a thought that kept her entertained ahead of the grim reality of what Nick had to say—once again—to the American public.

A light came on over the camera, and Nick was given the sign to begin.

"My fellow Americans, at eight thirty p.m. eastern time, a gunman opened fire at a gathering of soldiers at Fort Liberty in North Carolina, killing three and injuring more than seventy-five, two with life-threatening injuries. The perpetrator of this tragic event was Corporal Tyson Briggs, a five-year Army veteran who'd argued with other members of his squadron earlier in the day before being asked by his supervisor to leave and cool off. The next time anyone saw him was in an auditorium full of soldiers gathered for a comedy show. He used his Army-issued M-16 to inflict maximum carnage on his fellow service members before being shot and killed by military police.

"My administration stands ready to aid the Fort Liberty community during this difficult time in any way needed. I've directed Secretary of Defense Tobias Jennings and acting Army Chief of Staff General Roger Kaull to work with Fort Liberty's commanding officer, General Hilary Stern, to make the full resources of the federal government available for the affected service members and their families. In addition, General Stern has ordered the post chaplains to assist anyone who requires counseling. We will stand by our men and women in uniform always, but especially after such a tragedy.

"Earlier today, an email was issued by Secretary Jennings to all service members in the wake of the situation with the former Joint Chiefs of Staff. Service members were offered the opportunity to separate from the military with a dishonorable discharge if they feel unable to serve under my command. From what we've been told by his colleagues, Corporal Briggs was furious about the discharge being dishonorable and was asked to leave his workplace to get himself together. Needless to say, I'm shattered to have been in any way connected to Corporal Briggs's despicable actions.

"Samantha and I are devastated by these events and our hearts broken for the families reeling from this horrific tragedy. In the coming days, we'll visit Fort Liberty to express our condolences in person. For now, we ask our fellow citizens for their prayers on behalf of the brave servicemen and servicewomen who lost their lives or suffered grievous injuries. We also ask you to pray for their families.

"We'll have more information in the coming days. In the meantime, we ask you to pray for the Fort Liberty community and for all our servicemen and servicewomen on duty around the world tonight. Good night and Godspeed to those we lost today and those fighting for their lives."

"And we're out."

Nick removed the microphone and the powerpack that had been clipped to his belt and handed them to the technician. "Thanks, Josh."

"No problem, Mr. President."

Of course Nick knew his name, and judging by the young man's smile, he appreciated the courtesy of being recognized by the most powerful man in the world.

"We've done what we can here," Nick said, with his hand on Sam's lower back. "Let's get back to our place."

"I'm with you, Mr. President."

"Thank God for that."

THE PHONE RANG several times during the night as the Fort Liberty death toll rose to six servicemembers. Four men and two women were dead. They ranged in age from nineteen to twenty-seven and had five children among them. One had been engaged to be married in three short weeks. Another had just returned to duty after a year away to battle cancer.

Each person had a unique story, a family who loved them and so much more to give.

Nick's heart broke all over again every time the phone rang with an update.

"What are you thinking?" Sam asked after the third call.

"Maybe I should step aside if they hate me enough to kill people."

"What would that solve? Gretchen would become president, and people would have the same beef with her as they do with you. And who knows what she'd be like as president? At least with you, we know what we're getting."

"We know that. Other people don't. That's the problem."

"So let's work on that. Let's do more interviews so people have a chance to get to know us better, something more in-depth where we invite the reporter in to really get a feel for us and our family and what we're about."

His hand landed on her forehead.

"What're you doing?"

"Checking to see if you have a fever."

She whacked his hand away. "Stop. I'm serious."

"So am I. Who are you, and what've you done with my first lady?"

"I'm your wife, the person who loves you more than anything or anyone, and I'm tired of this narrative that you're an illegitimate president. You're the only president they've got for the next three years, so let's make sure they know exactly who you are and what you stand for. They can even follow me at work."

"You're terrifying me."

Sam laughed. "I'm serious!"

"I know. That's the part that's terrifying—you welcoming a reporter to dissect our lives and follow you around at work is the last thing I would ever expect you to do."

"I live to surprise you."

"Well, you have."

"We need someone big to talk to us," Sam said. "Like Oprah."

"Do you think she'd do it?"

Sam laughed. "Yes, Nick, I think she'd be interested in doing an in-depth interview with the president and first lady, and I'd love to meet her. We used to watch her show every day when I was in college. I was addicted. Run it by your people, and let's make it happen. The sooner, the better."

He rolled onto his side and put his arm around her. "Look at my first lady go."

"Watch out for her. She's a tiger with a rusty steak knife when people say mean things about her husband or do horrible things to others because they don't know the first thing about their commander in chief."

Laughter shook his body. "Easy, tiger. No stabbing allowed."

"I'm allowed to think about it, though, right?"

"Of course."

She placed her hand on his face. "I know this is awful and horrible and tragic and every other terrible thing. But it's not your fault, Nick."

"I know."

"Do you? Do you really?"

"I'm working on it. It's hard to stomach that it was tied to me, even indirectly."

"Try to think of it this way. It was tied to the office you hold. Not you. It was tied to the Constitution and how it addresses transfer of power. Not you. It was tied to the treasonous actions of senior military officers who should've known better and done better. Not you."

As he listened to her, he felt the unbearable tension start to ease a bit. "You're right."

"Duh, I know I'm right."

"Now you sound like Scotty."

"Scotty sounds like me."

"Heaven help us."

"Everything I said is the truth. What happened at Fort Liberty, as tragic and horrifying as it is, is not your fault."

"As commander in chief, I feel responsible for those service members."

"It's okay to feel responsible for them—as you should. It's not okay to blame yourself for what happened to them."

"Thank you for the reminder."

"Any time you need to hear it. Now come here and let me hold you so you can try to sleep."

He rested his head on her chest, and she ran her fingers through his hair as her hand made soothing circles on his back. "Your TLC is having the opposite effect from what you intended."

"Tell him to stand down. It's sleep time."

"He only knows how to stand *up*. He doesn't do stand down."

"Close your eyes, and let it all go so you can rest."

"Two of my three eyes are closed."

Sam's body rocked with laughter. "That's so gross."

"Nothing gross about it, my love. In fact, you often say, 'Oh, oh, oh,' when he shows up."

She smacked his shoulder.

"I speak only the truth," he said as he pressed his hard cock against her leg.

"Let me at it."

"What's this you say?"

She pushed on his shoulder to make room for her hand to slide down the front of him and wrap around his erection.

Nick gasped from the immediate charge of desire. "What is happening?"

"I want you to sleep, and he is *standing* in the way of that. I know how to make him stand down."

"Oh, that sounds intriguing. Do tell."

"How about I show you instead?"

"Even better."

He closed his eyes and tried to follow her advice to let it all go as she stroked him with slow, deliberate movements designed to drive him crazy, all the while continuing to run her fingers through his hair, sending shivers down his spine.

"Samantha."

"Hmmm?"

"I love you."

"I love you, too."

His hips came off the bed as he raised himself on his arms so he was hovering over her as she continued to stroke him. "I don't know what I'd do without you. Without this."

"I'm right here, love. Always."

He kissed her as he came, moaning against her lips from the surge of desire and love. After he broke the kiss, he gazed down at her sweet face, illuminated by the glow of a nightlight. "I need to clean you up."

"I've got it. You rest."

She scooted out from under him as he turned onto his back, his body throbbing from the release. At the worst of times, only she could make him forget the ever-present worries for a few blissful minutes.

When she slid back into bed, he held out his arms to her, and she rested her head on his chest.

"Try to sleep," she said. "You've done what you can for now. Tomorrow is another day."

Tightening his arms around her, he exhaled. He was still sick over the violence at Fort Liberty, but Sam was right. He'd done what he could, and he'd have to face it again in the morning.

FREDDIE CRUZ WAS at his desk at five a.m., determined to find out as much as he possibly could about the man who used to command their squad. He started with a regular Google search and worked his way through the voluminous coverage about his attempts to murder Sam, the trial and the sentencing.

In addition to the newer articles, Stahl had been quoted many times as part of investigations and other MPD business. Knowing now that most of what he'd said was probably lies was hard to swallow even days after the new information came to light.

He went back further, finding a mention of Stahl's graduation from McKinley High School more than thirty years ago. That was the only mention of his life before he joined the department.

Next, he accessed city databases to find his birth certificate, listing Richard and Donna Stahl as his parents.

He did an internal search for Donna Stahl and hit paydirt with stories about domestic violence accusations she filed against Richard and then later how she was charged for abusing her son, Leonard. He had a sick feeling as he read through the list of injuries thirteen-year-old Leonard had withstood at the hands of his mother—a severe concussion, a fractured jaw, a lacerated forearm that required forty stitches, bruises all over his body and several unexplainable burns.

Freddie felt like he'd found the explanation for why Stahl had turned out to be such a sadistic monster. He'd been raised by one.

There were reports from child welfare employees who'd recommended removal from the home long before the final incident had resulted in Stahl moving to his father's home.

Donna Stahl had been charged with multiple felonies and had served fifteen years in the same prison her son was now in before being released.

Over the next hour, Freddie used every resource at his disposal to find her current location. When he struck out, he decided to call Sam's favorite probation officer, Brendan Sullivan, to see if he had any info on where Donna might be. Since it was still early, he left a message for Brendan.

"What's up?" Gonzo asked.

Freddie had been so engrossed in his task that he hadn't heard his friend approach. "Digging into Stahl a bit. I found out why he went to live with his father at thirteen." He handed Gonzo a printout of the report on the incident that had put him in the hospital. "His mother beat the crap out of him."

As Gonzo read the report, his expression never changed. "This explains a lot."

"I know."

"But it doesn't excuse anything he's done."

"I agree."

"Good work, Freddie."

"Thanks. I'm trying to figure out where the mother is now, and I'm going to read more about the brother who went missing."

"Let me know what you find."

After Gonzo walked away, Freddie searched for the reports about Michael Stahl, Leonard's half brother. The fifteen-year-old had gone missing while walking home from school. There'd been no witnesses or anything for investigators to work with when the teenager went missing. His parents and friends had reported that he was a happy kid with lots of friends and interests, that no one disliked him that they knew of and that he got good grades in school.

Freddie wondered if Len had hated Michael because he was happy and well-adjusted.

It was a theory worth looking into.

According to articles he found about the teenager's disappearance, Michael's parents had done everything they could to find their son, including annual events to keep his name in the news and regular contact with the MPD. They'd had age-progression photos created and papered the neighborhood with flyers.

The family's efforts had ended with Richard's death and then his wife Karen's a couple of years later, leaving only Leonard and his half sister, Cindy.

Gonzo came out of the office. "I just talked to Malone's informant, looking for more info on how he knew to point us in Stahl's direction on the missing women. He said it was a conversation he overheard about how the cops had one in their ranks who'd done his friend's sister dirty and probably a bunch of others, too. The guy had a real problem with women, and everyone knew it. Malone's informant, who doesn't want me to

know his name, said he worked his way into the conversation
to ask which cop the guy was talking about. He said, 'The same
one who tried to kill the first lady.' Malone's guy asked how he
knew, and the other guy said, 'People talk. That's been word on
the street for a long time.'"

"Wow," Freddie said. "So people knew about Stahl and did
nothing?"

"They probably figured we'd take care of our own, so what
was the point in reporting it?"

"I can see that. Still, they could've called the tip line and
reported it anonymously."

"Sure, but, playing devil's advocate, maybe they were afraid
we'd figure out who they were and come after them. They
might've had their own skeletons to keep hidden and weren't
willing to risk their own necks to report him."

"True." Freddie shared what he'd learned about Michael
Stahl's disappearance. "Gone without a single trace for more
than twenty-five years."

"How can that not be related to Stahl?" Gonzo asked.

"There's no way it isn't related."

IN THE MORNING, with Nick next door dealing with the Fort
Liberty shootings, a wildfire in Southern California and
flooding in Kentucky, among other things, Sam checked in
with Freddie.

"Hey," he said. "I was going to text you to see how you guys
are doing. I just can't believe the news about the tomatoes or
what happened in North Carolina."

"I know. That's awful, and Nick is blaming himself because
it was tied to the situation with the Joint Chiefs."

"I heard. All the news shows are focused on the gunman's
rants to his coworkers ahead of the shooting."

Sam had intentionally left the TV off. "Of course they are."

"Plenty of pundits are saying this falls squarely at the feet of
the disgraced former Joint Chiefs, who put the wind in this
guy's sails with their actions."

"I'm glad someone is saying that."

"A lot of people are. If they hadn't done what they did, this guy wouldn't have thought it was okay to kill his fellow service members."

"It's all so senseless," Sam said. "I can't stop thinking about their parents getting that news, thinking their kids were safe on a military base, far away from conflict. It's so horrible."

"It really is. I'm sorry it happened and that Nick feels responsible. If anything, that shows what a compassionate leader he is."

"Try telling that to the people fueling this illegitimacy fire. He said last night maybe he should just step aside, and I reminded him that another unelected leader is in line behind him, so it wouldn't solve the problem. It would only make the country more unstable."

"Look at you becoming the adroit political wife."

"That's a big word for such a young grasshopper."

"What is? Political?"

"Adroit," she said with a laugh. "I'm not even sure I know what that means."

"Savvy."

"Ah, yes, I am that."

"Cripes, that was a softball."

"And I hit it out of the park."

"Whatever. So do you have to go there?"

"Yes," she said, sighing. "Nick is figuring out when."

"I don't envy you guys that task. So why'd you call me, anyway?"

"Because I miss you and your sharp wit."

"Try again."

"I'm wondering about what's up with the search at Stahl's house."

He filled her in on everything he'd learned earlier in the day about Stahl's background and the disappearance of his half brother.

"How much you want to bet he was involved with that?"

"We have no doubt. Brendan Sullivan had no info on where

Stahl's mother lives these days, and I can't find any sign of her anywhere."

"Maybe she changed her name after prison."

"That's a possibility. How do you feel after hearing what he went through as a kid?"

"Sad for someone who tried to kill me."

"I felt the same way. While it doesn't excuse the things he's done, at least there's a scintilla of reason behind it. In other news, they've discovered paperwork for a storage unit. We're awaiting a warrant to get in there. We're terrified about what we might find."

"God, I can't even imagine."

"The forensic excavation teams have arrived to work the site in his yard. Haggerty and his squad are working around the clock."

"Has the media caught wind yet?"

"Not that I've heard, but Public Affairs is in all-day meetings with the brass to figure out timing on that. You could ask Jeannie what's going on."

"I'll do that. Thanks for the update. I think."

"And get this, Stahl's sister is threatening to file suit against the department because we kicked her and her kids out of the house. I sort of felt for her when I met her yesterday. She's caught up in his stuff the same way we are."

"I guess that's true. None of this is her fault, that we know of. Thanks for keeping me in the loop. Anything else?"

"Gigi's hearing is this afternoon."

"Oh right. I knew that. I'll call her after this. How does she seem?"

"Resolute, determined to get through it and get back to work."

"I'm glad to hear that. How's Cam?"

"Wired tighter than I've ever seen him. He hates that she's going through this because of his ex."

"And like we said about Nick, Cam needs to know it's not his fault that Jaycee couldn't handle him breaking up with her."

"We've all tried to tell him that. I don't know what'll become of him if the IAB hearing doesn't go her way."

"What three officers are hearing the case?"

"Jeannie, Captain Andrews and Officer Offenbach, who's been moved to IAB since he was busted for lying."

Sam's heart sank when she heard Offenbach was part of it. He blamed her for the demise of his career and his marriage after she discovered he was having an affair while he was supposed to be at a conference. It would give him great pleasure to ruin the career of one of her detectives. "It'll come down to Andrews." The explosives captain was known for being tough but fair. He kept his cards close and wasn't known for socializing with other officers.

"He has no agenda."

"That we know of. What if he's one of the people silently seething over me and my new situation and all the attention I get because of it? If that's the case, how much would he enjoy taking his frustrations out on one of my people?"

"I don't think most people care that you're the first lady."

"I'm sure a lot of them think it's total bullshit that I'm trying to do both jobs, that I'm a camera hog or an attention whore or whatever else they've come up with."

"I don't think it's that many people, if any."

"I'm certain it's more than we think. Anyway, I'll call Gigi and prop her up."

"I'm sure she'll appreciate it."

"Anything else going on?"

"We have a court date for the preliminary hearing in the Blanchet case next week. The next day, there's another hearing in Spencer's case."

"Have Angela and the other families been notified?"

"Malone talked to all of them today."

Sam added a call to her sister to her to-do list. "How's Elin?" She'd been concerned about Freddie's wife since she'd had a recent miscarriage.

"Better. She's getting some of her sparkle back."

"I'm glad to hear it. It takes a while."

"Do you always think about the one you lost?"

"You never forget them, but after a while, you don't think about the loss every day. It becomes more like a dull ache than a sharp pain."

"That's good to know. I'm looking forward to the dull ache."

"You're young and healthy and can try again soon. Stay focused on knowing you can conceive, which is a very big deal. It'll help."

"Thanks, Sam. I appreciate the insight."

"My insight is free of charge to you any time you need it."

His snort of laughter made her smile. She hated to hear him down.

"I'll keep you posted on all the things," he said. "And I hope you're able to enjoy the vacation a little despite the craziness."

"I worry that we'd be bored without the craziness."

"Wouldn't it be nice to find out?"

"Yeah," Sam said, laughing, "it would be."

"See you soon at the beach. We can't wait."

"We're looking forward to it, too."

CHAPTER SEVENTEEN

E ager to get her obligations to others satisfied so she could
get back to being on vacation, Sam called Gigi.

"Hey, Sam. You're supposed to be on vacation."

"I am, technically."

"Such a tragedy about the shooting. We're thinking of you
guys."

"Thank you for thinking of us. I was calling to check on you
before the hearing."

"I'm doing okay. Cam is a mess. But I'm doing what I can
with him."

"I'm sorry to hear that. I wish I had a magic wand to make
this go away for you guys."

"We wish you did, too, but we'll get through it. My plan is to
tell the truth about what happened and how I felt I had no
choice but to kill her to save myself. That's all I can do. If it
costs me my career, then so be it. At least I'm still here."

"Your strength is impressive, Gigi."

"What else can I do? I've had several close calls lately
that've made me appreciate life even more than I already did. I
have my health, my family, my relationship with Cam and
friends like you who I love and value. At the end of the day,
what else is there, you know?"

"That's all there is."

"We get so caught up in a job like ours that we forget it's just a job. One of millions of jobs we could be doing. That's what I keep telling Cameron. It's just a job."

"You're right, and we do forget that."

"It's a special job," Gigi said, "that takes fortitude not many people have."

"That's also true. And you have it in spades. I'd hate to lose you on my team, but I'm glad to know you're okay no matter how it turns out."

"I have the truth on my side. I was attacked and assaulted in my own home. I had no doubt she would kill me if I didn't kill her first. I wish more than anything that none of it had happened, but if it had to, I'm glad I came out alive."

"We're all thankful for that, Gigi." Sam heard a male voice in the background. "Is that Cam?"

"Yes, that's him."

"Could I speak to him?"

"Sure. I'll hand the phone over to him."

"Good luck today, Gigi. Let me know how it goes."

"I will. Thank you so much for checking in."

"Of course."

"Here's Cam."

"Hey," he said.

"Hi there. What's this I hear about you being so tightly wound that people are worried you might implode?"

"Because I'm a serious implosion risk."

"Did you hear what Gigi said about this being just a job and how grateful she is to be alive and in love and surrounded by people who care?"

"I did, and she's amazing. But we already knew that."

"I know you're blaming yourself for this, but that doesn't help Gigi. She needs you to be strong for her and to support her no matter the outcome. If it goes bad for her on the job, she needs to know you'll still be there and be able to find a way to live with that."

"I'm trying, Sam. I really am. But the thought of her losing her job because of my ex..." His deep sigh said it all. "I suppose you've heard that Offenbach is one of the three officers on the panel."

"I did, and I'm sorry that my history with him might impact the outcome for Gigi, but you've got Jeannie on your side, and Andrews has a reputation for being tough but fair."

"I really hope that's true."

"I'm worried about you, Cam. You need to hold it together for your own sake as much as Gigi's."

"I know, but thank you for the reminder. I thought I'd seen everything after all the years on the job, but this…"

"I understand. It's all too much."

"Yeah, it really is. If she loses her career because of me…"

"It wouldn't be because of you. Tell me you know that."

"I do, but indirectly."

"What happened because of Jaycee isn't your fault, but if you blow up or do something stupid because of what she did, then that's on you."

"That's good advice, and I'll try my best to follow it."

"Put all your focus on Gigi and what she needs right now. Let's get her through this and back to work where she belongs."

"That's the goal, and I appreciate the pep talk."

"Hang in there and keep me posted."

"We will. Thanks, Sam."

"Any time."

She ended the call feeling as if she'd done what she could to prop up Cam and Gigi on a difficult day. Before she called Angela, she wanted to talk to Captain Malone.

"Hey, you're on vacation. Why're you calling me?"

"That's rude."

"Haha, just kidding. What's up?"

"I'm worried about Dominguez and the IAB hearing."

"Yeah, me, too."

It didn't help to hear he was worried, too. "Offenbach will try to screw her to get back at me."

"That's the fear, but Andrews and McBride will be there to override him."

"Will Andrews side with Gigi?"

"We can only hope. I'm her rep before the board, and I'll do everything I can for her."

"Thank you for looking out for her."

"She's an excellent detective and dedicated officer, which I'll remind them in my opening statement."

"I feel better knowing you're on it."

"She's got your lawyer friend Andy coming as well. Try not to worry. I don't let good people get away. How's Nick holding up with the Fort Liberty situation?"

"He's upset and doing what he can. Today, he has to call the families. I don't envy him that."

"Ugh, no kidding. Why do people want that job so badly?"

"Beats us."

"And the tomatoes... Are you okay?"

"Just a little bruise where one hit me in the face, but otherwise, I'm fine."

"That was scary. The Secret Service must be rattled."

"They are. I'm also getting updates on the goings-on at Stahl's house."

"It just keeps getting worse. We're waiting on the warrant for the storage unit. I'm terrified of what's in there."

"How's Haggerty holding up?"

"He's doing a great job, but working like a madman."

"I'll text him."

"I'm sure he'd appreciate the support."

"I'll let you get back to it."

"Try to enjoy the downtime, Sam. You've certainly earned it."

"Easier said than done when your husband is the POTUS, and your ex-coworker is a potential serial killer."

"That's a heck of a sentence."

"It's a heck of a life. Take care, Cap."

"You, too."

Sam sent a text to Lieutenant Haggerty. *Heard you and your team are doing heroic work. I'm thinking of you and sending support. Let me know if you need anything.*

Then she called Angela.

"Hey, I'd ask you how it's going, but you're all over the news."

"Awesome."

"Are you okay?"

"I'm fine. The shooting is far more upsetting than a few tomatoes."

"Still, that must've been shocking."

"It's all shocking, and Nick is beside himself because the shooter was heard before the shooting going off about having to work for an illegitimate president."

"That has to be so awful for him."

"It is, but I keep telling him that he hasn't done anything other than what his country asked of him, and if people don't like it, that isn't on him. He gets that intellectually. Emotionally is another whole story."

"I hate when people use that word to describe him. His ascension to the presidency happened exactly the way the framers intended."

"You sound like a social studies teacher."

"I read that on the *Washington Star* editorial page a few weeks ago."

"Ah, I see. Well, the reason I called is that I heard there's a hearing in Spencer's case next week, and I wanted to check in with you."

"Yes, Captain Malone called yesterday to let me know. He's such a nice guy."

"He's the best. How're you feeling about it?"

"I'm okay. I know it's all part of it, and I want justice for Spencer and the other families."

"You don't have to go to every hearing, Ang. Trace and I can do some of them."

"I may take you up on that."

"Please do. Don't put yourself through anything you don't feel you can handle. We're right here for you."

"I know, and that's getting me through."

"How's my Jack Sprat?" Sam asked of her young nephew, who'd been so close to his late dad.

"He's okay. Good days and bad days. Lots of questions at bedtime."

"Poor guy. I can't wait to squeeze him on Friday."

"We're really looking forward to it. It'll be a nice change of scenery for us."

"And you're all set to ride out with Tracy and Mike, right?"

"Yep! They're picking us up at four thirty."

"Can't wait for you all to get here."

"Are you having any relaxation time?"

"We're fine. It's all good." There was no way Sam would talk about her wonderful marriage to her newly widowed sister.

"Glad to hear it."

"I'll see you soon. Love you."

"Love you, too. Thanks for checking in."

Sam closed her phone and went to the front door to speak to the agent on duty, who was someone she hadn't seen before. "Hi there. Would you mind asking Vernon to stop by when he can?"

"Of course, ma'am."

"Thank you. And remind me of your name?"

"Oliver, ma'am."

"Nice to meet you, Oliver. Welcome to the team."

"Thank you, ma'am. It's an honor to work on your detail."

"You say that now..."

The young man with the light brown hair and hazel eyes laughed. "Everyone I know is envious of my very cool job."

"Good for you. Congratulations."

"Thank you, ma'am. Vernon will be right over."

"Thanks."

Exactly two minutes after she closed the door, a knock sounded. Sam opened it to find Vernon. "Thanks for coming by. Come in."

He stepped inside. "Everything all right?"

"Why do you wear a suit even at the beach?"

He rolled his eyes. "Because I'm *working*. Is that why you wanted to talk to me? To ask why I'm wearing a suit?"

"Nope, but that question occurred to me when you came in. You could at least lose the tie."

"What can I do for you this fine morning, ma'am?"

She glared at him to register her disapproval of the dreaded *ma'am*. "I was wondering about what happened with the tomatoes and if there's any trouble for you guys over it."

"Headquarters is unhappy, to say the least. Brant is taking it hard. We had people all over the place outside the restaurant, but we didn't see that coming. And we should have. We apologize."

"You don't have to apologize. You guys do such a great job. I suppose it's inevitable that you can't predict everything."

"Having the first lady struck in the face by a flying tomato is a very bad day at the office for us. It never should've happened."

"Did you get the person who did it?"

"We did, and she's being charged with several felony counts, including assault of a public official."

"Is that me? Am I a public official?"

Vernon flashed his usual smile. "That, you are."

"Huh. Interesting. Did you find out why she did it?"

"You know why."

"Because he's unelected."

"Yes."

Sam took a seat on a stool at the kitchen bar. "I want to understand that point of view. I really do, but all I see is a man who stepped up to serve his country first as vice president and then as president. He was confirmed by the Senate to be vice president, with the whole world fully aware of the VP's primary role."

"True, but people who don't agree with his politics will harp on anything they can to make things difficult for him. It's just the nature of our system."

"Do you think he's in real danger of being harmed by something much more serious than a tomato?"

"We're doing everything we can to keep you and your

family safe. That goal occupies the majority of our waking hours."

"And we appreciate you all so much. But tell me the truth, Vernon. Are there a lot of threats against him?"

His brief hesitation said it all. "I don't want you to be frightened."

"Too late," she said with a small smile. "It's a lot, this job of his." Sam laughed. "If that's not the understatement of the century. I see him giving it his all, you know? I see his empathy and compassion and heartbreak after things like what happened at Fort Liberty. And to know there're people out there who'd rather see him dead than in office... That's almost unbearable."

"I know it is, and I don't want you to live with that kind of fear. Despite what happened last night, you're surrounded by the best security in the world. Never doubt our commitment to protecting you all."

"I don't doubt that. Not for one minute. It's the lunatics who have me on edge. People who'd throw tomatoes at the first couple because they don't agree with his politics or his trajectory or whatever they're beefing about. Today, it's tomatoes. Tomorrow, it's bullets."

"We're having agency-wide discussions about what needs to happen to shore up the gaps that resulted in the tomatoes. I assure you we're taking this very seriously."

"That's good to know. Thank you for the info."

"I'm here any time you have questions or concerns."

"That makes me feel much better. We're so thankful for you and all your colleagues."

"We know you are. The first family are family to us. It's an honor to work with and for you."

"Thank you, Vernon."

"Any time, Sam."

After he left, she sat on the sofa and stared out at the ocean, which was frothy with surf today. She thought about the enormous burden placed on the shoulders of the Secret Service agents charged with keeping the president and his family safe. It was a job she couldn't do. She'd be stressed all the time about possibly missing something that cost someone else their life and plunged the country into turmoil.

What an awesome responsibility—and it took special people to bear the weight of that obligation.

CHAPTER EIGHTEEN

A t the house next door, Nick was making the worst kind of phone calls. The first two had broken him, listening to sobbing parents trying to make sense of the unimaginable.

"Are you ready for the next one?" Terry asked.

"As ready as I'll ever be."

Terry punched in the numbers for the family of Specialist Jessica Olinger. "Mrs. Olinger? This is Terry O'Connor, chief of staff to President Cappuano. He wondered if he might express his condolences on the loss of Jessica."

"I don't want to talk to him or anyone from the government."

The line went dead.

Nick exhaled a deep breath.

Terry dialed another number.

As Nick spoke to the family members of the dead and wounded, some were happier to hear from him than others. Four chose not to take his call.

"I'd like to not have to do that again," he said when they were done, three hours after they started.

"Right there with you," Terry said. "That was brutal."

"When are we going to Fort Liberty?"

"We're looking at Monday. I'll let you know for sure when I finalize the plan. Will Sam be able to come?"

"I'm sure she'll try, but she's due back to work that day."

"I don't have to tell you that she'll be criticized—and so will you—if she's not there."

"No, you don't have to tell me that. I'll do what I can, and so will she. Are we done here?"

"For now."

"Are you going back to DC?"

"Later this afternoon."

"Can you come back this weekend with Lindsey?"

"I'll let you know. She's been feeling lousy all week. She might want to stay home."

"Hope it's nothing serious."

"I don't think it is. I'll keep you posted."

"Sounds good. Give her our regards."

"I will."

"Thanks for coming out last night."

"No problem." Terry had gotten to the door when he turned back. "I know you're taking the loss of the service members—and why it happened—hard, and with good reason. But you're an amazing president, and you're just getting started. Over time, you'll show them how lucky they are to have you, and this illegitimacy nonsense will die down. Just keep doing what you're doing. Okay?"

Nick had never heard his chief of staff sound so emotional. "Thank you, Terry. I needed to hear that."

Terry nodded. "I'll talk to you tomorrow, hopefully not before."

Laughing, Nick said, "Yeah, hopefully not before."

"Go enjoy the evening with your wife. You've done what you can for the families and the country."

"Will do."

For a few minutes after Terry left, Nick stayed seated behind the desk, where he'd given several network interviews earlier in the day. He turned his chair to face the view of the beach. Almost four months after taking the oath of office, he was still amazed by how much happened in one day in America and how much of it was his concern.

The wildfires raging out West, the flooding in Kentucky, the shootings at Fort Liberty... Each crisis required a vigorous response from the federal government and his administration. Just when they had one thing handled, another required his urgent attention. The rapid-fire pace made his head spin as he adjusted to the relentlessness of it all.

What amused him, at times, was that the same people who disdained the government, him, how he became president, etc., were the same ones on camera after a crisis wondering why it was taking so long for the government to arrive and fix everything. The irony wasn't lost on him. Some people hated the government, but they still called 911 in an emergency and were damned glad someone showed up to help.

He needed to get out of the White House and spend more time with regular people, to listen to their concerns and assure them that an actual adult was in charge. The thought of being away from Sam and the kids for even a night had been keeping him from doing what needed to be done.

Before he lost the thought, he called Terry.

"Didn't I just see you?"

"You did, but I was thinking after you left. I have to get out with the people if I expect them to change their opinion of me. I need to be more than just a talking head. I have to engage with them directly. We never got to campaign for office, and I'm not suggesting anything like that, but I want to set up some events at various places around the country where people can spend actual time with me, ask me their questions and get to know me as a person and not a face on a TV screen."

"Is this in addition to an Oprah-level interview?"

"It is. And I want Gretchen out there doing the same thing."

"We'll start working on it."

"I'd rather not be gone for more than a night or two at a time."

"Understood."

"Thanks, Terry."

"Go back to your vacation, Mr. President."

"Yes, sir."

They laughed as they ended the call.

He got up to return to his vacation next door, already in progress.

Brant was waiting for him outside the makeshift office. "If I could have a moment, sir."

"Of course." Nick stepped back into the office.

Brant followed him and closed the door. "I want to apologize for the incident last night. It was completely unacceptable, and it won't happen again." The younger man wore his blond hair in a close buzz cut. His blue eyes were always intense. Today, his chiseled jaw pulsed with tension, and he looked like he hadn't slept in days.

"Thank you for the apology, Brant, but we don't blame you or the other agents. We know you do everything humanly possible to keep us safe."

"I'm sick over it, sir. When I think about what could've happened…"

"I don't want you to be sick over it. I'm sure you're reviewing every aspect of the incident and figuring out ways to prevent it in the future."

"We are. That's our sole focus in addition to the usual security mission. The person who threw the tomatoes has been arrested and charged with multiple felonies. We plan to make an example of her to deter others."

"I have full confidence in you, the other agents and the agency as a whole. What happened last night doesn't change that for me or Sam."

"That's very forgiving of you, sir. Is she all right?"

"She's fine. Just a small bruise."

"I'm sorry, sir." He seemed like he was on the verge of tears.

Nick went to him and put his hands on the younger man's shoulders. "When was the last time you took a break, Brant?"

He shook his head. "This is no time for that."

"Maybe it's the perfect time. You're an outstanding, dedicated professional, but everyone needs a break to recharge once in a while. I want you to take some time off."

Brant's jaw shifted as he looked down at the floor. "I'm afraid they'll replace me as your lead agent."

"I won't let that happen. You're the only one I want by my side for this wild ride, and I'll do everything in my power to keep you where you belong."

"Thank you, sir. You're too kind."

Nick removed his hands from Brant's shoulders. "This is a marathon we're running together. You have to take care of yourself so you can take care of me. Okay?"

"Yes, sir. I'll speak to my supervisor when we get back to Washington."

"I'll hold you to it."

Brant stood up straighter and seemed to recover some of his usual fortitude. "I appreciate your time and your loyalty, sir."

"And I appreciate your hard work. I'm ready to go next door."

"Yes, sir. Give me one minute to make that happen."

Even to go to the house next door, the Secret Service needed a minute. Sometimes Nick wanted to let himself out a random door and make a run for it, just to see what would happen. Only because he could end up dead did he reject that impulse. But the urge showed up quite frequently as he adapted to life inside the gilded cage.

One might think there was little difference in the cage of the vice presidency versus the presidency itself. One would be wrong. The presidency was far more confining, and the loss of his ability to move freely, to come and go as he pleased—for the rest of his life—was something he was still adapting to.

A knock on the door preceded Brant's return. "We're ready for you, Mr. President."

He followed Brant and two other agents as two others took the rear, which was twice as many agents than had accompanied him the day before on the same route.

The tomato incident would result in the cage closing even tighter around him, which was the very last thing he wanted.

.   .   .

MALONE MET Gonzo on the way into the pit the next morning. "PG County detectives found your pizza box in a dumpster about three blocks from the dorm. There was one clean box mixed in with three greasy ones."

"So we're not exactly looking for a rocket scientist here."

"Right. They brought all four boxes to our lab for analysis. I've also got the warrant for Tori Stevens's checking account and have requested canceled checks for the last four months."

"Did you sleep last night, Cap?"

"Not much. This situation with Stahl is keeping me awake at night."

"What's happening there?"

"I haven't heard anything new this morning. The forensic teams are working the scene under Haggerty's supervision."

"When is the department going to issue the statement?" Gonzo asked.

"This morning. We were trying to wait for more info, but we're getting a lot of questions about what's happening at the house. It'll be a few weeks before the remains are identified and next steps determined. The chief is reviewing the final draft of the statement now."

"I can't even think about what kind of nightmare this will be when people find out."

"We're preparing for worst-case scenario."

"Which is what?"

"The mayor or city council demanding the chief's immediate resignation."

"Do you think they will?"

"Would you? If you were them?"

Gonzo sighed. "I really hope they don't go straight to nuclear when we're doing everything we can to get answers for those families."

"Exactly, but we're still preparing for the worst."

"Will he resign?"

"He hasn't said yet what he'll do. He's playing it all by ear while trying to keep his focus on the investigation."

"The faster we get answers for the families, the faster the

heat will die down. People already know what Stahl is capable of, so they won't be surprised to learn there's more."

"There is that."

"Hang in there, Cap. We've gotten through a lot as a team, and we'll get through this, too."

Malone gave Gonzo's shoulder a squeeze. "Thanks, Sarge. I'll let you know when the checking account info comes through."

"I'll call Tori Stevens's parents to check on the status of her attorney."

"No need," another voice said. "I'm here."

Gonzo turned to find a man with his hair combed back from a face that most people would find handsome, wearing what had to be a five-thousand-dollar suit. Not that Gonzo knew much about custom suits, but even his untrained eye could spot high quality.

"Miles Kerr." He extended a hand to each of them. "Where can I find Sergeant Gonzales?"

"That'd be me."

"Excellent. How soon can I meet with my client?"

"We'll bring her upstairs shortly."

"Wonderful. Now if you could tell me why she's here, I'd appreciate that. Her mother was understandably distraught, so it was hard to get the full gist of what's taken place."

"She's being held pending counsel for arraignment on assaulting a police officer because she kicked one of our officers."

"Hmm, okay. What else?"

"We're looking at her for involvement in the death of Rachel Fortier, who'd been dating Gordon Reilly."

"What does that have to do with my client?"

Gonzo wanted to roll his eyes over how unprepared the guy was, but he resisted the urge. "Tori dated Gordon for years at home in Wisconsin, until they went to college in different states and agreed to see other people while they were apart. At least Gordon agreed to that. Tori says she didn't, even though he believed they had an understanding."

Kerr gave him a skeptical look. "So you think my client, a college student in Georgia, had something to do with the death of a college student here?"

Gonzo never blinked when he looked the guy in the eye. "I do."

"Huh, well... That's a bit of a stretch, don't you think?"

"I don't think so."

"What evidence do you have to tie her to this crime?"

"Are you aware that Tori was harassing Rachel for months via text? So much so that Rachel got a new phone number that Tori eventually got ahold of and started the whole thing up again?"

"I hadn't heard about that."

"I didn't think so. We're working on putting the pieces together and will have more info later today."

"You've already held my client longer than you're allowed to."

"We've been waiting for you, Counselor."

Kerr didn't like that answer, but Gonzo never blinked as he stared him down. Eventually, the lawyer looked away.

"I'd like to see my client."

"Right this way."

He led him to one of the interrogation rooms, turned the light on and told him to wait there. Normally, he'd ask someone else to fetch Tori from the basement jail, but he looked forward to seeing if a few nights in jail had humbled the young woman.

When he appeared outside the cell where she was being held with six other women, she met him with a wild-eyed look.

"You have to get me out of here."

"The attorney your parents sent is upstairs."

He nodded to the sergeant who ran the jail to unlock the door.

"Please extend your arms," Gonzo said.

"Why?"

"So I can cuff you."

"Why are you treating me like I'm some sort of criminal? I

don't belong in this place with..." She glanced over her shoulder. "Those people."

Nope, Gonzo thought. *The time in jail hasn't done a thing to humble her.* He wondered how years in the can would look on her, because he was certain she'd had something to do with Rachel's death. He just had to prove it.

"Your arms."

She stuck them out.

He cuffed her and led her to the stairs.

"When can I leave? I have homework to do."

"You're our guest for now."

"What? Don't I have rights?"

"You sure do. That's why I'm taking you to see your attorney. Because you have the right to legal representation."

"I have the right to my freedom, too."

"Which shall be granted to you if and when a judge deems it should be. In the meantime, you're our guest." He opened the door to the interrogation room. "Meet your attorney, Miles Kerr. Mr. Kerr, your client, Tori Stevens. I'll leave you to get acquainted. Let me know when you're ready to continue our earlier discussion."

"You have to get me out of here right now," Tori said to the lawyer.

"Have a seat."

"I don't want to sit!"

Gonzo closed the door.

She was Kerr's problem for the time being.

CHAPTER NINETEEN

While she waited for Nick to return, Sam took a call from his dad, Leo. "Hi there."

"Hi, Sam. Sorry to disturb your peace and quiet."

"When does the peace and quiet start?" she asked with a laugh.

"I'm sorry that it's been less than restful. The headlines are disturbing."

"Yes, they are."

"Because of that, I was calling to make sure you're still up for having the boys this weekend. It's no problem at all if you're maxed out."

Brayden and Brock Cappuano, Nick's seven-year-old brothers, were due to arrive with Scotty and the kids Friday afternoon. Leo and his wife, Stacy, both had to work over the weekend and would be unable to join them.

"We're looking forward to having them," Sam said.

"Really? Because they're a lot."

Sam laughed. "They'll keep our kids busy and occupied, and we've got the beach to entertain them all. We can't wait."

"You're too kind. The boys are out of their minds with excitement about a weekend away from Mom and Dad."

"That's so cute. We'll make sure they have a great time."

"Thank you again for having them. We'll meet the detail in New Carrollton as planned at four."

"I'll let the agents know you're good to go. We'll send pics and make sure they call you both nights before bed."

"Thanks again, Sam."

"Our pleasure."

When she ended that call, she found a text response from Lieutenant Haggerty. *Can you talk?*

Who hadn't she talked to that day? She placed the call to Haggerty. "Hey," she said. "How's it going?"

"Ugh, Sam. This is unbelievable. Human remains in the backyard, concrete holding cells behind the walls we took down with DNA everywhere we look in the basement... A little shop of pure horror."

"God," she said on a long exhale. "How's your team holding up?"

"We're exhausted and only about halfway done with processing the scene. And then there's the storage unit."

"I heard about that."

"I can only imagine what might be in there."

"What can I do for you?"

"I just needed to vent. I know you're on vacation."

"I'll be back early next week, and in the meantime, my team is available to support you in any way needed. Just get with Gonzo about what you need."

"He's been helping. We're running on fumes, and the paperwork alone will kill me."

"Ask for help, Max. And encourage your team to see Dr. Trulo after you're done there."

"I've already talked to him about that."

"Good."

"It's just so fucking shocking, you know? That someone we worked closely with... I don't have to tell you."

"No, you don't."

"This is going to be bad when it goes public, Sam."

"I know. My stomach is in knots over it."

"Mine, too. I'd better get back to it. Thanks for checking in. I appreciate it."

"Call me any time, Max. I mean it."

"Will do. Thanks."

Sam had no sooner slapped her phone closed than it buzzed with a text from Freddie. *Cristen Hans Reid has gone public with the fact that we're looking at Stahl for the murders of her sister and several others.*

"Oh fuck," Sam said as she read the text.

"What now?" Nick asked as he approached the sofa where she was seated.

"One of the women I saw the other day has gone public about the new investigation into Stahl—before we were ready for that."

She's going off on how the MPD was sitting on info that could've solved her sister's case years ago, that the murderer was among their ranks while her family lived with unbearable heartbreak.

That text was quickly followed by one from Helen, the chief's admin. *All-hands commander meeting at fifteen hundred. All commanders are urged to attend.*

She glanced at the clock on the mantel. The meeting was in fifteen minutes. "Commander meeting at three," she told Nick. "I know we're supposed to be on vacation, but I need to attend that meeting."

"I understand. I just spent half the day dealing with my job."

"We suck at vacation."

Turn on the news, Freddie texted.

Sam reluctantly reached for the remote and turned on the TV to find the woman she'd met the other day standing in front of a podium.

"For all this time," Cristen said, "the person who took my sister from us might've been working as a police officer in Washington, DC. He once headed the division that investigates murders. How ironic. I want to know what the MPD knew and when they knew it. This man has been convicted of twice trying to kill the woman who's now our first lady. She came to my house the other day in her capacity as the lieutenant in charge of the Homicide division to inform me that new information has come to light that could tie Leonard Stahl to my sister's disappearance and presumed murder. Has she known all along that she isn't the only one he targeted? I know I speak for all the other families who had loved ones go missing in the District around the same time as my sister did. We want answers, and we want them *now*."

"Holy shit," Sam whispered.

Reporters shouted questions at her, many of them involving Sam, her visit to the woman and what she'd said about Stahl.

"I don't blame her, per se," Cristen said. "She was doing her job by coming to inform me of the development, and I appreciate the update. But since she was there, I have nothing but questions, and I know I'm not alone in that. Like other families, we've waited years for news of our missing loved one. Parents and grandparents have died without ever knowing what became of their daughters and granddaughters. If the MPD has suspected Stahl of these murders and is only now telling us, it's a travesty."

"Whoa," Sam said. "We just found this out, and I told her that. Son of a bitch."

Nick's hand covered hers. "I'm sure the department will come out with a statement in response to her allegations."

"We should've said something before now," she said. "But they were waiting until they knew more about what was at the house. Now we've lost control of the story."

Her phone rang with a call from Malone.

"Hey."

"Have you heard?"

"I'm watching it now."

"Can you do the three o'clock meeting?"

"Yes, I'll be there."

"Thanks."

He was gone before she could say anything else.

· · ·

S AM USED her laptop to log on to the meeting with a link that
Malone emailed to her.

"Thanks for joining us, Lieutenant," Chief Farnsworth said.

"No problem."

"We've got everyone here except Lieutenant Haggerty, who's
been excused. Thank you all for joining us for an update on
where we stand with the Stahl investigation. As you know,
forensic teams are on-site at his home and have uncovered
human remains. After taking down a wall that appeared new,
Haggerty and his detectives have found two rooms that
appeared to be holding cells. Today, the sister of one of the
missing women went public with our suspicions that Stahl is
responsible for the deaths of numerous women.

"We've put together a statement that describes what we've
found thus far and what we're doing to expedite the
investigation. There's a quote from me included in the
statement that says we understand and acknowledge that the
families involved have already waited too long for justice for
their missing and presumed murdered loved ones, but that this
is painstaking work that'll take time to complete. I said we've
only recently learned of Stahl's potential involvement in these
cold cases, that we're sickened by these crimes and committed
to a full accounting of every violation committed by Leonard
Stahl while he was pretending to be an upstanding police
officer.

"I expect pressure from city hall to resign. I won't do that. I
intend to clean up every aspect of Stahl's mess before I even
consider leaving. If they want me out, they'll have to fire me.
His crimes occurred partially on my watch, and I'll see it
through to the bitter end. I've been in consultation with former
Chief Williams, who's as shocked and outraged as the rest
of us."

Sam was relieved to hear the chief say he intended to stay
in the fight. The mention of Don Williams brought back many
childhood memories tied to her father, who'd been close
friends with the former chief. As far as she knew, Williams was

living in Phoenix, where he'd moved after retirement to be closer to his children and grandchildren.

Williams hadn't attended her dad's funeral because he'd been ill at the time. He'd sent a card expressing his profound sorrow over the loss of his close friend and colleague.

"I'll be the face of this story for the department," Farnsworth continued. "No one else is to speak to the media. Please make sure your teams are aware of that directive, as I have no doubt every member of the department will be subjected to public commentary and potential reporter interest. I'm the only one authorized to speak to the media. Full stop.

"Thank you all for your attention to this matter and for your support this week. It's meant a lot to me, Deputy Chief McBride, Captain Malone, Lieutenant Haggerty and his team as we work our way through this process. I also want to remind everyone that Dr. Trulo is available to anyone who needs him.

"We understand this is a lot for the men and women of our department to absorb. It's always extra disappointing when we learn that one of our own isn't on the same team as the rest of us. We've had more than our share of that lately, but I assure you that I'm committed to rooting out the rot in this department. That's all I wanted to say. Thank you."

"Thank you, Chief," McBride said. "And may I echo everything the chief said. We're here to support our team in any way we can, and we'll get through this together."

"That's all," Malone said. "We'll put out an all-staff message summarizing this meeting. Let us know if there're any questions or concerns from your people."

Sam signed off the meeting and sent a text to Joe Farnsworth's personal cell phone. *Just wanted you to know I'm thinking of you, and as always, you have my full support. Thank you for your determination to stay in the fight. We need you right now, but please take care of yourself in all this.* She added a heart emoji and sent the text.

Then she went downstairs and turned on the TV, looking for coverage of the chief's news conference.

Capital News Network covered it live. The chief read the statement Public Affairs had drafted and then added his own sentiments, including much of what he'd said in the commander's meeting.

"What do you have to say to Caren Hans's sister and all the other families?" a reporter asked.

"I empathize with all the families affected by this man's actions. My own family, right here in this building, has been impacted by him. Lieutenant Holland and her sisters were like nieces to my wife and me as they grew up. Their father was my closest friend. When Stahl attacked her, he attacked my family."

Sam winced even as his words touched her deeply. The last thing she needed was more reminders to the rest of the department of how close her family had always been to the chief and his wife. That closeness had led to an ongoing feeling, among some of her colleagues, that she benefited from nepotism. Even though her father had died, her "uncle" Joe was still the chief. To which she said, *Whatever.* She worked her freaking ass off on the job and always had. At times, she felt as if she worked harder than most so she wouldn't be accused of favoritism.

In her opinion, her last name had caused her more trouble than any benefit it might've provided. Stahl hated her because he hated her father. Others had accused her of unfair advantages, and she was always up against the challenge of being a woman in a largely male profession.

"My department is taking these new allegations against Stahl extremely seriously. We will stay on this case until every victim has received the justice they deserve."

"What would you say to people who consider your department incompetent?"

"The MPD is made up of four thousand hardworking men and women. In any organization of that size, you'll have a few who don't play by the rules. We will fully prosecute anyone who breaks the law after having sworn to uphold it. Our recent arrest of former IT Lieutenant Bill Gibbons is an example of that. He's someone I considered a friend until it was learned that he assisted Stahl in some of his criminal activities. We have a zero-tolerance policy for lawlessness within our own ranks, and I assure the public that the rest of us are hard at work every day to protect this city and its citizens. As disgusted and revolted by these new allegations as you are, I promise you that we are more so."

He paused, resting his hands on the podium. "I've devoted my entire adult life to the District of Columbia and its residents. It's been the greatest honor of my life to wear this uniform and this badge in our nation's capital. Most of the people who work with me in this department feel the same way I do and show up every day to do a difficult, often thankless job.

"Do we always get it right? Absolutely not. We screw up far more often than we'd like to, but most of us come in each day with the best of intentions and the goal of doing the right thing. Twelve of our officers have made the ultimate sacrifice on the job. Others have been severely injured, their lives changed forever by a bullet or a knife or even a car intentionally hitting them. Many have been traumatized by things they've seen and experienced in the line of duty. We see things... every day... things that change us forever.

"I hear the drumbeat of people calling for my ouster, who want to blame me for every law-breaking cop who ever came through these doors. I understand the desire to hold me accountable for the misdeeds of those who report to me. I accept responsibility for the good, the bad, the terrible, the heartbreaking and everything in between that happens on my watch. You can lead the charge to remove me, but I promise you that won't deter people who are determined to break the law while the rest of us work to uphold it. Those people will always exist. A new leader won't share my intense commitment to right the wrongs of the past. This is personal to me in a way it wouldn't be to someone else. Trust me when I tell you that every ounce of my energy and fortitude is directed toward ensuring every victim of Leonard Stahl's—and their families—receive justice long denied. That's all I've got to say at this time. I'll update you the minute we have new information."

Sam wiped tears off her cheeks as she watched him walk through the main doors to HQ.

"We've just heard from Metro PD Chief Joseph Farnsworth," the anchor said, "who's expressed his determination to stay on the job despite the growing calls for his resignation or ouster as the full extent of imprisoned former Lieutenant Leonard Stahl's crimes comes to light. Dan, what would justice look like to families of the missing women? He's already serving two life sentences with no chance of parole."

"For many of them," Dan said, "I'd imagine justice would come from their bodies being found after all this time, of Stahl being tried and convicted specifically for taking their lives. I spoke to Cristen Hans Reid earlier, and this is what she had to say about that."

"For me," Cristen said in a recorded clip, "it doesn't matter that he's already in prison. I want him to stand trial for killing my sister. I want a jury to find him guilty of that particular crime. I want him punished specifically for her death. And if others within the MPD knew what he did, I want them punished as well. I won't rest until the people who took my sister from me pay for their crimes."

Nick sat next to Sam on the sofa and rested his hand on top of hers. The heat from his hand made her realize how cold hers was. "Are you okay, babe?"

"I think so."

"What do you think of what she said?"

"I agree with her. Just because he's in prison for what he did to me doesn't mean his other victims have gotten justice. I'm glad he's going to be charged for all the other things he did, including the burying of reports and cases he didn't feel like dealing with. So what if he's already serving life in prison? I want him found guilty for what he did to Calvin Worthington's family and Carisma Deasly's and for framing Eric Davies on rape charges. I want him convicted for everything he's done. I want justice for all his victims."

"I'm worried about the toll this is taking on you."

"It's not about me."

"Samantha, come on. Of course it's about you. This has to be bringing everything you went through with him back to the surface, although I'm sure it's never far from your mind."

Sam had chosen not to tell him about her recent dream because it would upset him, and she couldn't bear to relive it. "I try not to ever think about him or what he did to me."

"Which has to be much more difficult at times like this and when you learn what he did to—or didn't do for—others." He leaned in to kiss her cheek. "I can see that you've been crying."

"It's all very upsetting. I'd never say otherwise. Hearing the chief just now... He made me so proud to work for such a good man. That's what caused the tears."

Nick put his arm around her. "I'm sorry you're all going through this. It's outrageous."

"Yes, it is, but I'd rather know the full extent and give those families as much closure as we can."

"And that, right there, is what makes you the best cop I'll ever know."

"I'm not the best."

"Yes, you are, and you have to let me think so."

"As long as you only say that to me."

"I'd say it to anyone who'd listen, but I know you don't want that."

"You're right. I don't."

"We've got a few more days until the rest of the family arrives. What do you feel like doing?"

"After I take care of a couple of emails to my team and check in with Gonzo, I'd love nothing more than to light that fire and snuggle with you while we watch all the movies we've been saying we need to see."

"That sounds perfect to me. Let's do it."

CHAPTER TWENTY

Gonzo was about to go knock on the door of the interrogation room to move things along when Sam called. "I guess you've seen the latest?" he asked her.

"I have. I watched the chief's presser. He did a great job."

"What was the commander's meeting about?"

"An update to us on the Stahl case and a request from the chief that I've sent to all of you by email, reminding everyone that he is the only one authorized to speak publicly about the case. Pass that along to our people if you would."

"I will, and thank God he's willing to do it."

"I know, right? I feel for him at times like this. He's tied for first with my dad as one of the best cops I've ever worked with. He doesn't deserve all the shit that happens around there."

"No, he doesn't. None of us do. Speaking of shit around here, I heard that Forrester's office is moving ahead with charges against Ramsey for smashing into your SUV. They're working with the FBI on the investigation and looking to really make an example out of Ramsey, who not only attacked the first lady but two federal agents with his actions."

"I'm glad he's getting what he deserves, but it's just more bad press for the department at a time when we really don't need it."

"It's also proof that we prosecute our own. It's a good

message to send to anyone thinking about skirting the rules or assaulting people."

"I guess. How's it going with the Fortier case?"

"Our prime suspect is currently conferring with her attorney. Wait till you get a load of this guy. He handed us cards that noted he graduated from Harvard Law last May. He's a pompous ass."

"Oh, my favorite kind of lawyer."

Gonzo laughed. "I can't wait to watch you chew him up and spit him out."

"I shall look forward to making a meal out of him."

"I gotta go deal with him and his ass of a client."

"Good luck with that. Keep me posted."

"Will do."

After Gonzo ended the call, he gestured for Cruz to join him as they met with Tori and her lawyer.

"Gird your loins," Gonzo muttered.

"Ew."

He snorted out a laugh and knocked on the door. "Time's up."

"I was just about to come find you," Kerr said with a big smile, as if they were meeting at a country club rather than a cop shop. "We're ready for you."

Gonzo wished he was allowed to punch the smug look off his face, but alas, that sort of behavior was frowned upon. "It's customary for the attorney to sit next to the client."

For fuck's sake. How green was this guy?

Kerr jumped up so quickly, he nearly knocked over the chair and the one next to it as Tori eyed him warily.

Gonzo would be wary, too, if he were her. The guy was a boob.

When Kerr was settled on Tori's side of the table, Gonzo nodded to Freddie.

He turned on the recorder and made mention of who was in the room.

"I'd like to pick up where we left off previously," Gonzo said. "After you harassed Rachel to the point where she had to change her phone number, how'd you get the new number?"

"Objection," Kerr said. "You can't prove she harassed anyone."

It took everything Gonzo had not to laugh and roll his eyes. "Save your objections for court, Counselor." He placed the printouts that showed the texts Rachel received from Tori, as well as the accompanying texts from Tori's phone, on the table. "As you can see, we can easily tie the texts from Tori to Rachel."

Kerr leaned in for a closer look.

"These are the texts that came from Tori's phone to Rachel's new number." Gonzo put more pages on the table. "In addition, we'd like to know who you recently wrote a ten-thousand-dollar check to."

Tori looked up at them in shock. "How do you know that?"

"We got a warrant for your financials. We're waiting on another that will give us access to your canceled checks. Unless you'd like to fill us in. That'd save some time."

She looked at Kerr for guidance.

He seemed uncertain of what to do, so Gonzo sat back in his chair and folded his arms to wait him out. Why should he make this easy for him?

"I'd, uh, like a moment alone with my client."

Freddie pressed Pause on the recorder before they left the room.

In the hallway, Gonzo glanced at his friend. "Can you believe this guy?"

"Objection!"

They cracked up laughing.

"What's so funny?" Malone asked when he joined them.

"Tori Stevens's defense attorney is a Harvard-educated doofus."

"Oh jeez. Well, here are the canceled checks."

Gonzo took the pages from the captain and looked through them, landing on the one he was most interested in, made out to Randy Bryant. He passed the page to Cruz. "Let's figure out who he is."

"On it."

While Cruz headed for the pit, Gonzo waited for Kerr to tell him he and Tori were ready for him to return.

"What're you thinking, Sarge?"

"I'm thinking Tori Stevens hired someone to either eliminate her competition or help her do it and was so arrogant about the whole thing that she didn't worry about leaving a paper trail."

Kerr opened the door. "We're ready to continue."

Gonzo pushed off the wall and followed him into the room, reengaging the recorder. "So who's Randy Bryant?"

Tori gasped before she realized she needed to keep her cool. "I have no idea."

"Then why'd you write a check to him for ten thousand dollars ten days ago?"

"I didn't!"

Gonzo sat across from them, keeping his pose as casual as he possibly could. What did he need to be tense about? He had her nailed to the wall. "Here's a copy of the canceled check drawn from your account. Detective Cruz is working on figuring out who he is. We'll find him within minutes, if it takes that long, so you may as well tell us who he is."

She again looked to her attorney to tell her what to do.

Gonzo could tell that Kerr had no idea what to tell her.

"This check you're referring to was written by my client?"

Gonzo stared at him for a second and then pointed to the printout. "Yes, it was written by your client, or I wouldn't have mentioned it."

Kerr looked to Tori. "Did you write this check?"

She crossed her arms and gave them a defiant look. "I don't want to talk about it."

Gonzo laughed. "That's not how this works, Tori. Did you hire Randy to hurt Rachel?"

The question obviously shocked her. Where in the hell had she thought this was headed?

"I have no idea who she even is!"

"Then why did you text her hundreds of times on two different numbers?"

"That wasn't me."

He glanced at the lawyer. "Will you please tell your client that we can prove she texted Rachel and wrote the check to Randy? Will you tell her that when we get Randy in here, he'll tell us everything to save himself?"

"He won't say a word," Tori hissed.

"Be quiet, Tori," Kerr said sternly.

Gonzo was glad the guy seemed to have at least a basic idea of how much trouble his client was in. He stood. "Welp, I guess we'll wait to hear what Randy has to say." He was reaching for the recorder to shut it off when Tori spoke up.

"Wait."

"Tori..."

Kerr seemed tense enough for everyone. Perhaps he'd paid just enough attention in law school to realize when shit was getting real.

"If I tell you what Randy did, does that help me?"

"Depends on what you had to do with what Randy did."

"Tori, don't say anything else," Kerr said.

Gonzo took great satisfaction in the thin film of sweat forming on the lawyer's upper lip.

"I need to get out of here! If I tell them what Randy did, they'll let me go."

Kerr's gaze collided with Gonzo's. "No, they won't."

"But he just said that!"

"That's not what he said. If you know how or why Rachel was killed, you're in big trouble. So keep your mouth shut."

"I want to go home," she said tearfully. "I have homework to do."

"If you'd like to make a statement about what happened, I'll be glad to tell the prosecutor that you cooperated in helping us figure out how Rachel was killed."

"What kind of time would she be looking at?"

"As an accessory to murder? That's a long stretch."

Tori's gaze darted between them as she tried to keep up. "What does that mean? A long stretch?"

"Tori, the evidence shows that you were involved in Rachel's murder," Gonzo said, "regardless of whether you were the one to press on her carotid artery or if you paid someone to do it for you."

All the color left her complexion as the reality of her situation seemed to sink in. "I didn't touch her!"

"But Randy did, didn't he?"

"I don't know! I don't know what he did!"

"Did he do what you asked him to?" Gonzo asked.

"I didn't ask him to do anything!"

"Why'd you pay him ten grand, then? Just for shits and grins?"

"I..." She wiped away tears as she swallowed hard. "He... he was blackmailing me."

Gonzo wanted to laugh at the sheer madness of this situation. It would be hilarious if an innocent young woman wasn't dead in the morgue because of Tori's jealousy. "He was blackmailing you. Okay... Let's start with how you met him."

She glanced at Kerr. "Do I have to tell him that?"

Kerr rubbed at his jaw, looking as if he were the one who was about to get arrested for murder. He clearly had no idea what she ought to do.

"Mr. Kerr, have you defended a client in a capital murder case before?"

"*Murder?*" Tori screeched. "I didn't murder anyone! I was with Gordon all night. Ask him! He'll tell you."

"You told me you left for a time to go for a walk. Did you meet up with Randy then?"

"I've never met him."

"How did you find him?"

"I... I don't think I should say anything else."

Gonzo gave her a minute to change her mind, but when it became apparent that she wouldn't, he stood. "I'll have someone escort you back downstairs."

"I can't go back there," she said, sobbing. To Kerr, she said, "Do something! You're supposed to be helping me."

"I, uh, need to confer with my senior partners about the best way forward."

"Maybe you could send one of them over here—someone who knows what the fuck they're doing!"

"Let's go," Gonzo said to her.

"You can't make me go back down to that dungeon! The other women are *monsters!*"

Gonzo took her by the arm and all but dragged her from the room. In the hallway, he turned her over to the Patrol officer standing guard outside. "Take her back downstairs."

Tori screamed like a banshee the whole way to the stairs. She threatened lawsuits that would end their careers and yelled about police brutality.

"I take it our friend Tori has realized she's totally screwed," Freddie said when Gonzo returned to the pit.

"Yep, and her jackass of a lawyer has no idea what to do about it." Gonzo rubbed at the back of his neck, which was aching. "What've you got on Randy?"

"I've got an address for him three blocks from the GW campus."

"Have we heard anything from the lab on the pizza boxes yet?"

"There were prints all over them."

"How much you want to bet they're going to be our friend Randy's?"

"I'd bet the entire farm."

"Let's go pay him a visit."

RANDY BRYANT LIVED on the third floor of a townhouse on 22nd Street Northwest in Foggy Bottom, near the State Department complex. Since Freddie had found a photo of him online, they recognized him as their guy when he answered the door. As described by their eye-witness, he was a big guy with buzzed dark hair and a goatee. He wore a Clash T-shirt, jeans and red Vans sneakers. "Can I help you?"

Gonzo and Freddie showed their badges. "Randy Bryant?"

"Yeah? What the hell? What do you want?"

"You're under arrest for the murder of Rachel Fortier," Freddie said. "You have the right to remain silent. Anything you say can be used against you in a court of law."

The guy had barely registered that he was being arrested before Gonzo had him cuffed.

"What the fuck? I didn't murder anyone!"

"That's what they all say, isn't it, Detective Cruz?"

"Sure is, Sarge. We hear it all the time."

"What the hell is going on?" another guy asked from inside the apartment.

"They're arresting me. Call my parents. Tell them to send a lawyer."

The roommate moved toward the door. "*What?*"

"Don't come any closer," Gonzo said to the roommate. "Or we'll arrest you, too."

"Where are you taking him?"

"Metro PD headquarters." Gonzo handed him a card. "Tell the parents to send the attorney there. He's going to need representation."

"What did he do?" the roommate asked.

Gonzo ignored him and followed Cruz and Bryant down the stairs.

"I don't know what you guys think you're doing, but I'll have your badges for this."

"That's another one we never hear, right, Cruz?"

"Never."

They stuffed him into the back seat of Gonzo's car and headed back to HQ.

When they arrived, Freddie took Bryant to be processed.

Gonzo returned to the pit and stopped short at the sight of Gordon Reilly sitting in a chair outside Sam's office.

He jumped up when he saw Gonzo. "They told me to wait for you here. Do you know who killed Rachel?"

The poor guy barely resembled the person they'd first met. His hair was a mess, his eyes red and swollen and his entire disposition one of utter devastation.

"We think we have an idea of what happened."

"Was it Tori?" he asked warily.

"She was involved."

"Oh God. That can't be true. She didn't even know Rachel."

Gonzo unlocked the office. "Come in. Sit down."

"She didn't know her," Gordon said again when he was seated in one of Sam's visitor chairs.

"No, she didn't, but she knew *of* her, and that was the problem. I'm sure Rachel must've mentioned that she was getting hostile texts from your ex."

"What? No, she never said anything about that to me."

"Really? Huh…"

"She knew that the situation with Tori was very difficult for me." He rested his chin on his hands, elbows propped on his knees. "I'd been with Tori since we were kids. I was really upset about how hard she took our separation and breakup. I was sick with guilt over it, which is probably why Rachel never told me that Tori was bothering her. Why didn't she tell me? I could've made it stop."

"I don't know that you could have, Gordon. Tori was relentless."

"Wait. Is this why Rachel's phone number changed?"

"Yes."

"Oh my God. She never told me any of this."

Gonzo showed him the photo from his friend Jeff's social media. "This is when Tori realized you'd met someone else."

Gordon's face went flat with shock. "She… she saw that?"

"We believe so. Rachel's problems with her began shortly after that."

"This is all my fault. If I hadn't gotten close to Rachel, she'd still be alive." He looked at Gonzo with utter devastation. "How am I supposed to live with that?"

Taking pity on the guy, Gonzo got up and went around the

desk to sit next to him. "This is a horrible thing. I'm sorry it happened to you. But you didn't kill her."

"Did Tori kill her when she left my room the other night?"

"We think she paid someone to do it for her. She might've met up with him when she left your room to take a walk."

"*What?* Oh my God. It just gets worse. Who did she pay?"

"We believe it was a guy named Randy Bryant."

"Who's that?"

"We're still figuring out who he is and how they connected. She recently wrote a ten-thousand-dollar check to him as well as other smaller payments over the last few months. We believe she might've been paying him to keep eyes on you and Rachel."

He dropped his head into his hands again. "How could I have known this person for all these years and not known she was capable of such a thing?"

Gonzo had no idea what to say to him.

"My parents always said she was a spoiled rich girl, but I didn't think that was true. She was oblivious sometimes, but never unkind." He looked over at Gonzo again. "Will she go to prison?"

"She'll stand trial on solicitation of murder charges."

"I just can't believe this."

Freddie came to the office door. "Uh, Sarge... Tori Stevens's parents are here."

Gonzo and Gordon stood and turned toward the doorway.

Tori's mother let out a sharp cry and surged toward Gordon. "This is all your fault! You drove her to this!"

Gonzo quickly got between them and stopped her from striking Gordon. He walked her backward out of the office as Cruz restrained the father. "Unless you want to be charged, I'd recommend you get control of yourselves."

"He did this to her!" the father cried. "He jerked her around and made promises he didn't keep. How could you do that to her?"

"Gordon, go on home." Gonzo continued to restrain Tori's mother. "We'll be in touch."

Gordon hesitated. "I never promised her anything. I was

eighteen years old. I wasn't ready to commit to forever with anyone."

"Go, Gordon," Gonzo said again, more firmly this time.

After Gordon walked away, he loosened his hold on Mrs. Stevens. "Are you two able to comport yourselves properly, or do I need to take you into custody?"

The two of them adjusted their expensive-looking clothing.

"This is all his fault." Mr. Stevens was tall, with salt-and-pepper hair and a tanned, youthful face. "If you knew the games he's played with our daughter…"

"It's been a nightmare for her and us." Mrs. Stevens was a bottle blonde with the same eyes as her daughter. Every inch of her was ruthlessly polished.

"You know what's been a nightmare?" Gonzo asked. "Rachel Fortier having to change her phone number because your daughter was harassing her so badly. Rachel Fortier had nothing to do with Gordon's relationship with Tori, and yet, she's the one who's dead. We have evidence that your daughter paid someone to kill Rachel and eliminate the competition."

"You've got to be kidding me," Mr. Stevens said with a mean-looking sneer. "She's a college student. What in the world does she know about murder? There's no way you can prove this."

A uniformed officer came into the pit with a printout he handed to Gonzo. "The prints on the pizza boxes are a match for Bryant."

"What does that mean?" Mr. Stevens asked.

"It means the man that Tori paid ten thousand dollars to can be tied to Rachel's murder. We're going to talk to him now. I won't be surprised if he gives up Tori as the mastermind of the whole plan. I mean, if it's a choice between spending the rest of his life in jail or turning on her, what do you think he'll choose?"

"You can't pin this on her," Mr. Stevens said, seething. "This is a screw job."

"The evidence doesn't lie, sir."

"Are you expecting us to believe a department that

harbored a murderer in its ranks for *years* is capable of pinning a murder on our daughter?" he asked.

"Believe whatever you want, but your daughter will be charged with accessory to murder and solicitation of murder. And if I were you, I'd get her a better lawyer than that schmuck Kerr. He doesn't know his ass from his elbow." To Cruz, he said, "Let's go talk to Bryant."

"Wait!"

Gonzo turned back to Mr. Stevens.

"What if she tells all? Would that help her situation?"

"Larry! There's no way she did this. *What're you saying?*"

"Shut up, Charlene. You know damned well she's capable of anything. You raised her that way."

"*I* raised her that way? Who spoiled her rotten and treated her like an entitled princess since the day she was born?"

Gonzo had heard enough. "As entertaining as this is…"

"If she talks, will it help?" Mr. Stevens asked again.

"Let me consult with the Assistant U.S. Attorney and see what she says. In the meantime, have a seat in the lobby. I'll come find you when I know more."

"We'd like to see our daughter."

"I'll see what I can do about that later."

Mr. Stevens didn't like that response. He was probably used to people hopping to his every command.

Gonzo waited until they'd walked away before he turned to roll his eyes at Freddie.

"At least we can see where she comes by her charm," Freddie said.

Gonzo snorted out a laugh. "No kidding. I'll call the AUSA." His phone rang with an out-of-state number. "Sergeant Gonzales."

"This is Rosemary Bryant. My son has been arrested."

"Yes, ma'am."

"What's he being charged with?"

"Murder."

Her cry of shock had Gonzo holding the phone away from

his ear. "How... How can that be? He'd never do something like that. He's an honor student at GW."

"Our investigation shows that he accepted a ten-thousand-dollar payment from a woman who wanted her romantic competition eliminated."

"There has to be some kind of mistake. He doesn't need the money."

"There's no mistake, ma'am. I'd recommend you find a good defense attorney for him as soon as possible."

"Where do I go for that?"

"The DC Bar Association should be able to recommend someone. If you don't have the means, we can call the public defender's office."

"Tell him I'm working on getting someone."

"We will."

"Please... He's my whole world. Please don't let anything happen to him. I don't know what I'd do..."

Gonzo's heart broke for her. He couldn't conceive of what it would be like to have his son charged with murder. Sometimes parents could do everything right and still have something like this happen. "I'll wait to hear from you."

"Thank you."

CHAPTER TWENTY-ONE

Gonzo ended the call and sat in Sam's desk chair, gazing at the photo of her and Nick from their wedding day.

As if he'd conjured her, Sam texted him. *How's it going?*

You picked a fine time to leave me, Lucille.

She responded with laughing emojis. *That bad?*

Worse. Two college kids accused of murdering the third in a love triangle gone wrong. Lots of devastated (and a few entitled) parents. Good times.

Ugh, sorry. Have you got it sewn up?

Just about. Very sad all around.

Isn't it always?

Yeah, I guess so. How's the vacation?

Much more stressful than we'd hoped for. Rather than coming back to work on Monday, I'll be going to Fort Liberty.

It's awful.

Sure is, and Nick feels responsible, even though he isn't. Tough situation. But we're coping.

Sorry for everyone involved. Such a tragedy.

Thanks. I'll be back on Tuesday for the first half of the day before the state dinner with the Canadian prime minister. (How is this my life?)

Is that a rhetorical question?

LOL, nope.

Enjoy the rest of the time away. It'll all still be here when you get back.

Oh joy! Thanks for covering. It helps to know you're in charge.

No problem.

Freddie came to the office door. "What's next, boss?"

"I'm calling the AUSA. Hang on." He put through the call to the office where the Miller triplets worked as the Assistant U.S. Attorneys. One of them was always on call.

"Faith Miller."

"Hey, it's Gonzo. I've got a case put together, and I'm ready for your input."

"Be right there."

"Thanks, Faith." To Freddie, he said, "She's on her way."

NICOLETTA RATTLED around in Collins's luxurious apartment all day, waiting for him to get home and tell her how the rest of her life would unfold. She hated feeling powerless over her own destiny, but she'd decided to put her faith in him and hope for the best.

Though she was tempted to snoop, she resisted the urge. He already had enough reasons to think she was beneath him. She didn't need to give him more.

She stood at the window overlooking downtown Cleveland, noting the Rock & Roll Hall of Fame next to the Browns stadium on the shore of Lake Erie. Even after living there for years, she didn't know the city much better than she had when she first arrived. She'd spent most of her time there trying to survive and thrive, so she hadn't given much thought to getting to know the place.

As she looked out at the lake in the distance, she thought about what Collins had said about trying to make amends with her son.

Her son, the president of the United States, of all things.

She burst with pride every time she told someone her son was the president and then shriveled in shame when she had to say, no, she hadn't been to the White House. Not yet, anyway.

As if she'd ever be invited there. Her bitch of a daughter-in-law wouldn't let her anywhere near Nick or the White House, especially now that she'd orchestrated Nicoletta's public downfall.

She must be very pleased with herself.

How could her gorgeous prince of a son have shackled himself to such a horrible woman? Nicoletta would never understand what he saw in a loudmouth cop with the class of a mule. If she could work her way back into her son's life, maybe she could help him see reason when it came to his wife.

Then she recalled what Collins had said about the path to Nick running through *her*. The thought of making nice with the woman who'd ruined her life made Nicoletta sick. She was seething at the thought of having to deal with that woman when she heard the door open in the foyer.

Though her impulse was to greet him after a long day on her own, she held her ground and let him come to her. A man didn't stay interested in a woman who made it too easy for him.

"Hi there," he said when he found her in the spacious living room.

"Hi. How was your day?"

"Productive. Yours?"

"Long and quiet."

"Well, I come with good news."

"What's that?"

"I had a long talk with the district attorney, and he's agreed to drop the prostitution charges as long as you sign a settlement agreement that ensures you're out of the escort business."

"What about my customers?"

"He didn't ask for that info."

"Were you surprised?"

"Stunned, frankly, but I think it might have something to do with the media onslaught since he charged the president's mother. It's been way more than he bargained for. I'm getting a similar vibe from the U.S. Attorney on the racketeering and money laundering charges. He said if you pay your back taxes and permanently shutter the business, he'd consider dropping the charges as well. There'll be fines, probation and community service required in both cases, but I negotiated for expungement after three years, provided you aren't arrested again."

"Your day was productive indeed."

"Best-case scenario all around." He gave her a side-eyed glance. "You'll have to tap into those offshore accounts to pay the taxes. That'll be a hefty tab."

Nicoletta hated to hear that. Those accounts held her nest egg, her backup plan. She wrapped her arms around herself.

"Is that a deal breaker?" Collins asked.

"I'm not sure which is worse. Being broke or being in prison."

"I think you know which would be worse."

"Do I? I've been struggling my whole life. For the first time, I have financial security."

"Which means nothing if you're locked up in a cell."

She took a deep breath and let it out. Being locked in that cell had been an all-time low for her. "I suppose you're right." If she played her cards right, she could retain enough to live frugally for the rest of her life. There were other accounts no one seemed to be aware of. Hopefully, she could keep them off the radar.

"What're you thinking?" he asked.

"That I should thank you for negotiating a way out of this for me."

"You're welcome. If you're willing to agree to both deals, my daughter Jaclyn, who works with me, will help us draft a statement to announce the resolution of your cases."

"Is that necessary?"

"It is if you want to get the media off your back so you can go home. They're still camped out at your condo complex."

"Will there be an uproar over me seeming to get special treatment?"

"Having to pay more than a million dollars in back taxes is hardly special treatment."

"I guess that's true."

"This is good news, Nicoletta. The best possible outcome."

"Then why do I feel so defeated?"

"Because you were running a booming business, and now that's over. You'll have to figure out what's next for yourself and how you want to spend your time."

The thought of starting over—again—was almost as overwhelming as being thrown in jail had been. How many times could one person reinvent herself before she ran out of ideas of how to go forward?

"Try not to worry. We'll figure it out."

"*We* will?"

"I'd like to help you, if you'll let me."

"Why?"

"Because." He seemed almost shy for a second. "I like you."

She laughed.

"Why is that funny?"

"I was wearing a prison jumpsuit when we met."

"And yet, I still liked you. I find you interesting."

Frowning, she said, "Is that because of who my son is?"

"That's part of it. I won't lie to you about that or anything. But I'm *intrigued* by you. Not him."

She heard a key in the door and turned toward the foyer.

"That'll be Jaclyn."

"You must've been pretty sure I'd take the deals."

"I had a feeling you would, as the alternative is unthinkable." For the first time, he reached out to stroke her face. "Someone as beautiful as you are doesn't belong in prison."

He walked away from Nicoletta, leaving her breathless from the most innocent of caresses.

When was the last time that'd happened?

Never.

He returned with a gorgeous blonde woman wearing a red wrap dress and Jimmy Choo heels. "Nicoletta, meet my daughter Jaclyn. Jac, this is Nicoletta."

Jaclyn shook her hand. "Nice to meet you."

The young woman eyed her warily. She probably wondered what her father was up to bringing one of his clients to his home. Hell, Nicoletta was wondering that, too.

Over the next hour, the three of them sat at Collins's dining room table and hammered out a statement that would be released as soon as the judges signed off on the plea agreements. Jaclyn was polite and professional, but Nicoletta sensed distrust coming from the woman.

"Is there a chance the judges won't approve them?" Nicoletta asked.

"Always," Collins said, "but we should be okay in this case."

"Unless they want to make an example of the president's mother," Nicoletta said.

"That's always a possibility, but I don't expect that to happen."

"Well, hopefully it'll all be resolved soon, and you can get back to your place and your life," Jaclyn said as she packed up her laptop. "I could arrange for a hotel room in the meantime, if you'd like."

"She's fine here for now, Jac," Collins said with an indulgent smile. "I have plenty of room."

"Just trying to help." She seemed to force herself to look at Nicoletta. "Pleasure to meet you."

"You as well. Thank you for your help."

"You're welcome." She gave her dad a kiss on the cheek. "I'll talk to you later."

"Love you, sweetie."

"Love you, too."

As Nicoletta listened to them, it occurred to her that she'd never once had an exchange like that with her son, even though she loved him deeply. In her own way. Maybe her way wasn't the conventional way, but it was all she had.

"She's my middle kiddo," Collins said when he returned. "She's been such an asset to me at the firm, handling all the public relations stuff, social media and the like. I'm so clueless with that stuff." He poured amber liquid from a crystal decanter into a cocktail glass. "Drink?"

"Sure. Thanks." She sat on the sofa. "Your daughter wants me out of here."

"She's just being protective. That's how they are with me since my wife died. It's like the roles changed, and I became the child with three opinionated parents."

His words were full of affection and amusement.

"They won't want you spending time with the likes of me."

"The likes of you? What does that mean?"

"You met me in a jail, Collins. That's hardly the kind of meet-cute you see on the Hallmark Channel."

His brows furrowed with confusion that gave him a boyish cuteness. "What the heck is a meet-cute?"

She sighed with pretend exasperation. "You need to watch more romances."

"Do I?"

"A meet-cute is two people finding each other under the most adorable of circumstances, such as a woman being stranded in the snow, and a man comes to her rescue and offers to warm her up by the fire."

"Ah, I see. So what you're saying is that meeting in a jail isn't very cute?"

"That's what your kids will say."

"Let me tell you something about my kids. I'm very close to them. I talk to them every day. We went through hell together when their mother was sick and for a time after she died. That ordeal made us even closer than we were before. But we don't tell each other how to live our lives. I've been incredibly supportive of them and made their lives easier than mine ever was—and they know how lucky they are to not have student loans or to have to struggle to get by. They appreciate the lives they have and the person who provided them. And more than anything, they want me to find someone to spend what's left of my life with. They've set me up on countless blind dates with friends' mothers and aunts and cousins and what have you."

"I'm sure you're considered quite a catch by the mothers and aunts."

His face flushed, which was also cute. Hell, everything about him appealed to her, and to pretend otherwise would be ridiculous. "I guess. The thing is, none of them appealed to me."

"Why not?"

"How can I say this without sounding like a jerk?"

"Just say it. I know you're not a jerk."

"It's just that none of them was very... interesting or exciting."

It gave her tremendous satisfaction to hear him say that. "How come?"

He shrugged. "I don't know."

"Was your wife interesting and exciting?"

His handsome face lit up with the warmest smile she'd seen yet from him. It made her want to make him smile at her that way. "She was a firecracker."

"How so?"

"She had a very big personality and an even bigger laugh. She was the most joyful, funny, outgoing, nurturing, caring person you'll ever meet. Everyone loved her. I never knew what I might come home to. She was always holding a fundraiser for people in need on a moment's notice or hosting a pasta dinner for one of the kids' teams or whatever. I could barely keep up with her."

"It must've been hard to lose someone like that."

"Even though we knew it was coming, her death was a devastating blow."

"Had she been sick for long?"

"Three years. The last one was terrible. You'd think it couldn't get any worse, and then it would. Cancer is a nightmare."

"I'm sorry you lost her so young."

"It definitely changed the trajectory of my life. That's for sure. I expected to grow old with Deb, and then she was gone, and I was left to figure out what the next stage would look like. That was a struggle. Still is at times."

It was hard to imagine this cool, smart, urbane, successful, handsome man struggling over anything, but he'd clearly suffered over the loss of his beloved wife.

He turned on the sofa to face her and reached for her hand. "I find you interesting *and* exciting, Nicoletta, even if we didn't meet-cute."

She would soon be fifty-five years old and had never been swept off her feet or left breathless by a man until now.

"Funny," he said with a chuckle, "but you don't strike me as the speechless type."

"I rarely am, but you've succeeded."

"Is it possible you might find me interesting and exciting, too?"

"It's more than possible."

"I'd very much like to see where this might go. Would you?"

"I…" Normally, she'd be trying to find a way to let him down easy, but there was nothing *normal* about this man. "I believe I would."

His smile dazzled her, giving her the same feeling she got when she looked directly at the sun. He took her hand and kissed the back of it. "I only have one request if we're really going to give this a try."

"What's that?" she asked, sounding as breathless as she felt.

"I want you to make peace with your son."

DETECTIVE GIGI DOMINGUEZ had last worn her uniform at Skip Holland's funeral. One of the best parts of being a detective was that she could wear her own clothes. She'd found the uniform tight and restricting and didn't miss her days in Patrol when she'd had to wear it every day. She stood before the mirror in Cam's bedroom and took a critical look to make sure everything was where it belonged.

A low whistle had her spinning around to find Cameron standing in the doorway, with his arms crossed and gaze fixed on her. "Hot as *fuck*."

"Haha, sure. I've gotten flabby lately. I need to get back to the gym. The pants barely fit."

In the mirror, she watched him come across the room until he stood behind her, hands on her ass. "Don't say mean things about my favorite sexy cop. It annoys me."

She smiled at him in the mirror.

"Sexiest police officer in the history of sexy police officers."

"If you say so."

"I say so, and I've seen a lot of police officers. You've got them all beat."

"Thank you for the confidence boost."

He hugged her from behind. "You don't need me to boost your confidence. You're fine all on your own. You'll go in there today and knock their socks off with your poise and your certainty that you did everything you could to avoid having to use deadly force. If you focus on what you know to be true, you'll get through this."

Gigi leaned into his embrace, soaking up the love in every word he said to her. "You know what the best news is?"

"What's that?"

"No matter how this goes today, I get to come home to you and this and us."

"As much as I love what we have, I don't want to hear anything other than everything is fine, and you're cleared to go back to work."

She was fully aware that their relationship was riding on this hearing as much as her career was. Cameron would never be able to live with himself if she lost her career because of his ex-girlfriend.

Gigi turned to face him, placing her hands on his chest. "I was reading the report Gonzo sent on the Fortier case. It's very similar to what happened with Jaycee. Gordon Reilly told Tori Stevens he wanted to see other people in college, but she couldn't accept that. Gonzo is making a murder-for-hire case against Tori and the guy who did the killing. Just like you, Gordon had the right to tell Tori that he wanted something different. It was her choice to refuse to accept that. Now Rachel Fortier is dead, and Tori will spend most of her life in prison. What a waste it all is."

"It's funny that I've been working on that case and didn't make the connection to the similarities in our situation. But you're right."

"You did nothing wrong, and neither did Gordon Reilly or me with Ezra." Her longtime boyfriend had left her gravely injured after she'd told him she wanted to end their relationship. "We're all allowed to say when something isn't working for us. We're allowed to change our minds, to fall out of love, to take a different path."

"You're so fucking strong," Cameron whispered as he kissed her. "I love you, and I'm so, so proud of you."

"That means everything to me. I've got to go."

"I wish I could be there."

"I know, but it's better if you aren't. I need to stay focused, and you're a terrible, wonderful distraction."

His grin didn't quite reach his eyes the way it had before Jaycee attacked her, but she hoped it would again before too much longer. "Text me the second you get out of there."

"I will."

He picked up her hat and followed her out of the bedroom and down the stairs.

They took their own cars to HQ and walked in together.

Outside the morgue, Cam stopped her with a hand to her arm. "Love you," he whispered.

"Love you, too. Try not to worry."

He rolled his eyes. "Sure, no problem."

"I've got this."

"Don't let Offenbach throw you off your game. He blames Sam for his problems, but he knows it was his own fault that he got in trouble at home and at work."

"I can handle him." She stole a quick kiss. "Go to work."

He walked away, but he glanced over his shoulder twice before he disappeared around a corner.

"It's hard for him," Lindsey McNamara said.

Gigi hadn't seen her there. "It's excruciating. He blames himself."

"Which is too bad."

"I know," Gigi said with a sigh.

"I've worked with a lot of great women on this job. You're one of them. I wrote a letter to the IAB board to tell them that. I hope it helps."

A huge lump formed in her throat. "Thank you, Doc. That means the world to me."

"You did what any of us would've done under the circumstances. You defended yourself, and you survived. Stay strong."

"I will. Thanks again."

"My pleasure. I'm rooting for you to be back where you belong very soon."

"From your lips to God's ears."

Gigi left the kind medical examiner and headed upstairs to the IAB hearing room. "You must be Andy," she said to the attorney who stood when he saw her coming. She'd looked him up online so she'd recognize him.

He shook her hand. "Good to meet you in person."

"Thank you for being here."

"Of course."

They'd spoken several times on the phone and were ready to proceed, so they sat together to wait.

Captain Malone arrived a few minutes later and gave her a warm, reassuring smile.

Gigi was thankful to have him as her departmental advocate.

Twenty very long minutes later, Deputy Chief McBride came out of the room and gestured for Gigi to come in. She squeezed Gigi's arm, which helped to quell her nerves. Jeannie was a friend and an ally in this situation. Gigi had feared that Jeannie would be forced to recuse herself because of her encounter with Jaycee's mother, but the two incidents were being handled separately. Also, Jeannie hadn't been the one to shoot Jaycee's mother. Fairfax County SWAT detectives had done that.

Thinking about such things helped Gigi to stay cool as she

entered the room with Andy and sat in front of the three-person panel.

Officer Dylan Offenbach, who'd been busted from sergeant to Patrol after his transgressions, glared at her with barely contained contempt. He would be a problem, but she'd known that going in.

Jeannie began the proceedings. "We're here today to review the events of March sixth."

CHAPTER TWENTY-TWO

G igi listened to Jeannie's recitation of the events from the report Gigi had written, summarizing everything that'd happened from the second she returned from checking her mail to find Jaycee in her house. Much of it was hard to hear, especially details of the sexual assault. She kept her gaze down and focused on breathing as Jeannie got to the part where Gigi had backed up to her bedside table where her service weapon was kept, and with her hand behind her back, she'd withdrawn the weapon from the drawer and pointed it at Jaycee.

The minutes that'd followed were a blur as the two women had engaged in an epic struggle that had ended when Gigi shot Jaycee in the chest. In all the confusion, Gigi vividly recalled the moment she realized she wasn't going to die.

Captain Malone was next. "Detective Dominguez is one of the finest officers I've ever worked with or supervised. Her annual reviews have been stellar from both Patrol and Homicide. I have witnessed her struggle over what she had to do to save herself from Ms. Patrick's violent attack. The best officers are the ones who care so much that they punish themselves for doing what needed to be done. Detective Dominguez should be fully exonerated in this matter and returned to her position as soon as possible. Thank you."

"Thank you, Captain Malone," Captain Andrews said. "And

thank you for your attention to this matter, Detective Dominguez. I'd like to ask if you immediately recognized Ms. Patrick when you saw her in your home."

"Yes, sir. I'd seen her during an earlier altercation."

"Can you please describe that altercation?" Andrews asked.

"We were coming home to Cameron's place. She was on the stairs waiting for us. We'd gotten a protective order against her after she slashed Cameron's tires and made racially charged comments about me. She was in violation of the order, which we told her. Cameron told me to go inside so he could talk to her. I told her I was going to call Dispatch. I held off to give him a minute to deal with her, but I listened to what they said. I heard her tell him she was pregnant, and he said that wasn't true. He later told me it was another trick, another attempt to keep him tied to her."

"How did he know she wasn't pregnant?"

"He said it couldn't have been his because he hadn't been with her in months by then, and she'd be showing if she was pregnant with his kid. She threatened him, said he'd never see the kid, and he told her that if she was pregnant with triplets, that wouldn't matter to him. It was over between them. She said she couldn't believe he wanted me and not her. He said he loved me more than anything. That was..." She glanced up at the panel with a small smile. "That was the first time he said he loved me. Later, he said he hated that she was involved in that moment, but I didn't care. They were the best words I'd ever heard because I love him, too."

"Was Detective Green successful in convincing her to leave?" Andrews asked.

She wanted to ask why he hadn't read the reports. Maybe he had and he wanted to hear it from her. "We thought so, until a short time later when a brick came through the window and barely missed hitting us."

"I noticed in the reports that Ms. Patrick said she'd planned to marry Detective Green," Offenbach said, "but he was unaware of that. Is that true?"

"That's what Detective Green reported to me and others. He said they never once discussed marriage."

"So then how would she have gotten the idea that they were getting married?"

Gigi stared at him, uncertain of how she should answer that.

"I object to that question," Andy said. "There is no way Detective Dominguez could know what Jaycee Patrick thought or when she thought it."

"I agree," Jeannie said. "You can ask about what Detective Dominguez witnessed or heard, but you can't ask her what Jaycee Patrick was thinking or feeling."

"Very well," Offenbach said with a hard look for Gigi. "Were you seeing Detective Green while he was still dating Jaycee Patrick?"

"No, I wasn't. He'd ended his relationship with her before ours began."

"And you know that for certain?"

"I do."

"Is there a point to this line of questioning, Officer Offenbach?" Andy asked.

Gigi wanted to kiss him on the lips for asking the question she was thinking.

"I'm just trying to determine Ms. Patrick's motivation for confronting the detective."

"As the reports indicate," Gigi said, "her motivation was to get Detective Green to return to their relationship, after he'd told her that wasn't going to happen."

"Because of you," Offenbach said.

"No, because of him. He would tell you he'd realized it was over with her quite a while before he actually ended it."

"We'll have him come in to confirm the time line," Offenbach said.

"I fail to see how that's relevant to the matter before this board," Andy said. "Whatever occurred between Detective Green and his ex-girlfriend certainly had no bearing on my client or the incident at her home, which is why we're here.

The facts of that incident are irrefutable. Jaycee Patrick entered Detective Dominguez's home uninvited, threatened her, assaulted her and forced Detective Dominguez to defend herself in order to save her own life. Those are the facts in question here. What occurred—or didn't occur—between Detective Green and Jaycee Patrick prior to those events is irrelevant."

Gigi wanted to stand up and cheer for her on-point attorney.

"I'd like to know more about why you felt the need to use your weapon, Detective Dominguez," Captain Andrews said.

"As the situation in my bedroom evolved, Ms. Patrick became somewhat unhinged. That's the best word I can use to describe her demeanor. She dragged me upstairs, saying she wanted to see the place where I fucked her boyfriend—and those were her words, not mine. After she cut my clothes off me with a large knife, she pushed her fingers into me, saying she wanted to understand what I have that she doesn't. She... she said she wanted to know if my pussy was tighter than hers."

Gigi trembled as she recited the facts, feeling as if she were telling a story that'd happened to someone else. "Things went downhill from there. She got increasingly physical with me, swinging the knife around as she came toward me. I didn't think. I just went into survival mode by backing up to the table that housed my weapon." Her voice caught on a sob. "The last thing I wanted to do was kill her, but it was very clear to me that she would have no problem killing me."

"Thank you for your articulate recitation of the facts, Detective Dominguez," Jeannie said.

Gigi appreciated her kindness, knowing Jeannie had once been abducted and sexually assaulted on the job, so she understood better than most people would how difficult it was to talk about the assault, especially in a forum such as this.

"Are there any other questions for Detective Dominguez?"

"Just one," Offenbach said. "Detective, if you had this incident to do over with the benefit of hindsight, would you have done anything differently?"

Gigi glanced at Andy, whose expression was unreadable. "I... I've gone over it and over it a million times in my mind since that day, always looking for a way that this could've ended differently than it did, but I've never been able to see it unfold any other way. While I can't know for sure, it seemed to me that Ms. Patrick was very determined to kill me. If she couldn't have Cameron, then I wasn't going to have him either."

"As you mentioned earlier, it's not possible to know what Ms. Patrick was thinking," Offenbach said.

"No, it wasn't," Gigi conceded, "but I saw the way she was looking at me, as if she hated me more than anyone on earth and that it would be nothing to her to kill me. While I'd give anything for an outcome that didn't require me to fire my weapon or for her to be dead, I'm not sorry that I did what I had to do to survive. I love my life, and I'm thankful to still be here." She paused before she added, "I also want to say that I love my job and the people I work with. It makes me very sad to think about not being able to do the job I love anymore. If it comes to that, I'll be okay because I know in my heart that there was nothing else I could've done that day. That's all I wanted to say."

"Thank you, Detective Dominguez, for your candor and your courage in recounting such a traumatic event," Jeannie said. "We'll discuss this among ourselves and let you know our decision in the next few days. Thank you for coming in."

"Thank you for your time," Gigi said.

As she stood, her legs felt weak and wobbly.

"That went as well as we could've hoped," Andy said. "I think it's going to be all right."

She nodded to acknowledge Andy, but the lump in her throat made it impossible to speak. Whatever happened next was out of her hands.

CAMERON WAS GOING SLOWLY mad waiting to hear something from Gigi. It'd been two hours since they'd arrived at HQ. Surely, she must be done by now.

His desk phone rang with a call from an extension he didn't recognize. "Detective Green."

"Hey, it's Jeannie. The IAB panel has some questions for you. We wondered if you might come up to meet with us."

"When?"

"Now."

"Do I need representation?"

"Captain Malone and the attorney who represented Gigi have agreed to stay."

"I'll be right there." Cameron got up and went to Sam's office to check in with Gonzo. "IAB asked me to come up to answer some questions as part of Gigi's inquiry."

"Oh jeez. Do you have an attorney?"

"Andy stayed. Do you think I'll need him?"

"It never hurts to have him there. Good luck."

"Thanks."

This entire situation was beyond belief to Cameron. He'd spent his career building a reputation that was beyond reproach. The thought of his private life derailing the professional was surreal to him. He hated that the whole department—hell, the whole city—knew his personal business, that his ex-girlfriend had turned out to be a psychopath. He didn't use that word loosely. He could think of no other way to describe Jaycee's behavior from the minute he had kindly and gently told her that he was ending their relationship until the deadly confrontation in Gigi's bedroom.

What did it say about his judgment that he'd spent a year with Jaycee and never seen anything to lead him to believe she was capable of the things she'd done?

Everyone in his life had told him that what'd happened to Gigi wasn't his fault, but it sure as hell felt like it was.

Cam went upstairs to the second floor, his stomach in knots as he tried to anticipate what might happen at the hearing. He hadn't expected to be called to testify, even though Jeannie had warned him it was a possibility. He'd hoped that Gigi's testimony, on its own, would've been enough to shut down any further inquiry. However, Offenbach was the ringer in the mix, as he had a grudge against their squad and was probably enjoying the opportunity to retaliate.

Before he entered the room to which he'd been summoned, Cameron took a minute to breathe and calm himself. No matter what transpired, he could not and would not make this any worse for Gigi than it already was.

When he was as ready as he'd ever be, he walked into the room.

Andy Simone greeted him with a handshake. "Gigi did great. I think this is a formality to cover all the bases."

"Okay," Cameron said, feeling somewhat reassured.

"Detective Green," Jeannie said. "Thank you so much for joining us. Please have a seat."

Thankful for the presence of his close friend, he nodded to her and took the seat next to Andy.

Jeannie glanced toward Offenbach, confirming Cameron's suspicions. "Officer Offenbach, you asked to speak to Detective Green to resolve some outstanding questions. You have the floor."

"Detective Green, will you please tell us the timeline of your relationship with Jaycee Patrick and detail how it ended?"

"Of course. I met Jaycee through a friend and dated her for about a year before ending it months ago."

"Why did you end it?"

"Because I felt it had run its course."

"Was it also because you wanted to date Detective Dominguez?"

"My feelings for Detective Dominguez had nothing to do with my decision with Jaycee. I had known for quite some time that I wasn't happy with Jaycee and had waited for the right time to tell her it was over for me."

"And how did she react when you told her it was over?"

"Badly. She got very upset and screamed at me about promises I'd made to her that she would make me keep. I had never seen her behave the way she did that day. Her last words to me were, 'This is not over. This will never be over.'"

"Did you report her threats to anyone?"

"I didn't because I thought she was venting because she was upset. I never expected her to slash my tires, throw a brick through my window or attack my new girlfriend. In all the time I spent with Jaycee, I never saw any sign of that side of her. It was shocking, to say the least."

"Is it true that you'd asked Jaycee Patrick to marry you?"

"That's absolutely false. We never discussed marriage."

"According to her sister, Tanya, Jaycee had told her family you were engaged and even had a ring that she said you gave her."

"Not only did I never buy a ring for her, I never considered marrying her. As much as I enjoyed spending time with her, I didn't love her."

"Did you tell her that?"

"Only after she forced me to tell her the real reason I was ending things with her."

"Her sister told me Jaycee had a wedding venue booked."

"I found that out after I broke up with her. She never discussed that with me."

"It must've come as a shock to you to hear that," Jeannie said.

"To say the very least. That was when I first realized that something might be wrong with her in a medical or mental health sense."

"Did you alert anyone to your concerns?" Offenbach asked.

"No, I didn't."

"I'll bet you wish now that you had."

"That's enough, Officer Offenbach," Jeannie said. "The panel is directed to disregard that comment."

"If I may..." Cameron knew he ought to let it go, but how could he with so much riding on the outcome of this hearing? "I told her sister shortly after we split that I didn't propose to her or agree to a wedding venue or ever talk about marriage with her. I didn't specifically indicate a potential mental health concern, but I rather hoped her sister might realize something was wrong after I told her the truth. I felt like I'd done what I could to put them on notice of a possible problem. Her family was also aware of her actions after she slashed my tires and threw a brick through my window."

Jeannie glanced at Andrews and Offenbach. "Are there any further questions?"

The two officers shook their heads.

"Thank you, Detective Green," Jeannie said. "We appreciate your input."

"Of course, and if I may add... Detective Dominguez is an outstanding, dedicated detective with an incredible future ahead of her in this department."

Andy put a hand on his arm to stop him from saying anything else, which was just as well, because his voice was already wavering with emotion.

"That's all I wanted to say."

He got up and left the room with Andy.

"You did good, Cameron," Andy said. "I only stopped you so you'd quit while you were ahead."

"Thanks for being there and reining me in."

"You and Gigi have done everything you could. Now we just have to wait and hope it was enough."

Cameron would go mad waiting for the verdict.

He shook hands with Andy. "Thank you again for being here."

"No problem. I'll be in touch with next steps on responding to the lawsuit, but your testimony has given me an idea of how we might proceed."

"How so?"

"Jaycee's sister and family know about what she did with your tires and the brick. They know you didn't propose to her or agree to marry her. You told her sister you knew nothing about a wedding venue. There was indication of some sort of break with reality or delusional thinking that they either ignored or failed to properly address. We also have evidence of her mother acting erratically before the day she held Jeannie hostage. We can countersue them on those grounds."

"That feels a little dirty to me, if I'm being honest."

"I understand, but our goal is to get them to drop their suit.

If you countersue and show that you're willing to make their family's dirty laundry public, it might have them thinking twice about coming after you two."

"Let me talk to Gigi. I'll let you know about that."

"I'll wait to hear from you."

The two men shook hands. "Thanks again, Andy."

"No problem."

Cameron walked the attorney downstairs and said goodbye as Andy headed for the morgue exit, and then he went to the pit to get his head back in his job. Before he did that, however, he texted Gigi to tell her he'd been called upstairs to answer questions about his relationship with Jaycee. *It's all good, though*, he wrote. *Nothing to worry about.*

Thank you for doing that. I hate this.

Me, too. The waiting will drive me crazy.

Same.

Are we still talking to Dr. Trulo later?

Yes, he's coming by at seven.

I'll be home before then.

See you then. Love you. You're worth all of this.

I'm very lucky you think so. Love you, too.

CHAPTER TWENTY-THREE

G onzo came out of Sam's office to see that Cameron had returned. "How'd it go?"

"I think it was okay. Offenbach had questions about my relationship with Jaycee and the promises I made to her, which were none."

"Sam said that guy would be the ringer."

"She was right." Cameron rubbed the back of his neck, which was tight with tension. "Where are we, and what can I do?"

"Gordon is in the office. He's having a very hard time coping with what happened to Rachel. He's naturally blaming himself."

"I read the reports last night, and I really feel for him. He's living what could've been my worst nightmare with Gigi."

"That's an interesting point. Maybe you could have a word with him. He's in rough shape."

"Sure, I'd be happy to."

"Thank you. I'm waiting for Randy Bryant's attorney to arrive so we can talk to him. His prints match those on the pizza box that the PG County detectives found in the nearby dumpster, and the kid working the desk in the dorm has identified him as the guy who delivered the pizza to Rachel the night she was murdered."

"It's all coming together," Cam said. "What's the word from Stahl's?"

"More remains being recovered from his backyard."

"It's just unbelievable and believable all at the same time. I never worked with him, but after hearing all your stories, I guess I shouldn't be surprised."

"I worked with him, knew how horrible he was, but I'm still shocked by this latest development."

"I saw the news this morning. The whole world is coming for the chief on this."

"As if he wouldn't have stopped it if he'd known."

"I know. I never understand the rush to change the leadership at a time like this, when we need him more than ever."

"I don't get that either. He's the best possible person to guide us through these trying times." Gonzo stopped himself. "Maybe we should have a bunch of officers say that publicly."

"Probably couldn't hurt. Count me in."

"I will."

"I'll go talk to Gordon."

"Thanks, Cam. Keep me posted on what you guys hear from IAB."

"Will do."

Cameron stepped into Sam's office, where Gordon sat in one of the visitor chairs, staring blankly at the far wall. That he didn't even seem to notice Cameron had entered the small room said a lot about his state of mind. "Hey, Gordon."

The younger man glanced at him.

"I'm Detective Cameron Green. I work with Sergeant Gonzales and Detective Cruz."

"Hey."

"Do you mind if I sit for a second?"

Gordon shrugged. What did he care? The woman he loved was dead.

"I wanted to tell you that I understand a little of what you're going through. Something similar happened to me. My new girlfriend didn't die, thank God, but it was close. I just wanted you to know that I empathize with what you're dealing with and how guilty you feel."

"It's all my fault. Rachel would still be here if she'd never met me."

"It's not your fault, Gordon. You loved her. You never would've hurt her, and you had no idea Tori was capable of the things she's accused of doing."

"I've known her forever. I mean, I knew she was upset that I wanted to see other people in college, but to do this?" He shook his head. "How did I not see that?"

"Because she didn't want you to see it." Cameron realized that by talking to Gordon, he was helping himself, too. "I was with my ex for more than a year. I never saw anything but her sweet, accommodating side. After we broke up, I saw a whole new version of her. She'd reserved a wedding venue even though we'd never once talked about getting married."

"Whoa. That's effed-up."

"Sure was. I was shocked. And it just got worse until she took my new girlfriend hostage, assaulted her and forced my Gigi to kill her to save herself. It's been a nightmare. I came so close to losing Gigi, so I feel for you, man. I really do."

"It's the worst feeling to know Rachel is dead because she dated me."

"That's not why she's dead. It's because Tori couldn't accept your choice to see other people. That's on her, not you."

"Still..."

"Yeah, I get it. It's hard to not feel responsible."

"She was amazing."

"I'm so sorry you lost her."

"Thank you."

Cameron handed Gordon his business card. "Reach out if you need to talk to someone who understands."

"I will."

"As horrible as this is, it won't always feel this bad. Someday, you'll remember the good times, too. I promise."

"I hope you're right."

"Hang in there, okay?"

"Yeah, thanks again."

Cameron stood and squeezed the other man's shoulder before he left the room.

In the pit, Gonzo was talking to a man in a designer suit, who was a foot taller than Gonzo.

"There's no way you're pinning this on my client," he said in a thundering tone. "Do you have *any idea* who his father is?"

"Ask me if I care who his father is. The evidence has led us to your client, and he'll be charged accordingly."

"You'll regret this."

Gonzo stared at him without blinking. "I don't think so."

"We'll see about that." The lawyer turned and stalked off.

"Who's the father?" Gonzo asked when the lawyer was out of earshot.

"U.S. Representative Damien Bryant of Wisconsin's fourth district, representing Milwaukee," Cruz said.

"Well, that'll make for an extra shitty shit show."

"All our shows are shitty," Cruz said.

Gonzo grunted out a laugh. "True, but some are shittier than others. I wonder why the mother didn't tell me who the father was when she called. People tend to drop names at times like this."

Cruz clicked around on his computer. "Ugly divorce fifteen years ago followed by an uglier custody battle for Randy and his sister."

"Ah, that explains it. I'd better go brief the captain."

GONZO FOUND Captain Malone coming out of a meeting in the chief's conference room. "Could I have a minute?"

"That's about all I've got. We're fending off attacks from all corners since the chief's news conference about the Stahl case."

"How's the chief holding up?"

"He's resolute."

Gonzo followed Malone into his office and closed the door. "Two things. One, I'm hearing from a number of people that they'd like to make a statement in support of the chief from within the ranks. We'd like it to say that, at a time like this, the last thing we need is a leadership change."

Malone sat behind his desk as he pondered that. "I like it."

"We'll get to work on that."

"Keep it on the down-low until you're ready to go public with it. We'll make sure to use it to our full advantage. Great idea, Sarge. The chief will appreciate it."

"No problem. We thought it was important that the public —and the mayor and anyone else—hear it from the people who work for him."

"I couldn't agree more, but we need to act quickly. The pressure on him to resign is intense."

"We'll be quick. Second thing... We've pretty much got Randy Bryant nailed on murder-for-hire charges in the Fortier case. We'll be talking to him this morning. But there's a wrinkle."

"Isn't there always?"

"This is a big one. His father is a congressman from Milwaukee."

"Well, that doesn't change the facts, right?"

"No, it doesn't, but I wanted you to be aware that he's got a big-time lawyer talking about how he'll have our badges."

"Got it. Thanks for the warning."

Gonzo appreciated that the lawyer's empty threats had no effect on Malone. "I'll keep you posted."

"Thanks."

Gonzo left Malone's office and returned to the pit, where Cruz and Green were working at their desks. "Green light on the petition in support of the chief, but he wants us to keep it on the down-low until we're ready to go public. He said we need to act quickly."

"We'll get on it," Cruz said.

"What did he say about Representative Bryant?" Cameron asked.

"That who Randy Bryant's father is doesn't change the facts. Let's get him and the attorney in a room and get this one finished up."

"Do you want the AUSA?" Cruz asked.

"Yeah, give them a call and get someone over here."

Gonzo went into Sam's office and grabbed the case file that contained printed reports of everything they had so far tying Randy Bryant and Tori Stevens to the murder of Rachel Fortier. His phone rang with a call from a number he didn't recognize. "Sergeant Gonzales."

"This is Caroline Fortier, Rachel's mother."

"Yes, ma'am."

"I was wondering if there's any news in my daughter's case."

"We think we know what happened."

"Can you tell me? The not knowing... It's... Well, it's all just devastating."

"It's not official yet, but we believe that Gordon's ex-girlfriend—"

"The one who was harassing my daughter?"

"Yes. We believe she hired someone to kill Rachel."

"Oh my God. How does a college student have the money for such a thing?"

"She's from a wealthy family."

"Good Lord."

"We plan to charge them both with capital murder."

After a long moment of quiet, she said, "I thought maybe knowing why and how would help, but it doesn't. My daughter was a beautiful person, inside and out. She didn't deserve this."

"We'll make sure they pay for what they did to her."

"Thank you to you and everyone working to get justice for my Rachel."

"I'll be back in touch after charges are filed."

"Thank you again."

"I wish there was more we could do."

"What you're doing is very important to us."

After they said their goodbyes, Gonzo sat for a moment behind Sam's desk, thinking about people like Caroline Fortier and Graciela Blanchet and how they showed such enormous grace during the darkest time in their lives. People like them made this awful job so rewarding. Though justice would never bring back their loved ones, it would at least give them some answers.

With Mrs. Fortier in mind, Gonzo went to the pit to grab Cruz. "Let's get this sewn up."

JOE FARNSWORTH HAD SPENT most of his adult life dealing with the worst the world had to offer. Murderers, rapists, child abusers, animal abusers, drug dealers... You name it, he'd seen it. After the revelations about his former deputy chief had come to light, that Conklin had sat on information that would've solved Skip Holland's shooting years ago, he thought he'd seen the lowest of the lows within his department.

More than anything, Joe had been hurt by what Conklin had done to Skip and the rest of them by not coming forward with what he knew. In the case of Leonard Stahl, anger was his primary emotion. He had never been this angry. Not once in his entire life had he burned with this kind of rage or wished another person dead the way he did that guy. He'd never imagined wrapping his hands around another person's throat and squeezing until the life seeped out of him until recently. Now he dreamed about choking the life out of Stahl for what he'd done to so many innocent people while pretending to be a police officer.

It had all been for show. Joe realized that now. Stahl had never done the job the way he should have, but the rest of them had been too damned busy to notice. Who had time to police their fellow officers when the crime outside their building was more than enough to keep all their four thousand officers working nonstop to keep their city safe? He took his department's responsibility to the District residents as seriously as he took anything, not to mention the millions of tourists who visited DC every year. It was Metro PD's job to keep the public safe.

They had failed at that mission because of one man.

Stahl wasn't the only one who'd disappointed Joe. There'd

been others. More than he cared to admit. Overall, however, the good had far outweighed the bad.

Until now.

They'd had a serial killer in their midst and hadn't had the first clue.

No matter how his Public Affairs team tried to spin it, there'd be no escaping the dark cloud that Stahl had put over him and the department. Everyone who was anyone was calling for Joe's head on a stick. He'd been so stressed that his wife, Marti, had insisted he see his cardiologist to make sure he wasn't about to have a fatal incident.

His heart had checked out fine, but not surprisingly, his blood pressure was higher than it should've been.

Joe leaned forward and pressed the intercom that connected him with his faithful admin, Helen. "Can you please ask Jake to come in?"

"Yes, sir, right away."

He'd repeatedly told her she didn't have to call him sir, but she insisted on affording him the respect of his position.

Even if he didn't deserve it.

Five minutes later, he was still staring at the far wall of his office, not seeing anything but the red haze of pure rage.

A knock on the door forced him to blink as Jake came in.

"Hey, you wanted to see me?"

"I want to go to Jessup." Stahl was serving his two life sentences at the state prison in Maryland.

Jake stood with both hands on his hips. "Why?"

"I want to look him in the eyes and ask him why."

"What will that solve?"

"I don't know, but I need it. Will you come with me?"

Jake didn't want to. That was as obvious as the nose on his face. Joe and Skip used to tease Jake about being the handsome one in their group. Women had loved Jake, but he'd never wanted anyone but Val. That seemed like a hundred years ago now. Life had a way of kicking the innocence out of you.

"Yeah, okay."

"It's not an order."

"I know. When do you want to go?"

"Now. Right now."

"Give me ten minutes to tie up some loose ends. I'll meet you outside."

"Thank you."

"Sure."

In the past, Joe would've asked Skip to make a run like this with him, but Skip was gone, and Jake had tried his best to fill the massive void that Skip's death had created for Joe. Jake and Skip had been close, too, but not like Joe and Skip had been from the day they first met.

They'd been brothers to each other, and he'd give anything for Skip's wisdom and sage advice right now. He'd always known what to do. Even after his devastating injury, Skip had been Joe's go-to guy when he didn't know what to do about something.

Joe gathered his phone and keys, grabbed his jacket and headed out of the office. "I'm not sure if I'll be back today," he told Helen, "but I'll check in after a bit."

"I'll be here and will let you know if anything comes up."

As he started to walk away, he turned back to her. "Thank you, Helen, for a million and one things over the years and for your unwavering loyalty."

His comment seemed to catch her off guard, and for a moment, he feared she might cry. "Thank you, sir. It's an honor to work with and for such a fine man."

"I'm not sure I deserve such praise."

"You absolutely do, and don't let anyone tell you otherwise."

Now it was his turn to swallow a lump in his throat. "Thank you, Helen. I needed that."

"Any time you need to be reminded, I'm right here."

He gave her a nod and a warm smile before he walked away, thankful for the people he could count on. That number seemed to get smaller with every year he spent as chief of police. In six months, he'd become the department's longest-serving chief. If he made it six more months. With the way things were going lately, he'd be lucky to make it six more days.

He exited through the morgue to avoid the media gathered outside the main door. They were coming for his jugular lately, not that he could blame them. His department had handed them enough juicy stories to keep them satisfied for years to come. It wasn't that he didn't understand the impulse to blame the guy at the top. He got that. He really did. It was just amazing to him, he thought as he got into his department-issued SUV, that they didn't get that he would've done *anything* to stop Stahl's reign of horror.

If only he'd known about it.

If he had, there was *nothing* Joe wouldn't have done to stop him.

He'd said as much in multiple interviews as he expressed his anguish over the trail of heartache Stahl had left in his wake.

The passenger door opened, and Jake got in, bringing a blast of early spring chill with him. "Sorry to keep you waiting."

"I wasn't waiting long. Let's get this done."

CHAPTER TWENTY-FOUR

The two men didn't exchange another word until Joe had parked in a visitor spot outside the prison in Jessup.

"What's the plan?" Jake asked.

"I'm going to ask to see him and then try to get him to confess to what he's done so we can get answers for the families."

"What makes you think he'll just tell you?"

"Maybe he's proud of what he's done. Since he's serving two life sentences with no chance of parole, he might take perverse pleasure in spilling his guts."

"Are you prepared for him to tell us to go fuck ourselves?"

"I am." Joe waited to see if Jake had other questions before he reached for the door handle.

"Wait."

Joe paused and looked over at his friend.

"What if you're giving him perverse pleasure just by coming here and trying to get him to talk?"

"Then so be it. At least I'll have tried."

They got out of the car and went inside, showing their badges to the security officers.

"We'd like to see Leonard Stahl."

As they signed in, surrendered their weapons and walked

through the metal detector, the young officer asked, "You worked with him?"

"Unfortunately, yes," Joe said.

"He's a piece of work. Always getting into it with someone around here."

"That sounds about right," Jake said.

"I heard the latest. I'm sorry you guys are dealing with that. My dad was MPD."

"Who was your dad?" Joe asked.

"Keith Brady."

"I remember him. A fine officer. How is he?"

"He passed two years ago. Cancer."

"I'm very sorry to hear it." Joe withdrew his wallet and handed the young man a card. "If you have any interest in following in your dad's footsteps, let me know."

"Oh wow. Really?"

"Really. We're always in need of high-quality individuals to join our ranks."

"I'll definitely get in touch. My first name is Logan."

"I'll look forward to hearing from you, Logan."

Another officer appeared to escort them into the prison.

As they followed him, Jake glanced at Joe. "You're a good man, Joe. Don't let what anyone else has to say make you question that."

"Thanks. I try."

"You succeed more often than you fail."

They were shown to a room that had a glass wall down the middle of a row of tables with telephone connections to the other side.

"If you'll wait here," the guard said, "I'll get him for you."

"Thank you."

They waited for more than twenty minutes before Stahl was escorted in, wearing an orange jumpsuit that sagged off a frame that was much thinner than it used to be. He'd also lost most of what was left of his hair and had quit shaving. A large purple bruise took up most of his left cheek. The mean, beady eyes were the same as ever, though.

"To what do I owe the pleasure?" he asked with a smarmy grin after he picked up the phone. "I couldn't believe it when they told me the two stooges had come a'calling."

"I'm sure you've heard about what's going on at your house," Joe said.

"My sister is very unhappy with getting the boot, so yeah, I've heard. How'd you know to look there?"

"A little birdy told us."

"Could be one of so many birdies."

"Why'd you do it?" Jake asked.

"Because I could."

"You need to do better than that," Joe said, forcing himself to stay calm when he wanted to smash through the glass and follow through on his neck-squeezing fantasy from earlier.

"Why do I have to? What does it matter now?"

"It matters to the families of the women you killed," Joe said.

With his free hand, Stahl pretended to wipe away tears. "The poor, poor families who let their daughters grow up to be drug addicts and hookers. They got what was coming to them."

"No one deserves to be murdered," Joe said.

"You would think that. You sit in your ivory tower and worship your God on Sundays and always do the right thing. What a boring way to live."

"You think your way is better?" Jake asked. "How's prison life treating you?"

Stahl shrugged. "It's not so bad."

"We hear you're making as many friends in here as you did on the outside," Jake said.

The beady eyes narrowed. "I did just fine out there, and I'm just fine in here."

Joe pointed to his cheek. "Getting that must've hurt."

"You oughta see the other guy. So you fellas came way up here to see little ol' me, thinking I'd spill the tea on my dirty deeds simply because you asked me to?"

"We hoped you might still have a shred of decency left in you," Joe said through gritted teeth.

"Nah, that's been gone since long before you met me."

"What happened?" Jake asked.

Stahl shrugged. "What didn't happen? You guys were so chummy with each other, you never looked outside your own little circle to see what was going on with the rest of us. You never so much as once considered including me in anything."

"Because you acted like you hated our guts," Joe said, "and that was long before any of us got promoted over you."

"It wasn't an act. Do you think I haven't met other guys like you and Skip and Conklin? A bunch of frat boys having the time of your lives together while everyone else was struggling to get by."

"We were all making the same money."

"But it wasn't the same for the rest of us, was it?"

"Are you trying to tell me that you felt left out of the boys club, so you decided to become a criminal while wearing the badge?"

"It was so easy," Stahl said with a nasty smirk. "Candy from a baby."

"You still haven't said why," Jake said.

"Does it matter?"

"It might," Joe said, starting to lose patience.

"Do you remember Luke Starling?"

Joe sat up straighter. "What about him?"

"He was the first one to show me how there was a whole other world to be found for guys in uniform. People would pay for access, for favors, for just about anything they wanted or needed from us. And they remembered when you did them a solid. They were always happy to return the favor."

Joe felt sick. He'd liked Luke Starling. "Was he a killer, too?"

"Wouldn't you like to know? He was also the one who told me how you guys talked about me when you thought no one was listening."

"So we talked about you," Jake said. "That's what turned you into a murdering scumbag?"

"It made it easier not to care about the same things you do. And the killing thing? That didn't start here." Evil radiated off him in waves that Joe could almost feel, despite the thick glass between them. "Taking someone's life... It's the most natural high you can get, watching the existence seep out of them... I got addicted to the power the way your boy wonder Gonzales got addicted to drugs. After a while, you start to *need* it, to crave it. You wouldn't understand."

"Thank God that's true," Joe said.

"Ah, you and your God... You're too good to be true, Joe, and yet, all around you are flawed souls who can never live up to your pious expectations."

"My expectations have nothing to do with piety and everything to do with upholding the *law*—you know, the job we're *paid* to do!"

Jake's hand on his back was a reminder to keep his cool.

"Tell us where all the bodies are so we can bring some peace to the families," Joe said.

"Why would I do that?"

"Because it's the right thing to do."

Stahl threw his head back and laughed. "You're gonna have to do better than that. Why should I help you? I'm already doing life with no chance of parole for trying to kill your darling little niece."

"With one phone call, I can arrange six months in solitary confinement so you can think about where you buried the bodies."

The threat stole some of Stahl's cockiness. "That's cruel and unusual punishment."

"So is kidnapping and murdering for the fun of it and then leaving families to wonder for years what became of their loved ones. So is pretending to work cases and not even doing the most basic investigations. So is collecting a taxpayer-funded paycheck for doing nothing. Shall I go on?"

"You always were such a killjoy, Joe. Do you ever loosen that tight sphincter of yours and have a little fun?"

"What happened to your brother Michael?" Jake asked.

Stahl hadn't seen that question coming. His face lost all expression. "I have no idea."

"Really?" Joe asked. "So when we dig up your backyard, we won't find his remains?"

"No, you won't. I had nothing to do with his disappearance."

"We don't believe you," Jake said. "We think you know exactly where he is."

"Well, I don't, and I had nothing to do with any of that other stuff either."

"I'll be making that phone call about solitary the minute I walk out of here. Let me know when you're ready to talk." Joe put the phone down and stood. "Let's go."

When they were outside in the cool March air, Joe didn't slow down until he got to the SUV, where he stood for a long time as he processed the last hour.

"What're you thinking?" Jake asked.

"After I have him thrown into solitary, I want to rip his life apart from the second he was born until today. I want to know every single thing there is to know about him and every crime he's ever committed."

"That would take months, even years, and a ton of resources."

"I don't care what it takes. His victims deserve the truth. *We* deserve the truth, and I want you to handle it personally. Once we know everything there is to know about Leonard Stahl and his crimes? Then we'll retire."

SAM WOKE from a deep sleep to sun streaming through the window. She blinked several times before her eyes could cope with the glare, and then she took in the view of the dunes and the ocean in the distance. All her life, the ocean had called to her. From the first of many days she'd spent at Ocean City as a kid, to college weekends at Rehoboth and Dewey to Bora Bora to the recent beach trips with her own family, the sight of the ocean calmed and soothed her.

Their lives were a tilt-a-whirl of nonstop drama, demands and stress, but this... This was heaven.

She glanced over her shoulder to confirm she was alone in bed.

Nick was probably at his morning briefing, so she burrowed under the covers, hoping for a few more minutes of peace before she let in the world and its many problems.

How often did she get to lounge around in bed? Hardly ever, which made this sort of morning, the last one before their family arrived, feel that much more luxurious.

She had dozed off again when she felt the mattress sag behind her.

Nick snuggled up to her and put an arm around her, kissing her bare shoulder. "I thought something was wrong when I got back and you weren't up yet."

"Hmm, just enjoying the quiet while I can before the madness starts."

"How do you feel about breakfast in bed?"

"I feel very good about that."

"Coming right up." He kissed her shoulder again before he got up.

Nick returned a few minutes later with a mug of steaming coffee.

Sam sat up, pulling the sheet up over her bare breasts, and took the mug from him. "Thank you."

"My pleasure. My wife looks very well rested."

"Your wife loves it here."

"We should buy this place."

"No, we shouldn't."

"Why not? We love it here, and it has room for everyone."

"Why bother with owning it when we can rent it any time we want?"

"I suppose you're right."

"I'm the wife. I'm always right."

His smile was a thing of absolute beauty, the only view that could compete with the ocean for top billing. "I walked right into that trap."

"You're still new at this marriage thing. You've got plenty of time to improve."

"I'm glad you've decided to keep me around."

"What do I smell burning?"

"Oh shit."

She laughed as he bolted from the room to rescue breakfast. Sam loved that the president himself was attempting to cook breakfast for her. She wished the rest of the world could see the man she lived with and know his heart the way she did. They had no idea how lucky they were to have a man who cared so much about others as their president. He understood their struggles and wanted to make things better.

Her phone rang, bringing her back to reality. She took the call from Avery Hill. "Morning. How's our girl?"

"Better every day, although she's moving slowly. This baby had better be on time, or she might burst."

"We can't let that happen." Sam felt the old familiar pang of yearning to know what it might be like to carry a baby to term, even though she'd long ago accepted that her life was in no way conducive to caring for a newborn. Not that she'd object if it happened, but she'd accepted that it probably wouldn't.

"The reason I'm calling is to give you guys a heads-up that your mother-in-law's attorney has entered into plea negotiations on the federal and state charges. He's aiming for restitution, probation and community service. He'll probably succeed."

"I'm not sure what to think of that. As much as I want her locked up and sent away for forever, it's hard on Nick to have her in jail, even if she deserves it."

"I get that."

"Are people going to scream about her getting a sweetheart deal if she pleads out?"

"I'm not sure what the response will be. It's fairly common, as you know, to try to avoid trials with plea deals, especially in cases of first-time criminal defendants."

"It boggles my mind that this is her first time."

"First time she got caught, no doubt. There's one other thing..."

"What's that?"

"The U.S. Attorney in Cleveland passed along a request from the defendant to speak with her son."

"Isn't that highly unusual?"

"Highly, but he knows I'm personal friends with both of you, thus he reached out to me."

"That's not going to happen," Sam said as Nick came into the room carrying a tray.

"I thought you might say that, but I wanted to give you the message."

"Which you've done. Please respond accordingly."

"Will do. I'll see you tomorrow."

"See you then."

Sam slapped the phone closed with a loud, satisfying smack.

"Uh-oh. Who was that, and what did they say to piss you off?"

"Nothing." She forced a smile for him as he placed the tray on her lap. "This looks yummy."

"The toast is a bit well done."

"Just how I like it."

Nick went around to his side of the bed and stretched out next to her to share the meal. "Tell me what's wrong. Your eyebrows are all furrowed, and you're frowning. I don't like when my first lady frowns."

"I don't want to tell you, because you have enough to deal with. I took care of it."

He took a bite of crispy bacon. "Took care of what, Samantha?"

"Don't make me tell you. It's our last day alone, and I don't want to spoil it."

"If you don't tell me, I'll worry about what you're keeping from me."

"Ugh, I hate this!"

"I'm okay, love. Just tell me what's going on, and we'll deal with it the way we always do—together."

"Your mother wants to talk to you."

He froze midbite, his warm expression going blank. "Oh. About what?"

"Who cares what she wants to talk to you about? There's no doubt she's trying to use her connection to you to weasel her way out of this mess she's in. I want her nowhere near you."

"She has to know I can't do a thing to help her without making a mess for myself."

"I'll talk to her," Sam said. "Don't worry about it."

"Samantha... You shouldn't talk to her any more than I should."

"Let me find out what she wants, and we'll go from there. If she's asking for help with her legal problems, I'll shut that right down."

"You don't have to do this."

"Yes, I do. If she's slithering out from under her rock and coming for you, she'll have to go through me."

"I'm ridiculously turned on right now."

"Shut up."

"No, really. Look."

Sam glanced over to find him fully erect and lost it. When she came out of the laughing fit, he'd removed the breakfast tray and snuggled up to her.

"I fail to see why this is so funny."

That set her off all over again.

When she was otherwise occupied, he nudged the sheet aside and gently bit her nipple.

That startled the laughter right out of her. "Dirty trick, love," she said as she buried her fingers in his hair.

"Do I have your attention?"

"You do."

"Excellent." He moved closer and tended to both breasts before moving down to make sure she was fully on board with what he had in mind.

She was.

Twice.

While he kissed his way back up the front of her, she held

out her arms to him as he pushed into her. "Nothing is better than this."

"Nothing, and I still don't know how you do that."

He nuzzled her neck and made her shiver. "Do what?"

"You know."

"Say it."

"Make me come like a firecracker not once but twice."

"I love when you talk dirty to me."

"How is that dirty?"

"It's *so* dirty."

The third time, he was right there getting dirty with her.

Sam held him tightly as they came down from the highest of highs. "It's still funny that me dealing with your mother turned you on."

"Three orgasms later, and you're still laughing at me."

"I'm laughing *with* you."

"I wasn't laughing!"

"Because all the blood in your body was heading south so you weren't thinking clearly. Otherwise, you surely would've found it funny."

"Yes, dear."

"Aw, see? You're getting better all the time at this marriage gig." She patted him on the head the way she would an obedient puppy. "I think I'll keep you for another year."

"Oh phew. I was worried about whether my contract would get renewed."

"It was a close call, but the trifecta just now put you over the top for renewal. You'll want to keep that up to ensure a fourth year."

"I'll do what I can for my person."

"That's trademarked in all uses and formats."

He rested a hand on her face. "Thank you for this week. I needed it so badly. I need more of it in the future."

"Same. Let's make sure we get away together once in a while. The world will still function without us."

"Will it, though?"

They laughed.

"It'll have to," he said. "Because I'm taking more time alone with my wife, no matter who has anything to say about it."

"You won't hear me complaining. So what's the schedule for next week? Are we going to Fort Liberty?"

"I guess not. General Stern said she thinks it might be better if we didn't come right now."

"She actually said that?"

"Not to me, but to the Defense secretary. She said tensions are running high, so it might not be the best time for us to visit."

"When did you hear about this?"

"At yesterday's briefing."

"Why didn't you tell me?"

He raised his head from her shoulder. "Because it's... demoralizing. That the Joint Chiefs planted seeds of doubt about me that now have service members asking me to stay away." He shrugged. "What kind of commander in chief am I if I don't have the support of the military?"

"You are an amazing commander in chief, and you'll show them that in time. There may be a few people who have gripes with you, but I refuse to believe it's the entire military."

"Terry said the same thing."

"Terry is a smart guy, and so is your wife. You should listen to us."

That earned her a small smile.

"I know it's hard not to take these things personally, but you have to keep reminding yourself that two times you stepped up when your country needed you. You did what was asked of you, and you've risen to the occasion at every turn. Will everyone love you? Nope, but that's on them. If they knew you, *really* knew you like I do, they'd adore—" She stopped short. "Are you getting hard again?"

Nick gave her a cheesy grin and shrugged. "What can I say? My wife is hot when she defends me."

"I hope they never find out you're a sex addict."

"Only when my lovely wife is naked and saying nice things

about me. Or when she's breathing or sleeping or brushing her hair or—"

Sam kissed him. "You're a very silly commander in chief."

"Don't tell anyone that, okay?"

"Your secrets—all of them—are safe with me."

CHAPTER TWENTY-FIVE

The next morning, Chief Farnsworth came into the pit.

Gonzo startled at the sight of the chief. "Hello, sir. What can we do for you?"

"Are you holding Randy Bryant?"

"We are. We've built a case implicating him in the murder for hire of Rachel Fortier."

"You need to release him. Immediately."

Gonzo stared at the chief. "May I ask why, sir?"

"The directive came right from U.S. Attorney Tom Forrester. He said Bryant is to be released immediately."

"We can prove that he participated in a murder."

"Release him." The chief turned and walked away, leaving Gonzo staring at his back.

"What the fuck?"

"What happened?" Cruz asked.

"Farnsworth just ordered me to release Bryant. He said it came right from Forrester."

"Uh, we have the guy on murder for hire."

"I told him that."

"What're you going to do?"

Gonzo glanced at his friend. "The chief ordered me to release him, so that's what I'm going to do."

"But, Gonzo—"

"Believe me, I know. But what the hell am I supposed to do when the order comes from the chief himself?"

Cruz stared at him, looking as shocked as Gonzo felt.

"He didn't say anything about Tori, did he?" Cruz asked.

"No, thank goodness."

"What the hell is this?"

"I don't know, but I'm going to find out. Go release Bryant."

"I, uh, okay."

Gonzo was reeling as he went into Sam's office and called Captain Malone's extension. "I need to see you," he said when the captain picked up. "Urgently. Sam's office."

"On my way."

"Thanks."

Gonzo put down the phone and waited for the captain as a roaring sound echoed through his ears. He'd been ordered to free a murderer. That was definitely a first.

Malone came in and shut the door behind him. "What's up?"

"The chief just ordered me to release Randy Bryant. He said the order came from Forrester."

"What?"

"That's what we said, too. Cruz just went to see to the release. I'm not sure if the congressman father had something to do with it, but I thought you'd want to know."

"You're right. I want to know."

"So, um, we're still releasing him?"

"If the chief said to, then we are."

"And no questions asked?"

"I'll talk to him and see if I can find out more."

"What if Bryant kills someone else after we release him?"

"I don't know what to say."

"Tori Stevens is being arraigned again tomorrow on additional charges that she orchestrated the death of Rachel Fortier. What do I say when the judge asks who did the actual killing? Our case against her isn't as strong without him."

"You can still charge her with arranging it."

"It'll never fly at trial without the coconspirator, and you know it. What am I supposed to tell Rachel's heartbroken mother?"

"Let me talk to the chief. I'll be back to you shortly."

"And we're still releasing Bryant?"

Malone paused before he said, "Yeah, we are."

JAKE MALONE LEFT THE PIT, feeling as confused as Gonzales was about what was going on. He went to the chief's suite, where Helen was at her desk, even though it was an hour before her shift started He pointed to the chief's closed door. "May I?"

"Let me check." She picked up the phone. A few seconds later, she said, "Go ahead." As he walked toward the door, she said, "Jake."

She'd never once called him by his first name.

He turned back to her.

"Something's happening. I don't know what it is, but it feels... bad."

"How so?"

"I don't know. A vibe. I've never seen Joe so stressed. All this stuff with Stahl... I worry he's going to drop dead. His wife is worried, too."

That was more than she'd said to him in the more than twelve years he'd known her combined. Helen didn't tell tales out of school. "I'll talk to him."

"Thank you."

Jake knocked, walked into Joe's office and took a closer look than usual at his old friend. Helen was right. He looked rough.

"If you're here about the Bryant kid, I told Gonzo to spring him."

"Why?"

"Because Forrester said it was important."

"And that was enough to spring a kid we've got nailed on murder for hire?"

"In all these years, Forrester has never asked me for anything. He wanted the kid sprung. We sprung the kid."

"Joe... Are you serious? Our case against Tori Stevens isn't anywhere near as strong without Randy Bryant. Are you going to be the one to tell Rachel Fortier's parents that we let her murderers walk?"

"I..." He looked up at Jake. "The whole world is coming for me right now. Tom Forrester has always had my back. He said this was urgent, so you'll have to take it up with him."

"Don't mind if I do. Our Homicide detectives are upset, and with good reason. They've busted their asses to build this case, and now you're telling them to let it go? How do they live with themselves if they do that?"

"*How do any of us live with ourselves after the things that've already happened?*"

In the thirty years they'd been friends and colleagues, Joe Farnsworth had never yelled at Jake Malone. The outburst left Jake shocked and concerned.

"Joe..."

"Leave me alone, Jake. I gave an order. I expect it to be followed. That's it."

Jake left the office, slamming the door behind him to let his friend know his true feelings about his bullshit order.

"Is everything all right?" Helen asked as he walked by.

"No, Helen, it isn't all right."

He went straight to his office, grabbed his keys and left the building without a word to anyone. On the way to Forrester's D Street Northwest office, Malone called Sam.

The phone rang five times before she picked up, sounding winded. "Hey, Cap. What's up?"

"You won't believe me if I tell you."

"Okay..."

"The chief ordered Gonzales to release the guy who did the Fortier murder for hire."

"Oh my God. Why?"

"He said Forrester asked him to. I'm on my way as we speak to ask Forrester what the fuck is going on. We have much less of a case against Tori Stevens, who orchestrated this whole thing, without the guy who did the deed."

"Jesus. What's he thinking?"

"I don't know, but he just took my head off when I asked him that very question."

"Do you think I should call him?"

"I wouldn't. He's loaded for bear right now. He said the whole world is coming for him, and Tom Forrester has never asked him for anything in all the years they've worked together."

"I'm speechless."

"Right there with you."

"Let me know what Forrester has to say?"

"I will. Sorry to bother you on vacation."

"Please, don't worry about it. Of course I wanted to know about this."

"You might check in with Gonzo. He's beside himself."

"I can only imagine. I'll call him."

"I'll be back to you later."

"Okay."

Malone found street parking three blocks from the USA's office and hoofed it, keeping his head down against a cold, brisk wind. Spring was taking her own sweet time showing up this year. The cherry blossoms were behind schedule, putting everyone on edge about whether a late frost might doom them. He'd rather think about things like cherry blossoms than wonder what in the actual fuck was happening with the Fortier case.

Inside the U.S. Attorney's office, he was stopped by security.

He showed his badge.

"We'll need you to surrender your weapon to proceed into the building, Captain," the young security officer said.

Malone wanted to tell him where to go, but that wouldn't help his mission. He turned over his weapon, emptied his pockets and walked through the metal detector. "Where can I find Forrester's office?" He hadn't been there in years and couldn't recall.

"Third floor, to the left, the suite at the end of the hallway."

"Thank you."

While he waited for the elevator, Jake tried to calm his emotions so he could have a rational conversation with the man who prosecuted MPD cases. Under no circumstances could he lose his shit with Forrester.

He emerged from the elevator and followed the signs to Forrester's office, where a young man sat outside the door.

"May I help you?" he asked.

Jake showed his badge. "Captain Jake Malone with the MPD to see Tom Forrester."

"We don't have you on his schedule."

"That's because I don't have an appointment."

"Mr. Forrester is in meetings all day today. I'm only to interrupt him for an emergency."

"This is an emergency."

"Can you please tell me what you consider an emergency?"

"Your boss has ordered us to release a murderer, and I want to know why. I'm not leaving here until I see him."

The young man's Adam's apple bobbed in his throat. "Please have a seat."

"I'd rather stand."

"I, um, I'll be right back." He went into the office and closed the door.

Jake stared at that door so intently, his eyes watered as he fought the temptation to barge in there and demand the information he wanted. As five minutes passed and then ten, the temptation grew exponentially. He'd taken a step toward the door when the young man emerged.

"He'll see you, but he only has five minutes."

"That's all I need." Jake brushed past the guy and stormed into Forrester's office as the USA came around the desk with his hands up. "What the fuck, Tom? What the actual fuck?"

"I can't discuss it, Jake," Forrester said in his distinctive New York accent. He looked terrible, as if he'd been up for days. "I'm sorry, and please pass along my apologies to your detectives as well."

"What do we say to the victim's parents? They're calling every day to ask if we have the killer in custody. So far, we've been able to say yes, we do. But if we release Bryant, we have much less of a case against the mastermind."

"I'm sorry."

"I'm giving Rachel Fortier's mother your phone number so you can explain this to her."

"I can't tell her any more than I've told you."

"This stinks to high heaven. We find out the kid's father is a congressman, and the next thing we know, the USA is telling us to release the kid? What's going to happen when the media catches wind of this? Which they will, because the parents will go public."

Forrester ran a trembling hand through salt-and-pepper hair.

That's when Jake realized the other man was scared. "What the fuck is happening, Tom?"

"I can't."

They engaged in a visual standoff.

After a long moment, Tom blinked and looked away. "I'm sorry. Please tell your people..."

"Save it. This is fucking bullshit, and when it comes back to bite us in the ass, we'll tell the truth about what happened."

"Do whatever you need to."

"Unbelievable."

Jake turned and stormed out, brushing past the young man standing outside the door so quickly, he nearly knocked him over. In nearly thirty years on the job, he'd never experienced this level of outrage—and that was saying something. He called Sam.

"How'd it go?"

"I know as much after seeing him as I knew going in, except for one thing. Forrester is scared."

"Really? He's the most unflappable person I've ever known."

"That's my impression as well. Whatever this is, it's big."

"Are you going to release Stevens, too?"

"No," Jake said, deciding in the moment. "We'll do what we can to make a case against her without Bryant."

"That'll be tough."

"I know, but I refuse to let them both go. The order was for Bryant."

"A good defense attorney will get Tori's case tossed at preliminary."

"Her attorney is a boob. If the case against her gets tossed, it won't be by us."

"This is all so crazy."

"This might be the week that takes me right into retirement."

"Don't say that."

"I mean it. I'm as fed up as I've ever been. The day we start releasing murderers is the day I've had enough of this shit."

"Don't do anything hasty. Whatever is going on, it's not like Forrester to do something like this. Give him a minute to work it out. We can always detain Bryant again later."

"If we can find him."

"I'm so sorry, Cap, but please don't bail on us when we need you most. It's apt to get worse before it gets better."

"That's my fear."

"Do you think it has something to do with Stahl?"

"I have no idea, but it wouldn't surprise me. I've got to deal with the fallout of this disastrous decision. I'll talk to you later."

"Call if you need me. Any time."

"Thanks."

As he drove to HQ, he vowed to do everything they could to lock down the case against Tori Stevens. With Bryant or without him, they'd make sure she paid for Rachel Fortier's murder.

Scotty Cappuano had counted down to Friday all week. Well, he always counted down to Friday, but this week had moved more slowly than most. He couldn't wait to get to the beach and to see his parents. He knew it wasn't cool for a fourteen-year-old to miss his parents when they were away for one short week, but he'd waited a long time for parents. He really, really loved his. They were the best, and he'd missed them this week.

After he got home from school, he quickly packed the rest of his stuff and Skippy's. He put Skippy's harness on her and grabbed the dog seat belt they'd ordered online to keep her safe in the car.

As if she knew there was about to be an adventure, she was super excited, dancing all around him and nearly making him trip a couple of times as he finished packing.

Reluctantly, he grabbed his backpack with homework that needed to be done before Monday. If he saved it all for Sunday night, he'd hate himself. If he ever grew up to be president, the first thing he'd do was outlaw math, followed by homework.

He checked the clock on his bedside table. The twins would be home any minute. "Let's go downstairs, Skipster."

The dog faithfully followed him everywhere he went, even into the bathroom, which amused him to no end. You knew that someone really loved you if they wanted to go to the bathroom with you. She'd even go into the shower with him if he'd let her, but that's where he drew the line.

Having a dog was one of his favorite things *ever*. Her smiling, happy face greeting him every morning from her spot next to him in bed was the best way to wake up, even if he had to go to school.

He also loved having a younger brother and sister.

As he headed for the stairs from the residence to the first floor, he ran into Eli coming the other way.

And he loved having a big brother.

"Going to meet the kids?" Eli asked.

"Yep. You?"

"Gotta do it while I can."

"They love seeing you when they get home," Scotty said.

"They love seeing you, too."

Scotty had a bit of hero worship for Eli. He was the coolest guy ever, and Scotty got almost as excited as the twins did when their older brother was due home from college at Princeton.

"Can I ask you something?" Eli said as they went down the stairs together.

"Sure."

"Do the twins seem weird to you since I brought Candace home?"

Shit, Scotty thought. He'd wondered if Eli had noticed his siblings' frosty reaction to his wife. "Maybe a little?"

"It's more than a little. They won't even talk to her or look at her. What's up with that?"

"I think they might be jealous of her."

Eli stopped short and turned to Scotty. "Why?"

"Um, well... They used to have your full attention. Now they have to share you with someone else."

Eli rubbed at the stubble on his jaw as he contemplated that. "Aw, jeez. They don't have to share me. Candace is someone else to love them."

"They don't know her well enough to see it that way. Hopefully, in time, they'll come around, but if you're asking my advice..."

"I am. Of course I am."

Scotty felt seven feet tall to have someone like Eli ask for his advice. "I'd be careful not to be too... you know... cozy with her while they're around. Just until they get used to her."

"Ah, I see. That's a good point. We'll dial back the PDA a bit for now."

"That'd be good. You know you're like their whole world, right?"

"Not anymore. You and your parents are as important to them as I am. I get jealous that you guys have so much time with them."

"But you're the rock-star older brother when you come home." Scotty looked up at him, feeling shy when he added, "For all of us."

Eli gave him a warm smile. "I can never wait to see any of you."

"Amazing how families are made, huh?"

"It really is, and I'm thankful for you guys every day. I know my babies are well loved here."

"Don't let them hear you call them babies."

Eli laughed. "I won't. Don't worry. But that's what they'll always be to me. I was thirteen when they were born."

"I get it."

Eli gave him a quick hug that took Scotty by surprise. "You're the best." He ruffled Scotty's hair. "I'm glad my babies have you to keep them entertained when I'm not here."

Scotty fixed his hair, pretending to be annoyed when he was thrilled to be around Eli. "They keep me entertained, too."

"Here they are. Coming in hot!"

The twins came rushing through the door, dragging backpacks as their detail followed.

"Can we go to the beach now?" Alden shouted when he saw Eli and Scotty waiting for them.

Aubrey dropped to her knees to hug Skippy, who was very patient with them.

"Right now," Eli said. "Go put your school stuff away and grab your suitcases."

They went flying up the stairs, screaming with excitement for the weekend adventure.

"This is gonna be fun," Scotty said, excited to hang with his cousins, too. Technically, Nick's brothers were his uncles, but he thought of them more as cousins since he was older than them.

He ran up the stairs to grab his stuff.

It was time to get this show on the road.

CHAPTER TWENTY-SIX

S am wanted this taken care of before the kids arrived, so she'd asked Avery to set up the call with Nick's mother for noon. This was the last freaking thing she wanted to deal with any day, let alone when she was down to her final hours alone with Nick before the rest of the family joined them.

Nick was next door, attending his last meeting of the day, and even though they couldn't wait to see the kids, they were looking forward to a quiet afternoon before the chaos.

She sat on a barstool in the kitchen, staring at her phone, waiting for it to ring with a call from the last person on earth she wanted to talk to.

When the 216 area code popped up on her screen five minutes past the appointed time, Sam let it ring a few times before she picked it up. "This is Sam."

"It's me. Nicoletta."

Sam loved that the woman sounded nervous. Good. She should be. "What can I do for you?"

"I, um... I was hoping to talk to Nick."

"About what?"

"That's between my son and me."

"I'm afraid that's not how this is going to go. If you want to get to him, you have to go through me. You'll tell me what you want with him, and I'll decide whether that conversation happens or not."

"Does he know you're acting as his gatekeeper?" Nicoletta asked in a testy tone.

"He sure does. He said it was up to me, so make your case, and I'll decide."

After a long silence—so long, Sam wondered if she was still there—Nicoletta said, "I want to make amends."

"Could you be more specific?"

"For everything! For all the heartache I've caused him from the time he was born."

Sam had to admit she was surprised to hear Nicoletta admit she'd caused him heartache his entire life. "And how do you plan to do that?"

"I'd like the chance to apologize to him and to ask for a fresh start. I'd... I'd like to be in his life."

"What caused this sudden change of heart?"

"He's my son, and I love him."

Sam couldn't contain her snort of laughter. "You have a strange way of demonstrating your so-called love for him."

"I should've known you'd be like this," she said bitterly.

"Like what? Protective of the man I love? And when I say I love him, I show him that every day of his life, so he knows the difference between your kind of love and mine."

"Never mind."

"You're giving up kind of easily, aren't you?"

"What's the point? You'll never let me near him, so why bother wasting the time to convince you?"

"Why bother? Hasn't that been your motto all along? If you want things to change, you need to convince me you're for real, and that'll take some doing in light of the way you've treated him since the day he was born."

"I love him! I have always loved him. Was I ready to be a mother at sixteen? No, I was not. Did I fuck it up every which way? I did, and I regret that. I've always regretted that, but after a while, the cuts are so deep, there's no fixing them."

"So you set out to make the cuts deeper?"

"Not intentionally. I know you have no reason to believe me, but I mean that. I never meant to hurt him. He's... Well, he's the best thing I've ever done, even if I had nothing to do with him turning out the way he did."

Sam couldn't believe she was starting to believe the woman. "Is this because he's president, and you want to use his position to better your own?"

"No, it's not. I'm ridiculously proud of him. My heart swells every time I see him on TV, looking so handsome and commanding."

"Mine does, too," Sam said. "I love him more than anything in this world. More than my own life. He's the best person I've ever known, and that's saying something, because before him, I would've said my dad was. But Nick is even better than him, and my dad set a very high bar."

"He's been too good for the likes of me his whole life."

"Yes, he has. If I let you have access to him, I need to be certain you aren't going to cause him more pain. He's suffered over you being in trouble and in jail. He wished he could help you, even though he knew he couldn't do that and survive politically as well as ethically. So you need to be sure. If we let you in, you get one chance. If you fuck it up, that's it. Game over."

"I understand," she said, seeming as if she was speaking through gritted teeth.

"Do you? Because I mean it when I say I will personally make sure you can't hurt him. At the first sign of your usual bullshit, you're gone."

"I get it."

"I need to think about this and talk to him about it."

"How long will that take?"

"As long as it needs to. This is a big ask on your part."

"Fine. I'll wait to hear back from you, then."

"I'll let you know either way." She gave her phone a very satisfying slap closed, relieved to be done with that conversation.

She'd no sooner had that thought than Nick came in the

front door, smiling when he saw her.

He came over to kiss her. "Why are you all tense?"

"Because I just talked to your mother."

He straightened, going tense himself. "What did she say?"

"She wants you in her life and is willing to do whatever it takes to achieve that goal, including no longer being an asshole."

"Did you believe her?"

"She did seem somewhat... sincere. She said she loves you, has always loved you, and is so proud of you, her heart wants to burst from her chest when she sees you on TV as president."

"Oh, well... That's nice to hear."

Sam ached for the little boy inside him who'd waited his whole life to hear that his mother loved him and was proud of him. "What do you want to do?"

"That's up to you."

"No, babe," she said softly, "it's up to *you*. I'll support you in whatever you decide."

"Even if I decide I want to see her?"

"Even if."

"Let's go sit together. I want to hold you."

"Lead the way, my love."

He took her hand and walked them to the sofa, where he stretched out and brought her down with him, wrapping his arms around her. "That's better."

Sam rested her head on his chest and breathed in the familiar scent of home. "Much better."

"I know you don't want me to see her."

"I don't want her to hurt you. Whether you see her or not is entirely up to you."

"Would you be with me if I did?"

"Try and stop me."

His low rumble of laughter made her smile. "And you'd promise not to bring your rusty steak knife?"

"That's asking an awful lot of me."

"I know it is."

"Fine," she said in a dramatic tone. "If you insist."

"I'm afraid I do, as bloodshed in the Oval Office would be unseemly."

"You're not seeing her there. Anywhere but at the White House, which is exactly what she probably wants. We can go to the house on Ninth Street."

"Yeah, that would be better. As long as you'll be there, I suppose I could let her make her case."

Sam had known he'd say that even if she'd wished he would tell the woman to go away and stay gone. He didn't have that in him, which was one of a million reasons she loved him so much. "After I let her stew for a couple of days, I'll set it up."

"Not until after the Canadian PM's visit."

"Right. I'll tell her no Chanel No. 5 either."

"That'd be good. Thank you for running interference for me."

"Always."

GONZO WAITED for Kerr to arrive before he had Tori brought up to an interrogation room. An older man arrived with Kerr. He was tall, with gray hair and a distinguished air about him. "This is one of our senior partners, James Teller," Kerr said. "James, meet Sergeant Gonzales and Detective Cruz."

As Gonzo shook hands with the man, he was thinking, *Oh shit.* A senior partner would know what he was doing, unlike Kerr.

He led them to the interrogation room, where a Patrol officer watched over Tori, who was shackled at the hands and feet.

Freddie turned on the recorder.

Kerr introduced her to Teller.

"Are you going to get me out of here?" she asked the older man.

"I'll do everything I can for you, sweetheart. Try not to worry." To Gonzo and Freddie, he said, "Is it necessary for her to be shackled? Who's she a threat to?"

Gonzo looked at Freddie and gave a quick nod, authorizing him to uncuff her.

Tori rubbed her wrists dramatically.

It was all he could do not to roll his eyes. He had that urge a lot when he was with her.

"Now what we have here, fellas, is a misunderstanding," Teller said. "My client never met Rachel Fortier."

Gonzo put the pages of text messages sent from Tori to Rachel on the table, turning them so Teller could see them. "She may not have met her, but she harassed her for months after seeing a post on Facebook that linked the man she thought of as hers with Rachel. We asked Rachel's mother why she didn't block Tori, and she said her daughter wanted to be able to show Gordon how his ex-girlfriend was behaving, when the time was right. According to Rachel's mother, she thought Tori was pathetic, not dangerous."

Tori did not like being described as pathetic. Her face got very red, and her breathing deepened. The transformation was so complete that Gonzo could picture her arranging a murder.

Gonzo put a printout of the post that had started the trouble on the table. "After the Facebook post went live, Tori paid more than three thousand dollars for someone at GW to keep tabs on Rachel and to keep her posted on the status of Gordon Reilly's relationship with her. We believe Tori knew Randy Bryant from the Milwaukee area, where they both are from. Here are the canceled checks and the texts she exchanged with Bryant, as well as proof of a ten-thousand-dollar payment and a forty-two-minute phone call Tori had with Bryant the day before Rachel was found dead. We believe Tori and Randy made their plans to kill Rachel during that phone call.

"We also have an eyewitness who can put Bryant in Rachel's dorm at the time of her murder and can tie his prints to a pizza box that the eyewitness said he was carrying when he came to Rachel's dorm, and a print matched the one found on Rachel's neck. The medical examiner has determined that Rachel died because her carotid artery was compromised."

"So where is he?"

"His case is separate from Tori's." Gonzo made sure he never blinked as he held Teller's gaze.

"I'd like to speak to my client, please."

Freddie turned off the recorder as they got up to leave the room.

"That guy is no idiot," Freddie said when they were in the hallway.

"My thoughts exactly."

"Can we pull this off without Randy?"

"We're going to try like hell."

They waited a long time before Kerr came to the door to summon them.

When they were back inside, Freddie reactivated the recorder, again noted who was present and then sat next to Gonzo.

"We'd like to make a deal," Teller said.

"What kind of deal?"

"Tori will plead guilty to harassing and stalking Rachel, but that's it."

"That's nowhere near enough."

"That's our offer."

"I'm not sure if you're aware how this works, Mr. Teller, but we're the ones who offer deals, not you."

"You can't put my client anywhere near Rachel Fortier on the night she was murdered."

"Actually, we have a forty-eight-minute period in which she was somewhere other than Gordon Reilly's room. That time frame coincides with the time of death provided by the medical examiner. When we get the ping data from her cell phone, I believe we'll see she was either at or near Rachel's dorm at the time of the murder."

"You can't prove she laid a finger on that woman, so you can't charge her with murder."

"We can and will charge her with murder for hire and accessory to murder." Again, Gonzo met the other man's intense gaze. "Randy Bryant is prepared to testify that Tori paid him to kill Rachel."

Gonzo prayed that Cruz wouldn't react to the bald-faced lie.

To his credit, Cruz remained silent.

Gonzo had no idea if this gambit would work, but he was determined that someone would pay for Rachel's death. If he had to choose between Tori and Randy, he would've chosen her as the one who orchestrated it. "We'll consult with the AUSA and let you know what they're prepared to offer."

When they emerged from the room, Gonzo said, "Go see what you can do to slow down Bryant's release. We don't need him posting something about being released before we can nail this down."

"Got it. Thankfully, cell reception is almost nonexistent in the interrogation rooms."

"Let's hope so."

Gonzo went to Sam's office, closed the door and called Faith Miller. "This is Gonzo. I've got a situation, and we need to act fast. Can you help me?"

"Lay it on me."

He walked her through the latest developments.

"Are you saying that Tom Forrester, *our* Tom Forrester, ordered Bryant's release?"

"Yep, but Tori and her lawyers don't know that. If we move fast, we can get her to plead to murder for hire and accessory to murder and lock it down before they find out Bryant was released."

"I'll want seventeen to twenty years for that."

"Done."

"I'll write it up and get it over to you."

"Do you need Forrester's approval?"

"Probably, but I'm not going to ask for it."

"Thank you, Faith."

"Be right back to you. Will take me about fifteen minutes."

"I'll be watching for it."

Freddie appeared in the office door. "Bryant was released twenty minutes ago."

"Son of a bitch." Gonzo was regretting the cold pizza he'd had for lunch. He got up and headed for the door.

Cruz stepped aside to let him pass so he could retrieve a Tums from his cubicle.

"We've got a matter of minutes before this blows up in our faces."

"What did Faith say?"

"She needed fifteen minutes." Gonzo's phone rang. "This is her. Hey, Faith."

"I copied and pasted from an earlier case. It should be in your email."

"You're the best. I owe you one."

"It seems to me like we owe you one. I'll see what I can find out about why Forrester ordered Bryant released."

"Let me know."

"Will do."

Gonzo grabbed the plea agreement off the printer and glanced at Cruz. "Let's go."

CHAPTER TWENTY-SEVEN

While Sam waited for her guests to arrive, she took a walk through the house to make sure everything was ready for them. She'd spent the morning distributing towels and checking sleeping arrangements on the second floor of the house where they were staying as well as a house across the street where Angela and Tracy would stay with their families.

Scotty had texted to say they were on their way and again after they picked up Brayden and Brock in New Carrollton.

Nick had spent much of the day next door dealing with president things. She hoped he'd be back in time to greet the kids when they arrived.

She went downstairs to check the oven, where two huge pans of lasagna she'd made were baking. She'd also made blueberry muffins and chocolate chip cookies. After taking a bite of one of the cookies, she realized she should've let the White House bakery provide theirs. Before they moved out of the White House, she was determined to learn the secret to those incredible cookies, as well as the chicken salad.

When she was satisfied that everything was in order, she went to stand at the huge windows that overlooked the beach and the ocean in the distance. The weather would be ideal for the weekend, with temperatures in the seventies for the first time that year. She'd texted with Angela earlier and was looking forward to giving her, Jack and Ella a change of scenery. They hadn't been anywhere since that terrible weekend at Camp David during which Spencer had died in his sleep after taking illegally acquired pain pills poisoned with fentanyl.

Sam shuddered, recalling Angela's panic as she'd come into their cabin to say that Spencer wouldn't wake up. The nightmare day that'd followed, as they'd learned Spencer wouldn't recover, was one none of them would ever forget.

Sam wondered if or when they'd ever go back to Camp David. At some point, she needed to discuss that with Nick, because he'd loved it there before disaster struck. Maybe they could eventually return to the presidential retreat and try to make new memories there.

Her phone rang with a call from Avery Hill. "Hey, how's it going?"

"I thought you'd want to know that Shelby is in labor."

The news struck a note of panic in Sam. "Already? Isn't it too soon?"

"They said any time after thirty-six weeks is safe, and that's right where she is."

"Oh wow. Tell her we love her, and we can't wait to meet your little one."

"Me, too. It's all so... overwhelming. And I feel somewhat useless."

"Just hold her hand and keep telling her she's amazing. That's what she needs right now."

"I can do that."

"Call me later?"

"I will."

"Love you guys."

"You, too."

As Sam closed her phone, Nick came through the front door. "Shelby's in labor."

"Is that okay?" he asked.

"Avery said they said any time after thirty-six weeks is good to go, and she's right there."

"Well, that's a relief," he said before his expression changed. "Fuck. The state dinner."

"Oh jeez. Well, knowing Shelby, everything is set to go in a binder full of pink tabs and sticky notes."

"I'd better let Terry know."

"I'll hit up Lilia. Between the two of them, it'll be fine."

He gave her a kiss. "I hope so."

While he called Terry, she reached out to Lilia, her White House chief of staff.

"Hi there. How's the beach?"

"Gorgeous, but the vacation has been a bit more stressful than we expected."

"I know. I'm sorry."

"Did you hear Shelby is in labor?"

"I did. She was in her office when her water broke."

"Oh wow. Nick hates to think about work at a time like this, but he's concerned about the state dinner on Tuesday."

"She's given me everything I need to step in for her, so we're all set. I'm going to skip the beach this weekend so I can stay here and make sure everything is good to go."

"Thank you for that, but we'll miss you guys out here."

"We'll miss you, too. Rain check?"

"You got it. I hear a gaggle of voices outside. I think the kids are here. I'll talk to you on Monday—and thank you, Lilia."

"No problem."

Nick returned to the room. "Terry says Lilia's got it."

"Yep."

"I feel much better knowing that."

"Me, too."

The front door opened, and chaos erupted as four excited young kids came bursting through the door, all talking at once, as they dragged small roller bags and stuffed animals. Brayden had a pillow tucked under his arm.

Scotty, Eli and Candace followed, carrying more stuff, with Skippy bringing up the rear.

Sam and Nick hugged and kissed the kids and handed out room assignments.

"Can we go to the beach?" Alden asked.

"As soon as you stash your stuff upstairs and put on some shorts."

He took off like a rocket for the stairs, with Aubrey, Brayden and Brock in hot pursuit.

"They're bonkers," Scotty said as he allowed Sam to hug him again.

"I missed you so much."

"You were too busy kissing to miss me."

She bopped him on the head. "That is not true."

"The kissing or the missing?"

They shared a laugh that gave her the warmest feeling of joy she'd ever experienced. The joy that came from being his mother was different from all other kinds. "I really did miss you."

"Missed you, too, Mama. Now, which room is mine?"

When Gonzo and Freddie returned to the interrogation room, Gonzo was relieved that no one immediately accused him of being a liar, which meant their secret about Randy being willing to testify was still safe. He also noted that Tori had been crying, probably because her attorneys had told her she was fucked.

"The Assistant U.S. Attorney said this is a now-or-never deal." He put the page on the table so Teller and Kerr could read the charges against their client and the proposed sentence of seventeen to twenty years. "You've got ten minutes to take it, or we'll offer the deal to Bryant."

"What does it say?" Tori asked as tears streamed down her face.

"You'd be pleading guilty to murder for hire and accessory to murder and would serve seventeen to twenty years in prison." Teller spoke to her as if she were a little girl. "You'd be risking life in prison without the possibility of parole if we went to trial, sweetheart."

Tori wailed at the words *seventeen to twenty years in prison*. "I never touched her!"

"No, you paid someone else to do it, which is a felony." Gonzo's heart beat so hard, it was like a bass drum in his ears. It all came down to this. If Tori didn't agree to the deal, they might never get justice for Rachel.

She bent over the table, head on her folded arms, sobbing. "I can't go to prison. I just can't. I didn't do anything."

Gonzo looked to the two attorneys, hoping one of them would explain this to her.

"They have the man who can testify that you paid him to kill Rachel, honey," Teller said. "You'd be found guilty at trial, so you'll want to take this deal. If you behave in prison, you could be out a lot sooner and start your life over again. It's a good deal."

"Six minutes," Gonzo said.

Tori wailed louder.

Kerr squirmed in his seat as if he had itchy hemorrhoids or something.

The thought nearly made Gonzo laugh out loud. "Four minutes. Are we taking the deal to Randy, Tori, or do you want it for yourself?"

Her head whipped up. "What about what she took from me? Does anyone care about that?"

Gonzo looked her dead in the eyes. "No, we don't care about that. You took her *life* from her. It's not comparable."

"He was *mine*, and she knew it!"

"Two minutes, Tori. Take the deal or roll the dice at trial. We don't care either way."

Teller handed her his fancy pen. "Sign the deal, sweetheart. I promise you'll be all right."

Gonzo wanted to ask him how he knew that, but again, he didn't care. She would get everything she deserved and then some.

Tori took the pen and stared at the sheet of paper as tears fell on it.

Luckily, Teller noticed that and moved it out of the line of fire. He pointed to the line. "Right there, Tori."

Tori signed her name.

Gonzo and Freddie exhaled at exactly the same second.

Luckily, Kerr and Teller were dealing with their client and didn't notice their relief.

"We'll get this over to the AUSA and see you in court."

"Can I go home now?" Tori asked.

Gonzo stared at her, incredulous. "No, you can't."

"But I did what you wanted! I signed the paper."

"And confessed to two felony charges. You're not going anywhere for a very long time."

As Gonzo followed Cruz from the room, the sound of her shrieks filled him with satisfaction. They'd scored half a victory, and half was better than nothing.

He hoped Rachel's mother agreed.

When they were back in the pit, Freddie turned to him. "Holy. *Crap.*"

"Right?"

"I thought I'd have a heart attack waiting for her to sign it before Kerr got on his phone and saw that Randy was sprung."

"Same. My blood pressure was dangerously high."

"That was masterfully done, Sarge."

"Shut up."

Freddie laughed. "I mean it. It was!"

"Whatever you say."

"Listen, I'm not kidding around here. If you hadn't told her what you did about Bryant, she could've walked. I'm not sure I would've had that idea."

"Yes, you would have."

"Well, it never crossed my mind until you said it."

"I was praying that you wouldn't suddenly look at me or something."

"I had to stop myself."

They cracked up.

Malone came into the pit. "What's going on?"

Gonzo handed him the signed plea agreement. "We've got Tori."

"Great job, guys. I guess one is better than none."

"That's the thinking. I'll call Mrs. Fortier to update her."

"I'll get this back to Faith for you," Malone said. "Really well done. I was afraid the case would implode without Bryant."

"Sergeant Gonzales was masterful in making sure that didn't happen."

"Shut *up*, Cruz."

"He was," Freddie said again. "He totally nailed it."

"No, you can't have a raise," Gonzo said, embarrassed by his friend's effusiveness.

"Thank you both for a job well done," Malone said. "It's a relief to have a partial victory."

"I still want to know why we had to release Bryant," Gonzo said.

"You and me both," Malone replied as he headed to his office.

"I have to call the mother," Gonzo said.

"You want me to do that for you?"

"It's nice of you to offer, but I'll do it. Thanks for being my wingman in there."

"Always a pleasure, Sarge."

"If you hug me, I'll punch you."

"I'm not going to hug you. Go away. Make your call."

Laughing, Gonzo went into the office and shut the door. He sat behind the desk and sent a text to Sam before he made the call. *Got Tori to plead to MFH and accessory. 17-20 inside.*

He'd tell her the details later. It was better not to put such things in writing.

GREAT NEWS, Sam replied. *I was worried.*

That meant she'd heard about Bryant being sprung. They'd have *a lot* to talk about when she returned from vacation. *You and me both. Now I gotta call the mother.*

Hugs, friend. Thanks for all you do.

Sure thing.

Because it wouldn't get any easier if he put it off, Gonzo dialed Caroline Fortier's number and waited for her to pick up.

"Hello?"

"Mrs. Fortier, this is Sergeant Gonzales in Washington."

"Do you know what happened to my daughter?"

"Yes, ma'am," he said. "We do."

As he told her the story, she broke down into sobs. "We told her to go to the police about the harassment, but she didn't want to be involved with it. She said the ex-girlfriend was no threat to her, so what did she care?"

"By all accounts, your daughter was a wonderful person. Everyone in the dorm said the nicest things about her. I was struck by her roommate, Harley, saying they got off to a rough start that lasted all of a week because you couldn't *not* love Rachel."

"That sounds about right," she said, sniffling. "You said Tori hired someone. Will that person be charged, too?"

Gonzo closed his eyes as he said, "We're working on that part. I wanted to tell you about Tori, though. She was the mastermind."

"What does it say about me that I'm heartbroken for her parents, too?"

"It says you're a good person who didn't deserve to lose your wonderful daughter in such a senseless way."

"Thank you for that. It's very kind of you. We're not sure how to go forward from here."

"It's not the same thing at all, but I lost my partner on the job more than a year ago. All I can tell you is it's a one-day-at-a-time journey."

"I'm sorry that happened to you."

"Thank you. Another thing I'd tell you is to be careful relying on any sort of medicinal relief. That didn't work out well for me at all."

"Are you doing better now?"

"Much better, and grateful that my wife and colleagues stood by me during the struggle."

"I appreciate you sharing that with me. It helps."

"I know you're not local, but my boss—"

"You mean the first lady?"

"Yes," he said with a chuckle, "that's her. She and our department psychiatrist have started a grief group for the families of violent crime victims. I'll confess that at first I was skeptical, but I've been a few times, and it's helped. If you're interested, I could send you information about when and where the meetings are."

"I'd appreciate that. At some point, we'll have to come there to recover Rachel's belongings. Perhaps there'll be a meeting while we're there."

"Please feel free to get in touch any time, and I'll keep you apprised of the hearings, too. There'll be one coming up for the judge to approve the plea agreement."

"I'll look forward to hearing from you. Your mother must be very proud of you, Sergeant. Thank you again for your kindness to us during this terrible time."

"You're welcome," he said, touched by *her* kindness.

As he always did after closing a case, he marveled at the examples of incredible grace and resiliency he witnessed from victims' families. If someone killed his wife or son, he wouldn't respond with grace. That was for sure.

He shuddered at the mere thought of such a thing. He'd barely survived losing his partner. There was no way he'd survive losing Christina or Alex. And now there was a baby girl on the way who'd probably make him her bitch. He couldn't wait.

The thought of Christina made him want to talk to her. After he put through the call, he winced, realizing she was probably asleep.

"Hey," she said, sounding sleepy and sexy.

"Sorry to wake you."

"It's okay. I was dozing while watching TV. Another long one for you, huh?"

"Yeah, but we mostly closed the Fortier case."

"Mostly?"

"That's a long story. I'll tell you when I get home. I just have to write it up, and then I'll be outta here."

"There's dinner for you in the fridge."

"You're too good to me."

She snorted out a laugh. "It's nothing fancy."

"It is if you made it."

"Okay, then. We'll see what you think of it."

"I'll be home soon."

"I'll be here."

"Counting on that, babe."

"Are you okay, Tommy? You sound... off."

"It's been a heck of a day around here."

"When isn't it?"

"More so than usual today. I'll tell you when I see you. How're you feeling?"

"Fat, nauseated and swollen. You're going to throw me over before this is done."

"Never. I'd be nothing without you, and you know it."

"That's not true, but I'll let you say nice things about me." She yawned. "Sorry."

"Get some rest, babe. I love you."

"Love you, too."

He put down the phone, determined to get the reports done so he could get home to her. It wouldn't matter that she was asleep. Being near her was enough to bring him the kind of peace and comfort he needed after a hellish day like this one.

Freddie came to the door.

"I thought you'd left."

"Randy Bryant has been murdered."

CHAPTER TWENTY-EIGHT

T hey were quiet as Gonzo drove them across town in his car. The words *what the fuck?* cycled through his mind on repeat. Four hours after Randy had been released from their custody, he was dead. How was that going to come back to haunt them and everyone who'd been involved with his release?

"Will this tank our deal with Tori?"

Gonzo gripped the wheel tighter. "I don't know. It might. She signed it thinking we had Randy to testify against her. I took a chance lying to her, and now it's blowing up in my face."

"We've still got plenty to tie her to Rachel's murder."

"But now she and her attorneys will know we don't have the smoking gun."

"Yeah."

Gonzo's stomach churned with heartburn and an overall sick feeling over how a case that'd seemed somewhat simple at the outset had blown up in their faces. He called Malone over the Bluetooth. "Cap, we have a problem."

"What now?"

"Randy Bryant has been found murdered down by the river."

"Come on. You've got to be kidding me."

"I wish I was."

"What the fuck is happening here?"

"No idea, but we're on our way. I'll update you later."

"Send me the address. I'll meet you there."

"Cruz is texting it now."

"Thanks."

The line went dead.

"I'm glad he's coming," Gonzo said. "This feels above our pay grade."

"Right? A congressman's son is arrested on murder-for-hire charges, then the USA orders us to release him, and now he's dead, all in the scope of a couple of days."

"This is crazy even by our wide definition of the word." Gonzo's phone rang, and he took the call from Sam. "Hey."

"How's it going?"

"You won't believe it. We released Bryant's son and now he's been murdered."

"Whoa. I can't get my head around this."

"Right there with you."

"Keep me posted."

"We will."

"WHAT NOW?" Nick asked after she ended the call.

She glanced toward the stairs to make sure the kids were still upstairs getting washed up for dinner after an hour on the beach. "Remember how Forrester ordered us to release Randy Bryant, the congressman's son?"

"What about it?"

"The son has been murdered."

"Whoa. Didn't he just get sprung today?"

"About four hours before he was found dead."

"Oh shit."

Sam bit her thumbnail as she pondered the fallout. "They used the threat of him testifying to make a deal with the woman who masterminded the murder for hire."

"Will that deal fall apart now?"

"It could. A judge hadn't signed off on it yet."

"Crap. If you need to deal with work, I can feed the troops."

"That's okay. Gonzo and the others are on it. There's nothing I can do from here."

Angela, Tracy, Mike and their kids arrived just as Sam was preparing to serve dinner. "You're right on time," she said as she hugged her sisters, brother-in-law, nieces and nephews.

"What's up, Flotsam?" her nephew Jack asked with a big grin that revealed a missing front tooth.

"Not much, Lo-Jack, and what happened to your tooth?"

"The tooth fairy needed it. I got five bucks!"

"Five bucks? That's outrageous, Jack-o-Lantern."

"Tell me about it," Angela said. "It was a tooth fairy shakedown."

"It's inflation," Jack said as he ran to greet Scotty and the other kids.

"How does he know about inflation?" Nick asked with a laugh.

"This is what happens when we send them to school," Sam said.

Angela nodded as she poured a glass of the decaffeinated iced tea Sam had brewed for her. "School is the root of all evil if you ask me. He's learned words I thought I wouldn't hear from him for *years*."

"Oh no," Sam said as she tried not to laugh.

"Oh *yes*."

"It's possible he might've heard some of them from me."

"Sam!"

"What can I say? I love a good swear word."

"What's my beloved done now?" Nick asked as he reached for a Sam Adams in the fridge.

Angela glared at her sister. "It's possible she's taught my sweet, precious, innocent Jack some naughty words."

Nick laughed as he kissed the top of Sam's head. "Yes, it's very possible. We're working on it. Scotty's got his college paid for thanks to the swear jar."

"You're supposed to be on my side, mister," Sam said.

"I'm on the side of truth, babe."

Angela laughed.

Sam hadn't realized how much she'd needed to see her sister laugh the way she used to before disaster struck.

"What?" Angela asked when she caught Sam watching her.

"It's nice to see you laugh again."

"Feels good to laugh. Keep it coming this weekend, okay?"

"I'll do what I can for my people."

WHOEVER HAD KILLED Randy Bryant had sent a message. He was unrecognizable. If it weren't for the red Vans sneakers, Gonzo wouldn't have been sure it was him, but the student ID confirmed it.

The body had been dumped behind a warehouse by the Potomac.

"Who called it in?" Gonzo asked the Patrol officer who'd met them.

"Night security guy." The officer pointed to a man being tended to by EMTs. "He's shook up because he recognized those red sneakers. The victim's dad owns the place, so he's seen him around."

As they walked over to talk to the security guard, Gonzo glanced at Freddie. "Find out where Congressman Bryant lives locally."

Freddie pulled out his phone and got to work.

"You found the body?" Gonzo asked the older man, who was indeed shaken up. He had white hair and a ruddy complexion that indicated he either worked outside a lot or was a big drinker. Gonzo wasn't sure which it was.

He wiped tearful blue eyes with a tissue a female EMT handed him.

"What's your name?"

"Dennis Coughlin." He dabbed at his eyes. "Kid can't be more than twenty years old. I got grandsons that age. Who could've done such a thing?"

"Are there security cameras down here?"

"Only in the front."

So whoever had dumped Randy there had known they wouldn't be seen. "What goes on at this place?"

"They fabricate parts for ships or something like that. I'm not really sure."

"How long have you worked here?"

"About six months. Thought it would be an easy retirement gig. Now I'm not so sure."

"Have there been other incidents that were concerning or questionable?"

"Nothing like this, but they're secretive about what goes on inside the big building. We're told to stay out of there. Our job is to work the perimeter and keep out trespassers."

"What's the name of the company?"

"Capital Retrofitters."

"Who do you take orders from?"

"Gavin Daugherty, the director of security."

"Where can we find him?"

"He's not here. I can give you his number."

Gonzo wrote down the number Dennis provided from his phone. "Did you call him to tell him a body had been found on the premises?"

"I texted him. I haven't heard back."

"So you're the only one here tonight?"

"Yes."

"Did you see anyone back here?"

"I didn't see anything. All I can tell you is when I did my eight o'clock rounds, he wasn't there. When I came back around at nine, he was."

"Do you follow the same routine on every shift?"

"For the most part. We all do."

Gonzo handed him a business card. "Have your boss give me a call."

"I'll tell him."

Freddie went to meet the medical examiner team.

After Gonzo took down Dennis's address and phone number, he asked the EMTs if he was okay to be released.

"His BP is very high, Sarge."

"Why don't you take him in, just to be sure?"

"That's not necessary," Dennis said. "I'm not supposed to leave the place unattended."

"It's crawling with cops, and I'd feel better if we had a doctor look at you." Gonzo didn't want the man dropping dead on his watch. "Better safe than sorry."

Dennis released a deep sigh. "If you say so."

Gonzo nodded to the EMT, who helped Dennis get settled in the back of the ambulance. "If you think of anything else I should know, you've got my number."

After the ambulance pulled away, Gonzo called Captain Malone. "I'm at the scene where Bryant was found. Someone is sending a message with the way this kid was killed. I wouldn't have recognized him if he hadn't been wearing the same sneakers he had on earlier. Student ID in his pocket confirmed his identity." He told him everything he'd learned from the security guard.

"What're you thinking?"

"Do we know who picked him up when he was released?"

"I'll find out."

"We need Crime Scene here. Is anyone available?"

"Haggerty has released most of his team back to regular duty while the forensic people do their thing at Stahl's. I'll send them over."

"After we get them started, Cruz and I will pay the father a visit." It also occurred to him that he'd have to call Bryant's mother, who'd seemed sweet and sincere when she'd told him Randy was her whole life. God, he wasn't looking forward to that.

"Damn," Dr. Byron Tomlinson said as he stood over the bloody body. "Do we have a positive ID?"

"Randy Bryant," Cruz said. "Age twenty, a student at GW, originally from the Milwaukee area."

"Any clue what landed him here?"

"Nothing solid yet," Gonzo said. "But a time of death would help tremendously."

"I'll get it for you as soon as I can." Byron gestured to his team to prepare the body for transport. "Did I hear this kid was in our custody earlier on the murder-for-hire case but was cut loose?"

"You heard correctly," Gonzo said.

"Is that going to be a problem?"

"Your guess is as good as mine, man."

"The father lives in Adams Morgan," Freddie told him.

"As soon as Crime Scene arrives, let's pay him a visit."

ON THE WAY to Adams Morgan, Malone texted Gonzo to say someone named Hal Summers had picked Randy up when he was released from custody. Gonzo handed his phone to Cruz. "Figure out who that guy is."

Two minutes later, Cruz said, "He's Bryant's chief of staff and a longtime operative in Wisconsin politics."

He took a call from Malone. "What's up, Cap?"

"I just got off the phone with Tori Stevens's attorney. Apparently, the word is out about Randy being dead, and they plan to contest the deal."

"Great." Heartburn made Gonzo's chest burn. "How did they hear about Randy?"

"I asked, but he refused to say."

"This entire case stinks like ten-day-old dog shit."

What had seemed like a simple murder-for-hire case—or as simple as such things ever were—had descended into chaos.

"We'll be skinned alive when the media catches wind that we had him in custody, released him and now he's dead, along with our case against Tori Stevens," Gonzo said.

"The release isn't on us," Malone said. "The USA will have to explain that one. I'll give him a heads-up to let him know Bryant is dead. Call me after you talk to the congressman."

"Will do." Gonzo ended the call, feeling as tense as he had in longer than he could remember. He hated the thought of their case imploding, especially when he was covering for Sam while she took a much-needed vacation. He didn't want her coming back to a mess that she'd have to help clean up, even if it wasn't a mess of their making.

"I've seen a lot of crazy crap on this job," Freddie said. "But Forrester ordering us to release Bryant is right up there."

"I know. Nothing about that makes sense. Since when are we in the business of letting murderers walk out the door?"

"It makes me think Bryant's father has something on Forrester," Cruz said.

"That's a possibility. But what would a congressman have on a U.S. Attorney?"

"Who knows? Could be anything."

"It's weird, though. Randy was arrested a couple of days ago, and his father has enough on Forrester to get him to order Randy released? How does that happen?"

"I have no freaking clue."

JAKE WASN'T SURPRISED to find Joe still in his office long after nine o'clock. He'd heard that Marti had brought him dinner and made him eat it before she left. Joe had barely said a word on the ride back to town after their visit with Stahl, but he'd made the call to request that Stahl be moved to solitary confinement to contemplate his sins.

Maybe some time in the hole would give him a conscience.

Jake wasn't optimistic about that.

"What's up?" Joe asked.

"Randy Bryant has been murdered."

"The guy Forrester ordered released?"

"Yep."

Joe's reaction was one of exhaustion mixed with disbelief. "No way."

"According to Gonzales, whoever did it sent a message. The kid was nearly unrecognizable."

"Have you told Forrester?"

"I wanted to ask you how you want us to handle him."

"I'll call him. He better be ready to explain this, because I've got enough to deal with without getting blamed for this, too."

"There's one other thing."

"I'm almost afraid to ask."

"The deal with Stevens may be in jeopardy. Word is out that Bryant is dead, and her attorneys are claiming that nullifies our deal with her."

"The hell it does. We've got her nailed on murder-for-hire charges with or without Bryant's testimony."

"Gonzo told them we had him and he was willing to testify. Now they know that wasn't true. They say that nullifies the deal, since the threat of Randy's testimony was the thing that convinced Tori to take it."

"Can we prove she was the mastermind of the plot to kill Rachel Fortier?" Joe asked.

"Yes, but—"

"No buts. The deal goes forward."

"I'll talk to Faith about it."

"Thank you."

"Let me know what Forrester has to say."

"I will."

Jake returned to his office feeling more unsettled than he had since they'd found out Conklin had known all along who'd shot Skip—and why. Something else was happening, and he had no idea what. He didn't like the not knowing. He called Faith Miller's cell number.

"Hey, Cap. What's up?"

"Have you heard that Randy Bryant, the guy Tom ordered us to release earlier, was murdered?"

"What? No. Oh my God."

"Have you heard any more from Tom about why he ordered the release?"

"I haven't been able to reach him. I've tried for hours, but he's not picking up on either of his phones."

"Do we need to send someone to check on him?"

"I'm not sure what to do. I just got off the phone with my sisters, and we agreed to give him another hour to get in touch before we sound any alarms. He told his assistant he was leaving for the day around six, which is early for him, but he could've had a meeting outside the office. The weird thing is no one is picking up his home phone. I tried his wife's cell, and it went right to voice mail. It's odd for them to be off the grid. They have two daughters in high school. Tom jokes about how he and his wife, Leslie, are their bitches."

"Something isn't right. Since when does a U.S. Attorney order a murderer released, and then the guy turns up dead a couple of hours later? Not to mention the dead guy is the son of a U.S. congressman. And now we can't find the USA."

"I agree. It's weird."

"I'll send my detectives to his house. Do you have an address?"

Faith recited the address, which was in Gaithersburg.

Since it was so far out in the suburbs, he decided to call Gaithersburg police to ask for a wellness check at the Forrester home.

"I'll be back to you," he said to Faith. "Let me know if you hear anything."

"I will."

Jake called his equivalent in the Gaithersburg Police Department to request the wellness check.

"Tom Forrester, you said? The U.S. Attorney?"

"Yeah, but keep it on the down-low, will you? We're not sure what's going on. He's off the grid and so is his wife, which his team tells us is highly unusual."

"I'll send some officers out to take a look and get back to you."

"Thanks, Cap."

"No problem."

Jake returned to Joe's office to update him. "Do you think we should notify the Feds?" Jake asked.

"And tell them how Forrester ordered us to release a murderer, and now the kid is dead? I'd rather keep that to ourselves until we figure out what the hell is going on."

"Right. I'll let you know what Gaithersburg comes back with."

"I'm going home. Call me with any updates."

"Sure." Jake started to leave, but something had him turning back. "Are you okay?"

"Never better."

"If I can do anything…"

"You're doing all you can, and I appreciate it. I'll see you in the morning."

As Jake watched his good friend walk away, noting the hunch of his shoulders, he hoped that everything he was doing would be enough.

CHAPTER TWENTY-NINE

Gonzo and Freddie arrived at Congressman Bryant's home to find a crowd gathered outside that included several beefy-looking security guys with earpieces. Since when did congressmen have such a robust security presence? Most of them complained about not being able to afford DC residences while maintaining homes in their districts. As he gazed up at the fancy townhouse, it was clear that wasn't an issue for Bryant.

They showed their badges, and Gonzo introduced them. "We'd like to see the congressman."

"He's not taking visitors right now," one of the guards said.

"We're not visitors. We're cops, and we want to see him."

"He's not available."

"Let me tell you how this works. We ask to see him, and you get him for us, or we go to a judge and swear out a warrant for his arrest. Unless you want to see your boss on the eleven o'clock news in handcuffs, you'd better go tell him we're here." Gonzo consulted his watch for the time, which was creeping toward ten o'clock. "You've got five minutes to produce him."

The other guard used his chin to tell the first one to go get the guy.

"Thank you," Gonzo said to him after the first guy went inside.

"Used to be on the job. I get it."

"Whereabouts?"

"New Haven."

Five more minutes passed before the first guard returned with another man, who Gonzo assumed was the congressman. It had better be him. The guy was about five eight with a mostly bald head and a red complexion, as if he'd been drinking or crying.

"I'm Damien Bryant. I understand you're asking to see me?"

"That's right. Can we talk inside?"

He glanced back toward the house. "Um, sure. I guess."

They followed him past the two security guards, up the stairs to the townhouse. Once inside, it was clear from the roar of voices that a crowd had gathered.

"In here," he said, leading them to a small room off the foyer.

The security guards brought up the rear and stood outside the door after Bryant closed it, sealing them off from the noise.

"Who are all the people?"

"Friends, colleagues, supporters. They came when they heard about Randy."

"How did you hear about Randy?" Gonzo asked.

"A friend called."

"How did he or she hear?"

"I'm not sure." He ran a trembling hand through what was left of his hair. "I still can't believe it. My son..."

"Here's the thing, Mr. Bryant." Gonzo deliberately refused to call him Congressman. "Randy's body was found less than an hour ago, so how did you or anyone know Randy was dead?"

"I'm... I'm not sure how they knew."

"You didn't ask where *they* heard the news?"

"All I heard was that my son was dead. After that..." His eyes filled, and he looked away. "I'm sorry. I'm in shock."

"U.S. Attorney Forrester ordered your son released from MPD custody earlier. Do you know why?"

"I have no idea. I had only learned that Randy was in

custody when I heard he'd been released. I figured it was some sort of mistake."

"What's your relationship with Forrester?"

"I don't know him."

"If we learn otherwise later, we can charge you with obstructing a homicide investigation. So I'll ask you again, what's your relationship with Forrester?"

"I, uh... I'd like to consult with my attorney."

"Then you'll have to come downtown with us to wait for him."

"Is that really necessary?"

Gonzo stared at him without blinking. "It really is."

"I'll need to tell the others I'm leaving."

"I assume your guards can take care of that for you. And why does a congressman from Wisconsin require private security anyway?"

"I need to consult with my attorney."

"Let's go," Gonzo said, resigned to a long night.

MALONE CALLED when they were on the way to HQ with Congressman Bryant in the back seat. His security detail was following in a separate vehicle since Gonzo had refused to allow them to ride in his car.

Gonzo took the call from Malone off the Bluetooth so they wouldn't be overheard.

"No sign of Forrester or his family at the Gaithersburg house."

"He doesn't have security?" Gonzo asked.

"Apparently not. I'm trying to track down his personal assistant to see what he can tell me. I've also got a call into the FBI and the U.S. Marshals."

"We're on the way in with Bryant's father."

"The congressman?"

"Yep. We're meeting his attorney at HQ."

"I see how it is. I'll let Joe know that the congressman will be our guest."

"Good idea."

"See you when you get here."

"Could you ask Faith to come in?"

"Will do."

As he drove the rest of the way to HQ, Gonzo was certain they were missing something big. When they were stopped at a light, Cruz showed him his phone where he'd typed a message saying the same thing Gonzo was thinking.

"Same."

What, though???

Gonzo shrugged. He had no idea and was no closer to understanding it than he'd been earlier. The Fortier case was solved, as far as he was concerned. He was able to tell her parents what had happened to her and why. But if Randy Bryant's mother asked him why her son was dead, he wouldn't be able to tell her.

Not yet, anyway.

When they arrived at HQ, Cruz escorted Bryant into an interrogation room to await his attorney's arrival.

Gonzo went into Sam's office to call Rosemary Bryant. She sounded sleepy when she picked up the phone.

"Ms. Bryant, this is Sergeant Gonzales with the MPD."

"I hope you're calling to tell me you made a big mistake arresting my son."

"No, ma'am, that's not why I'm calling. Your son was released from custody earlier today, and I'm sorry to have to tell you that he was later found murdered."

"That's not possible."

"I'm sorry, ma'am, but we've confirmed it's him."

"My son is asleep in his childhood bedroom as we speak. I'm looking at him right now. I picked him up at the airport two hours ago."

Then who in the hell was in their morgue, and why did the congressman think his son was dead?

"Ma'am, we have Congressman Bryant in our custody. He's under the impression that his son has been killed."

"I'm sure he thinks that because he orchestrated it as it

would mess up everything for him to have his son charged with murder. I've learned to be one step ahead of him and ensured my son was picked up by someone I trust when he left police custody. At my instruction, he dropped Randy at Reagan National Airport for the flight home. I'm not sure who's been killed, but it's not my son."

Gonzo felt like his head might explode. *What the hell?* "Thank you for that information, ma'am, and I'm sorry for the confusion. I'm glad to hear your son is all right." If for no other reason than it made him available to testify against Tori.

"Whatever's going on, Sergeant, I promise you my ex-husband is smack in the middle of it."

"That's good to know."

"There is nothing that man won't do to gain and keep power, even kill someone else to make it appear his own son was dead."

A chill went down Gonzo's spine at the thought of doing such a thing. Where would they have found someone with Randy's general build and hair color, wearing the same sneakers Randy had on when he was released from custody?

"Thank you for the information, ma'am. Please keep your son there until you hear from me."

"Don't worry. He's not going anywhere."

"I hope you understand that despite being released earlier, he's still facing serious charges here in DC and may need to turn himself in to keep from making things worse. If he'd be willing to testify against the ringleader of this murder for hire, he may be able to reach a deal for immunity. But that deal will have a time limit attached to it."

"I'll get him back there in the next day or two. You have my word."

"I'll hold you to it."

As he put down the phone, Malone and Faith came to the office.

Gonzo waved them in. "You won't believe what I just learned."

"What?" Malone asked.

"That's not Randy Bryant in our morgue. He's in Milwaukee with his mother, sleeping in his childhood bedroom."

"Then who the hell is in our morgue?" Malone asked.

"I have no idea."

GONZO WENT to talk to Byron Tomlinson. "Our guy from tonight just became a John Doe."

"I thought you had an ID."

"So did we, but it's not him. They bashed his face in, so we'd assume it was him based on the student ID in his pocket and his signature red Vans."

"Why would someone want you to think one guy was dead when it wasn't him?"

"Maybe to get a kid off a murder-for-hire charge. We've got a congressman in the interrogation room who thinks his son is dead, and it's possible he ordered the hit on the son. But the mother, who's bitterly divorced from the father, says the son is asleep in his childhood bed in Wisconsin."

"What the fuck?" Byron asked.

"That's the question of the day. If you could work on getting me an ID of John Doe, that'd help tremendously."

"I'm on it. Hopefully, his prints are in the system. I'll let you know."

"Thanks, Doc."

When Gonzo returned to the pit, Cruz met him with a printout of information about the congressman.

"Give me the summary."

"He's serving his tenth consecutive term, has several influential committee assignments and is cozy with the leadership. He's a big Second Amendment advocate, a supporter of cutting Medicare and Social Security and is active in a number of organizations that support veterans. His constituents seem to like him. He spends a lot of time at home in Wisconsin, courting their favor, showing up to local sporting events and high school stuff. He's very much a presence in his district.

"The divorce from the wife, fifteen years ago, was ugly, as was the custody battle that followed for five-year-old Randy and seven-year-old Lauren. In the end, the ex-wife got full custody, and he got visitation. I went back a year on his social media and don't see a single mention of his kids, which leads me to think they might've been estranged. One other interesting thing—for the first time since he was originally elected, he's facing a very significant primary challenge from a younger guy who says he's tired of business-as-usual politicians who talk a big game at home and then do their own thing in Washington. The polls have them tied, with five months until the primary."

"Interesting. So he's fighting for his political life even though he's everything to everyone in his district, but has no relationship with his kids. Is there anything you found linking him to Forrester? Because how is there *not* a connection there?"

"I couldn't find any connection between him and Forrester."

Faith came up to them. "That's because the connection was confidential." She held up a sheaf of papers held together by a binder clip. "Tom was investigating him for campaign finance irregularities at the request of the attorney general. He'd been asked to keep it confidential and to handle it personally."

"How'd you find that out?"

"Through inside channels. The info is legit. I can attest to that."

"Huh," Gonzo said. "So let's take this one step at a time. The AG asks Forrester to investigate Congressman Bryant for possible campaign finance irregularities, but asks Forrester to see to it himself. Is that unusual?"

"Highly," Faith said. "The U.S. Attorney rarely tends to cases on his or her own without staff involvement. Almost everything is assigned to an AUSA."

"Okay, so Forrester digs in, Bryant's son is arrested, Forrester orders us to release him, Forrester and possibly his family go missing, a kid who is supposed to be Randy Bryant turns up dead, and the real Randy Bryant is in Wisconsin. Have I missed anything?"

"That about sums it up," Freddie said as Faith nodded.

"Let's go have a talk with the congressman."

"What's the plan?" Freddie asked.

"We'll let him dig his own hole before we tell him what we know."

CHILDBIRTH TOTALLY SUCKED. As her labor extended into a tenth hour, Shelby tried to remember why she'd thought it was such a good idea to have a second child at age forty-two. She was too old for this and was feeling every second of her age as the agony wore on.

An epidural had saved her sanity, but it had slowed things down, as she'd been told it might.

Poor Avery was a wreck, but he hadn't left her side for more than a few minutes since they arrived. Their sweet Noah was with Shelby's sister and asking every five minutes if his baby had come yet.

Shelby would be a mother of two if this little one ever decided to appear.

"Is it normal for it to take this long?" Avery had run his fingers through his hair so many times, it stood straight up.

"Come here."

"I'm here."

"Closer."

He leaned in close enough for her to fix his hair. "My mama was in labor with me for thirty-six hours."

"Come on. How is that possible?"

Shelby shrugged. "The baby comes when the baby is ready."

"Is that why you're late for everything?"

"No," she said on a laugh. "Noah is why I'm late for everything. I was never late once in my life before he arrived."

"Should I expect that to get worse when we have two?"

"Most likely."

He kissed her. "Good thing I love you so much."

"It's a very good thing."

"In case I forget to tell you later, you're a badass at this childbirth thing."

"I don't feel like a badass. I feel exhausted."

"You're doing great."

The doctor came in a short time later, did yet another internal exam and declared her ready to push.

Things kicked into high gear after that.

After Noah, the process was familiar, but still scary.

Avery was right there to hold her hand, to prop her up when she felt like she couldn't do it and to be the first one to see their baby when she finally made her appearance at ten o'clock.

Shelby and Avery cried as they beheld the face of their little angel.

"She's absolutely perfect," Avery said. "As pretty as her mommy."

"No, she's prettier. We have a little girl, Avery."

"I heard."

"What's her name?" a nurse asked.

"Meet Maisie Rae Hill," Shelby said. "Named after my grandma and Avery's."

"That's a beautiful name for a beautiful girl," the nurse said.

"Thank you." Shelby looked up at her husband. "We have a son *and* a daughter."

"Yes, we do, and I couldn't be happier or more in love with my sweet little family. But tell me this... Will she wear any color other than pink?"

Shelby gave him a saucy look. "What do you think?"

Gonzo entered the interrogation room to find the congressman with another man sitting next to him. The lawyer had white hair and a stern countenance.

"I demand to know why my client is being detained at a

police station on the day his son was murdered," the lawyer said.

"Your name?"

He put an embossed business card on the table in front of Gonzo. "Jason Fallow."

Gonzo recognized the name of the prestigious firm and noted that Fallow was a partner.

Freddie started the recorder and recited the names of the people present.

"Your client is here because he was unable to tell us exactly how he heard his son had been murdered when the body hadn't even been found yet," Gonzo said.

"I told him I don't know!" Bryant said.

"You don't know how you heard your son was killed?" Fallow asked him.

Clearly, Bryant hadn't been expecting that from the lawyer.

"One of my people told me."

"You'll have to do better than that, Mr. Bryant," Gonzo said.

"I can't remember who said it. I was in shock. It was devastating news."

"Did you ask U.S. Attorney Forrester, who was personally investigating you for campaign finance irregularities, to order the MPD to release your son after he was detained as part of a murder-for-hire investigation?"

He *really* hadn't been expecting that.

Bryant's mouth flopped open and then shut just as quickly.

"What I'd like to know is what you have on Forrester that would've made him do such a thing while he was investigating you?"

Bryant gave him a defiant look. "I don't know what you're talking about."

"Sure, you don't."

"What're you accusing my client of?" Fallow asked.

"I'm not sure yet, but I've got a body in my morgue and a U.S. Attorney missing along with his family. I'm thinking your client knows exactly where the USA is, and he knows what happened to his son because he ordered the hit."

"I did no such thing! He was my *son!*"

"When was the last time you saw Randy?" Gonzo asked.

"A few weeks ago, when I told him I was cutting him off because his spending was out of control. We argued. He didn't think it was fair that I wasn't going to help him anymore while he was in college."

"Perhaps that's why the ten thousand dollars Tori Stevens was willing to pay him to kill Rachel Fortier looked good to him," Gonzo said.

"My son didn't kill anyone!"

"Actually, he did, and we can prove that."

"Well, it doesn't matter now. He's gone." Bryant dropped his head into his hands. "It's devastating."

"With a significant primary challenger giving you a run for your money, it must've been upsetting to have your son facing charges in a murder-for-hire plot."

"Yes, it was upsetting, but not because of my career."

"When had you seen Randy before your meeting about his spending? Had it been a year? Two? Five? Longer?"

"I don't know. It'd been a while."

"Was that because your kids don't speak to you anymore after you divorced their mother and fought her for custody of them, even though you live mostly in Washington these days?"

Again, his mouth did that flapping thing.

"Where's Tom Forrester?" Freddie asked.

"How would I know? I barely know him."

"But he was causing you some grief with his investigation, wasn't he? And then he orders your son released from custody when we've got him nailed on murder charges. How is that a coincidence?"

"I'd like to confer with my client," Fallow said.

Freddie turned off the recorder and followed Gonzo from the room.

"There's no doubt in my mind the congressman is up to his neck in this whole thing," Gonzo said. "I want to talk to his security guy. The one who was on the job."

"I'll put him in a room."

Cruz returned ten minutes later. "He's in interview two. His name is Kent Sanders. Faith is in observation, and I have a Patrol officer coming to stand outside the room to make sure the congressman stays put."

"Thanks." When the Patrol officer arrived, Gonzo said to Cruz, "Come with me to have a word with Sanders."

They burst into the room, taking the larger man by surprise. He looked nervous. Good.

"Mr. Sanders, we believe the congressman was involved in his son's murder and the disappearance of U.S. Attorney Tom Forrester and his family. What do you know about that?"

"You forget that I know how this works, Sarge. I'm not saying shit without an attorney."

"Well, we know the congressman is up to his eyeballs in this, and he's conferring with his attorney now. He's probably going to tell us he wants a deal, after which he'll toss the people who helped him commit his crimes under the bus. I assume the bus will run over you and your sidekick first after he starts talking. But that's fine. If you want to leave it in his hands..." Gonzo and Freddie headed for the door.

"Wait."

Gonzo bit back a smile as he turned back to him.

"What would my deal look like?"

"That'll depend on what you tell us."

Sanders crossed his hands on the table and then stared down at them. "I'll tell you everything, but I want immunity."

"Stay with him," Gonzo said to Cruz as he went to talk to Faith.

She met him in the hallway. "I'll give him immunity. I want to know where my boss is."

Gonzo nodded and reentered the room. "Immunity has been granted by the AUSA."

"I want to hear it from them."

Gonzo went back to the door to admit Faith. "This is Assistant U.S. Attorney Faith Miller."

"I'll give you full immunity from prosecution, provided you

tell us where USA Forrester and his family are and who arranged the hit on Randy Bryant."

Rather than return to the observation area, Faith stayed in the room.

"Bryant was losing his shit over the investigation into his finances, and then his son was arrested. The arrest was big news back home. He's fending off his first serious challenger and the guy is gaining in the polls. He asked us to pick up Mrs. Forrester and her daughters and put them up in hotel for a few days."

"Where are they?" Faith asked.

"At the Washington Hilton. We were told to take good care of them, which we've done."

"I'm notifying the FBI to go get them," Faith said as she typed on her phone.

"Forrester was told to go to work as usual, to pretend nothing was wrong and to tell the AG there's no case against Bryant. And then Randy was arrested, and the congressman completely lost it. He told Forrester if he ever wanted to see his family alive again, he'd order the MPD to release Randy. Then he told us to pick up Randy and deal with him."

"And you took that to mean murder him?" Gonzo asked.

"Yes."

"No one questioned that he was ordering the murder of his own son?"

"He hated the ex-wife and his kids for making him look like a shitty husband and father."

"Which he was."

Sanders shrugged. "It wasn't my job to judge him."

"When your boss ordered you to commit murder on his behalf, did either of you balk at the order?"

"I said I wouldn't do it. I don't do murder."

How honorable that he has limits, Gonzo thought. "But someone else on your team was willing?"

"For fifty large, yeah."

"Who was it?"

"Aaron Peterson."

"Where will we find him?"

"At the congressman's place."

Gonzo glanced at Freddie. "Don't go alone."

"I won't." Freddie got up and left the room.

"What's a congressman from Wisconsin into that requires him to have full-time security?"

"What isn't he into? Gambling, guns, prostitutes and drugs, mostly. He's in deep with one of the Mexican cartels, and he's constantly afraid they'll kill him. That's where we come in."

"What would you say if I told you the person Aaron Peterson killed wasn't Randy Bryant?" Gonzo said.

That seemed to genuinely surprise Sanders. "It wasn't?"

"Nope. It was someone posed to make us think it was Randy, with his trademark red sneakers, and his face bashed in so we couldn't be sure."

"I can't explain that. Does the congressman know it wasn't Randy?"

"I'm not sure what he knows."

"Maybe Aaron got cold feet or something."

"Or maybe he wanted the congressman to *think* his son was dead when he wasn't, so we'd do exactly what we're doing by hauling him in here and making him explain himself."

"Maybe. The congressman is an asshole. We all hate him, but we like the money, so we put up with his shit."

"You'll have to testify to all of this in court," Faith said.

Sanders looked at her without blinking. "That's fine."

"Where's Tom Forrester?" Faith asked.

"I honestly don't know."

"Take me through the whole thing, from the top," Malone said as the clock edged closer to midnight.

"Forrester was investigating Damien Bryant for campaign finance irregularities at the behest of the AG. Bryant knew the investigation would bear fruit, so he had Forrester's wife and daughters 'detained' until Forrester reported to the AG that there was nothing to the investigation. Then his son was arrested, and he completely freaked out when the news broke back home, where he's facing a formidable challenger. He demanded that Forrester get his son released or his family would be harmed."

Malone crossed his arms as he processed the details. "That explains why we were told to release him."

"I feel better knowing Forrester was protecting his family," Gonzo said, "and not out of his goddamned mind."

"The congressman also ordered his security people to 'deal' with the son, except they killed someone else. The son is in Wisconsin. I'm waiting for Tomlinson to tell me who's in the morgue."

Tomlinson walked into the pit. "He's a well-known drug dealer named Zachery Calder. His prints were in the system from multiple arrests."

"Let me find out if he was one of the congressman's guys," Gonzo said.

He returned to the room where Sanders waited. "Does the name Zachery Calder mean anything to you?"

"Yeah, Z is one of our guys. Why?"

"He's the one Aaron killed instead of Randy."

"Oh, come on. No way."

"Way. Stay here."

Gonzo returned to the pit. "Sanders has identified Z as one of their guys." He went into Sam's office, found his notes on the place where Randy Bryant lived and called the number he'd been given for Randy's roommate.

When the guy answered, Gonzo introduced himself. "I was wondering if anyone came there today saying they needed some of Randy's clothes to bring him in jail."

"Yeah, a guy named Aaron came by and said Randy needed some of his stuff. I let him in."

"What did you give him?"

"He asked for his student ID because he needed a second form of ID for the cops, T-shirts and a pair of the red Vans that are his favorite. Randy has several pairs of those."

"Thank you."

"Hey—I heard Randy was dead. Is that true?"

"Just a rumor. He's with his mom in Wisconsin."

"Oh God. That's a relief. I've been trying to call him for hours."

"Thanks again for your help."

Gonzo went back out into the pit. "Randy's roommate confirms that someone named Aaron came by to get some of Randy's clothes earlier and specifically asked for his student ID, which was found in the pants pocket of the body, and a pair of the red Vans that Randy likes. The roommate let him in."

The Patrol officer who'd been assigned to the congressman's interrogation room came into the pit. "The lawyer says they're ready to talk to you."

"Shall we lay some wagers on the congressman offering us a deal?" Gonzo asked, buzzing with adrenaline after putting together the pieces of this strange and baffling case.

"I'd wager if I didn't agree with you," Malone said.

Faith returned to the pit. "Forrester's wife and daughters are safe in FBI custody. They haven't heard from Tom."

It was a relief to know Forrester's family was safe. "Let's see what the congressman wants," Gonzo said.

"Mind if I tag along?" Malone asked.

"Please do."

"I'll be in observation," Faith said.

They entered the room to find the congressman looking much less cocky than he had earlier, which gave Gonzo tremendous satisfaction. "This is Captain Jake Malone. You asked to speak to us?"

"My client would like to make a deal," Fallow said.

"What kind of deal?" Gonzo asked.

"The kind in which he tells you what he knows about the Forrester family and his son's death."

"Oh, well, we've already rescued Forrester's wife and daughters from the Hilton, and we know who killed his son. It was your pal, Aaron, who's being picked up as we speak."

Watching that news land on Bryant was among the more satisfying moments in Gonzo's career.

"How... how do you know that?"

"Your guy Sanders helped us fill in the blanks."

"He'd never!"

"Oh yes, he would. When you offer someone immunity in exchange for information, you'd be surprised how chatty they get. So as you can see, your offer is of no use to us. We'll be charging you with numerous felonies, including kidnapping, unlawful detention and contracting murder, to start with. I'm sure there'll be much more before we're finished, because Sanders also told us about the guns, prostitutes, gambling and drug dealing. Not to mention the campaign finance case Forrester has built. Someone has been a *very* busy boy."

Bryant's jumped to his feet. "Wait a minute! You can't prove anything!"

"Sit down, Damien," Fallow said, "and stop talking. Now."

"You might want to listen to him before you make it worse," Gonzo said as he followed Malone to the door. "Oh, and, Mr. Bryant? Your son's not dead."

EPILOGUE

On Saturday morning, Sam received word from Cameron that Gigi had been returned to full duty by an IAB vote of two to one. *Offenbach fought hard to have her busted down to Patrol and suspended without pay for ninety days, but Andrews said Gigi never deviated from her original story and declared the shooting self-defense. We've also decided to countersue the Patrick family in the hope that they'll drop their suit against us.*

All good news, Sam replied. *I'm so relieved.*

Us, too. Thanks for all the support.

Of course!

Did you hear that more than 2200 officers signed a letter in support of Farnsworth?

I knew about the letter because I signed it, but that's an amazing show of support. More than half of the department.

Agreed. We hope it helps.

See you Monday.

See you then.

So far, their weekend with the family had been great. Friday night had been about lasagna, board games and laughter. Sam and Nick sat up late into the night with Scotty, Eli, Candace, Angela, Tracy, Mike, Brooke and her boyfriend, Nate, who was on Eli's Secret Service detail, but was off duty for the weekend with his girlfriend's family.

Right after Brooke and Nate first arrived, Nate said, "Thank you for having me, Mr. President, Mrs. Cappuano."

Nick had shaken his hand and said, "We're Nick and Sam here, Nate."

Nate's eyes went wide. "I can't."

Everyone else had laughed.

"You must," Nick had said.

"I told you." Brooke had linked her arm with Nate's. "If you're gonna hang with my family, you can't be a Secret Service agent."

"I'll, um, I'll try, sir," Nate had said.

"Try hard," Nick had replied with a grin.

Freddie, Gonzo and the rest of the squad were at work cleaning up the paperwork on the case they'd closed in the early hours of that morning, so they wouldn't make it to the beach. Nick and Sam had ended up with a smaller group than they'd planned on, which was fine.

They spent all day Saturday at the beach, enjoying the first warm weather of the season, followed by a bonfire with s'mores on Saturday night.

Sam got up early Sunday to read the reports Gonzo and Freddie had written on the Fortier and Bryant cases and still couldn't believe the wild chain of events that had led to the arrest of Congressman Bryant and several others in his inner circle.

She was so absorbed in reading the twisted trail that had led to the congressman's arrest that she didn't hear Nick come up behind her or even know he was there until he kissed her neck and startled her.

"Morning," he said. "I was sad when I woke up alone."

"Sorry. Freddie texted me overnight to be on the lookout for reports that would tell an unbelievable story. He was right about that."

"What happened?"

Sam gave him the highlights.

"I know Bryant from when I was in the Senate. That's unbelievable."

"Sure is. You know what else is unbelievable?"

"What's that?"

"They've recovered nine bodies from Stahl's yard so far, and they're not done yet."

"God, that's awful. I'm sorry, Sam."

"He's like a nightmare that refuses to end. Freddie said the warrant for the storage unit finally came through, so they'll be taking that on as soon as they get some sleep."

"I'm glad you're not there to have to deal with that."

"I doubt they'd let me even if I was there."

Her phone rang, and she took the call from Freddie. "Hey, I figured you'd be asleep by now."

"Sam…"

"What? What's wrong?"

"Tom Forrester has been murdered."

Don't be mad at me for leaving you there! I've got a wild story in mind for the next book, *State of Suspense*, coming in 2024. When I started writing *State of Bliss*, I'd imagined a fun, quiet, light-hearted novella about Sam and Nick's vacation. I wasn't far into it when I realized that wouldn't be realistic. When are their lives ever quiet? I added the murder at GW, and we were off to the races with a whole new plan. I enjoyed giving Gonzo more of a starring role in this one than he's had before. As always, writing this couple and this series is a total thrill ride for me as I never know where it's going until it happens. Like when Randy Bryant was "murdered." I was like WTF is that now? Haha! That's how my mind works, and I don't ask any questions. I just follow the crazy muse wherever she decides to take me.

Reminder to join the Fatal/First Family Series group at *www.facebook.com/groups/FatalSeries* to keep up on all the latest news with the series. We've got some fun stuff coming in the new year, so make sure you're in that group and/or on my newsletter mailing list at *https://marieforce.com* so you don't miss anything. Join the State of Bliss Reader Group at *www.facebook. com/groups/stateofbliss/* to dish about this book with spoilers permitted.

A huge thank you to my amazing team: Julie Cupp, Lisa Cafferty, Jean Mello, Nikki Haley, Ashley Lopez and Rachel Spencer for their help behind the scenes. To my editors, Joyce Lamb and Linda Ingmanson, first-line beta readers Anne Woodall and Kara Conrad, and continuity editor Gwen Neff, I appreciate you all so much!

Thank you to the Fatal/First Family Beta Readers: Jennifer, Karina, Irene, Kelly, Ellen, Elizabeth, Maricar, Mona, Amy, Gina, Jennifer, Sarah, Jennifer, Marti and Phuong.

As always, a HUGE thank you to Capt. Russel Hayes, Newport, RI Police Department (retired) for his wisdom and insight. Russ is always available to me at a moment's notice, and I couldn't (and wouldn't) write this series without his input.

As we wind up another wild year, I'm incredibly thankful for all the readers who love this series and this couple as much as I do. Your enthusiasm for their story keeps me going, and I appreciate you all SO MUCH. Looking forward to 2024!

Happy holidays to you and your family, and all my best for the New Year.

Much love,

Marie

ALSO BY MARIE FORCE

Romantic Suspense Novels Available from Marie Force

The First Family Series

Book 1: State of Affairs

Book 2: State of Grace

Book 3: State of the Union

Book 4: State of Shock

Book 5: State of Denial

Book 6: State of Bliss

Book 7: State of Suspense (Coming April 2024)

Read Sam and Nick's earlier stories in the Fatal Series!

The Fatal Series

One Night With You, *A Fatal Series Prequel Novella*

Book 1: Fatal Affair

Book 2: Fatal Justice

Book 3: Fatal Consequences

Book 3.5: Fatal Destiny, *the Wedding Novella*

Book 4: Fatal Flaw

Book 5: Fatal Deception

Book 6: Fatal Mistake

Book 7: Fatal Jeopardy

Book 8: Fatal Scandal

Book 9: Fatal Frenzy

Book 10: Fatal Identity

Book 11: Fatal Threat

Book 12: Fatal Chaos

Book 13: Fatal Invasion

Book 14: Fatal Reckoning

Book 15: Fatal Accusation

Book 16: Fatal Fraud

Contemporary Romances Available from Marie Force

The Wild Widows Series—a Fatal Series Spin-Off

Book 1: Someone Like You

Book 2: Someone to Hold

Book 3: Someone to Love

The Miami Nights Series

Book 1: How Much I Feel *(Carmen & Jason)*

Book 2: How Much I Care *(Maria & Austin)*

Book 3: How Much I Love *(Dee's story)*

Nochebuena, A Miami Nights Novella

Book 4: How Much I Want *(Nico & Sofia)*

Book 5: How Much I Need *(Milo and Gianna)*

The Gansett Island Series

Book 1: Maid for Love *(Mac & Maddie)*

Book 2: Fool for Love *(Joe & Janey)*

Book 3: Ready for Love *(Luke & Sydney)*

Book 4: Falling for Love *(Grant & Stephanie)*

Book 5: Hoping for Love *(Evan & Grace)*

Book 6: Season for Love *(Owen & Laura)*

Book 7: Longing for Love *(Blaine & Tiffany)*

Book 8: Waiting for Love *(Adam & Abby)*

Book 9: Time for Love *(David & Daisy)*

Book 10: Meant for Love *(Jenny & Alex)*

Book 10.5: Chance for Love, *A Gansett Island Novella (Jared & Lizzie)*

Book 11: Gansett After Dark *(Owen & Laura)*

Book 12: Kisses After Dark *(Shane & Katie)*

Book 13: Love After Dark *(Paul & Hope)*

Book 14: Celebration After Dark *(Big Mac & Linda)*

Book 15: Desire After Dark *(Slim & Erin)*

Book 16: Light After Dark *(Mallory & Quinn)*

Book 17: Victoria & Shannon (Episode 1)

Book 18: Kevin & Chelsea (Episode 2)

A Gansett Island Christmas Novella *(Appears in Mine After Dark)*

Book 19: Mine After Dark *(Riley & Nikki)*

Book 20: Yours After Dark *(Finn & Chloe)*

Book 21: Trouble After Dark *(Deacon & Julia)*

Book 22: Rescue After Dark *(Mason & Jordan)*

Book 23: Blackout After Dark *(Full Cast)*

Book 24: Temptation After Dark *(Gigi & Cooper)*

Book 25: Resilience After Dark *(Jace & Cindy)*

Book 26: Hurricane After Dark *(Full Cast)*

Book 27: Renewal After Dark *(Coming 2024)*

The Green Mountain Series

Book 1: All You Need Is Love *(Will & Cameron)*

Book 2: I Want to Hold Your Hand *(Nolan & Hannah)*

Book 3: I Saw Her Standing There *(Colton & Lucy)*

Book 4: And I Love Her *(Hunter & Megan)*

Novella: You'll Be Mine *(Will & Cam's Wedding)*

Book 5: It's Only Love *(Gavin & Ella)*

Book 6: Ain't She Sweet *(Tyler & Charlotte)*

The Butler, Vermont Series

(Continuation of Green Mountain)

Book 1: Every Little Thing *(Grayson & Emma)*

Book 2: Can't Buy Me Love *(Mary & Patrick)*

Book 3: Here Comes the Sun *(Wade & Mia)*

Book 4: Till There Was You *(Lucas & Dani)*

Book 5: All My Loving *(Landon & Amanda)*

Book 6: Let It Be *(Lincoln & Molly)*

Book 7: Come Together *(Noah & Brianna)*

Book 8: Here, There & Everywhere *(Izzy & Cabot)*

Book 9: The Long and Winding Road *(Max & Lexi)*

The Quantum Series

Book 1: Virtuous *(Flynn & Natalie)*

Book 2: Valorous *(Flynn & Natalie)*

Book 3: Victorious *(Flynn & Natalie)*

Book 4: Rapturous *(Addie & Hayden)*

Book 5: Ravenous *(Jasper & Ellie)*

Book 6: Delirious *(Kristian & Aileen)*

Book 7: Outrageous *(Emmett & Leah)*

Book 8: Famous *(Marlowe & Sebastian)*

The Treading Water Series

Book 1: Treading Water

Book 2: Marking Time

Book 3: Starting Over

Book 4: Coming Home

Book 5: Finding Forever

ABOUT THE AUTHOR

Marie Force is the #1 *Wall Street Journal* bestselling author of more than 100 contemporary romance, romantic suspense and erotic romance novels. Her series include Fatal, First Family, Gansett Island, Butler Vermont, Quantum, Treading Water, Miami Nights and Wild Widows.

Her books have sold more than 13 million copies worldwide, have been translated into more than a dozen languages and have appeared on the *New York Times* bestseller list more than 30 times. She is also a *USA Today* bestseller, as well as a Spiegel bestseller in Germany.

Her goals in life are simple—to spend as much time as she can with her "kids" who are now adults, to keep writing books for as long as she possibly can and to never be on a flight that makes the news.

Join Marie's mailing list on her website at *marieforce.com* for news about new books and upcoming appearances in your area. Follow her on Facebook at *www.Facebook.com/MarieForceAuthor*, Instagram at *www.instagram.com/marieforceauthor/* and TikTok at *https://www.tiktok.com/@marieforceauthor?*. Contact Marie at *marie@marieforce.com*.

Printed in the USA
CPSIA information can be obtained
at www.ICGtesting.com
LVHW042310250424
778512LV00026B/467